MW00831635

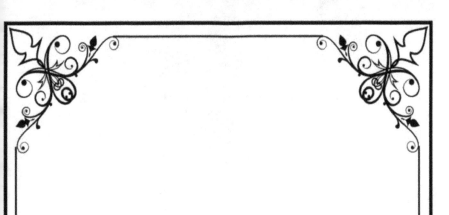

ENTANGLED

PRINCE OF THE DOOMED CITY:

BOOK 2

FIRE
WYRM
BOOKS

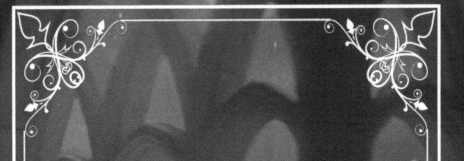

ENTANGLED

PRINCE OF THE DOOMED CITY:

BOOK 2

Cover illustration by Amira Naval

For Leo and Aurelia,
magical in every way.

1

NOT EVERY BOOK IN VESPRE LIBRARY WILL TRY TO kill you. But most of them will if given half a chance.

I'm down on the sixth floor of the library, walking slowly along the curved bend of bookshelves. My fingers hover mere inches above battered spines. Magic prickles against my skin, twines through my senses. Dangerous magic.

Closing my eyes, I let my inner senses deepen. I don't have to *read* the books to *feel* the spell they contain. It's almost like a song—a unique, rhythmic pulse in the air that vibrates against my soul. In most of these books, that vibration is broken. In some of them, it's dead entirely.

But in the last book on the shelf, the rhythm is perfect, strong. That's the book that contains the Noswraith.

I open my eyes, take a step back, and look at that collection of oddly mismatched volumes. Twenty-five of them—which means this Noswraith has broken its bindings and been rebound twenty-five times. That's relatively few compared to some of the nightmares imprisoned in this library. I let my gaze roam from the shelf in front of me around the curving wall, then across the open space of the central citadel to the bursting casements on the far side. So many shelves, packed to brimming. And this is only one floor!

I shiver and continue, leaving one collection of nightmares behind and moving on to the next. The individual cases are a good fifteen feet tall, so I'm obliged to climb a ladder to inspect the uppermost shelves. Looping my arm through the top ladder rung, I let my fingers trail along the spines in front of me, extending as far as I can reach. Broken magic hums unpleasantly against my skin, like the stink of a rotting corpse. My stomach turns. Gods above, I really shouldn't be doing this! My training as a Vespre librarian began less than a week ago. I shouldn't be wandering the library alone, much less working with Noswraiths even in this limited capacity.

But there's no one else to do the job. Nelle Silveri, the senior librarian, is diligently creating a fresh binding for the Hungry Mother, the Noswraith that broke its binding two nights ago and went on a rampage through the city. I managed to catch it with a temporary binding, but even with the Prince of Vespre's assistance, it wasn't very strong. If we're to avoid another breakout, Nelle must create a proper binding, and soon.

I close my eyes—and for a moment, I'm back in the streets of Vespre City, watching the Hungry Mother bear down upon me. A lurching, hulking being of pure horror, with long, dragging arms, blazing eyes, and two sagging, withered breasts. I hear her voice in my head once more, subtle as poison: *Come to my arms . . .*

Hastily I pull my awareness back to the present, blinking as bookshelves come into focus. I'd known this job was dangerous, of course. The life expectancy of the Vespre librarians is shockingly low. But after what I saw the other night . . . well, there's good reason Vespre is known as the *Doomed City*.

However, doom might be averted for another day if we all pitch in and do our part. Mixael and Andreas are hard at work up on the first floor, writing out numerous small bindings. After the Hungry Mother's outburst, there was a surge of rebellion throughout the library as many of the smaller Noswraiths redoubled their efforts to break their spells.

I lack the skill to rewrite bindings, newcomer that I am. But I can walk the stacks and check the spellbooks for signs of breakdown. I've already collected four compromised volumes on my little trolley, which I will deliver to Mixael and Andreas for inspection. Maybe they won't need immediate attention; I'm not experienced enough to know for sure. But Mixael urged me not to take risks.

"If you get even a *whiff* of breakage, grab the book and send it on up!" he'd said. "Better safe than sorry." I hadn't missed the concern shimmering in his eyes. They all know I shouldn't be given a task like this.

9

Something prickles beneath my fingers.

I stop. I've reached the end of a shelf of battered, broken books. I take a closer look at the final volume on the shelf—a little book of dark brown leather, bound with yellow cross-stitch threads up the spine. I bring my fingers close to that spine again and sense that peculiar vibration of magic I've been learning to discern. This volume definitely contains a Noswraith, but . . . there's something wrong. Something more than just the weakness I'd sensed in the four books on my trolley. I don't know how to describe it; there aren't words in my limited vocabulary suited for moments like this. There's a subtle *wrongness* here, like a breeze blowing through the house when you know all the windows should be shut for the night.

And that breeze carries a stench of rot.

Gooseflesh rises on my neck. I stare at that spine. The other four books I'd gathered were weakened and gave off a sense of fragility. This book, however, now that I study it more closely, looks as though black mold is eating away at the leather and yellow threads. But that's not mold; it's *spellrot*.

What will happen if I pull it off the shelf, place it in my trolley, and try to carry it up to Mixael? Will it disintegrate entirely? I suck on my teeth, wracked with indecision. Mixael was very clear in his orders—bring back *any* compromised book. And *don't* try any fancy heroics! Despite my nearly-successful effort to bind the Hungry Mother the other night, the other librarians have warned me against overextending my fledgling abilities. Overconfidence can too easily lead to small mistakes. Too many small mistakes could leave the door open to a Noswraith inhabiting my mind, leaving me dead . . . or worse.

Like Vervain.

I draw a long, steadying breath, my nostrils flaring at the stink of rotten magic. Then, firming my jaw, I reach into the satchel resting against my hip and touch my weapons—a blank book and a gray quill pen. *My* quill pen, a gift from my fellow librarians, bestowed on me with great ceremony just yesterday. The quill has a spell on it—so Mixael explained to me—that lets it write without the need to be dipped in ink. A useful tool for a librarian of Vespre.

Drawing confidence from the feel of that feather under my fingers, I come to a decision. I withdraw my hand from the satchel and, gripping the ladder rung tight with my other hand, reach for the compromised spellbook.

The moment my fingers close around it, I know my mistake. This book is even more fragile than I realized. Spellrot has eaten deep into the binding, and at the barest touch, the delicate threads holding the pages together crumble. I try to pull it from the shelf, but it falls to pieces, landing in chunks on the floor at my feet, dusting the base of the ladder with debris. I stand there, poised high on the rungs, looking down in dismay.

I know what I've done. I've broken the spell.

The Noswraith is loose. And it's close.

"Gods save me!" I whisper, more an expletive than a prayer in that moment. Hastily, I slide down the ladder. My feet thump on the floor, scattering more book dust, but at least now I'm on firm footing, not precariously balanced some ten feet in the air. Heart in my throat, I look around me. The curved balcony rail is a few feet in front of me, a guard against the empty drop down the center of the citadel into the dark, shadow-lost floors below. Pale starlight glitters through the crystal dome high above, and many pale lanterns set in sconces at intervals between the bookshelves light up this whole floor nearly as bright as day, only . . .

Only now there's a shadow over everything—an *overlay*. It's like peering at the world through a pair of dark glasses. I blink several times, trying to clear my vision. It's no use.

I've been pulled into the Nightmare Realm.

My body is somewhere close by, just on the other side of reality's veil. Asleep. Vulnerable. Here, my mind is alert, but I'm alone. Mixael and Andreas, six stories overhead, are still in the waking world. They can't hear me through the veil, no matter how I shout.

I clench my teeth, reach into my satchel, and withdraw book and quill. It's too late to rewrite the old binding, but I can write a new one. I've done it before. But first I've got to find this Noswraith and, if possible, figure out its name.

Leaving the trolley behind, I walk along the curving shelves, keeping them on my left. Here and there corridors branch off from the main floor, leading away from the citadel center into catacomb like passages lined with more shelves. I walk lightly on my toes, ears straining for the faintest disturbance. It's eerily silent. Of course, one expects silence in a library. But always before there's been the hushed, distant whisper of the other librarians going about their work: Andreas sheafing through loose pages—Mixael whistling as he scampers recklessly up and down the book lifts—Nelle muttering to her wyvern, who responds with little *meeps*.

On this side of reality, however, all is painfully still.

My knees shake so hard, I grab a bookshelf for support as I peer down one of the branching passages. A lantern on a sconce illuminates a bookshelf some twenty feet away, like a little floating world of light in that darkness. No sign of a Noswraith.

I skitter by the passage and continue around the curve of the main tower. My book is open across one arm, and I keep my pen poised above the first blank page. *"Write it back into the pages,"* I whisper. Then I stop. *"Write it back into the pages,"* I whisper again.

My own voice echoes inside my head, but . . . but there's no sound in the air around me. Only silence.

I open my mouth and try to speak again, my tongue dry, my throat thick and tight. With an effort, I quaver, *"Boo."* Then again, with more force, *"Boo!"* Then, filling my lungs, I scream, *"BOO!"*

Nothing.

Silence.

Oppressive, smothering silence.

I'm starting to shiver.

A skittering movement draws my eye. Turning sharply, I peer out over the balcony rail, across the empty space to the shelves on the far side of the tower. There's something there, something moving in the darkness. Crawling along the shelves, nimble as a spider. I can't see it very clearly, not from this distance. It's more of an *impression* than anything else—an impression of long limbs, weirdly jointed. Of a broad, smooth forehead and no place for eyes. Of curving horns, batlike ears, and long, clattering claws.

Fear jolts in my veins. But no . . . no, I'm all right. I draw a steadying breath, hold it fast. In this moment, I'm all right, I'm safe. It's all the way across the citadel, so far away it can't even know I'm here. I've got time to gather myself, to begin writing a binding. I'm going to be—

It turns its head.

Though it has no eyes, I feel it *looking* at me.

I have merely a second to grasp this fact before the Noswraith springs from the bookshelf to the rail and poises there, its knees arched as high as its chin, two large, black wings unfurling at its back. Starlight falling from above gleams on massive tusks jutting up from that huge underjaw. The jaw falls open, and a long, forked tongue rolls out and laps the air.

The next moment, it soars out into the open space, spreading its wings and angling straight at me.

A scream bursts from my throat—a scream without sound, lost in perfect silence. Some part of me knows I need to stand my ground and write, that writing the binding spell is my only chance. But I can't. Instinct takes over.

I turn on my heel and run.

I can't hear the Noswraith, but I *feel* it land on the rail, *feel* it leap to the floor and begin a loping gallop behind me, just at my heels. I *feel* when its own momentum around the curve carries it up the bookshelf so that now it runs sideways along the shelves, knocking books to the floor behind it. Books which fall with a *thud, thud, thud* of vibration but without making a sound. I feel it all so vividly, like it plays out in my head, a stage production I observe from a distance, all happening to some alternate version of myself, not my *real* self at all. And maybe . . .

A faint flicker of hope sparks in my heart. Maybe it feels that way because somewhere, in some other layer of reality, I *am* standing firm, I *am* writing, crafting a spell. If I can only stay alive in *this* reality long enough to give my other self time . . .

Long taloned fingers slash at my hair. Hot breath burns the back of my neck. Another scream bubbles in my throat, soundless and impotent. In desperation, I turn and dive down one of the side passages. It's too dark. A pale white candle glows in its sconce further down, but no matter how many steps I take, it never seems to get closer. I hurtle toward it nonetheless, some mad, panic-stricken part of my brain convinced that if I can just reach that sphere of light, I'll be safe.

The floor dips suddenly.

My arms wheel as I stagger and fall headlong. Something flies over my head. I feel the tear of talons through my hair, scraping my skull. That blow could have taken my head off if it had landed true. I tumble, roll down the steeply inclined floor. I have no sense of up or down, nothing but a mad jumble.

Finally, I stop.

I lie on my back, staring up into utter darkness.

Panting yet unable to hear my own breaths, I pull my bruised and battered body upright. Candlelight flickers, still painfully far away. I crawl to one side, find a bookshelf, feel leathery spines under my fingertips. Gripping the edge of a shelf, I pull myself to my feet.

It's so silent. So still.

The Noswraith is here. And I can't sense it at all.

I press my back against the wall, the edge of a bookshelf digging into my shoulder blades. I'm no longer holding my book; I must have dropped it somewhere in my flight. Does that mean I'm not writing anymore in the waking world? Am I trapped in this Nightmare, alone, unarmed? No, not wholly unarmed—I still hold my quill in one hand.

Time to move.

I slide sideways, keeping my back to the shelves, inching my way toward the candlelight. My feet trip, struggling to find footing on the steep, downward slope of the floor, a slope which does not exist in the waking world. I grip the shelf behind me for support.

Something heavy falls on my shoulder.

I turn. Look.

Candlelight gleams off the edge of long, black talons.

My heart surges to my throat just as I'm flung to the ground. Weight presses into my shoulders, and sharp points pierce through the fabric of my gown, through the flesh of my shoulders, down to the bone. Pain floods my senses, and I try to scream, but can't. My hands flail uselessly against unseen arms.

I've dropped my quill.

Some small part of my brain must still be thinking rationally, for I stop trying to yank at those unseen hands and instead reach out, feeling along the ground beside me. My fingertips brush plumy feathers. I reach a little further, grasp hold.

Suddenly the darkness of the Nightmare peels away, revealing a face. Semi-humanoid, crowned with arching horns that curl back from a smooth, eyeless forehead. The browbone juts sharply above a blunt, slitted nose. The skin is glossy black like polished ebony, gleaming in the distant lanternlight. The massive underjaw opens and shuts, spittle falling in my eyes. That hideous head bends toward me, and the long, forked tongue licks my face, its razor edge cutting my skin. I try to scream again, choking on my own silence. That wide jaw widens still more, ready to bite my entire head off.

I do the only thing I can think of in the moment—I jam my quill nib deep into that lashing black tongue.

An explosion of ink fills the monster's mouth, spattering in my face, pouring down its throat. The Noswraith rears back. The heavy pressure of its hands leaves my shoulders, and I don't hesitate even a moment. I roll to one side, hit the wall, push myself up onto my hands and knees. The Noswraith is flailing, shaking its head, spattering ink every which way. I open my mouth and, to my amazement, discover I have a voice again.

"Silence!" I scream. The word rings in the passages, growing with every reverberation. I can see ripples of energy, bouncing off

the candlelight and returning.

The sound strikes the monster. It explodes in a mist of black droplets.

2

I BLINK THREE TIMES, LONG AND SLOW.

With each rise and fall of my eyelids the darkness of the Nightmare retreats.

I come back to full consciousness, sitting on the floor in the stone passage, my back pressed against a bookshelf. Candlelight flickers directly over my head, not many yards distant as it had seemed just a few blinks ago. It's bright enough that I can read the titles on the spines of the books across from me. The shadows around me no longer writhe with living energy.

I let out a huge sigh and lean my head back against the uncomfortable lip of a shelf. Then, dropping my chin, I let my gaze fall to the book in my lap. While in the Nightmare, I'd lost track of it, but on this side of reality, I'd somehow managed to hold on. Hands trembling, I lift it, feel the new *weight* of it. A shifting, prowling, furious sort of weight.

I caught the Noswraith. Not for long, I'd guess—without its proper name, any binding I create will soon disintegrate. But long enough to get it up to Mixael, who can create a stronger binding.

Groaning, I get to my feet, sway, find my balance. A wan smile pulls at the corner of my mouth. My heart is still pounding, my shoulders throbbing. My body wants to believe what happened was more than a dream, that I truly was battered and bruised by those awful talons. But I'd survived. The horrors of Vespre Library haven't devoured me yet.

I make my way back up the passage. The floor is *not* slanted as it had been in the Nightmare. Emerging from the passage into the main floor, I face the open citadel center. In my mind's eye, I see again that awful, winged monster angling toward me across the empty space. There's nothing but glittering starlight now, and books surrounding me. A comforting sight. Or it would be if I didn't know what all those books contain.

I turn right, take three steps toward where I'd left my trolley . . . and stop short.

My heart thuds against my breastbone.

Oh no.

The Prince is there. Between me and my trolley.

He's dressed in long, trailing, purple robes, which open at the throat and sweep away in flowing sleeves from his elbows, a very Aurelian style of dress. His arms are crossed over his chest, and one shoulder leans casually against the wall between two bookshelves.

His right foot crossed in front of his left leg, his whole stance easy, graceful, and insouciant. But I don't miss the faint impression of dark circles ringing his eyes. Not even his fae glamours are strong enough to hide the aftereffects of the curse under which he suffers. The curse which very nearly killed him just two nights ago.

I choke back a surprised yelp and drop a dignified curtsy. "Prince," I say, my voice calm, measured. When I rise, I take care to fix a little smile in place—a faint, meaningless smile that does not reach my eyes, but which serves to disguise any traitorous expression that might try to flash across my face. "I did not expect to see you, sir. How are you feeling?"

The Prince doesn't answer for a long, long moment. Then, after a pregnant pause: "Irritable."

I raise my eyebrows. "Oh?"

He nods, thoughtfully, as though coming to a hard-won conclusion. "Yes, irritable. It never fails to irritate me when subordinates ignore direct orders and step in where they are ill-prepared to offer help, threatening to undo the precarious safety of this entire island. That's just the sort of thing that puts me in a foul frame of mind."

The spellbook I'm holding bulges suddenly against my stomach as the Noswraith rebels against its binding. I gasp, my arms tightening. The Prince's gaze snaps from my face to the book. A whole babble of excuses rises on my tongue. After all, the Noswraith broke loose the moment I touched the book! I had to do something, hadn't I?

23

But the truth is, he's right. In retrospect, I ought simply to have made note of where the compromised book was located and gone to tell Mixael directly. I shouldn't have tried to remove it, seeing what state it was in. It was arrogance on my part, and even more arrogance to try to craft a spell on my own.

I swallow my excuses and hold out the book to the Prince. It gives another jolt, nearly jumping from my fingers. He snatches it from me and, without looking at it, tucks it under his arm.

"Did you know the name?" he asks.

I shake my head. "I . . . I thought it might be *The Silence*. Andreas mentioned it during drills the other day. But I couldn't remember the proper name, the binding name."

"*Nahual.*"

"Pardon?"

"*Nahual.* That's the name. *Silence* in old Vaalyun." He narrows his eyes ever so slightly. "You were on the right track."

His tone is begrudging, but warmth floods my cheeks. The Prince is not one to give praise, and he particularly despises me. Anything like approval is rare from him. "If you'll spell it out for me, I'll finish the binding," I say, my voice bolder than before.

His eyes narrow still more. "I think not. You've done enough for one day, Darling."

Before I can react to his misuse of my last name, he turns on his heel and strides away. "Come!" he calls over his shoulder. "Bring your findings. You'll need to update Mixael on what you've done, and while you're at it, you can apologize to him for putting everyone at risk."

Whatever pleasure I'd felt a moment before fades under this bitter censure. With a sigh, I obey the Prince's command, fetch my trolley, and push it to the nearest book lift. There I unload my small stack, pull the ropes and levers, and send the lift all the way up to the first floor. The Prince stands close at hand, watching me, still holding my newly written spell under his arm. I wonder why he doesn't send it up with the others. Does he not trust my work?

Painfully aware of his scrutiny, I don't look his way, but go about my task with crisp efficiency. When I'm done, I turn to him, fold my hands, and offer him another blank smile. He answers with a grimace of his own, then turns without a word and starts for the spiral stair. I have no choice but to follow, hastening up the winding steps behind him. The gaping chasm of the citadel yawns below me. I take care not to look out over the rail.

We've climbed no more than a story or two, when suddenly the Prince grips the banister with both hands and doubles over. A hiss bursts through his teeth followed by a groan. Startled, I hasten up a few steps until I stand on the tread behind him. My hand reaches out, hesitating before touching his white knuckles. "Are you all right?" I ask.

As though in answer, his other hand suddenly loses its grip on my spellbook, which falls, bounces off a step, and lands another step down, pages fluttering open. I have a brief, flashing glimpse of a taloned hand stretching out, of a muscular arm straining to get free.

Quickly I snatch up the book and slam its cover shut. It bucks in my grasp, rippling and contorting, trying to force itself back open. I press it against my stomach, using all my strength to hold it shut. For a few moments, I stand there, resisting. Then the book relents. My binding holds. For now.

Breathing a sigh, I open my eyes, meet the Prince's gaze. He's sunk onto the step, sitting with his elbows resting on his drawn-up knees, his head heavy and sagging. His glamour has slipped, revealing lines of pain in his face. He holds my gaze for a long moment. Am I mistaken, or is he trying to reassert his glamour? I can almost feel the flutter of magic in the air around him. It doesn't work. With a groan, he drops his head, hiding his face in his hands.

I chew my bottom lip. At last, uneasy in the long silence, I whisper, "You're not well."

"You noticed, did you?" He shoots me a dry look between two fingers before letting his head sink again. "It's this curse. It seems to be getting stronger."

I nod. Momentarily I consider pushing past him and continuing up the stair. But that seems both foolish and unkind under the circumstances. Instead I take a seat beside him, close to the rail. The book churns in my grasp again. I push it hard against my stomach, trusting my spell to hold a little longer at least.

I sit there, beside the Prince of the Doomed City. And I wait.

He lets out a sigh. Turning my head just slightly, I study the part of his face I can see behind his hands—one ear, the line of his jaw, a bit of a cheekbone. He's alarmingly handsome, even without glamours. His human blood does not diminish his beauty even in the slightest. But it's his human blood that's slowly killing him.

"You really have no idea who cursed you?" I'm not entirely certain what makes me ask the question. My voice sounds painfully loud after that long silence.

The Prince sits still as stone for such a long time, I begin to think he'll ignore me entirely. Finally he shakes his head. "If I did, I would have gone about curse-breaking a long time ago."

I watch the way his cheek tightens, the way the cords in his throat tense and relax and tense again. Why does the sight of his pain have to make that gods-blighted nurturing side of me rear up with such force? I want to place a hand on his shoulder, to offer what comfort I can. But I wouldn't dare such informality with a Prince.

Besides I know perfectly well how bitterly he hates me. I killed his mother, after all.

I lower my gaze to the spellbook resting on my knees and idly trace the edge of the cover with one finger. "Do you know *why* you were cursed?"

The Prince drops one hand and turns his head to fix me with a level glare. "You're quite the Nosey Nelly today, aren't you?"

I shrug. "Just making conversation."

"Mightn't you choose a less intrusive topic? The weather perhaps. Or palace gossip. I understand our own Mixael is hopelessly in love with Captain Khas, or so Lawrence informs me."

I snort. It's a good ploy, but not good enough. "So that means you *do* know. Or at least, you suspect."

The Prince growls and rubs a hand down his face. Then, resting both elbows on his knees, he stares down the stairway we've just climbed. "I do." He raises one eyebrow and casts me a sharp glance. "Care to guess?"

It's not a very nice game. But then most of the games played by the Lords and Ladies of Eledria aren't nice. "If I had to guess," I say slowly, "I'd say whoever did it was trying to make you ineligible for the throne of Aurelis."

His brows draw together in a tight knot. He turns away from me quickly.

I continue, choosing my words with care. "I would guess your half-human blood already made you vulnerable. That there was opposition to any future claim you might have to Lodírhal's throne. I would further guess that after . . . after the death of your mother, you became more of a target."

Everyone knew the moment Dasyra died that her Fatebound husband, King Lodírhal, could not survive long after. They were destined by the gods to love, live, and die together. His seemingly immortal fae life immediately began to fade at the moment of her passing.

That was five years ago now. When last I saw him, Lodírhal was starting to wither. Everyone knew he couldn't last long. Soon his throne will pass to his heir. Not to his son. Nor to his niece, Estrilde. No, it would pass to his favorite, his warrior champion: Lord Ivor Illithor.

A burning rush floods my cheeks at the mere thought of that name. Ivor. Beautiful, golden, glorious Ivor. Hastily, I shake my head and concentrate on the present conversation. "Am I correct in guessing that your curse began in the last five years?"

The Prince chuckles, a dark, bitter sound. "Your aim is true, Clara Darling. You've hit the bullseye dead-on. Yes, the curse fell soon after my mother's death. As a result, any chance I may have had of inheriting my father's throne was stripped from me. I was already considered something of a liability, but so long as I commanded both fae and human magic, I was too powerful to be easily toppled. Now . . ."

Now, thanks to the curse, any time he uses his human magic, it nearly breaks him in two. What used to be his greatest asset has become his direst burden.

What must it be like to live this way? Suffering from a curse like a disease, all the while knowing someone had done it to you deliberately. Then again, that's the way of life in Aurelis. It's a cutthroat world of courtly bloodthirst. I served under Princess Estrilde long enough to observe more than I liked of the Lords and Ladies and their intrigues.

Princess Estrilde.

Princess Estrilde, who had long sought to be named her uncle's heir.

Though I have no liking for my former mistress, who was always cruel and capricious, I still struggle to imagine her going so far as to curse her own cousin. Then again, perhaps I'm being too generous. Estrilde sold my Obligation to the Prince, after all, and had me sent off to the Doomed City without batting an eye. And all because Lord Ivor deigned to smile my way.

Ivor . . .

I close my eyes, hug the spellbook a little tighter. Then, regaining my composure, I turn to the Prince once more.

He's looking at me. "Your mask slipped," he says.

A flush roars up my cheeks. I blink several times and force my smile back into place. "Pardon?"

He points, wiggling the end of his finger in a circle. "There. That little smile of yours. The one you're always hiding behind. It slipped for a moment. I could see you were thinking something worrisome. What was it?"

"Nothing," I answer too quickly. "Nothing at all."

The Prince raises an eyebrow. "I could *oblige* you to tell me, you know."

He could. Of course he could. And, because he owns my Obligation, the command would be absolute. I would be forced to answer, like it or not. To confess that I was thinking about Lord Ivor and his beautiful smile and chiseled jaw and muscular frame. Wondering if he still remembers the girl he'd singled out for attention among all the human servants in Aurelis. Wondering if he thinks of me, wondering if he misses me.

The last thing I need is for the Prince to know any of that!

I shake my head. "I was simply wondering something. That's all."

"Wondering what?"

"Whether or not you *want* your father's throne."

The Prince raises an eyebrow. "You're wondering whether or not I *want* my rightful inheritance? Whether or not I *want* to be seen by my own father as a worthy successor to his kingdom? Whether or not I *want* to be both accepted and respected among the courts of Eledria, to wear a crown and prance about in golden robes, lording it over all I survey?" He cups his chin in his hand, tilting his head slightly as he looks at me. "That's what you're wondering?"

I shrug. "It's just . . . if you *were* to inherit, you would have to leave Vespre. And I wondered if you'd want that."

"Oh! Now, yes, I can see how you'd be confused. What a dilemma!" The Prince snorts. "Only a fool would leap at the chance to leave this gods-forsaken island, this land of gloom and rock-gnawing trolls."

He can mock me all he likes. I'm a good observer of human nature; I am the daughter of a novelist after all. And while the Prince's nature may be only *half* human, I can't help thinking it's the dominant half. There's conflict in the set of his cheek, in the depth of his eye, in the bitterness of his voice. While he may pretend otherwise, I suspect he might actually care more about Vespre and its denizens than he likes to admit. And if he were to take his father's throne, if he were to leave Vespre . . . how long would the city last without him?

The Prince turns sharply, catches my eye again. "Stop it."

"Stop what?" I ask, blinking innocently.

"Stop thinking better of me," he growls. "Stop thinking I have any sort of altruistic guiding star keeping me here. Vespre is my father's punishment on me for being less than I should be. A punishment he bestowed long ago, long before any curse fell. I'm here because I was sent here to be out of everybody's way. I feel no loyalty to this city, its inhabitants, or its gods-blighted library. No more than you do."

He stands suddenly. With one hand he grasps the banister, catching his balance; the other he extends to me. I hesitate a moment before slipping my fingers into his, allowing him to help me to my feet. I start to pull away, but his grip tightens. He draws me a step closer, gazing intently into my eyes.

"You shouldn't think better of me than I deserve, Clara Darling." His voice is low, simmering. "Nor should you think better of yourself. We're none of us here because we wish it, because we want to see good done and people spared unnecessary suffering. We're prisoners—same as the Noswraiths themselves, and equally as dangerous. If ever given the opportunity to burst free, we'll burst all right . . . and gods help those left in our wake!"

My lips part. I want to protest. I want to tell him to speak for himself, not to presume he knows me, knows my heart. But how can I? The truth is, I'm here for ten more years as I serve out the term of my Obligation. The moment my sentence is up, I'll be scampering for home. And I'll spend the rest of my life trying to forget Vespre and its people. Trying not to wonder what happened to them . . . or what will happen to the worlds at large if the Noswraiths ever break free.

I drop my gaze, looking down at the Prince's hand gripping mine.

Slowly, his fingers loosen their hold. Then he reaches for the spellbook I'm still holding, pulls it from my grasp, and tucks it under his arm. Without another word, he turns, continues up the spiral stair. I stand some moments, watching him go.

Only when he's rounded the bend out of sight do I lift the edge of my skirts and follow.

THE PRINCE

WHY DO I DO THIS? WHY DO I TORTURE MYSELF like a damned fool?

I grip the stair rail hard, each step more ponderous than the last. This simple act of putting distance between us feels like hauling dead weight. Everything in me urges to turn around. To return to her side. Simply to be in her presence.

But that's not the plan.

Gods damn me, I should have left her in Aurelis! Why did I allow Nelle and the others to talk me into fetching her here? Granted, we're dangerously understaffed and in desperate need of new mages. I'd somehow thought it would be easier, though. Maintaining my reserve. Keeping out of her way. It's a big library, after all.

And yet . . . and yet . . .

No matter the work to be done on any given day, I'm inevitably drawn to wherever she happens to be. Whether she's walking the stacks, practicing lists of names with Andreas, or laboring under a particularly tricky binding, it doesn't matter. I'll catch myself moving in, near and nearer, her name on my tongue, ready to be spoken.

Generally, I'm quick to amend the situation. I turn on heel, march at once for whatever remote corner of the library I can find. But within hours it all starts over. Somehow, without conscious effort on my part, there I am again. Near her. Just around a corner or up a flight of stairs. But always near.

I know well enough what's happening. I know the gods and their little games. But I'm not so weak-willed as they seem to think. I won't be manipulated. I won't be a plaything for the amusement of distant deities.

I reach the topmost floor, stride from the stairwell, and make for Mixael Silveri's desk, which happens to be nearest to me. "Silveri!" I bark.

He looks up from his work, blinking unfocused eyes, bleary after too long focused on small scripts. "Yes, Prince?" he murmurs as I drop the spellbook containing Nahual on his desk. "What's this?"

"The new librarian's handiwork. Check it over. Make certain she's not left us with a poorly set trap ready to spring."

Mixael hefts the little volume in one hand. "Feels solid enough. She's quite a skilled mage, our Miss Darlington. Did you show she—"

"I'm in no mood to hear a litany of the girl's proficiencies. So long as she's not causing active harm, we must count ourselves fortunate."

Mixael's brow puckers slightly. But he shrugs and turns back to his work.

"And Silveri?"

"Yes, Prince?"

"Give her the rest of the day off."

He shoots me a confused look. "There's an awful lot of work to be done. I was hoping to have her walk the stacks down to the eighth floor and possibly try her hand at a—"

"She's getting reckless. Thinks she's advanced beyond her training. Maybe a day home with her people will clear her head." When he looks ready to protest further, I finish with a severe, "That's an order, Silveri."

Mixael sighs but knows better than to gainsay my wishes. "Very good, Prince."

I turn, leaving him at his desk, and cross the floor to my own private office. Stepping inside, I shut the door behind me and stalk across the room to my overflowing desk. There I sit. For some while. Unconsciously rubbing my chest with one hand. My heart is beating that inexplicable rhythm again. The rhythm which has not left me since that night . . . the night I saw her for the first time, and . . . and . . .

Growling, I reach for a box half-hidden beneath a sheaf of loose parchment. I pull it to me, pop the lid, and gaze down at the red plume quill nesting in a bed of silk inside. My mother's quill.

I cannot forget how she died. The brutality of that death.

I cannot forget who brought it about.

This is the reason I fetched the girl here. Her magic, left unchecked, was too unstable. Here I can keep an eye on her, make certain she doesn't work more of her dark mischief. And in the meanwhile, why not put those powers of hers to good use?

Yes. This is why she is here. The only reason.

Not because the thought of her in Estrilde's thrall, serving at my cousin's whims like some mere handmaiden galled me.

Not because the memory of her wrist caught in my hand burns so vividly, sometimes I cannot breathe.

Not because the image of her face has haunted my waking hours and plagued my dreams every night these last five years.

No. It's because she's dangerous. She might not seem it, with her big dark eyes and her demure little smile, and her innocent questions. But she's one of the more dangerous creatures I've ever encountered.

I look down suddenly, realize I'm rubbing my heart again. With a groan, I pull my hand away, then drop my head in my palms. This has been much harder than I anticipated.

A knock at the door.

"What?" I snarl.

The door opens. Lawrence appears, balancing a tray on one hand. "Teatime, sir. As usual."

I lean back in my chair, watching as my Obligate sets his tray down atop a pile of grimoires and half-written spells. He plucks a quilted cozy from the shiny black teapot. Curling steam escapes the spout. "I saw Miss Darlington on her way out from the library in a hurry," he says, placing a silver strainer across a cup and swirling the pot gently. "Is she to be away the whole day?"

"With any luck," I growl.

"How nice for her." Lawrence pours a stream of black liquid through the strainer, which catches stray tea leaves. "And how does she fair in her training these days, if I may be so bold to inquire?"

I scowl up at him from under my brow. "Why this interest in the new librarian?"

"Oh, no reason at all, sir. No reason at all." He sets the teapot down and, though it's within easy reach, picks up the teacup and offers it to me. "Will you be dining alone this evening?"

I snatch the cup, slopping tea over the edge. "What else would I be doing?" I down the contents in a single draught, ignoring the burn.

"I simply wondered if I ought to order a meal for one or . . . ?"

"I have no intention of changing my dining habits." Wiping my mouth, I set the cup down with a clatter on the tray and wave for it to be taken away. "You're to go about your business as usual."

"As you wish, sir." He picks up the tray and turns to leave.

"Lawrence."

My Obligate looks back over his shoulder, both eyebrows raised. "Sir?"

"Order dinner for two."

His lip twitches ever-so slightly at the corner. "As you wish, sir."

CLARA

3

M Y FIRST TASK UPON REACHING THE TOP FLOOR
is to fetch the books I'd sent up the lift and take them
to Mixael's desk. When I get there, I see that the Prince
has already dropped off my book with the unfinished spell. There
are seven other spellbooks already piled at Mixael's elbow, but he's
pushed them aside and is paging slowly through mine, careful not
to let the Noswraith out.

He looks up from his work, his eyes rather bloodshot in the
pale light from his lantern. A grin flashes across his face, and I'm
once again struck by how *pretty* he is. I'd been told that he has fae
blood in him, that his mother, Nelle Silveri, is an *ibrildian* like the
Prince himself—a half-human, half-fae hybrid—and possessed of
a unique blend of magic as a result.

Mixael sports rather less fae blood than his mother as his

father was fully human, but he is nonetheless a strong magic-user. And unnaturally pretty. Annoyingly pretty, for all his ginger hair and freckles, and long, scrawny limbs. All those features might make for a plain young man under other circumstances, but not Mixael Silveri. And his grin is downright melting. I can't help smiling in response.

"Well, now, Miss Darlington," he says, closing my book around one finger. "I've just been enjoying a rather thrilling read. Did you write all this up since I sent you down to the sixth floor? You're quite the scribbler, you know! It's all due to that new quill of yours."

That last bit is tongue-in-cheek, but the rest he speaks with real feeling. I shrug and roll my eyes, pleased at his praise—praise which he offers freely, not grudgingly like the Prince. "Is the spell strong enough?" I ask, indicating the book with a jut of my chin. "I didn't know the name."

"Not to worry. There are an awful lot of names to learn. No one expects you to have them all memorized in less than a week."

He might not; the Prince certainly seems to! He seems to expect me both to work miracles and to fail everyone all at the same time.

I place my four gathered books on top of Mixael's already towering stack. "Sorry to add to your workload."

"*You* haven't added to it. The library does that all on its own." He sighs, sets my spellbook aside, and taps it with one finger. "But this is a surprisingly good piece of spellwriting. It'll hold old *Nahual* for a good few weeks, I would guess, once I've got the name-binding in place. How did you think of it?"

I open my mouth, but no words will come. I remember my father complaining about questions like this every time he came home from some high society function. *"How do you think of those incredible stories?"* people would ask. As though any writer ever actually knew the answer to such a question!

The truth is, while writing that spell, it didn't feel as though I was writing at all—it felt as though I *lived* the encounter. In a way, I did, for if the Noswraith had killed me in the Nightmare Realm, I would have died here as well. My physical body may not have had its face bitten off, but I would have been found down on the sixth floor somewhere, limp and lifeless.

Thus what I'd written in the spellbook, I'd also experienced in the Nightmare. And when I succeeded in defeating the Noswraith in written form, I was able to bind it into the book itself. Not everyone can think and write so quickly off the cuff. Mixael has confessed that he himself must think through a spell in excruciating detail before attempting to write it down. Generally, he concentrates his efforts on rebinding old spells, sometimes with small elaborations, but primarily dependent on the original author's text. Nelle also is disinclined to spontaneous creativity. Andreas is better at it, but prefers writing his bindings in verse, which doesn't lend itself to quick spellcasting.

By comparison, my work may be raw and rough—but I'm fast. And I'm able to think on my feet and come up with words, even when the Noswraith is actively attacking my mind. I've managed it with two smaller wraiths now. With time, will I be a match for one of the Greater Noswraiths too?

Mixael is still waiting for my answer. "I'm not sure," I say slowly. "I just . . . I just *wrote* it. That's all. Didn't even know I was doing it, not exactly."

He presses his lips and nods. "You're a mage in the making, Miss Darlington, and no mistake."

He doesn't seem upset by the fact that I'd accidentally set the Noswraith free. Perhaps the Prince didn't tell him.

"I've mostly finished my rounds on floor six," I say, turning to go before the conversation can take an uncomfortable turn. "I'm heading back down now but wanted to be sure you got these first."

"Actually," Mixael says, stopping me in my tracks, "the Prince told me to tell you to take the rest of the day off. He says you ought to go home, visit your people."

"What?" I whirl to face him, shocked. "I'm to go *home?*" As an Obligate, I am by law permitted one day off per month to visit my own world, to do what I can to maintain connections with my old life. My last visit home was only a week ago—the day before the Prince purchased my Obligation from Princess Estrilde and whisked me away to Doomed City. I've scarcely had a chance to think about anything but survival since then. "But . . . but there's so much that needs doing!"

"True." Mixael shrugs. "There always is. The worst is cared for now, however." He indicates his stack. "You can't do much with these. Your little bit of unexpected spellwriting notwithstanding, you're not ready to tackle rebinding most of these bad boys. Andreas and I will be too busy to drill you, and my dearest maternal figure will be all day at the Hungry Mother's binding."

"But I can keep walking the stacks. I can keep searching for more weakened spells."

Mixael pulls a face. "Gods save us, one would think you didn't actually *want* to go home! Is that it, Miss Darlington? You prefer to spend your day with the Noswraiths?"

"No, but—"

"In my experience, it's best simply to accept gifts from the Prince and not ask questions." He smiles again, his face once more transforming into something much too pretty for a rangy, freckle-faced youth. "We'll be fine without you for one day at least. Andreas and I have enough to keep us busy. If any other Noswraiths break out, we'll deal with it."

Still I hesitate. "If you're sure . . ."

"Sure, I'm sure." Mixael waves a dismissive hand. "Besides, it doesn't matter if *I'm* sure. The Prince has decreed that you, Miss Darlington, should have a day off, so a day off you shall have. Go along with you now! Enjoy yourself."

Though I try to hold it back, a real grin breaks through my habitual mask smile. This is not at all what I expected when I woke up this morning. I might even feel a twinge of gratitude toward the Prince.

"Just one thing," I say. "How do I get off the island?"

I stop in my room long enough to change into a simple mulberry gown and cloak: both items of clothing which belong to me, not part of the extensive wardrobe provided by my new Obliege Lord. I try not to take anything from Eledria back into my own world when I visit.

Once I'm suitably dressed, I hasten through the palace to the front entrance. Word must have been sent of my coming, for the massive stone doors stand open—luckily for me, as I don't think I'd ever be able to budge them on my own. I step out onto the front porch and look down to the street below.

A carriage pulls into view. Apparently, the Prince always orders his carriage to take the Obligates to the nearest Between Gate on their off days. In Aurelis, there are numerous Between Gates set into the walls surrounding the palace itself. Here in Vespre, there are none . . . an added layer of precaution against the Noswraiths, no doubt.

I shiver and pull my cloak tighter around my body as I watch the carriage lumber along the street, pulled by six awful creatures in silver-studded harnesses. *Morleth*—Darksteppers. Bigger than horses, with massive cloven hooves and awful spines protruding through their thick, braided manes. Serpentine tails lash irritably, and sharp yellow teeth flash through the foam on their muzzles. Appropriate beasts for a world like this one.

The driver pulls the morleth to a halt, then turns his craggy head up to me and tips his hat deferentially. His face looks as though it's carved from pure granite, a huge slab of forehead heavily overhanging small, pale eyes. When he smiles, his teeth glint like faceted gemstones.

He's a troll. A troll in a top hat. Just when you think you've seen everything, Eledria finds a way to surprise you.

I make my way down the fifteen front steps. They're built on a scale much too large for me. I must either jump from one step to the next or sit down and scoot my bottom over the edge of each like a toddler. The other night, when Mixael and I raced out into the city to chase down the Hungry Mother, I chose the former method. Today, I choose the latter. It's a bit undignified, but at least I won't run out of breath.

The troll watches my descent. It's impossible to read an expression like his, but I get the distinct impression he's amused. When I reach the base, I straighten my skirts, lift my head, and attempt to regain a shred or two of dignity as the troll climbs down from his driver's box and moves to open the carriage door. He pulls out the little box step and steps to one side, bowing slightly at the waist.

I hesitate. "Um . . . would you mind very much if I rode up front with you?"

Troll faces are notoriously difficult to read, but his eyes glint a little, I think with surprise. *"Gorar trok?"* he says. Then he coughs, shakes his head, and tries again. "You want sure to, miss hooman?"

His accent is strong, his syntax a little odd. But the meaning is clear enough. "Yes," I reply with a firm nod. "If it's not too much trouble." The idea of riding in that dark carriage by myself is much more unnerving than the idea of riding beside the big troll.

Am I wrong, or does he look pleased? "Good, miss hooman," he says, and pushes the box step back inside and closes the carriage door. Then he indicates the little bars leading up the side of the carriage to the driver's box. *"Hira groart."*

I scramble up to the seat, then squish as far to one side as possible when the troll climbs up the other side. There's not a lot of space left once he takes his place, though he does his best not to crush me. At least I'm slim.

I grip the edge of the seat, and when the troll inquires, *"Jiror?"* I nod. With a slap of the reins, the morleth lurch into motion. I clutch the seat, a little gasp escaping my lips. "Hold arm at need if, miss hooman," the troll says, offering me another gem-studded grin.

I nod and slip my hand through the crook of his elbow, gripping hard. Gods above, just a few short days ago I could never have imagined sitting comfortably beside a troll, arm in arm, behind a team of monsters!

The morleth trot down the steep road leading away from the palace into the city. Vespre is built on a vast mountain . . . or rather, it appears to be *carved out* of the mountain. The palace dominates the topmost peak, and the rest of the city rings it in descending circles down into deep valleys, lost in shadow. We soon come to a street so steep, it's practically sheer. My eyes widen. How in the worlds can the carriage navigate such a sharp incline without losing grip and rolling end over end?

"Jirark, miss hooman," the troll says suddenly. "Hang on!"

I just have time to tighten my grip when the morleth suddenly surge forward. Rather than descending into the street, they speed out into empty sky. Their cloven hooves *clip* and *clop*, striking the air brightly as they prove the truth of their name—*Darksteppers*. Walking on a path of pure darkness, the morleth carry the carriage up and up, away from the city into the purple sky. We climb higher and higher until the towering buildings look like toy models far below, and the air is thin and cold and crisp. I pull my cloak tight and lean into the troll driver's arm, glad for his proximity.

As the morleth level out, I find my gaze searching the drifting clouds overhead for signs of beating wings. The last time I made this trip, coming the other direction, we were attacked by a flock of minor Noswraiths called frights, which very nearly succeeded in tearing me to pieces. Were it not for the Prince's quick and powerful magic, I would certainly have perished.

I shudder and resist the urge to bury my face in the troll's arm.

"You is *gruaka* girl," the troll says, abruptly breaking the silence between us. I look up and meet another unsettling, sparkling smile. "Come to Vespre City. Doomed City. Help our *Jirot*, our—how say?—our Prince."

"Oh. Yes." I wonder what *gruaka* means. A compliment? An insult? "It's, um . . . it's been very interesting."

The troll chuckles. I'm not sure how well he understands me, but that chuckle sounds sincere. "Not many *kurspari* last in Doomed City," he says. "*Urksta* bones—how say?—*snap!*" He chuckles again, and this time I think it rather unpleasant. "But you *gruaka*, you make the brave. Maybe you no *urk* too easy."

53

I shudder. "I hope not."

The morleth have settled into a steady, rhythmic gait by now. From this height, I can see the ocean. The Between Gate, Mixael told me, stands on the far shore beyond the channel. That shore belongs to Noxaur, he says—the Kingdom of Night. Not a place to linger. But the librarians of Vespre enjoy special privileges as long as they don't wander.

"Story tell of new *gruaka*," the driver says, breaking the silence again, his tone strangely conversational. "You face the *Nartorak*. The Dream-Scary. All on your ownsome in middle of street. Troll eyes spy you. Troll eyes see *gruaka* girl and the Nartorak hag. You make the brave with little . . ." Here he mimes writing with a pen.

So the trollfolk of Vespre talked about the new librarian girl up at the palace, did they? And I was observed doing battle with the Hungry Mother. The driver sounds impressed. Pleased, even. I cast him a short glance. "I . . . I don't make *much* brave. I make more fear."

The troll grunts and shrugs. "There be troll saying which go: *Kaurga-hor, gruaka-hor*. It be in small-bite speak: *More fear, more brave*."

We lapse into silence once more. I listen to the unsettling sound of morleth hooves striking pure darkness. Soon we're out over open water. In the distance, through the mist, I can just see the shore of Noxaur. "Have you always lived in Vespre?" I ask after a while.

"*Korkor*," the troll responds. "Me and me *torumblar*—how

say?—*mar* and *tar* and *ortolarok.*"

I know the word *mar*—it means *mother.* I've heard it before, spoken from the mouths of four troll children. Orphans, who looked to me with their sad, soulful little eyes and claimed me as their mother. My heart suddenly feels heavy. I haven't seen the children—Dig, Har, Calx, and Sis—since before the Noswraith outbreak. I don't know where they are, what happened to them. When I've asked Lir, my maid, for information, she merely sniffs and turns up her nose, saying, "It isn't your business, Mistress, what becomes of trollings. Be glad they're gone. Little pests."

"May I ask you a question?" I say suddenly.

The driver grunts again. *"Korkor."*

I take that to mean yes. "It's about . . . about orphans. In Vespre, I mean." I give him a close look. Based on Lir's reactions to the orphans, I'm not sure how this driver will take my questions.

"Irrr?" The sound is open, mildly curious.

I forge on. "I'm told that trolls do not care for orphans. That if a troll child loses its parents, no other troll will take it in."

"Korkor," the driver says, nodding, his stony face as impossible to read as ever.

"I want to know why. Why are they not cared for? Why will no one help them or let anyone else help them? Are they considered bad luck or something?"

The troll casts me a quick, sideways glance. I feel his arm stiffen beneath my fingers and hope I've not offended him. He's silent for a while, but finally draws a long breath. "It be *Morar tor Grakanak* who care for no-*mar* and no-*tar* ones. God of the Deeper Dark—he choose small ones for his own. If troll to take god's trollings, god must *obghat*—how say?—*punish*."

I frown, turning this over in my head. "You're saying that to adopt an orphan is to thwart the will of your god?"

"*Korkor.* Is bad do."

I'm silent for a long while. Finally, I venture, "And if I were to take such children in, even at their own request, I would be opposing your God of the Deeper Dark?"

"God choose who be his own, who belong to *mar* and *tar*. God choose, not troll." There's firmness in his tone, implying absolute certainty.

"But isn't it possible the God of the Deeper Dark might provide a *new* family for the children? That he might choose to give them a new *mar*, for instance?"

He shrugs again. "I know not much of gods and god ways. I good troll. I do as *mar* say when I small trolling. I do as *mar* say as big trollman. I not ask the Deep Dark askings."

This I take to be the troll equivalent of, "I'm no theologian—I do what my priest says and don't worry about it too much."

I sink once more into silence, allowing the clip-clop of the morleth hooves to fill my ears even as cold air whips my cheeks. It'll be a relief to get home again, a relief to be back in familiar surroundings.

The carriage begins its descent at last. "*Hirak, gruaka* girl," the troll driver says, nudging me gently and pointing. I look where he indicates and see the long pier stretching out from the shore. Soon after, the carriage draws level with the pier, and the morleth's hooves clop onto planks.

The driver clambers down and offers me a hand, which I gratefully accept. My feet are a bit unsteady, but I catch my balance and straighten my shoulders. I take a few steps, then turn suddenly, a shiver in my gut. I catch the driver's gaze. "You'll be here when I return?"

"*Korkor, gruaka* girl. *Korkor.*"

I nod, offer a weak smile, and turn to face the long pier and the dark shore waiting at its end. I'd not realized when first coming that the shore belongs to Noxaur. I'd never been to the Kingdom of Night before, but I've heard plenty of stories and glimpsed folk of that dark realm when they've visited Aurelis. None of what I've heard has made me want to know it better.

The Between Gate is not far off, however. I'd not seen it when first coming this way, for the gate leading from Aurelis had simply deposited me in the middle of that rocky beach at the end of the pier. But apparently the Prince has an agreement with King Maeral, guaranteeing the safety of his librarians as they travel to and fro. I should be safe.

Steeling myself, I set off at a brisk pace along the pier. Lanterns hung at ten-foot intervals from tall poles offer little pockets of light, but in between each lantern, it's painfully dark. I reach the end of the pier—no more lanterns. I stand for several moments, waiting for my eyes to adjust. When I'm finally able to see again, seemingly endless shore stretches on either side of me. Black rocks litter the sand, some of them enormous boulders which, under the half-light of the moon, look almost like the spines of ancient dead creatures.

Off to my right, on a promontory above this rocky beach, I see the gate.

Grasping my skirts in both hands, I pick my way across the beach. With every step, I become more and more aware of hidden gazes watching me from shadowed crevices. I ignore them and focus on my goal, climbing up to the promontory. Salt stings my eyes, sand grits in my teeth, and as I reach the top of my climb, a chill sea breeze whips through my cloak and bites my skin.

The gate stands before me, a huge circle of black, sea-blasted stone. It's tall enough for a centaur to stand beneath comfortably. I feel pathetically small as I approach. There's no gate guard here like at Aurelis, no horned Lyklor to turn the dial. I find the dial myself in the lee of the gate, a massive thing, set with a hundred or more different marks around its circumference, each indicating a different destination. I find the mark that represents my own home gate, and for a moment, fear I won't have the strength to turn the huge dial and work the magic. My first feeble attempts are about as effective as trying to budge a mountain.

Then something seems to shift ever so slightly, and the whole mechanism turns almost too fast. I pull hard on the lever to keep it from swinging around right past my gatemark. Once the dial is set, I wait a few breaths, studying the air within the stone arch. Finally,

I see it—a shivering ripple in the fabric of reality, like an iridescent veil only just visible to the naked eye.

A little thrill races down my spine. I've never been given an extra day off before! Won't Oscar be surprised to see me? Perhaps he won't have sunk so deeply into a stupor of depression. Perhaps he'll even seem like himself again, if only for a short while.

I gather my cloak about me and step under the gate arch. The ripple I'd sensed intensifies: the way between worlds is opening. I gaze out across the dark waters of the channel, through the murk and mist to where, just for a moment, I glimpse the island of Vespre and the distant peak of the Doomed City. Starlight glints off the library's crystal dome.

I catch my breath.

Then the Between Gate opens wide. I close my eyes as I'm hurtled across worlds.

4

NO MATTER HOW MANY TIMES I DO IT, TRAVELING between worlds never gets any less unpleasant.

It's worse this time—somehow the journey from Noxaur to my own world is more harrowing than traveling from Aurelis. Perhaps it's because the gate is not in good repair, the magic in the stones slightly faded, roughed up by the elements. Ordinarily, I feel a sense of very precise blades cutting away the topmost layers of my skin.

This time, I feel as though my entire body is being stretched in a long, thin string, then stretched some more, then pulled and pulled, until I'm almost certain I will snap. It doesn't actually *hurt*. I can't describe it in terms of pain; words like that are simply insufficient. The stretching continues until I'm sure I feel part of my essence still on that promontory above the ocean, while the rest of me is worlds and worlds away, trying desperately to pull myself together. There's a moment of excruciating resistance.

Then, with a sensation I can only describe as *pop!* I find myself standing in my own home.

I collapse to my knees, sucking in labored breaths. The world spins uncomfortably around me, and I'm obliged to close my eyes and cradle my head in my hands, waiting for the dizziness to pass. Slowly, my equilibrium returns. I peer through my fingers at the familiar square living space with its sparse furnishings. Early morning light falls through a grimy window, shining on Mama's old chair as it rocks back and forth gently, disturbed by the energy of my sudden appearance. The familiar creak strikes my senses like a haunting strain of music. I can almost imagine Mama sitting there in her accustomed place, her hands folded, her gentle face gazing up at me in welcome.

The image fades all too soon. Mama is long dead, after all. There's little else here to remind me of her, just her chair with its broken runner and the little porcelain shepherdess on the mantel with her smashed face and colorful frock.

I pick myself up. The room is quite cold, no fire on the grate wards off the winter chill. I'm glad I wore my cloak. All is painfully still. Empty. "Oscar?" I call, my voice echoing. "Oscar are you there?"

As though in answer, there's a sudden clatter at the front door. I whirl around just in time to see it open. My brother steps into the little foyer, removing his hat as he comes. He stops short in the doorway, and his eyes lock with mine.

"Oscar," I say. "It's me."

Like the sun bursting through a cloudy sky, his face lights up. "Clara! As I live and breathe!" My brother tosses his hat carelessly at the coat tree, not bothering to retrieve it when it misses and lands on the floor. Instead he lunges across the room and wraps me in a great hug. It's so unexpected, I let out a yelp of surprise, then wrap my arms around him, wincing at the frailty of his delicate, bony body.

"You're up early," I say, pushing back and looking him in the eye. It's so strange to see him flushed pink and smiling. "Are you feeling quite yourself?" I laugh, pretending to tease as I press the back of my hand to his forehead.

Oscar snorts and bats my hand away. "None of your clucking, mother hen!" he says with a laugh so like the one I remember from our childhood, it makes my heart skip. "This little chick is cock of the walk these days, and I've no need for a sheltering wing."

I frown. "What were you doing out before dawn?"

"If you must know, I never went to bed. I've been up all night, because . . . well!" He grabs my hand and leads me to the middle of the room where he bids me stand and wait. Then he fairly scampers to the battered bureau on one wall, rummages for something inside one of the drawers, and returns to shove it into my hands. "See?" he says, his voice fairly bursting with excitement. "Make of that what you will!"

His exuberance is catching. I can't help grinning as I say, "What is it?" and look down at what I'm holding. The grin fades into slack-jawed surprise.

It's a copy of *The Starlin.* The most popular literary magazine in the city. Right across the top, just beneath the main header, is a title in bold, ornate type: *Black Heart Beating.* Beneath that, printed in a more modest size yet unmistakable—*A Tale of Terror by Oscar Darlington.*

"Oscar!" My eyes widen as I look up, catching his gaze. "You . . . you got a story accepted by *Starlin?*" When last I'd visited, my brother had been scribbling away at some illegible manuscript, lost in a haze of addictive substances and despair. The transition from that to this—to an upright, smiling brother and a published work of fiction, all in a mere seven days—it seems impossible!

Oscar's grin widens. "It was like a miracle," he says, squeezing my hand. "I wrote it the day after you left, then took to haunting Wrankan Street. That very evening I managed to collar Mister Bazzard; you know, that old bulldog bastard who used to be Dad's editor? He recognized me and tried to shake me off, but I couldn't be shook, not this time. I made him look at the story, and lo and behold! He liked it."

Laughing brilliantly, Oscar throws himself into Mama's old chair, rocking it back and forth so violently that I fear the broken runner will snap right off and send him toppling. "I was paid twenty silver for it. Feels like a fortune after all this time, let me tell you!" He leans forward in the chair, beaming up at me, and clasps his hands. "I feel it, Clara. I feel my luck turning at last. This is the first of many! The ideas are practically *bursting* in my head, just waiting to be written down. And old Bazzard will be slavering for them after today. I won't be able to write them fast enough to please him!"

"Oh, Oscar." I look from him to the magazine and back again. My heart is beating fast, like it wants to soar out of my breast. But a thin thread of worry keeps it tethered in place. "It's wonderful, so wonderful, but . . . but . . ."

He lifts an eyebrow and laughs again, this laugh a little darker than the last. "But what, sister mine? Out with it! What deluge would you like to send to spoil my parade?"

I hesitate. I've never been directly involved in the publishing world, but I grew up in the household of a famous novelist. I don't remember a time when an editor read one of Dad's stories, liked it, and published it all in less than a week. There were always board reviews and editorial passes, revisions, typesetting, proofs, the works.

But I can't deny it: that's Oscar's name on the cover of *Starlin Magazine.*

"After all these years," I murmur. My brother published his first story when he was no more than fourteen years old, and the whole city erupted with excitement as the glowing reviews poured in. But ever since . . . well, ever since my Obligation, ever since I was spirited away to Eledria, he hasn't managed to write a single publishable work. Many times, he's accused me of cursing him, and sometimes, depending on the depths of his despair, he even believed it.

Perhaps the curse—if there ever was such a thing—is finally lifted.

"What, Clara?" he demands, pulling my attention back to him. His lip curls with a hint of bitterness. "Didn't think I had it in me anymore?"

"Oh, Oscar, of course I—"

"No, no." He raises a hand, cutting me off, and leans back in the rocking chair again. "I can't blame you. I was starting to doubt myself. But that's all changed now!"

There's something in his eye—a brightness that looks strangely familiar, though I can't immediately place it. I take a step closer, trying to get a better look. "What changed?" I ask gently.

He flashes me a roguish grin, tilting his head so that his brown curls tumble over his forehead. "I'm in love!"

I'm not entirely certain what expression flashed across my face. Before I can get my features back under control, Oscar tosses back his head and barks a laugh, rocking the chair so far that it hits the wall behind him. When he brings it back level again, I see a flash of shimmering green in his eye. It's not just a trick of the morning light.

A stone drops in my stomach.

"Don't look so startled, sister mine," Oscar says, with a wink. "While you may have no room for romance in your life beyond your staid affection for our esteemed Doctor Gale, the Darlington family is well known for its grand passions!"

I draw myself a little more upright. I shouldn't take offense. It's not a fair statement; my affection for Danny Gale is certainly not *staid*. It's just that I've known him my entire life. I care about him deeply, and while perhaps it will never be a *grand passion*, that doesn't make it any less real.

I take my seat on the stool by the hearth. It was always my place when we were little—me on the stool, Mama in her rocking chair, Oscar sprawled on the floor, chin in his hands, feet kicking behind him. We'd huddle close to the fire, soaking up whatever warmth we could from the meager coals, drawing more warmth from each other.

I reach out now and place a hand on Oscar's knee, leaning toward him. "All right, out with it." I make my voice light, teasing. "Who's the lucky girl?"

An eyebrow slides up his forehead. "Wouldn't *you* like to know."

"As a matter of fact, I would. Is it someone I know?"

"Hardly!"

"How did you meet?"

At this, Oscar simply laughs. He rises and goes to the bureau again. His back is to me, and I can't see what he's doing.

But then I watch him tilt his head back, his hand upraised in a familiar gesture. I go stiff. I've seen others perform that same maneuver. In Eledria, on certain nights, when the fae sought to embrace extra levels of madness.

Slowly I rise and approach Oscar just in time to see him pop a little stopper on a tiny crystal bottle and shove it deep into one of the bureau's recesses. I duck around him, my hand darting fast, and grab the bottle, backing away too quickly for him to react. I hold it up. Greenish liquid glitters in the morning sunlight.

Rothiliom. Nectar of the *rothli* blossom, taken in droplets to the eyes. In concentrated preparations, it can send even the fae into raving lunacy, but along the way, they experience such transports of joy and passion, any risk is worth the reward.

"Oscar, where did you get this?" I gasp and grab him by the arm. He looks down at me, his gaze unfocused. Now that I'm close enough, I can see the green swirl moving through his irises, like twin snakes forever eating their own tails.

He snatches the bottle roughly from me, closing it tight in his fist. For a moment, his expression twists into something so vicious, I almost don't recognize him. Then it melts back into a smile of pure sunshine. "You should see the look on your face, sweet sis! You look like spinster Aunt Joseline seeing her first—"

He finishes so crudely, I flush bright red. This only makes him laugh harder. I lunge for his hand, but he turns from me and dances across the room, holding the bottle behind his back, always just out of reach. "You're it!" he cries, giggling like a schoolboy in the play yard.

"Oscar, I'm serious."

"You're always serious, Clara. So very serious! Always seeing the worst and the darkest when there's such a lot of beautiful things out there in the worlds."

Worlds. He used the plural: *worlds.* Ordinarily, Oscar doesn't acknowledge the reality of multiple worlds. He prefers to put his head down, focus only on himself and his immediate needs, disregarding anything that is inconvenient or uncomfortable to remember.

Worlds.

And he's clutching an Eledrian tincture in his fist.

"Oscar," I say, trying to keep my voice from sounding too heavy, "you can't keep taking that. It will kill you."

He perches on the table, pulls his legs up in a crisscross, rests an elbow on one knee, and cups his chin in his hand, looking for all the world like a capricious little imp. "I'm not sure I mind so much if it does," he says. His eyes sparkle, and once again I catch the gleam of *rothiliom.* "I tell you, I don't mind *dying* so long as I truly *live* in the meantime. Ah, Clara! You don't know what it's like! To feel the best parts of yourself trapped so deep, beyond your own reach. To be less than you ought to be, broken and crippled, then suddenly . . . *free.*"

I pull in my dry lips, wetting them with my tongue. An image passes through my head, a recent memory: I'm standing in Biroris Hall at the Court of Dawn, wearing a blue-violet gown. Princess Estrilde looms before me, her hand grasping my throat. Her magic reaches inside of me, penetrating my head. And suddenly, something is loosed. Like a dam broken to let the river run free. I'd felt power flooding through me, power I'd not realized I possessed, but which welled up from the deepest places of my soul.

It was like coming alive.

I close my eyes, turn away from Oscar. My hands knot into

fists, clutching folds of my gown. That night my whole world had changed. Not for the better. Power like that always takes a toll.

Slowly, I lift my head and face my brother again. He gives me a narrow look, silently promising to spring up and flee if I move too fast. He's like a wild creature of the forest, so delicate, so beautiful, but dangerous.

I take a slow step. "Who gave you the *rothiliom,* Oscar? Was it . . . was it this new love of yours?"

He tilts his head to one side and shrugs. "Maybe."

My stomach pitches. An Eledrian. One of the fae folk has crossed over the boundaries into this world and visited my brother. But why? And how? For the most part, the fae don't bother with humans. It's been centuries since there was any regular communication between the worlds. I could have gone my entire life without knowing the fae even existed had I not inadvertently broken the Pledge and brought the wrath of Eledria down on my head.

"There you go again," Oscar says with a snort. "You look like you've just sucked a lemon. Spit it out, sister mine!"

Taking it slow so as not to startle him, I move around to the other end of the table and sit on the edge. We turn to look at one another, and I hold his gaze. For a moment, that manic light flickers, and I glimpse the shadows that lurk in the depths of his pupils. Living shadows that writhe and roil in his soul like nightmares longing to break free.

"I just want you to be careful," I say quietly, resisting the urge to reach out to him.

He tries to smile again, but it's a little less brilliant than before. "I know. But *I* don't want to be careful. Not always. Not ever. I want to live and live and live some more. I want to know how it feels to burn bright as a meteor, even if it means I must extinguish faster than I otherwise would. I want to make my name in this world, a name that will live on long after I'm gone."

Like our father.

Like Edgar Darlington, legend of the literary world. Even when his excesses and debauchery brought ruin upon the family, his name was celebrated in every circle of society, both high and low. His stories in *The Starlin* made that magazine a bestseller every two weeks, putting money in the pockets of his publishers even as his family starved.

He was brilliant. He was burdened.

He was monstrous.

I drop my chin and stare down at my own hands twisted in my lap. Funny how I hadn't thought much about Dad in such a long time. Sure, I remember his existence, remember how unpleasant he made our lives. . . but for the most part, my memories of him are shut away behind a thick, locked door in my mind. A door I have no desire to open.

With a shake of my head, I lift my gaze firmly back to Oscar. He's studying my face rather too closely behind the sheen of *rothiliom*. I don't like it. I hop down from the table and begin bustling about the kitchen, snatching up a rag and wiping down anything within reach. There's grime enough to keep me busy, and I'm glad for it, glad for any pretext to escape my brother's scrutiny.

"You were out and about early today," I say, determined to change topics. "Anything in particular to drag you out of bed before the crack of noon?"

"Well, *The Starlin* came out yesterday. You know what that means."

"I'm not sure that I do."

"Reviews." There's an edge to Oscar's voice that brings my head whipping around fast to look at him. "*The Wimborne Observer* always posts reviews from Filverel and Luris and a few other notables the day after a major publication like this. I'm keen to see what they've written about *Black Heart Beating*."

Again, my stomach pitches. I know too well what a fickle friend a reviewer can be, what power they wield over the heart of any author. I watched my father suffer the highs and lows of next-day reviews more times than I can count. And the lows were always so much lower than the highs were high.

"There you go with the sour mouth again." Oscar waves a derisive hand. "Are you assuming the reviews will be bad? Some supportive sister you are!"

He hops off the table, heedless of my forlorn, "Oscar, please!" and snatches up his hat and coat where he'd left them on the floor.

I drop my cleaning rag. "Where are you going?"

"To buy a copy of this morning's *Observer*," he tosses back over his shoulder as he pulls his coat on. "I, at least, am not afraid of what others might think. I know my own worth!"

He speaks the words boldly enough, but I'm not fooled. Clutching my cloak close, I dart after him, ducking out onto the street. "I'm going with you. I could use the fresh air."

Oscar grunts in neither agreement nor denial. But he doesn't argue when I tuck my hand in the crook of his arm. "Are you not going to lock the door?" I ask as he sets off down dingy Clamor Street, his pace hurried and a little unsteady.

"A friend might pay a call," he answers with a shrug. "Or might not. One never knows, does one? But I leave the door unlocked all the time just in case. Chin up, sissy!" he adds, chucking me under the chin. "It's not as though we've got anything worth stealing in that house, now do we?"

I can't argue. But I wonder about this friend of his. Might it be the same individual who brought him the *rothiliom?* How long has this "friendship" been going on? Had it begun before my last visit? Or has Oscar struck up this acquaintance within the last week? I'm not sure which idea concerns me more.

I try to push these thoughts aside as Oscar leads the way to King Dain Square, where Mister Durdles keeps a magazine stand and peddles his wares to middle-class society gentlemen looking for a little light reading to enjoy over their morning coffees and crumpets. How many times have I walked this way with Oscar in the past, sent to fetch a copy of *The Wimborne Observer* for Dad the day after a big publication? Those memories of morning jaunts with Oscar are dear to my heart . . . but so often colored by the darkness waiting at the other end.

I try not to think about that now. Better to simply enjoy this unexpected day off and time with my brother. While I know Oscar's high spirits are the result of the *rothiliom* in his eye, it's good to see him smiling and happy, to hear him making the same old jokes he used to make, to put up with his teasing and sometimes biting wit. Just to have Oscar be *Oscar,* not the painfully thin phantom so lost inside his own tormented head.

We arrive at King Dain Square, and Mister Durdles smiles when he sees us coming. "Good morning to you, Miss Darlington!" he says, doffing his hat. "We've not seen you 'round much these last many months."

"No, indeed, Mister Durdles. My work keeps me away from town," I answer with a smile and a polite nod. This is the story we tell when necessary—that I took a position as a governess to some landed country gentleman, instructing his four daughters in reading, writing, arithmetic, and history. Only Oscar, Danny Gale, and his sister, Kitty, know the truth.

"Ah!" Oscar exclaims without so much as a nod for Mister Durdles. "Look, Clara! It's here!"

"Now, now, young master!" Durdles growls, snatching the magazine out of Oscar's shaking hands. "I know your ways! If you wants to read it, you'd better pay first. I won't have you standing in front of my stall, paging through the whole gods-saved thing till I've seen the glint of your coin."

Out of habit, I reach for my money pouch, only to remember that I don't have one. It's not as though I keep human currency on me in Vespre.

"Don't worry, Clara, I've got it," Oscar says cheerfully, withdrawing a coin purse. "Remember, I'm a rich man these days!"

He'll burn through whatever pittance *Starlin* paid for the story in short order. But I merely nod and smile, and Oscar hands over his coin and takes his magazine. Then, putting his back to the vendor, he begins leafing through the pages, one after another. My stomach churns, knowing the next few moments could spell either delight or disaster.

"There!" Oscar exclaims at last. He rolls the magazine cover back and holds the article up close to his face, hiding his expression from view.

"Let me see," I urge, tugging gently at his arm. He doesn't budge. For several long moments we remain like that. My heart seems to have stopped, poised on the brink of suspense.

Then Oscar lowers his arm. "Bastards." His face has gone white as a sheet. He breathes the word through clenched teeth once again: "Bastards!"

I feel as though I've been stabbed to the gut. "What does it say, Oscar?" I ask gently, trying to pry the magazine from his numb fingers. "Please, tell me."

He shakes his head. Then, with a wordless growl, he tosses the magazine to the ground, shakes off my hold on his elbow, and stomps away, shoulders hunched and shaking. I kneel, pluck up the magazine and quickly scan the article. The words seem to blur under my eyes. Only one passage stands out from the others:

Like his father before him, young Oscar Darlington chooses the short format to explore universal themes of death, egoism, and evil. Though one might question whether the son was born with comparable talent, this first attempt at mimicking the brilliance of the late Edgar Darlington is suitably impressive. One may hope that, given time, the son will become the equal of the father.

"Oh." I let a breath escape my lips. Then, in a tight whisper, I echo, "Bastards!"

"Hey! Mister Darlington! Are you all right sir?"

Mister Durdles's voice breaks through the thrumming in my ears. I turn on my heel in time to see my brother just as his knees buckle. Dropping the magazine, I leap to his side, catching hold of him just as he crumples in on himself. He's too heavy for me, and we both sink to the ground, right there in the middle of King Dain Square.

"Quick, get help!" I cry, turning to the magazine vendor.

He, in turn, shouts to one of his runner boys, "Get down to Westbend Charity and fetch a doctor!"

I hold my brother's head in my lap, stroking his cheeks. I've seen this kind of thing happen before with the fae. One moment, they're high on *rothiliom*, the next, it's as though the life has been sucked out of them. They collapse, sometimes for days on end, scarcely moving or breathing, barely existing. How much worse will the comedown be in a human?

"Oscar! Oscar, can you hear me?" I switch from caressing his cheeks to patting them sharply until they turn bright red. It's no use. His face is deathly pale as though he's seen a ghost. Perhaps he has. The ghost of our father. The ghost that haunts us night and day, long after his death . . . his death . . . his . . .

I scream.

Stabbing pain shoots through my head, like fire-heated needles. I clutch my temples, curl over Oscar's limp body. Another stab of pain comes hard on the heels of the first. Then another. And another. Between each stab, I see . . . glimpses . . .

Kneeling at the feet of a shining figure.

A sword upraised.

Blood dripping from its edge.

And beside me . . .

Lying broken and twisted on the paving stones . . .

Something dark stirs inside my head, behind my screams, behind my pain. Something dark and violent. Something alive.

"Clara?" A familiar voice rings out in the cold air.

I just have time to lift my face, to gasp out a single word: "Danny!" Then I fall beside my brother in the street, and shadows close in upon me.

5

T HERE NOW, I THINK SHE'S COMING TO."

The gentle voice sounds muffled, distant, as though speaking through layers of heavy drapes. I frown and turn my head toward the sound, trying to force understanding into my brain, trying to push my way through those curtains as I come slowly awake.

I'm lying at an uncomfortable angle. My head is propped on something soft, but my neck aches, and my shoulder is pushed up awkwardly. Where am I? Not the paving stones in King Dain Square. No, this is at least more comfortable than that. I breathe in, inhaling the scent of furniture polish and delicate lavender soap.

"Clara? Clara, dearest, can you hear me?"

Kitty. Kitty Gale. Relief floods my heart as I recognize the voice of my oldest friend. Then I frown. I don't like for Kitty to be upset, to be bothered by things she cannot help or even fully comprehend. Kitty doesn't need to know about Eledria. About Obligations. About fae bargains and fae vengeance.

About Noswraiths.

"Here, let me give her some of this."

Another familiar voice, warm and a little husky on the edges, always tinged with sorrow. Danny. Danny is here. That thought is enough to make me breathe easier. Danny will help. Danny always helps. He'll tend to Oscar, and—

Oscar!

A burning stink fills my nostrils. I gasp, choke, and my eyes flare open. Danny's face hovers just above mine, summer-blue eyes bright with concern. He's holding smelling salts under my nose.

"Ugh!" I groan and push his hand back. But the powerful vapors have done their work, pulling me fully into consciousness. I see now where I am, lying on the stiffly upholstered lounger in the Gales' front parlor. How I came to be here, I could not say.

"Danny!" I cough, shake my head, and try to sit upright, hastily correcting myself, "Doctor Gale."

"Don't try to sit up, sweet Clara." Kitty's voice draws my gaze beyond Danny to where his sister hovers anxiously. "You've had a nasty turn. You and Oscar both! But you're here now; you're safe. Oh, Danny!" She clutches his shoulder. "Are they sick? Is it grey fever?"

"Don't fret so, Kitty," Danny says, gently pushing his sister back a step or two. "Give her room to breathe. Miss Darlington has had a dizzy spell. There's no sign of any sickness in her or her brother."

It's strange hearing Danny referring to me as *Miss Darlington*. I'm not sure I'll ever get used to it. We've been so close, all four of us, since we were children. But over the last five years, a gulf has opened between me and Danny; a gulf of worlds. I'm not sure we'll ever manage to cross it, to find a way back to each other.

"Where's Oscar?" I demand. My voice sounds so strangely weak and tremulous. I push upright on the pillow, and the room spins, forcing me to close my eyes. I remember then the stabbing pain in my head. It's gone now, the pain and . . . and something else. A memory? Or an *almost* memory. Something I can't fully recall.

"There, there, Miss Darlington." Danny's voice is soothing despite its forced formality. "Oscar is resting in my room. He's all right, though a sight worse off than you. He seems to be experiencing the aftereffects of some potent drug." These last words are spoken reluctantly, as though it's too dark a thing to mention in the presence of ladies.

Kitty, however, paces across the room, flinging up her hands. "Opium!" she growls. "What is the poor fool boy thinking? Does he want to die young? I suppose he thinks it'll be romantic, more suited to his artistic soul!"

I shake my head and meet Danny's eye. "It's not opium."

He looks grave. "I thought not. There seems to be some kind of residue in the corners of his eyes. Something I've not seen before." He hesitates before adding, "It's green."

81

Green and no doubt glowing. I've seen it before when Princess Estrilde returned to her rooms after a particularly boisterous night of dancing and mayhem. Her eyes would be crusted with green for days afterwards.

"It's *rothiliom*." I lower my voice and cast a quick side-glance at Kitty. "It's Eledrian."

Danny's face goes even graver than before. He turns to his sister and says quietly, "Kitty, would you mind bringing tea for Miss Darlington?"

"I'll ring the bell. Hominy will bring it."

"I would appreciate it if *you* would bring the tea. You know best how Miss Darlington likes it. And perhaps you could look in on Oscar while you're at it."

Kitty pauses, her brow puckered. She glances from Danny to me and back again. I'm never entirely certain just how much Kitty is aware of the real circumstances around my month-long disappearances. In person, we maintain a strict pretense that I really am just a country governess. Sometimes I think Kitty has played the game so long, she truly believes it.

In this moment, however, I see a flash of comprehension cross her face, followed quickly by a flash of fear. She nods, her cheeks a little paler than before, and slips from the room, shutting the door behind her.

Danny turns to me again. It's funny—his face is so familiar to me that I often forget how handsome he truly is. Compared to the glory of the fae Lords and Ladies he's quite plain, of course. But the dimple in the corner of his mouth, glimpsed only when he offers a rare smile, transforms his entire face.

There's no sign of that dimple now, however, when he fixes his serious gaze upon me. "Now, Miss Darlington," he says, maintaining that formal mode of address even in private. "Tell me what's going on."

"I'm not sure." I drop my gaze, staring at my knotted fists in my lap. "I've not seen Oscar like this before. He cycles through highs and lows, of course, but not *this*. He claims he's in love. And I think his lover is the one who brought him the *rothiliom*."

"So," Danny hazards, "you think his lover is Eledrian? But how can that be? Doesn't that go against the Pledge?"

I shrug ruefully. "I honestly can't tell you. I understand little about the Pledge and how its laws pertain to the folk of Eledria. All I know is that Oscar couldn't have come by *rothiliom* in this world."

"That's not entirely true." Danny sits back thoughtfully in the chair he's drawn up close to the lounger. He catches and holds my gaze earnestly. "There are places even here in the city where folk gather who know a thing or two about Eledria. There are those who claim even to travel between the worlds, and I've heard tell of a 'Miracle Market' where Eledrian goods are bought and sold. Is it possible Oscar may have found his way there?"

A shiver rolls down my spine. "I suppose so. I suppose anything is possible. I'm so little here, I have only such brief glimpses into his life! My impression has been that he rarely leaves the house. But I don't know where he goes when he does leave. He doesn't confide in me."

"No, nor me," Danny admits. "I make it my business to check in on him whenever I'm able, but he rarely opens his door to me these days. I've not observed him to have any friends or visitors. Certainly no . . . no women."

I nod. "How is he? After his fainting spell, I mean?"

"As well as can be expected. I know nothing about this fae drug, this *rothiliom*. Do you know if it's addictive?"

"To the fae, no. To humans . . . I don't know."

"Was it the drug alone that made him faint?"

I draw a long breath. I don't want to remember that moment in the square, don't want to remember the words of that review. But they're burned across my mind. Slowly, I shake my head. "He had a story published in *The Starlin*, yesterday. Filverel and Luris posted a review in the *Observer* this morning."

"A bad review?"

"No . . ." I look down at my hands again, twisting my fingers together. "It compared his work to Dad's. I'm not certain a negative review could have hurt him more. He forever feels crushed beneath the weight of Edgar's memory. Both personal and professional." I lift my gaze, peering out from under my lashes. "At heart, you know, he's still that little boy locked in the cellar. I'm not sure . . . I'm not sure he'll ever really get out again."

Danny holds my gaze long and hard. Then he reaches out and takes my hand, his fingers closing tight around mine. "You did. You got out."

A shaky, mirthless laugh escapes my lips. "I suppose if there's any good to be had from my being taken to Eledria, it's that I made a final break from my past."

And that's the truth. Isn't it? For while I remember the facts of my childhood, while certain key moments remain clear in my memory, all the *feelings* associated with those facts, those moments, have faded. Or they had faded until . . . until . . .

Until that moment in King Dain Square.

I blink—and in the darkness behind my eyelids, I feel again that stabbing pain. Not as sharp this time, not as bad. But in that momentary flash, I'm once more kneeling on the paving stones in front of my house. Sticky blood stains my hands, the stink of iron fills my nostrils, and powerful fingers grasp the hair atop my head.

"Clara?"

I draw a breath and come back to the present. Danny leans forward in his chair, his brow puckered with concern. Dear Danny! Always so kind, so solicitous. So dependable. Gazing into his eyes, I feel some of my fear and anxiety melt away.

"You're back sooner than I expected," he says, squeezing my fingers.

"Yes." I open my mouth to offer an explanation, then close it again. How can I begin to explain anything about my new circumstances? The idea of telling Danny about the Prince of Vespre, about the library full of Noswraiths, about my own new and terrifying role—all the changes that have come about in the seven days since I last saw him—it's too much. "I was given an extra day," I finish instead. It's lame and explains absolutely nothing.

And I can tell by the look in Danny's eye that he knows I'm hiding something.

Pulling my hand free, I rise, brush past Danny, and go to the window. Elmythe Lane lies before me—the nice, ordinary street of row houses, all neat and respectable. The very *realness* of them threatens to overwhelm me. This is the *real* world, after all. The world I belong to. A world far from towering palaces carved from mountain stone, far from possessed grimoires and living nightmares. Away from devastating fae lords and capricious fae princesses. Away from all those strange terrors that have become my new *real*.

I can escape. Ten more years. Just ten more years, and Elmythe Lane may become my world again. I can marry Danny, move into this very home, keep house for him, order meals, warm his bed, raise his children. Forget the darkness of Vespre and the worlds beyond.

Why does that thought feel more like a dream than ever before?

Suddenly I'm aware of Danny's presence close behind me, just at my shoulder. I close my eyes, bite my lower lip . . . and the next moment, he's taken hold of my elbow and turned me around to face him. "Clara." His warm voice makes my cold heart melt just a little. "What's wrong? Can you not tell me?"

I dip my chin, shake my head.

"It's not just Oscar, is it," he persists.

"Isn't Oscar enough?" I reply with a bitter laugh. Then I roll my eyes to the ceiling, blinking back tears. "I'm sorry, Doctor Gale! I've taken you away from your duties at Westbend Charity, haven't I?"

He shakes his head. "My shift was nearly over anyway. Besides, I'm glad to be here, glad to help."

"Well, I'm quite all right now, I promise. And as for Oscar . . . may he stay a little while? Until he's recovered his strength? I fear he won't wake up before it's time for me to go."

"Of course, Clara. Of course, Oscar will stay as long as he's willing to. We're always ready to open our home to him. I hope you know that. We're here for him, here for you. Whatever you need."

"Thank you, Danny." I try to smile. "It's a great comfort."

His hand moves, shifting from my elbow to cradle my cheek. My eyes widen, flashing to meet his. "Clara," he says, his voice lower and rougher than before. His gaze drops, fixing on my lips. "Clara, may I kiss you?"

I shouldn't let him. It's not fair to him, not fair to me. He ought to have given me up long ago, moved on, found some lovely girl to marry. But here he stands—faithful as ever. Loyal and true. Danny. My Danny. My best and oldest friend.

I nod. Just slightly, just the barest inclination of my chin.

He doesn't hesitate. He closes the gap between us, pressing his lips against mine—lips as gentle and warm as he is. For a moment, they rest against my mouth, so soft.

Then he slips his hand around the back of my head and pulls me closer, deepening the kiss. My heart leaps to my throat, startled by this unexpected burst of passion. A thrill rushes to my head, down my spine, and for a few moments, I'm lost to that sensation.

Lost in a moment of heady sweetness, like wine taken a little too fast. I want more.

But I mustn't have it.

With a little gasp, I put up my hands, press against his chest. He resists for a moment, then releases me, allows me to take a step back. "I'm sorry!" I breathe. "I shouldn't . . . we shouldn't . . ."

"Sorry?" Danny echoes. He tries to draw me to him again, but I keep my hands firmly planted, my elbows locked. Then, with a quick shake of my head I turn away, back to the window, and wrap my arms around my middle.

"Clara, please." He speaks low, close to my ear. "Please, you know how I feel about you. You know my hopes, my plans."

"It's not right," I whisper. "I have ten years of Obligation left to serve. I can't get out of it. I don't . . . I don't even . . ."

I don't even know if I'll survive it. One of these months, Danny, Kitty, and Oscar might wait in vain for my return. The month will pass with no sign from me. Then another month. Then six months, a year, two years. Eventually they'll stop looking for me. Eventually they'll accept that I've been swallowed up by Eledria, never to return.

Perhaps it would be better for everyone to accept it now.

"Something's changed." Danny's voice holds an edge that wasn't there a moment ago. "Something's different about you, Clara."

My chin quivers with the effort to fight back tears. I firm my jaw, refusing to give in.

"What has happened?" Danny urges. "Tell me."

But I won't. I won't burden him with any of it. He doesn't need to know. It will only hurt him.

"You don't have to face it alone, Clara. I can still free you."

My eyes widen with horror. I whirl around, facing Danny. "No!"

"Why not?" He looks angry now, angrier than I ever remember seeing him. "You admitted yourself, there's a way to break your Obligation. I can do it. For your sake, I know I can!"

"No, Danny. No." My voice sounds positively ferocious in my own ears. But I *must* make him understand. "I could not bear it if you were to try and fail. If you were to become Obligated too. Think of Kitty! Think of Oscar! Think of all your patients at Westbend Charity who depend on you! I won't be responsible for their loss of you. I won't."

"It's not your responsibility. It's mine." He tries to cup my face with his hands, but I step back too quickly, putting distance between us. "I love you, Clara," he persists. "Is my love so frail, so meek, that I would not risk everything for your sake?"

"I don't *want* you to risk everything. I don't want it, do you hear me? I don't need to be saved. I will serve out my sentence. If you can't respect that, then . . ." At the flash of hurt in his eyes, I let my words trail away.

"I do respect your wishes," he says earnestly. "I always have. I always will. But I just . . . I don't understand."

"And I can't make you understand." I let out a long sigh. My limbs feel suddenly heavy. It's all I can do not to sink onto the lounger and bury my face in my hands. "I can't make you understand because I can't tell you everything. But please, Danny, please believe me. It's better this way."

He takes a step closer, hands outstretched. But I'm prepared. I dodge away, step briskly across the room. Spying my cloak draped across a chair, I snatch it up and draw it around my shoulders. "I need to be getting back. Please, watch over Oscar for me. I know he can be difficult, but he needs someone to care."

"You know I care." Danny hasn't moved from his place near the window. "I will always care."

The pain I see in his face nearly makes me relent and run to him. But I hold firm. "Goodbye, Doctor Gale," I whisper.

Then I open the parlor door. A little gasp bursts from my lips when I find Kitty standing there, tea tray in hand. Was she listening at the keyhole? How much did she hear?

"Oh, are you leaving already?" she asks, taking a quick step back. A confused blush stains her cheeks. "But you usually stay until sundown, don't you?"

"Not today, Kitty. I'm so sorry." The words tumble out in a rush. I pull my hood up over my head, pushing past her to the front door. "I'll return as soon as I can. Thank you!"

"Clara, wait!" Kitty calls after me. But I'm already out the door and shutting it behind me.

6

MY RETURN JOURNEY IS UNEVENTFUL.

The troll driver waits for me on the pier just as he promised. He looks so much uglier now after several hours away in my own world. Uglier and stranger, like a figure from a children's story. And the morleth are downright dreadful, with their spiny necks arched under their bearing reins and their fanged jaws chomping at their bits.

I shudder at the sight of them as I approach. There's always an adjustment period when I step between worlds. Usually it lasts only a few hours. Then my heart, mind, and body all sink back into the regular rhythms of life in Eledria. This time, however, I suspect it will take rather longer.

I opt to ride alone in the carriage rather than beside the driver. He doesn't seem offended. He assists me inside and shuts the carriage door firmly. The minute we're in motion, I regret my decision. Motion sickness makes my stomach churn.

Worse still, however, is the churning in my brain.

Over and over again, I see Oscar tilting back his head as drops of *rothiliom* fall into his eyes. Over and over again, I hear him speak of love, comparing his new passion to my feelings for Danny.

Over and over again, I feel the pressure of Danny's lips against mine.

My fingers move to touch my mouth. I bite my lower lip. He's never kissed me before. I've often wondered what it would be like to kiss him, how it would feel, how I would react. It's a change to our dynamic, for sure. Always before, the feelings between us have been unspoken. Acknowledged and accepted but unspoken and certainly unacted.

Now everything is different. He's kissed me. He's declared his love. And I . . .

I rejected him.

"But it's not as simple as that!" I whisper fiercely. "*Of course* I love Danny! *Of course* I want to be with him!"

It's true. I'm almost certain of it. Were it not for my Obligation, for those ten long years looming between us, I wouldn't hesitate to accept his embraces, to return them even. Would I?

Clenching my fists, I press my knuckles against my temples. So much for a relaxing day away from Vespre! It's almost as though the Prince *knew* a visit home would leave me glad to return to the Doomed City. A plague of Noswraiths would be a relief compared to desperate brothers and would-be lovers!

So my tormented thoughts spin round and round until finally the morleths' hooves hit solid paving stones, and the carriage lurches from a smooth, rolling progress into bumping, jostling misery all the way to the steps of the palace. I feel bruised and battered by the time the driver opens the door, pulls out the step, and offers his enormous hand to help me down.

I climb the palace steps slowly, wearily. A guard stands at the door and opens it for me, silent and stone-faced and intimidating. I pass through into the massive carved passages of Vespre Palace and shiver.

Shiver because it feels *familiar.*

I don't want that. I don't want familiarity; I don't want to be comfortable here. The moment a body becomes comfortable in Vespre is the moment they become vulnerable to all the dangers lurking in every shadow. I need to keep my guard up. Fear is like armor here. Fear will keep me alive.

I make my way through the winding passages back to my own room. It's a bit of a hike to get there. The palace itself is like a city—a big, empty city, so sparsely inhabited, one could wander the halls for hours and never bump into another living soul.

Thankfully, my room is not so empty, however. I've scarcely stepped through the door before a bright, silvery voice exclaims, "Mistress!" I turn, surprised to see my maid just emerging from inside the tall wardrobe set against the wall, her arms full of pale blue fabric.

It will never cease to amaze me that I have a maid at all. I'm supposed to be the servant here under the terms of my Obligation. Back in Aurelis, it would have been unthinkable for someone like me to be served by another. Here in Vespre, however, I have Lir—beautiful, otherworldly, bossy, and completely charming Lir. She's a troll, though I never would have guessed it if I hadn't been told. Unlike the vast majority of trolls I've seen, she is soft skinned and built rather more along the lines of a human, with perfectly proportioned limbs and a luxurious mane of hair. What sets her apart is her pallor—she is pure white, from the top of her head all the way to the soles of her feet. Even her eyes and eyelashes are white.

Her lovely face breaks in a suspiciously guilty smile at the sight of me. "I wasn't expecting you back so soon!" she says, carrying the bundle of blue cloth to the bed and laying it out. It's a gown—a magnificent gown with a high neck and very little back and nothing at all by way of sleeves. A gown that would have no place in proper society back home. A gown someone like me shouldn't be caught dead in.

I raise one eyebrow. "What is this, Lir? What are you up to?"

She looks down at the gown, blinking as though surprised to see it there. Then she turns her gaze back to me and offers another much too guilty smile. "Did you have a nice time in the human world today?"

"I did, thank you, and what are you doing?" I reply, not about to be deflected.

"What do you mean, Mistress?"

I point at the dress and give her a look.

"Oh. This?" She blinks at the dress again, bites her lip prettily, then turns to me and says all in a rush, "It's not my fault, Mistress! Word came from the Prince that you're expected to dine with him upon your return this evening, and I'm to make certain you are dressed appropriately. This is an appropriate gown for dinner with a prince, you must admit!"

"What?" I stand there, gaping in surprise. "I'm supposed to dine with him *tonight?*"

It doesn't make sense. The Prince has made it very clear that he wants nothing more to do with me than absolutely necessary. I'm here to be trained as a Vespre Librarian, to participate in the proper care and keeping of the Noswraiths and their grimoires. I'm meant to be useful . . . but I know perfectly well the Prince would much rather I was far, far away, out of his sight at all times.

"Why?" I blurt.

Lir's mouth curves in a knowing smile. "One shouldn't question the whims of princes," she answers serenely as she removes my cloak. Upon seeing the humble dress I wear underneath, she sniffs and adds, "I drew your bath. Best be quick and wash off all that . . . humanness."

A glance at her face tells me there's no point in protesting. Besides, after the day I've had, a bath sounds wonderful. I slip away to the washroom but pause in the doorway to tug off my shoes and stockings, frowning suddenly. "Lir?"

"Yes, Mistress?"

"I don't suppose you've heard anything of the children these last two days, have you?"

My maid turns a blank expression my way. "What children do you mean?"

I shoot her a glare. "You know perfectly well who I mean. I haven't seen them since the outbreak, and I'm worried. Do you know if they've tried to reach me?"

Lir's mouth firms into a stubborn line. "I'm sure I don't know."

"Well, ask around for me, will you? That's an order, Lir."

She holds my gaze for a long, resentful moment before finally inclining her head. "Yes, Mistress."

Figuring that's a battle won, for now at least, I retreat to the bathroom and make a valiant attempt to scrub away the stress of the day. But no matter how sweet the perfumed bubbles, no matter how warm and soothing the water, no matter how deep I sink into the enormous copper tub, my mind keeps flashing back to that moment in the street. To Oscar, lying so pale and still in my lap, his face twisted in torment. I hate that I left without seeing him again. I know he'll be in good hands with Danny and Kitty if he'll only allow them to help him. Which is unlikely.

With a groan, I sink under the water, let the scented bubbles close over my head. I stay there, holding my breath in the warmth, the quiet, the stillness.

And see the flash of a bright blade.

A head, hitting paving stones, rolling.

I surge up out of the water, gasping for air, rubbing my eyes with the heels of my hands. But the images are gone already. When I search, there's nothing there, only flashes of pain that recede the moment I stop pressing.

Heart pounding, I sink back into the water, blowing bubbles across the surface. I think I know what's going on. The Prince said that Princess Estrilde suppressed my memories upon my arrival in Aurelis Court. He's since lifted those suppressions but told me it would take time for the memories to return. Is that what's happening to me now? Are these my forgotten memories of the night when the fae folk came from Eledria to steal me away, to punish me for my sin?

Memories of the night after I somehow called a Noswraith to life . . .

"Mistress?" Lir's voice accompanies a tap on the washroom door. "You'll be late for dinner if you don't hurry."

I sigh. The last thing I want after a day like this is to dine with the Prince. What in the gods' names will we even talk about?

Reluctantly leaving my bath, I towel off and don a dressing gown before stepping into the bedroom. Lir sits me in front of the vanity and sets to work on my hair, prattling idly as she works. She talks about Captain Khas and the other trolls serving in the palace, about Lawrence, the Prince's manservant, and her many small grievances with him. All the little pieces of gossip she's accumulated throughout the day, none of it significant, all very bright and cheerful.

I frown suddenly, looking up at her reflection in my mirror glass. It occurs to me that I don't know anything *real* about her. In the seven days since my coming to Vespre, I've never bothered to ask Lir about herself. Granted, I have been *rather* busy these last few days, but still . . .

"Lir?" I say, meeting her gaze in the glass as she pauses over her comb and pins. "How did you come to work here in the palace?"

She hesitates a few moments before answering with a too bright smile. "The Prince gave me a position here."

There's something final about the way she says it. I want to push but decide to leave it for now. After all, there will be plenty of time to deepen our acquaintance over the next ten years.

There's no need for stays or petticoats with the beautiful gown Lir has picked out. I feel rather underdressed without proper structuring garments underneath. But when Lir finishes fastening me into the gown and pinning up my hair just so, then leads me to the mirror, I can't deny the overall effect is quite lovely. The dress fits well but doesn't hug my figure too closely to make me feel immodest. The bare back is a bit much, but it's the style in Eledria and appropriate for this context.

What would Danny think of me in a dress like this?

Hastily shaking that thought away, I give Lir a satisfied nod. "It's nice. Do you think me fit to dine with a prince now?"

"Certainly!" Once more, Lir flashes that knowing smile of hers. "You know, Mistress, the Prince rarely dines with his librarians."

I meet her gaze in the glass again and narrow my eyes. "What exactly are you implying, Lir?"

"Oh, nothing!" She trips away, pretending to tidy up the already spotless chamber.

I turn back to the mirror and give myself another once-over. My stomach knots uncomfortably. Is my maid seriously implying some sort of . . . of *preference* on the Prince's part? For *me*? Such nonsense! The Prince hates me; of that, at least, I'm quite certain. And a dinner like this is nothing more than a power play on his part. A pointless one too, as far as I'm concerned. I'm an Obligate—he is my Obliege Lord. He holds all the power in our dynamic.

A knock at the door draws my head around. Lir hastens to answer, and I glimpse two trolls standing just outside. "Mistress, your escort is here," Lir says. "Are you ready?"

"Yes." I turn and face the door, drawing my head up high. "I am ready."

I've grown more used to the twisting passages of Vespre Palace, but that doesn't help me this evening. I've never been to this part of the palace, and without the aid of the two troll guards marching before and behind me, would have soon been totally lost.

It feels as though we've walked a mile before they finally stop in front of a set of doors. Without a word, both guards depart, blending into the shadows and leaving me quite alone. I stand there in my pretty blue gown, looking around for some sign of another living soul. There's no one.

I face the doors again. The last time I was invited to dine with the Prince, it turned out to be in his private bedchamber. Following such an experience, I have no idea what to expect this time. I only know that I feel rather exposed and vulnerable in this backless ensemble.

Well, nothing for it. I can't stand here all night. I knock.

Immediately, the door opens, and Lawrence appears. The Prince's valet is a plain sort of fellow with a freckled face and a pleasant demeanor. Though he is also an Obligate, serving out a sentence for some Pledge-breaking infraction, he never seems displeased with his lot. He serves the Prince with a loyalty that would be endearing if the circumstances weren't so odd.

"Ah, Miss Darlington!" he says with a welcoming smile. "You're right on time. Do come this way."

I nod in response, lift the hem of my skirt, and step through the door . . . only to stop dead in my tracks. I'd expected a dining hall of some sort. But while there is indeed a large and long stone table set with ornate dinnerware, this is no hall. It's an enormous balcony extending over the city. Instead of a chandelier, there's a vault of twinkling stars in the vivid purple heavens above. Instead of wallpaper or moldings, there's a sweeping view across the island and out to the ocean horizon.

It's a magicked view, I realize after I've managed to suck in a few stupefied breaths. It must be magicked . . . because from where I stand, I can see across the water, through the mist, all the way to a distant glimpse of a golden city bathed in dawn light. Aurelis. The same magnificent golden palace where I spent the first five years of my life in Eledria, serving Princess Estrilde. I've never seen it from such an angle and can scarcely believe the vivid detail discernable even from such a vast distance. This viewing spell must be powerful indeed.

Why, I wonder suddenly, would the Prince want to dine within sight of the very kingdom that should, by right of blood, be his?

No sooner does this thought crossed my mind than I hear footsteps echo in the passage behind me. I turn to see the Prince himself stride into view, his elegant robes wafting like wings behind him. "Ah! There you are, Darling," he says, spotting me in the doorway. "I see you've made it to dinner."

7

ONCE AGAIN, I RESTRAIN MYSELF FROM CORRECTING his misuse of my name. Instead I sink into a deep curtsy and murmur, "Prince."

He waves this off. "None of that now. I'm much too famished for formalities. Gods, it seems an age since I've eaten properly! I trust you're hungry after your little jaunt to the human world. I've always found that mortal air works up a powerful appetite!"

Before I can get a word in, he takes hold of my elbow and deftly guides me out onto that enormous balcony, steering me toward the table. I give my arm a little shake, and to my surprise, he immediately lets go and saunters to the head of the table without a backward glance. His color is much improved since this morning. Has he fully recovered from his bout of sickness? Perhaps . . . but I also detect a gleam of glamour about him, which implies he's covering up something.

He drops into his chair at the head of the table, then motions with one hand. "Please, be seated."

I look up and down the table, noting that the only other place set is just to the Prince's right. Moving with purpose, I make my way to the opposite end from him and gracefully perch on the edge of the huge stone chair sitting there.

The Prince meets my gaze down the long stretch of tabletop. I blink blandly back at him. His eyes narrow. "Come now, Darling, don't be ridiculous. I'll shout myself hoarse if we're to have any conversation at all."

The muscles in my back tense. Any moment he'll issue an order, command me to rise and come sit in the place beside him. When he does, I'll obey him, of course; the terms of my Obligation will compel me. Resistance will lead only to pain, as I know from experience. When Princess Estrilde issued orders, I learned to jump into action.

The Prince tilts his head, his words hanging unanswered in the air between us. My heart beats a little faster, expecting at any moment for the command to come. Instead he stands abruptly, picks up the crystal decanter in front of him with one hand, snatches up two goblets with the other, and strides down the long length of the table. Once he reaches my end, he sets down the goblets, catches the back of the chair on my left, drags it out, and settles into a graceful lounge. Plucking up one of the goblets, he pours himself a measure of wine and takes a sip.

"Have some?" he offers then, holding up the decanter. When I don't respond, he goes ahead and fills my goblet. "And how was your day, Darling?"

I stare at him, my lips parted in a disbelieving O.

Before I can think of a coherent answer, the doors open once more, dragging my attention back across the balcony. Lawrence steps into view, followed by a stream of massive, stone-hided trolls carrying a series of silver trays. They circle the table, their heavy feet vibrating the floor with every step they take, yet their movements oddly graceful in a trollish sort of way. They arrange their platters before the Prince and me, lifting covers to reveal sumptuous dishes: cuts of red meat rubbed with spices and grilled to a charred finish, fruits and vegetables impaled on spikes and slow roasted in a shiny glaze, loaves of fresh bread with intricate patterns cut in their domed crusts to reveal glimpses of the soft insides, as well as soups, sauces, smears, and spices, all in a bewildering array. Far too much food for any two people.

Their task complete, the trolls line up, holding their heads high, their massive chests out, their arms straight and proper. They're wearing absolutely enormous uniforms complete with silver epaulets, and the whole effect is so incongruous, I have to press my hand over my mouth to keep from giggling.

"*Jah rifrok,*" the Prince says in a surprisingly convincing troll accent, nodding pleasantly.

The trolls respond with perfectly synchronized bows, like a wave going down the line. Then they turn and file out again without a word. Lawrence, standing at the door, asks, "Will there be anything else?"

"Not just now, thank you, Lawrence," the Prince responds with a wave.

His valet bows and exits, shutting the door behind him. And I am once more alone with the Prince of Vespre.

He stands and, taking up a pair of silver tongs, begins serving a gluttonously large portion of meat onto my plate. He adds some of the fruit and vegetables on the side, and even goes so far as to butter a slice of bread for me. All this he offers with great dignity before even starting on a plate for himself. At last he sits back, takes a large bite, chews, swallows, then looks at me. "Please, eat."

I can't find any appetite. But I don't want him to know. I pick up a fork and take a very small mouthful. It's so delicious, my hunger surges, and I force myself to keep from shoveling one unladylike bite after the other.

The Prince eats in silence for a little while before pausing and swirling his wine. He sniffs it delicately, then takes another sip before turning to me. "And how was your visit home, Darling?" he asks. "I trust you found everything as you expected?"

I pause, my cheek currently rather too full of vegetables. Why is he doing this? Why is he acting as though he isn't my lord and master, as though he doesn't control every aspect of my life via magical agreement? My stomach churns, and I wish that I'd not eaten so much. Chewing quickly, I swallow and pat my lips with a napkin. "It was nice," I say at last.

"Of course, I shan't be able to sanction extra days off on a regular basis," the Prince continues conversationally as he cuts his meat into tiny, perfectly even bites. "But after your efforts of the last few days, I rather felt you deserved it."

I don't know how to answer this. "Thank you?" I manage at last. It seems the only appropriate response.

He shrugs. Using the end of his knife he begins delicately arranging tiny bits of garnish on top of each bite of meat until each one looks like a perfect little culinary work of art. "And how are your people?" he asks, his tone all ease and familiarity.

Why do I get the feeling he's fishing? As though he already knows the answers but wants to see how I'll respond, whether or not I'll lie or withhold from him. "They're well," I say.

"You have a brother, yes? I seem to remember there was a brother somewhere about. A young fellow. How does he get on these days? Was he pleased to see you?"

He knows about Oscar? My heart gives a little hiccupping jump in my chest. But of course he knows, he apparently knows everything. And if that's true, he knows as well exactly what kind of state my brother is in. What is he trying to do? Rub it in my face?

I offer a cold little smile. "He is well," I lie.

"Glad to hear it."

I watch in silence as he eats those perfectly prepared bites of his. A coldness creeps over my soul. Could it be the Prince who gave my brother the *rothiliom?* But . . . but *why?* What could possibly be his motivation? The answer comes with chilly clarity: to torment me. To punish me. I took his mother from him . . . why should he not make sport of my brother in turn?

I set my utensils down with a clatter and grip the arms of my chair. The Prince looks up, his expression startled, then sets his own fork and knife down and steeples his hands. "What's wrong?" he asks, his gaze too keen for comfort.

I can't very well accuse him outright of getting my brother addicted to fae poison. "Nothing," I say and hastily pick up my fork, shoving a too large bite into my mouth. I roll it around uncomfortably, trying to find a ladylike way to chew, all the while painfully aware of the Prince's scrutiny.

He swirls his wine once more. "Tell me, Darling, is there anyone else in your life? Anyone besides family whom you visit on your return journeys, I mean."

For an instant, I'm standing back in the Gales' front parlor. Danny's hand is on the back of my head and his lips are pressed against mine.

I draw a sharp breath through my nose, forcefully swallow the too large mouthful, and grimace. Then, setting my fork down with rather more vim than necessary, I turn on the Prince. "Exactly what is the point of all these questions?"

His brows rise slightly, his expression much too innocent to be trusted. "Simply making conversation. It's what people do at dinner in civilized circles."

I shake my head. "You are *not* simply making conversation.

Don't tease me. I don't presume to *know* you, but I know you well enough to know you have a purpose in all that you do. So what's the purpose here? To all of this?" I sweep my arm in an all-encompassing gesture. "This dinner, this gown, this cordiality, this pretense?"

"Pretense?" He leans back in his chair, tilting it on its back legs. It's much too casual a posture for such a fine setting, and I half wonder if he'll go right over backwards. "No pretense. If you suspect an underlying purpose, that's resolved simply enough. You and I must work together at close quarters in the library. There are dangerously few of us, and the work we do is perilous. We need to know that we can depend on one another—all of us, at all times. You and I"—he tilts his goblet my way—"have not, perhaps, gotten off to the best of starts. Due to a variety of factors."

Due to the fact I killed your mother.

I look down, my heart seething. But the Prince continues, his voice as casual and easy as ever, though he must know his words are like poison to my ears. "We must learn to get along, like it or not. Even to trust one another, if possible."

I meet his gaze sharply. Then, very softly, but with careful enunciation I say, "Bullspit." It's a word I picked up from Nelle Silveri. A nasty word, a word that doesn't belong in a lady's vocabulary. A word that would make my poor mother roll over in her grave. It rather burns my tongue to speak it.

It does the trick. The Prince looks momentarily shocked. "Come again, Darling?"

"I said, bullspit. And I mean it. I know bullspit when I hear it. You haven't brought me here to get to know me, to build some sort of bond of trust between us. You should at least be honest with me."

"And why," he says, his voice suddenly low, "do you think I'm not being honest with you?"

"Because you want nothing to do with me." I try to keep my words level, but I can hear the edge of tension creeping in. "Because you don't trust me, you don't *want* to trust me, and you *never will*. You don't even want me here and only brought me under duress."

"I hardly think that's fair. I remember going through rather a lot of bother to fetch you."

"Only because you were desperate. Only because you're running low on librarians. You know I have what it takes to at least partially fill the gap left behind by Soran Silveri. And you don't much care if I survive to the end of my Obligation or not."

"And why would you say that?"

"You can scarcely stand the sight of me. Your request on my first night here made that clear enough."

He frowns. "What request was that?"

"That I keep out of your sight unless we are actively training."

"Ah!" He purses his lips, his brow furrowed. "Yes, well, that does sound rather like me, I'll admit. But I've changed my mind."

I level a stare at him. "Why?"

At this, at least, he finally looks uncomfortable. "Why?" he repeats. "Because I am a prince. Princes are notoriously fickle, are they not? Always changing their minds on a whim. Am I not allowed to be as whimsical as the next prince? Should I not be permitted to contradict myself upon occasion? I'll probably change my mind again at some point, then you won't have to bother yourself with meals like this."

I hold his gaze for a long, silent moment. Every instinct tells me to break it, to look away, to bow my head and submit to whatever this power struggle is.

Instead I open my mouth and say very quietly, "If you've changed your mind about seeing me, have you changed it about the children as well?"

"What children?"

"The troll children. Dig, Har, Calx, and Sis. Will you let them come back to me?"

He takes a sip from his goblet, swirls the wine, then sets it down. Slowly, he turns the goblet around, the little jewels adorning its base flashing in the starlight. "On that score I have not changed, no. In fact, I have set protective wards around your room to make doubly certain the little waifs don't return. It's time you learned the ways of Vespre, Darling, and respected those ways." He lifts his sooty lashes in a flash of violet. "Whether or not you agree with them."

Anger burns in my breast. I stand, fists clenched.

"Where are you going?" the Prince asks mildly.

"To bed," I answer. "I'm tired. It's been a long day." I ball up my napkin and toss it onto my plate. "Good night, Prince."

As I turn, however, his hand darts out, catches hold of my wrist. "No," he says. My eyes flick to meet his, and when I tug, his fingers tighten ever so slightly. "Stay."

"Is that an order?" I demand. "Are you *obliging* me?"

He holds my stare for a long moment. Then, abruptly, he releases my wrist and leans back in his chair, a sardonic smile curling his lip unpleasantly. He says nothing, merely takes another long sip of wine.

I turn to make my escape. On second thought, however, I whirl and pick up one of the full platters from the table. This elicits a grunt of surprise from the Prince. "What's this, Darling? A little midnight snack?"

I don't answer. And since he doesn't stop me, I simply walk away from the table, heart pounding, limbs trembling. My hands are full, so I kick the door three times, wait a beat, then call out, "Mister Lawrence?"

He opens the door and peers out at me. "Miss Darlington?"

"I should like to return to my room now."

Lawrence casts a look over my shoulder, his brow puckered. "Prince?"

"Take her away, my good man," the Prince calls easily, lifting his goblet and somehow managing not to slosh his wine. "The poor girl can only stand so much good company it seems. Let her return to her rooms and soothe her poor nerves."

My teeth set on edge. But when Lawrence smiles pleasantly at me, I answer in kind. "Allow me, miss," he says, offering to liberate me of my platter.

"No, thank you," I respond, and sweep through the door, leaving the balcony, the feast, and the Prince behind.

8

SOME SMALL PART OF ME HOPES THE PRINCE WAS lying when he said he'd placed wards around my room. Opening the door awkwardly with one hand while I balance the platter on my hip, I half expect to see little rock-hide bodies tumbling about the floor, clambering up the bedposts, jumping on the bed, and tossing everything from the wardrobe out onto the floor. I'd anticipated their delight at the sight of the food I'd stolen for them, how they'd rush at me, probably knock me off my feet in their enthusiasm.

But no. There's evidence of Lir's handiwork—a nightgown laid out on the bed, the fire in the grate stoked up, the lanterns hanging from the stalactites overhead turned down to dim. But Lir herself is not present. And there's no sign of the children.

The Prince spoke the truth after all. I'm alone.

With a sigh, I set the heavy tray of food down on the table near the window. After a last forlorn look around, I sit at my vanity and stare at my reflection in the glass. Slowly, I begin to take pins out of my hair and drop them in a little bowl. Every motion is calm, and my face is perfectly serene.

But inside, my head is spinning.

I don't trust the Prince. Why should I? He may be half human, but he's also half fae. He's got an agenda, of that I'm certain. And he's trying to get me to let my guard down.

I won't be fooled, though. I remember the three tenets of an Obligate's life in Eledria: *Never anger the fae. Never trust the fae. Never love the fae.*

At least I'm not in danger of loving the Prince of Vespre! But I've certainly angered him. That much I accomplished long ago, angered him in an unforgiveable way. And an angered fae is a deadly fae indeed. Thus, I dare not trust him. Not ever.

Released from its coils, my hair tumbles about my shoulders. I brush it vigorously, working out the stress and tangles of that long day. By the time I'm through, the shadows in my room are deeper than before. Or perhaps it's just a trick of the eye. I'm not sure. But I can't help feeling as though there's a *living* sort of energy in those shadows.

I set my brush down and deliberately fix my gaze on one particularly dark, dense shadow in the corner of the room beyond my bed, farthest from the fireplace. I could almost swear I see something sitting there. Something . . . not big. Quite slight, actually, with long, awkward limbs drawn up in odd contortions close to a shuddering body.

Dread shivers through my soul.

"Nothing is there," I whisper.

But it's not true. And that darkness is just waiting for me to climb into bed, to put out the lights. To lie there in the gloom, vulnerable.

I can almost, *almost* hear a voice whispering on the edge of my awareness: *He really loves you . . .*

With a little gasp, I rise from my seat. "That's enough!" My voice is loud, firm. The moment I speak, the shadows retreat and become nothing but shadows once again. Empty.

I change out of the beautiful blue gown into the nightgown. Then, with a last glance at the stolen food platter, I climb into bed, pull the covers up to my chin, and nestle deep into the pillow.

I should put out the lights. I know how—Lir taught me the word that will make the pale lanterns overhead extinguish. But I can't. I shut my eyes firmly and count to a hundred. Then I open them again and stare up at the spiderweb pattern of the canopy over my head.

A little growl rumbles in my throat as I sit upright, push the covers back and slide out of bed. Plucking a candle from the vanity, I light it at one of the wall sconces and set it firmly in a silver candlestick.

Night is not much different from day here in Vespre, the realm of perpetual twilight. For the most part, human members of the palace household, like myself, depend on the tolling bells to help us track the passing hours. But I do believe the hours closest to midnight are significantly darker, as the sky beyond the windows deepens from purple to indigo, and the stars stand out more starkly in their inky backdrop.

I hold my candle high. It's a white light, not like the warm, yellow fire from my own world, but *moonfire*—a colder, paler light that suits this world. For some moments, I stand in the middle of the passage outside my room, my heart pounding strangely. I look in the direction of the library.

Then, growling again, I turn and march down the passage, my stride purposeful and swift. I've made inquiries. I'm fairly certain I know where I'm going.

I reach the west wing without encountering a single soul. It's almost too easy to believe that Vespre Palace is abandoned, that I am the only living person remaining in a vast household of ghosts and memories. The air almost breathes of emptiness.

And just behind that emptiness waits the Nightmare Realm.

I set my jaw and continue, determined not to let fear sway me. I pass down a long hall with floor-to-ceiling windows on either side. There's no glass in these windows to separate me from the night air, and I know this wing of the palace is set above a great, precipitous drop of many stories. It's too easy to imagine the whole structure swaying beneath my feet. But I keep going, my gaze firmly set on the door at the far end.

When I reach the door and try the latch, it gives without resistance. Part of me hoped it wouldn't.

I push the door open and see a long stair spiraling up in front of me. I take a moment to draw one last long breath before I begin the climb. There are many windows on my left as I venture up, offering views of Vespre City under starlight. There are more windows on my right—barred windows set into heavy doors. The rooms on the other side are dark and, more importantly, empty. But I'm sure I've come to the right place. So I keep climbing, on and on, until I arrive at the very top of the tower. The very last chamber.

I step up to the barred window and peer inside.

A single lantern hanging from the center of the ceiling illuminates the room—a small, comfortable chamber, nicely furnished. There's a bed with a thick quilt neatly folded at the foot, and a plump, upholstered chair drawn close to a little fireplace. Tapestries line the walls, depicting peaceful, pastoral scenes, and a thick pile rug takes up most of the floor. Even this window through which I look is trimmed with lace curtains.

There are no other windows.

And there are no books.

A thin figure sits in the corner of the room. Not on the chair or the bed, but on the floor itself, pressed as tight into the corner as she can get. Her bare feet are tucked under her, her face is turned to the wall. It's as though she's hiding from the lantern light.

A low, ceaseless moan reaches my ears.

My throat thickens. I try to speak but can't. I want to retreat, to flee back down those stairs, back down the gallery of tall windows. Back to my room. At least the shadows waiting for me there are *mine*.

These shadows, this darkness . . . this doesn't belong to me.

My lips move, trying to form a name. It comes out a pathetic whisper. I clear my throat and try again: "Vervain?"

The figure in the corner starts, as though struck by a barb. She pushes even tighter into the corner, and her moaning redoubles.

My pulse throbs in my throat, a strange mixture of horror and heartbreak roiling in my gut. The last time I'd seen Vervain, she'd saved my life. She'd dragged me out of the clutches of the Hungry Mother and tried to reassert the broken binding over the Noswraith. The Noswraith who was her own creation. The dark child birthed from the depths of her own dark mind.

Guilt pricks at my heart as I gaze on the poor woman now. But I've come this far; I feel I must do what I came to do.

"I . . . I wanted to check on you," I say. "Nelle told me you were here. Mistress Silveri, I mean. They're all worried about you." My words sound so lame, so foolish in my own ears.

But unexpectedly, they seem to do the trick. The moaning stops. Vervain's arms, wrapped over her head, lower slightly. She turns her head, peering through straggling dark hairs. Her eye is bright and bloodshot in the lanternlight. It fixes on me.

"Hullo, Vervain," I say softly. "Do you remember me? I . . . I wanted to see how you're doing. I heard you were in a bad way."

There's a terrible sound, like a rasping bray, followed by a wet cough. Vervain's whole body convulses, her shoulders hunching up to her ears. But she turns slowly away from the wall, peeling back inch by inch, bone by bone, until she faces me. She sits cross-legged, hunched, her elbows resting on her bony knees. She wears a nightgown similar to mine but torn and shredded and bloodstained in places. Has she been hurting herself?

"Yes," she says at last. Her voice is clear, lucid. "Yes, thank you. I *am* in a bad way. Kind of you to notice."

I can't tell if there's bitterness in those words or not. There's a strange sort of calm in her bloodshot eyes as she blinks up at me. It's deeply disturbing. We stare at each other for some moments. I feel paralyzed by my own stupidity. Why in the seven gods' names did I come here?

"Clara," the pale woman says at long last, as though she's finally arrived at the solution to a difficult problem. "Clara. Darlington. The new talent. The Prince's little poppet."

I bristle. "I am the new librarian, yes."

Vervain nods slowly. "Take care, little poppet. The Prince is a dangerous one. Not safe. Not ever. Don't give him your heart unless you're willing to give him your soul as well."

"Thank you for the warning." I recall suddenly how Vervain had looked at the Prince once or twice when she didn't know I was observing—that expression of mingled adoration and hatred. But I am not her. "I don't intend to give my heart to anyone."

Vervain chuckles. "Ah, but that is the real tragedy of existence, is it not? We all of us think we have some sort of hold on our own hearts. We all of us think we have some sort of control over how and when and whom we love. But ultimately, we're prey to forces beyond our control. Each and every one of us."

As she speaks, she starts to turn from me, to curl over into herself once more, her arms over her head. But I have not yet gotten what I came for.

"Vervain," I say, very quietly. "Vervain, I have to ask you something."

There's no response at first. Then, slowly, Vervain uncurls and looks up through the bars again. Her expression is once more startlingly lucid. And so, so sad. "You want to know how I came to create a Noswraith," she says.

I feel as though I've been punched in the gut. But the words are out now, the question asked, as clearly as though I'd asked it myself. My hand trembles so violently that the candlelight wavers, threatens to go out.

Vervain pulls herself into a seated position, pressing her shoulders to the wall. She leans her head far back, as though exposing her pale, thin throat to a blade. I watch the muscles of that throat constrict as she swallows. "Tell me, girl, why do you want to know such a thing?"

"I need to know." I duck my gaze and draw a shaky breath. "I need to know because . . . well, because I don't know how I did it. I know that I did. Everyone seems to know, in fact. But I . . . I don't understand *how.*"

"You mean you don't *remember* how."

"I don't. I don't remember any of it. Or rather, it's like I don't *want* to remember."

"Well, of course not." Vervain snorts. When I glance at her, her

124

eyes gleam with bitter light. "No one in their right mind would want to remember such a thing. A Noswraith is born from the deepest pain—betrayal. And the heartbreak that follows betrayal." She shakes her head slowly, closing her eyes for a moment. "There is no worse pain."

I open my mouth, then shut it again. I don't want to ask.

Vervain's lashes rise, her slitted eyes glaring at me. "You're going to say, *But how were you betrayed, Vervain?*" She laughs, a low, growling sound. "No doubt they've told you my story. No doubt they've told you what I did and why I did it. But they don't know. They don't *know,* I tell you. They only think they do. But they've not lived my life, they've not walked my path. They've not experienced my betrayal."

She bends forward, and her dark hair falls across her shoulders, veiling the sides of her face. "The world betrayed me," she whispered. "The world that drove me to betray myself. Everything I was and everything I ever hoped to be. Drove me to the point of death. But I cheated them! I cheated them all. From that death, I brought forth life—the life of a nightmare. Born ravenous, born with an insatiable hunger."

I see it in my mind's eye again—the Hungry Mother, bearing down on me in the darkness of the nightmare-veiled streets.

Come to my arms, she'd crooned.

Her hunger had been palpable, the very need she exuded nearly enough to kill.

Vervain suddenly unfolds her limbs, rises. She stands a

moment, swaying, then wafts toward me. In the pale light of the lantern overhead, she resembles the Hungry Mother—not in physical appearance, but in essence. She approaches the window, and when I back away, she grasps the bars. "What is your betrayal, little girl?" Her teeth are very white, and her gums look black in the flickering candle's glow. "From whence does your darkness flow?"

I shake my head. "I don't know. I don't know, I tell you!"

"You don't know? Or you *won't* know?"

That's the truth. Whatever suppressed memories are trying to rise, I don't want them. I don't want to understand the *hows* or the *whys* of what I did, and I certainly don't want to remember doing it. I feel as though I'm balanced on the tip of a knife, poised between darkness and light, evil and goodness. As long as I hold my breath and close my eyes, I need not fall one way or the other. Better to stay in this place of between.

I cannot remember.

I dare not remember.

Vervain's chuckle brings me back to myself. "You'd best figure it out soon," she says. "I know what you've made. And I know how easily it may slip its bonds. Without its name, its true name, the name it was given by its mother on the day of its birth . . . without that name, not even the Prince can hope to bind it forever. It will break every chain, burst every spell. And then it will come for you. They always come for their makers. It will swallow you up, and there will be no hope for binding it ever again."

I back away, shaking my head, retreating down the steps.

Vervain strains at the window bars until I can see nothing but her one bright, bloodshot eye. "Remember, little girl!" she cries. "Remember!"

I turn and flee down the stair. Vervain's hollow laughter follows, biting at my heels.

9

THE NEXT MORNING, I REPORT TO THE LIBRARY AT six bells, yawning and bleary-eyed. My stomach is in knots of dread at the prospect of another magic lesson with the Prince, but to my relief, he isn't anywhere in sight. Instead Mixael asks my help reshelving a trolley full of newly rewritten binding spells.

Thankful to turn my attention to a relatively mundane task, I help Mixael load the book lift, then ride it down to the seventh floor. I feel a little guilty, for Nelle Silveri has been perfectly clear that the book lifts are for *books*, not *librarians*, but Mixael laughs off my concerns. He rides up and down the lifts without a care, even while his mother looks on and scolds. I wouldn't dare thwart the senior librarian's rules so openly. Still, I let Mixael talk me into it when she's not around. It's a relief to spare my knees a stair climb or two.

We set to work companionably, arranging the books in their proper places. It's not just the new bindings, of course—there's the old bindings too, now broken and empty, but always carefully preserved in their proper place.

"Why is it so important to keep the old spellbooks?" I ask Mixael at one point as I shove another battered volume into place. "I mean, the spells inside are broken, and the books themselves are on the verge of collapse. Does it really matter if we keep them?"

A few casements over, Mixael pauses, his brow puckered. "You know, I'm not entirely certain?" He slides a book into place, steps back, and frowns at it contemplatively. "It's probably something to do with residual magic," he says at last. "Though the spells are broken, some of the magic lingers on. The combined residue most likely adds to the strength of the current binding spell. So the more old volumes you have, the stronger the new volume should be." He shrugs and goes on with his work. "I don't know, Miss Darlington. It's just what we do, what we've always done. Best not to question such things too closely. These are living nightmares we're talking about after all."

With that he yawns hugely, covering his mouth with the back of his hand. He is particularly hollow eyed this morning. "Are you all right, Mister Silveri?" I ask.

He tries to toss me a careless smile but can't disguise the tired lines scoring his face. "Oh, don't you worry about me! I was up late into the night, is all. Working on a binding. One of the Big Bads down below was making some trouble. Since it's one we don't have the proper name for, it can be a bit of a bother to keep it properly bound up."

My stomach sinks. Though I answer Mixael's statement with a little nod and a sympathetic grin, I turn away quickly. He doesn't say it, and his expression is carefully neutral, but I'm almost certain that it's *my* Noswraith he's talking about. *My* dark creation, whose name I don't remember.

I chew my lip, staring at the spines in front of me but not really seeing them. Then, with a little quiver of my shoulders, I continue working, shelving to the end of my row. When I'm done, I wait for Mixael by the book lift. He joins me, and we ride it up to the first floor again, all without speaking. There's another trolley full of books waiting to be loaded, and we set to work, hauling heavy stacks. My muscles strengthen with every passing day in Vespre Library; I can carry up to eight fat grimoires at a time now. Who knew that being a librarian required so much physical prowess?

I'm shaking off a little smile at this thought when suddenly the big main doors of the library burst open. I turn and watch Captain Khas stride in. Mixael's face immediately lights up with a grin. Khas comes to an abrupt stop, and for an instant, I see embarrassment flash across her stern, porcelain face. There might even be the faintest hint of a blush.

"Good morning to you, good captain!" Mixael calls out brightly, hastening up to her. "What brings you to the library today? Looking for a little light reading?" He shoves his hands in his pockets, altogether boyish and charming as he peers up at her from under locks of red hair tumbled across his forehead.

Khas contrives to make her expression even more severe, determined not to react to Mixael's undeniable charm. "There's been a break-in," she says curtly.

Mixael's eyebrows rise. "A break-*in,* you say?" He tosses me a quick glance. "Generally, we're more concerned about things breaking *out.*"

But Khas shakes her head. "I've been following the trail all morning. It leads straight here. To the library."

At that, the flirtatious charm drains from Mixael's face. "Do you know who it was?" he asks, in a suddenly serious tone.

"Trollfolk, I believe," Khas responds.

At this, Mixael looks relieved. "Well, that's something at least. Thank you, Captain. I'll sound the alarm. We'll find the blighter, make no mistake!"

With that, he sets off to a set of bellpulls located near the door. I trail after him and whisper earnestly, "What exactly is happening, Mister Silveri?"

Mixael yanks on one of the bellpulls, which sets a series of bells ringing on all the different floors of the library. I cover my ears and wait approximately thirty seconds for the clamor to subside. Only then does Mixael turn to me. "We've had break-ins before. Mad Lords and Ladies of the various Eledrian courts who take a fancy to the idea of owning a pet Noswraith. Lord Luirlan of Solira was the last to try it. He was devoured by the Tall Man. We only ever found bits of him spattered between the eighth and eleventh floors."

He lets this sink in, leaving me by the bellpulls to rejoin Khas. She's barking orders at a series of troll guards as they enter the library. Though it's difficult to read the trolls' stony faces, I get the impression they're as sick to their stomachs as I am.

Andreas and Nelle arrive from different parts of the library, looking wide-eyed and serious. The Prince joins us last of all. I can't help a flutter of discomfort in my gut at the sight of him emerging at the top of the stair. I've not glimpsed him since our dinner last night. I don't know if he's avoiding me or not.

He certainly doesn't look my way now but strides swiftly over to Khas and Mixael. "Mister Silveri," he calls out. "Report, if you please."

Mixael whirls at the Prince's approach and hastily fills him in. The Prince directs his next several questions to Khas, who informs him of a breakdown in one of the warding spells on the southeastern hall. Listening in, I think through my mental map of the palace. I'm not yet very familiar with all of its vast and intertwined passages and wings, but I think I know which hall Khas is talking about. It's another one of those great, long, windowed galleries, extended over a huge drop. Whoever breached the wards on that hall would have had to first climb a good three hundred feet up sheer stone wall.

"Did they fly in, do you think?" the Prince demands, obviously thinking much along the same lines as me.

The captain shakes her head. "Impossible. An aerial assault would have been spotted from the watchtowers."

"And you're sure your lads weren't sleeping on the job?"

Khas looks offended. "My *hrukta* never sleep on the job."

The Prince pulls a face then turns to the guards and the gathered librarians. His gaze passes right over me as though I'm not there. "Mistress Silveri," he says, addressing Nelle, "you and your underlings will keep to the first floor for now. Have your quills and spellbooks at the ready and be on alert for a Noswraith outbreak. Otherwise, stand back and let Khas and her *hrukta* do their work."

Nelle grunts in agreement. Then she grabs my arm and draws me back, saying as she goes, "You heard the man. This way."

The four of us retreat to Nelle's cubical desk, built directly into the stone wall. There we huddle, watching the guards descend the spiral stairs, which seem far too small and rickety for beings of their size. Khas and the Prince exchange a few words before both of them disappear to the lower levels as well. It suddenly feels very empty up here on the first floor. And much too quiet.

I look around at my fellow librarians. Andreas, true to form, has taken a seat on Nelle's desk, pulled his legs up crisscross beneath him, and is already deeply engrossed in a book. Mixael paces, tapping his quill against his thigh. Nelle sits in her desk chair and absently strokes her wyvern, who keeps up a steady, nervous grumble.

"Does this happen often?" I ask in a low voice. "Break-ins, I mean."

Nelle grunts. "More often than you'd think." She sighs and leans back in her chair. "The folk of Eledria don't fully understand

Noswraiths, you see. They know they're dangerous, and they know they're contained in spellbooks. But they seem to think that because they're made of *human* magic, any fae worth his salt should be able to dominate them. And if one of the Lords or Ladies thinks they need an edge in one of their eternal conflicts, they'll send a thief around to our library to steal a grimoire or two. Sometimes, depending on their level of arrogance, they come themselves. Never turns out well for anyone."

"But don't you worry, Miss Darlington," Mixael puts in, casting me a reassuring grin. "Captain Khas will sort it out in short order. She's done it before."

His pacing tells me he's not as confident as he sounds. I remember a few nights back, when we'd all rushed out to hunt down the Hungry Mother. Mixael and I had seen Khas preparing to march into the city. The look on Mixael's face had been . . . revealing. Khas, as a troll, possesses no magic that can possibly work against a Noswraith. But that hadn't stopped her from launching herself into the fray and distracting the Hungry Mother. It wasn't a battle she could hope to win, but she'd not hesitated. In fact, she'd saved my life.

A smile tugs at my mouth as I watch Mixael now. He's so obviously in love with the beautiful troll! Everyone can see it . . . except perhaps for Mixael himself, who hasn't bothered to mention his feelings to Khas. I wonder how she would take declarations of love from a human librarian. Is it even possible for such a connection to thrive?

We wait in tense silence, hardly speaking to each other. Every few minutes, Mixael walks to the rail and looks down to the lower floors. Then he walks back, meets his mother's gaze, and shrugs, shaking his head. Andreas calmly continues reading, occasionally pausing to make notes. Nelle mutters, and her wyvern climbs down from her shoulders and sits at her feet, where it begins to groom its scales with loud, annoying slurps.

Finally Nelle says, "No point in just sitting around twiddling our thumbs. You two, take a page from Andreas here and make yourselves busy. Andreas, slide your bony behind off my desk so I can get on with some of these bindings."

The other two jump to obedience right away. Andreas gathers his books and papers, and both he and Mixael disappear to their own cubicles, plunging into whatever tasks they have waiting for them. I, however, don't have any work. I'm still too new to the library to be trusted with writing spells on my own, and I can't be sent down for shelving or to check for compromised volumes.

Both bored and uneasy, I drift back to my own desk, located on the opposite side of the floor from the others, all the way across the huge open space. The Prince says that while I'm still learning proper spell-writing technique, I'm too dangerous to allow near the others. Once I've acquired a bit more skill, I will presumably be given one of the many empty cubicles closer to Nelle and the others. For now, however, I feel quite isolated.

Puffing a sigh through my lips, I pull back the chair and take a seat before casting a last glance around the first floor. I can see the other three, all of them bowed over their work. They truly *belong* here and are so confident in that belonging. I can't help wishing I shared their confidence. It would be nice to belong somewhere. Anywhere.

Sighing again, I turn to my desk and scoot my chair in closer.

My feet hit something solid.

"Ouch," a little voice squeaks.

I yelp and push my chair back so fast that it nearly tips over. My heart gallops in my breast.

A face peers out from the shadows beneath my desk.

"You all right, girl?" Nelle's voice calls across the empty space.

I turn sharply and look across the rails to where she sits, peering out of her cubicle. With a quick nod, I raise an arm and offer a wave. The last thing I need is for her to come and check on me. "I'm fine!" I call out, sending a reassuring smile her way. "Just bumped my toe, that's all!"

Nelle grunts and turns back to her work. I glance toward Andreas and Mixael's desks, but neither of the other two librarians looked around at my cry. I could almost swear I hear the pound of troll feet down on the lower floors as Khas and her cohorts search for the library intruder. Up here, however, all is calm.

Swallowing hard, I ease out of my chair and down onto my hands and knees.

"Calx?" I whisper.

A stony face peers out at me from huge, pleading eyes. Then its mouth opens, flashing a wide grin full of tiny, gemstone teeth. *"Mar!"*

The next thing I know, the troll boy scrambles out from under the desk and throws himself into my arms. I'm nearly knocked flat but manage to catch my balance. Very aware of how exposed we are, I tuck in closer to the desk, hiding in the shelter of the cubicle. Calx, when standing at full height, doesn't come any taller than my knee, but he's a wide brick of a boy and extremely heavy. Holding him is like cradling a cinder block. I manage to scooch him off my leg before he cuts off all circulation, then I wrap my arms around him. He presses his head against my chest and sighs, *"Mar! Mar! Hroa tor kata, mar!"*

I have no idea what he's saying, but I stroke his back comfortingly. "What are you doing here, Calx?"

He gazes up at me, blinking hugely. "I look for *mar!*" he says. His voice is rough, like two stones being scraped together, but he speaks my language clearly enough. "*Mar* need me. *Mar* need brother and brother and Sis."

My heart swells. "Are your brothers and sister all right?"

Calx nods, then shakes his head. "Brother and brother and Sis need *mar*. *Mar* need brother and brother and Sis. And Calx!" he adds, pointing a thumb at his own chest for emphasis.

How am I supposed to respond to this? The truth is, the *last* thing I need in my life is another layer of complexity. And it doesn't get much more complicated than a whole passel of orphaned troll children! But the look Calx gives me is so beseeching, how can I deny him?

"Where are the others? Where are Har and Dig and Sis?"

A shadow comes over Calx's face. *"Guk jorton,"* he says. Then adds with emphasis, *"Guk, guk-guk."*

I have no idea what the word means, but something about the way he says it makes my skin crawl. "Can they come to me? Can they come with you?"

Calx shakes his head sadly. "Brother and brother and Sis no come. Want come. No come."

Something is wrong. I know it. Something Calx wants to communicate but can't with his limited language skills. My arms tighten around him. If only I could scoop him up and keep him safe! I close my eyes, press my cheek against the top of his hard little skull—and in the darkness behind my eyelids, I see Oscar. Not as I last saw him, manic with *rothiliom* light swirling in his eyes, but as the small boy I used to hold. In the darkness. On the cellar steps. Listening to the angry voices on the other side of the door. Light streaming under the door, shadows closing in all around. Caught in the middle, between that light and that dark, holding each other—

A heavy hand lands on my shoulder. "What have you found there, Darling?"

I twist in place, staring up into the Prince's face. His extremely beautiful, extremely stern face.

"Good job," he says around a smile that doesn't reach his eyes. "You've found our little troublemaker." With those words, he plucks Calx from my arms. Though I know the troll boy is tremendously heavy, he holds him up high and calls out, "Captain Khas! Your sneak thief has been apprehended. Call up your lads."

"Wait!" I scramble out from under the desk, tripping on my own skirts before finding my balance. I hold out my arms to Calx, who reaches for me, wailing a piteous, *"Mar! Mar mar!"*

The Prince turns deftly, whisking the child out of my reach. He fixes me with a stern look. "I believe I've made myself quite clear on this subject: *No* adopting troll children."

Protests pile up on my tongue, but I can't seem to speak any of them. Captain Khas reaches the top of the stair, and I see other trolls emerging from other stairwells all around the upper story of the citadel. They close in on us, blocking off any hope of escape even if I were mad enough to attempt it.

I turn to the Prince and clasp my hands. "Please. Please, they don't have anyone else. They're orphans!"

"I am well aware," he responds coolly. "I'm also aware of the consequences should we break the law of the Deeper Dark. Are you familiar with troll theology, Clara Darling? No? Then think twice before you go charging in where you do not belong."

Khas is upon us. The Prince turns and neatly deposits little Calx into her outstretched arms. The captain's mouth curls with sneering displeasure. "Your pardon, Prince," she says, holding the child at arm's length. "I had thought the boundaries secure. My *hrukta* will redouble their efforts, of that I assure you."

"Take care they do," the Prince replies. "I've had word from the *Hrorark*, and they have given me to understand that they won't suffer interference with the *grakanak-balja*. We don't need trouble with the Priestesses of the Deeper Dark, that's for sure!"

Khas tucks Calx under one arm and offers a crisp salute. Then she marches away, her guards falling into single file behind her, huge and lumbering. Their heavy footfalls make the floor shake all the way to the tower's foundations countless stories below. Calx, peering out from under Khas's arm, cries one last forlorn, *"Mar!"* before he and the guards disappear through the door, which shuts firmly behind them.

I stand at my desk, still as stone. Tears brim, and when I blink, escape in two drops, racing down my cheeks. Vaguely, I become aware of the other three librarians approaching. But I don't look at them.

Instead I whirl on the Prince. "How *could* you?"

He offers me a placid look. "Rather competently, I thought. And with some relief that the intruder was nothing worse than a determined troll waif. A much simpler problem to solve than a thief, that's for sure!"

How can he just stand there so coolly, after watching that child be carted away like so much unwanted garbage? I want to wring his neck. I want to slap his face. I want to cause him pain, real pain. "That *child* has lost his *mother.*" The words slice through my gritted teeth. "Does that mean *nothing* to you?"

For an instant, a spasm crosses the Prince's face. My stomach turns. It was a dirty blow, after all. The next instant, however, the expression is gone, replaced by his usual condescending smirk. "Go on, Clara Darling," he says, crossing his arms and widening his stance just slightly. "Go on, tell me more about these people, this city, this world. Tell me more how my leadership offends you, how my decisions go against your highly attuned sensibilities. Instruct me in matters of which you know nothing. Please. I'm listening."

Heat roars in my head, throbs in my temples. I feel as though something in me will burst. But I keep my voice low and level. "I may not know anything about this city or this world. But I do know that poor child is looking for someone to care for him. And why should he not be cared for? Because of a misguided belief that some distant god will care enough? Well, what if that god intends to show his care through the people he's placed in the child's life? Did no one ever consider that?"

The Prince holds my gaze for an endless moment. "What I consider," he says at last, "is the ultimate good of Vespre. Vespre cannot afford to be overrun by Noswraiths. Which means I and my librarians are responsible for the keeping and maintaining of the grimoires. That's it. Nothing more."

"What if I'm capable of more?"

He snorts and rolls his eyes to the crystal dome overhead. "Your urge to nurture and protect the weak will be the death of you, Darling!"

"I'd rather die for a good cause than live knowing I could have done more."

"But *I* need you to do more." He takes a step closer to me, uncrossing his arms as he comes. He seems suddenly much taller than before. Is he using a glamour to intimidate me? "I need you to do more *here*. In the library. I need you to do your part. The same as I need Nelle and Mixael and Andreas. The same as I need Captain Khas and Lir and Lawrence and every member of this household, who perform their roles to maintain the delicate balance of this entire city. What I do *not* need is to be battling the very trolls I'm trying to protect. What I do *not* need is for the *Hrorark* to be offended, to whip their followers into a frenzy. What I do *not* need are angry zealots storming the palace walls, breaching our defenses, infiltrating the library. What I do *not* need is a bloodbath."

He batters me with his words. As each blow falls, I seem to see the horrors he sees—visions of Vespre Palace crawling with trolls, of the library doors burst in, the librarians torn to pieces. Grimoires ripped from their shelves, pages shredded. Noswraiths breaking loose.

It all feels terribly real. And terribly possible.

He comes to the end of his verbal assault, and we stare at one another, neither of us moving, scarcely breathing. For just a moment, I feel as though I finally *see* him. Him and the tremendous burden bowing his shoulders. The burden that is this city, the burden that is this library and all the horrors it contains. No one should be made to carry such a burden alone. But he does carry it. Because no one else can.

I close my eyes, turn away. But when I'm free of the Prince's penetrating gaze, it's Calx I see in my head. His desperate little face. "I don't know about the rest of it," I say, looking up at the

Prince once more. My voice is softer than before, gentler, but edged with steel. "I only know those children need a mother."

He looks at me for a long, hard moment, and I almost let myself believe I see a flicker of understanding deep in his eyes. But I'm probably imagining it.

He turns abruptly in a sweep of long, trailing sleeves and marches for the nearest stair, tossing back over his shoulder as he goes, "Your services are not required here for the rest of the day. Return to your rooms, Clara Darling, and clear your head."

I draw a sharp breath, as though I've been slapped.

Then, firming my jaw, I ram my chair roughly back under the desk and storm out of the library. I refuse to meet Nelle's or Mixael's eyes as I shoulder between them, and I'm almost certain I feel the Prince's gaze burning into the back of my skull.

I pull the huge doors open, slip through, and let them slam shut behind me.

10

I RETURN TO MY ROOM. I HAVE NOWHERE ELSE TO GO. I feel like a child being punished, and I hate the feeling, hate the powerlessness of my situation, my inability to offer real help to Calx or his siblings.

Flinging open my door, I look around the room in vain hope that maybe, just maybe, the other troll children will be here, waiting for me. There's no one, of course. The room is empty.

I yank the door shut behind me and storm into the room, standing in the middle for some moments, breathing heavily, full of pent-up rage with no vent. Finally, I snatch a pillow off the bed, stuff it against my face, and scream as hard as I can. Then I scream again and again and again.

Suddenly, I'm on the floor. Sobbing.

Oscar! Oh, Oscar!

I'm so helpless. Helpless and useless, just like I've always been. Never able to do the right thing, never able to save him. I tried to protect him, I tried to be the shield he needed. But I couldn't be. I could never be enough. Not for him. Not for me. Not for anyone.

There was only one person who might have protected you . . .

I straighten, hiccupping on sobs, and push strands of hair off my damp cheeks and out of my eyes. Though I try not to, my gaze pulls to the dark corner of the room where, just last night, I'd believed something lurked. But the lanterns are lit, and the corner isn't dark. The room is full of light, almost as bright as day.

Shuddering, I wipe tears from my cheeks and rise. I pull the spiderweb curtains back from my window to look down on the city below. On all those concentric streets ringing the palace, leading down and down and down deeper still into the surrounding valleys, into dark crevices below the surface of the world. Trolls, after all, live as comfortably under the mountains as on them.

Inevitably, my gaze wanders to that section of destroyed city street where the white stone buildings are leveled and blasted black. Lawrence had told me it was a Noswraith's doing, from an outbreak last year. The same outbreak that killed Soran Silveri, Nelle's husband, Mixael's father.

How do the trolls feel about having their city used as a storage facility for Noswraiths? They wouldn't have had any choice in the matter. I don't pretend to understand the complexity of Eledrian politics, but I know it's been many a long age since trolls had kings and queens of their own. Vespre falls under the rule of Lodírhal of

148

Aurelis—a distant and uncaring sovereign, who decides the fate of subjects he's never even set eyes upon.

No one cares about the trolls. Save for the trolls themselves. And even they care nothing for their own needy orphans.

I put a hand to my forehead, rubbing hard. Then, coming to a sudden decision, I cross the room to my door and stick my head out into the passage. There's no one there. Drawing a deep breath, I shout as loud as I can, *"Lir! Leeeeeeeeeeeir! I need you, please!"*

The "please" sounds a bit ridiculous when shouted at that volume. Hopefully Lir will take it in the spirit in which it's meant. I step back into the room and pace in front of my window. My head is awhirl with anxious thoughts. I keep seeing little Calx pinned under Khas's arm . . . but in my mind's eye, his face morphs into Oscar's and back again, until I can't quite keep them straight. I press my knuckles against my temples, trying to drive the image out.

A light tap at the door. "Mistress? You called?"

I whirl and rush to the door, yanking it wide. "Lir! I'm so glad you're here!"

She smiles and allows me to drag her into the room. "I'm always happy to serve, Mistress. But why are you here at this hour? I would not have expected you to finish in the library so early. Did something happen? I heard about the break-in. That wretched *grakanak-balja*. Disgusting!"

I let go of Lir's hands and back away. "Lir, I need your help."

She smiles again. "Anything, Mistress! I'm always happy to help."

"I need you to help me understand about the . . . the *grack-ank-bal-ya*." I try my best to pronounce the series of sounds I've heard. I know my accent is dreadful, so I add for good measure, "The orphans. Calx and his siblings."

Lir draws back a step. Her smile is gone. She crosses her arms, looking suddenly austere. "There's nothing to understand. They're orphans. They don't belong here. They're pests. That's it."

"That is *not* it." I shake my head. "I've heard about the . . . the Law of the Deeper Dark." At this, she casts a sideways glance toward the door, as though she wants to escape. "Please, Lir," I persist, trying to angle myself between her and the exit. "I know that orphans are said to belong to the troll god, Lamruil. That to take them is seen as dishonoring to the god. Is this so?"

Lir nods. Her lip sticks out in what I first take to be a pout. Then I see it tremble. I cross the space between us and take her hands. Suddenly, Lir's eyes are swimming with tears. They catch in her pale lashes, glittering under the lantern light as she turns her face away from me. "Help me understand," I urge. "Please."

She takes a shuddering breath then dashes the heel of her hand across both eyes. "It's a sin to take orphans from Lamruil," she says finally. "For those who take them and . . . and for the orphans themselves. If they are taken, they can never reenter *Vagungad*."

I blink uncomprehendingly. "What is *va . . . vung . . .* ?"

"*Vagungad*."

"Yes. That. What is it?"

Lir licks her lips. "It's difficult to explain in your tongue. It . . .

it pertains to cycles of holiness. If one falls off the *gungad* for an infraction against the god, the *va* is damaged. Sometimes irreparably. One cannot reenter *Vagungad* with a damaged *va*."

I consider this, trying to make sense of the strange words via their context. "And . . . and if it's not your fault that your *va* is damaged?"

"It does not matter. A damaged *va* is still damaged, whether by something you did or by something done to you. And once you have fallen from *Vagungad*, you can never return."

There's something about the way she says it. I hesitate a moment before asking softly, "Is this what happened to you, Lir?"

She meets my gaze briefly, then looks away and nods. Another tear slips down her cheek and runs off her chin. "I was *grakanak-balja*." Her accent is harsher than before. More trollish. "I was without father or mother. *Orphan*." She spits the word. "I did not trust *ord grakanak*, the Law of the Deeper Dark. I did not trust my god to protect me. I sought outside of *Vagungad*, and I was taken in. Here. By the Prince. He accepted me into his household, gave me a place to live. Feno and Lialana, two of his servants, became my *tar* and *mar*."

I recognize those names: I've seen them carved into two of the empty desks in the library. Lir's adopted parents were two of the Vespre Librarians who long ago lost their fight to the Noswraiths. Leaving Lir alone. Orphaned for a second time.

"Did they . . . did they care for you?"

Lir offers a sad little smile. "They loved me." She sniffs and shakes her head. "I loved them too. But they died, and I am alone.

I am outside of *Vagungad*. I am outside my people. I have no place. I do not serve in the library like my human parents, for I am trollfolk—I cannot read or write. I do not return to my people in the city, for I am *va-lak*. I belong nowhere."

My heart aches at the sound of her voice, at the lost, forlorn, hollowness. Finally I start to understand Lir's distaste for the troll children—she sees them through the lens of her own self-condemnation and heartache.

I hesitate a moment. Then, giving in to impulse, I take her hand and squeeze it gently. "You *do* belong. Here. With me. I don't know what I'd do without you, Lir."

A spark reignites in Lir's eye. She looks at me through shimmering tears. "And I do serve you well, don't I, Mistress?"

"You do. You have been a good friend to me."

Lir blushes prettily and ducks her head. "I'm glad."

We stand there a little while, letting the moment simply be. But Calx's desperate face is still forefront in my mind. At last, though I hate to dig into what is obviously an open wound, I press deeper. "Do you regret your time with Feno and Lialana? Do you wish they had never been your *tar* and *mar?*"

"Oh no!" Lir answers at once. Then she stops, frowns, shakes her head. "That is . . . I wish not to be outside of *Vagungad*. But I would not take back my time with them. Never." She looks almost fierce as she says it, as though even to speak the words is rebellion. "It's just . . . humans are so frail. They die so easily." She looks at me solemnly. "It is better for troll children to stay in *Vagungad*. It is better for them to trust the Law of the Deeper Dark. It is hard, but trolls are made to be hard. We are made to *ttarmok*—that is, to bear with the pressure of worlds down in the deepest places. It is what makes us what we are."

"Lir," I say, choosing my words carefully. "Are you less of a troll because of your upbringing?"

She nods sadly. "Yes, Mistress."

I continue, knowing very well I'm venturing into unknown territory. "But mightn't you be looking at it the wrong way? Maybe you aren't less; maybe you're *more*. You've been shaped and formed by two worlds—troll and human. You are something from each and, therefore, greater than both. Stronger. Maybe you are even more *ttarmok*." I stab at the word a bit wildly, quite sure I've butchered the accent. But though Lir shakes her head, her eye brightens as she looks at me. "I don't pretend to understand. Not about the holy cycle, or about what you've been through. But I do know that Calx, Har, Dig, and Sis have called me *mar*. They have claimed me as their mother. I can't ignore that claim. No more than Feno and Lialana could cease to be your parents, even after death."

The tears brimming in Lir's lashes escape and roll down her face.

"Lir," I say, slowly, "can you tell me where I might find the children?"

She looks startled. Her body tenses, like a wild animal on the verge of flight. "Why?"

"Because I think they might be in trouble. I think Calx risked a lot to find me because he's afraid. For himself and his siblings."

Lir's expression darkens. She looks away. For a moment I fear she'll refuse to speak. Finally, however, she says, "Most of the Children of the Deeper Dark are collected by the *Hrorark* to serve in the City Below."

My heart shivers. I remember the Prince mentioning the *Hrorark* earlier today, though I'd not understood what he meant. Something about the way Lir says the word fills me with foreboding. "What kind of service is this?"

"They're made to collect the cocoons of the *hugagug.*"

"The what now?"

Lir looks uncomfortable. "The *hugagug.* The sacred moths which make their nests deep below the fiery river, down where the pressure is so great, it makes even a troll go strange in the head. Big trolls can't make it so deep—so they send children. Children small enough to crawl down the tunnels made by the *hugagug.*"

I struggle to understand what I'm hearing. "They send them after cocoons? Moth cocoons?" I shake my head. "But *why?*"

"For the *umog,*" Lir replies, as though this is answer enough.

I open my mouth. Then shut it again. I'm not sure I can take one more strange-sounding troll word just now. My head is already aching, trying to make sense of all this.

But one thing at least is clear: "So you're saying the children— *my* children—are being used for slave labor?"

Lir blinks then frowns. "It isn't slavery to serve the Deeper Dark."

"But they don't have any choice in how they serve."

At this, she merely shrugs. "The god chooses."

I don't begin to know how to combat this mindset. Lir speaks with such conviction, and I don't want to be disrespectful of her beliefs. But I also don't like thinking of those children being sent down into the dark and the heat and the pressure, crawling into tunnels to fetch some sort of cave-moth cocoons. Everything in me rebels at the notion.

"Tell me, Lir," I say, "do you know where they are? Can I at least see them?"

Lir shakes her head. "That wouldn't be a good idea, Mistress. If the children see you, it might . . . it might make them hope. Better for them to accept their place and stay within *Vagungad.* It's hard, but that's life. Life for a troll, anyway."

"And what would have happened to you if the Prince hadn't taken you in? Would you have been sent down under the fiery river too, searching for moth cocoons?"

"Yes. Very likely."

"And do you think you would have been happier?"

This Lir cannot answer. She stands there, open-mouthed, her eyes slightly unfocused, as though she's trying to see into a realm of possibility she's never fully considered.

Leaving her to think it over, I march to the wardrobe and take out my cloak, tossing it around my shoulders. "Where are you going, Mistress?" Lir asks, roused from her thoughts.

"I'm going to find the City Below. Alone, if I have to. And I'm going to ask everyone I meet where I can find the mines and the children forced to work in them. I'm going to ask and ask and keep on asking until I find someone who will tell me. Then

I'm going to find the children, seven gods help me! *All* seven of them, Lumruil too!"

"But, Mistress—"

"Yes?"

Lir opens and closes her mouth several times, making little half-hearted sounds. But when I take a step toward the door, she leaps in my way, squaring off in front of me. She's such a pretty thing, but in that moment, I'm reminded of just how very *troll* she is, tall and imposing.

"Stand aside," I say with as much authority as I can muster.

"The Prince won't like this." Her voice is tremulous, uncertain.

"The Prince doesn't like a lot of things." I shrug. "I said, stand aside."

Her chin quivers. Then, with a little gasp and a sob, she steps to one side, allowing me to pass. I march out the door into the passage and set off swiftly. I count each footstep that I take, holding my breath, hoping . . . hoping . . .

Suddenly, Lir is beside me. She slips her arm through the crook of my elbow and squeezes. "I'm with you, Mistress," she says softly. "I'm with you, come what may."

I smile. That's one victory, at least.

11

THE STREETS OF VESPRE ARE BATHED IN STARLIGHT. I've only ever been in the city proper one other time, on the night of the Hungry Mother's attack. Which was not exactly ideal for getting an honest impression of the city and its inhabitants. Then, there were either stampedes of terrified trolls threatening to pulverize my bones beneath their stomping feet, or utter silence as the city's denizens cowered in their homes, hoping not to be found by the ravening Nightmare.

This, however, is an ordinary day in Vespre. I see trolls going about their lives, presumably after typical troll fashion. I don't pretend to understand all that I'm seeing, but there's something about the bustle that feels comfortingly familiar. The beings I encounter may be huge, lurching creatures with faces of stone, who make the ground reverberate with every step they take, but they seem to be doing the same sorts of things one would expect of city folk back home. I spy a mother troll with a passel of trollings riding on her shoulders, possibly out for exercise, or maybe making a run to market. There goes a big trollman, carrying a massive boulder on his back. Is he taking it home to his family or hauling it for his employer? Who can say?

Lir leads me deeper, and I catch glimpses of troll life everywhere. There's a market square where vendors seem to be selling different varieties of rock, all arranged in interesting pyramids. Troll farmers draw carts behind them, piled high with more stones, and there are even what I take to be upper class trolls being carried on decorative litters or riding strange troll beasts the likes of which I've never before seen.

Everything about troll society seems to be concentrated on rocks. The trolls carry, cart, and collect rocks of all kinds, and while I can't tell them apart in the twilight, I get the impression there are many different varieties. Perhaps troll eyes, adapted both to the perpetual twilight above ground and the deep gloom below, are able to perceive subtleties of color and texture that I simply can't.

We pass one street corner where a big boulder stands. I'm struck by how like a living troll it seems. I can almost see the shape of hunched shoulders and a heavy head.

"That is a *vagob*," Lir says as we draw near, and nods at the boulder.

"A what?" I take a second glance.

"What you would call a *holy man*," she supplies.

So it's not a boulder? I look more closely and realize, what I had dismissed as merely an impression of hunched shoulders and a head are *exactly that*. Now that we're closer, I can even discern features in the face. It's a troll all right.

"Is it *alive?*" I ask.

"Oh yes," Lir answers, her voice reverent. "He is deep in the *Vagungad*. He will be stone."

We continue on our way, but I cast a last glance back at the *vagob* troll, wondering a little at that last phrase Lir spoke. Something about the way she said it makes me think it's a sacred saying. Perhaps troll religious practice is aimed at becoming more and more one with the stone that so dominates every facet of their lives. Perhaps this is why they care so little about orphans— if the ultimate goal is to become stone, then fleeting experiences like suffering or love simply don't matter. All that matters is the sedentary agelessness of rock.

We proceed a little further and pass by a group of trolls who seem to have come to observe the holy man. They cross to the other side of the road when they see us coming, and one of them calls out a hoarse, "*va-lak!*" The others growl and rumble a series of aggressive sounds that make my blood pressure spike.

Lir ducks her head and, holding my arm a little more tightly, hastens down the road. "What was that?" I whisper.

She shakes her head. "Most folk know I am *va-lak*—outcast. Not many trollfolk live in the palace; our faces are known everywhere in the city." She looks ashamed. "They know I am out of cycle. I will never be stone."

With that, she sinks into silence. I wonder as we progress deeper and deeper down the steep streets, down toward the City Below. I know that Lir, beautiful and delicate as a moonlit dream, is considered a *throwback* to the days before trollfolk fell from favor with Lumruil. Mixael explained to me that trolls like Lir, and Khas, and my own little Sis are rare, and when they occur, they are seen as lucky among their kind. But apparently Lir's outward appearance is not enough to spare her judgment from others of her kind.

Lir leads me to the lower parts of the city where the mountain's shadow falls, rendering all deep and dark as true night. Because the towering buildings on either side of me are carved from the living stone, I feel as though I'm venturing underground. Every now and then I look up, just to make certain I can still see the sky overhead.

We pass more trolls down in these deeper parts of the city. Lir is no longer the only one getting dirty looks. More and more often the clusters of trolls stop whatever they're doing and simply stare at us as we walk by. Several times, Lir draws me to her other side, putting herself between me and them.

"What's wrong?" I ask nervously after one particularly tense encounter. "I thought the trollfolk of Vespre welcomed the librarians? I thought they appreciated our fight against the Noswraiths?" There's definitely no appreciation in the faces of the trolls on this street.

"They are *Hrorark*," Lir says, rumbling the word like a miniature avalanche. Her face is uneasy. "They are believers of the Old Ways. They do not care for humans."

I shiver, remembering suddenly something the Prince had said on my first night in Vespre: *"There are trolls who follow the Old Ways. They think humans make for good eating."*

I look back over my shoulder at the last cluster we passed. They're still watching me.

"This way," Lir says suddenly. For the most part, we've taken streets that lead straight down from the palace. Now she ducks into a side avenue. We follow this, turn a few more times, make a few more plunges . . . and when next I look up for a glimpse of starlight, I discover we've gone so deep, I can no longer see the sky.

My knees begin to tremble.

The truth is, we've walked a *very* long way in the last two hours. I'm totally lost and twisted around. I can't even see the palace when I look back up the road. Utterly dependent on Lir, I cling to her arm like a frightened child.

"There." Lir points to a building ahead of us. It looks like a massive, unsightly stalagmite, jutting up from the ground. The windows and doors might have been bashed into place rather than carved. All of them are open to the elements—trolls don't believe in doors or shutters.

We creep up to the building and peer through the lowest of the windows. I'm just tall enough to see over the ledge if I stand on my toes. Inside is a huge, open space full of vats—massive vats, carved directly into the floor, brimming with what looks like molten lava.

Big trolls stand over them, stirring with enormous stone rods.

Little scurrying figures carrying large sacks on their backs race in and out of the harsh red light. I watch as one of them scurries up to a nearby vat and empties its sack into the molten sludge. Some weirdly shaped thing makes a *splat*. I try to follow that same figure away from the vats, to see where it goes. At the back of the huge chamber, I see a pit like an open, ugly mouth in the ground. It's maybe twenty feet in circumference. The little trolls run to it and clamber over the side, empty sacks slung over their shoulders. Now and then another one will pop out, its sack bulging.

So this is the mine Lir told me about. I stare into the red, hellish glare. Now that I've come this far, I have no idea what to do. I can't bear to think of Calx or any of his siblings in a place like this.

"What do they want the cocoons for?" I ask in a whisper. Lir turns to me, blinking with gentle perplexity. "It's just, I've never seen trolls interested in anything other than rocks."

At this, she snorts. "True enough, Mistress. But the *hugagug* cocoons are necessary. Once they're purified, the *umog* make thread from them."

"Thread?" I shake my head. "What do *trolls* need *thread* for?" Other than the palace trolls, I've never seen any of the denizens of Vespre wearing more than a loincloth.

"It's for the *grankan-umog*—the Priestesses of the Deeper Dark."

She says it as though this is all the explanation I could possibly need. She couldn't be more wrong.

Before I have a chance to question further, however, I'm startled

164

by the sight of a pale figure climbing up from the pit. She stands out among the rough, dark bodies among the vats, like a perfect little angel, fallen and trapped in this hell.

"*Sis!*" I cry, my voice echoing. Lir shushes me viciously, but it's already too late.

Sis looks around at the sound of her name. When she spies me, she throws down her sack, flings wide her arms, and shouts, *"Mar!"* The next moment, she's flung herself across the big chamber, between the vats, scrambled onto the windowsill and leaped into my arms. I drop to my knees and press the troll girl close. Sis wriggles and wriggles like a puppy, jumping at my face to kiss me. *"Mar! Mar mar!"* she cries, unable to contain herself.

Then another voice joins in: *"Mar! Torat, mar!"* I look up and see another small face peering over the windowsill. It's one of the older two troll brothers—Har or Dig, I'm not entirely certain which, for they look so much alike. I just have time to brace myself before he leaps from the window and knocks me onto my back, driving the breath from my lungs. Yet I instinctively wrap my arms around the solid troll boy, who rumbles, *"Mar! Mar!"* with as much enthusiasm as Sis.

"Be careful, you!" Lir growls, grabbing the boy and lifting him off me. He twists and turns in her grasp, but she is much stronger than he. "You'll break her if you're not gentle, you *balja.*"

The boy goes limp as a kitten, but keeps saying, *"Mar! Mar!"* and grinning wide enough to show all of his little gem teeth.

I pick myself up, one arm still wrapped around Sis. Suddenly,

I'm aware of many eyes on me—trolls peering from doors and windows up and down the street. When I turn and try to catch a glimpse of them, they retreat. It doesn't matter. I can *feel* the animosity all around me.

"Mistress," Lir says warningly as she turns in place. "Mistress, we can't linger here."

I stand, pulling Sis closer to me, and look down at the girl. "Are you all right?" I ask. "Are you safe?"

Sis's smile fades. She shakes her head and presses her face into my leg, clutching my skirts. *"Mar!"* she says, her voice a muffled sob.

I look from her to the boy in Lir's grasp. Then my gaze is drawn to the street behind Lir, where figures move toward us. Huge, lumbering figures. A dozen of them at least. And they're not ducking out of sight anymore. The foremost among them is pale and tall and beautiful as an angel, his skin fairly glowing in the dark. Though he is smaller than the big rough creatures at his back, he is somehow far more terrible.

"Grok kortarko ttermokjin!" he calls, his voice echoing among the stones.

Startled, Lir whirls around, spotting the approaching figures for the first time. "Mistress," she says, "get behind me."

I obey at once, holding tight to Sis.

The group draws closer. Now I can see the features of their leader, so perfectly chiseled, like a marble statue of some idealized demigod brought to life. *"Grok kortarko!"* he says, harsher this time.

Lir drops the troll boy and curls her fists. The boy scurries to

166

grab Sis's hand and pulls her away. I try to hold on and call out to them both, but they're much too frightened. They disappear back into the ugly building out of my sight.

The pale troll and his entourage are still advancing. *"Kortarko! Hrothtoli ror ithortor!"*

Lir stands tall, her shoulders back, her head high. By comparison to that pale man, she looks downright frail, but I know my maid is much stronger than she looks. Still, I can't expect Lir to defend me from all of those massive trolls.

"Brark hrar tark!" Lir stomps her foot hard enough to make the ground crack and shake and makes herself seem much wider than she is. It's a singularly trollish stance. *"Hrar hrar!"* she roars.

The pale troll man pauses, momentarily intimidated. He even takes a step back. Then, as though remembering suddenly that he's not alone, he advances again. The other trolls follow close at his heels.

"It's all right," I call out, my voice thin and piping. "I don't mean any harm. I just wanted to see the children, that's all."

The trolls stop. Their eyes swivel from Lir to me.

"Mistress," Lir says.

"What?"

"Don't talk."

I bite down on my lower lip, my heart jumping in my throat.

The first troll keeps coming, closer and closer, until he is almost nose to nose with Lir. His mouth opens, and I glimpse black teeth, sharp like shards of jasper. *"Kortarko,"* he snarls in a voice like a gaping chasm.

Lir tilts her head back to meet his looming gaze.

Then, gathering herself suddenly, she lunges at him, catches him by the shoulder and arm, and hurls him bodily through the air. I let out a startled scream as he flies right through the window of the mining building. There's a splash, a rush of heat, and droplets of molten lava falling everywhere. I hear a roar of either pain or anger—

And Lir scoops me off my feet.

She tosses me over her shoulder, and runs for all she's worth, away from the vats and the building, away from the pits and the trolls. Away from Calx and Sis and Dig and Har. My stomach is on her shoulder, and every jolting footstep she takes drives air from my lungs in painful gasps. I try to hold onto her shoulder, to prop myself up. I manage to lift my head, looking back the way we've come.

Trolls.

They're swarming after us—huge, lumbering silhouettes against the red light. They're faster than they should be, faster than I ever would have thought possible, like a living avalanche.

What have I done? What have I gotten us into?

"Hold on, Mistress!" Lir cries, turning abruptly. I have a flashing vision of the road up ahead blocked by more trolls standing shoulder to shoulder, forming a living wall. Lir avoids them, skirting to the edge of the road and leaping out into open air. For a moment, we soar, weightless.

Then we come down hard on the rooftops of the lower street. Lir takes the impact and rolls but loses hold of me. I tumble, faster and faster, convinced every bone in my body is about to be shattered. I try to stop myself, try to catch hold of something, but just keep tumbling until there's no more sloped roof. Empty space yawns below. I lash out with one hand, manage to catch hold of something. I'm suspended over a fifty-foot drop, my legs kicking wildly in midair.

"*Lir!*" I scream.

Her face appears above me, pale and frenzied, her white hair billowing like a cloud. She catches me under the arms and hauls me onto the roof beside her. I scarcely have time to draw a breath before she moves to pick me up again. Hastily, I put up both hands. "No! I can run!" I really don't want to end up draped over Lir's shoulder again.

For a half an instant, Lir looks as though she'll argue. Then, "This way!" she says and leads me back up the slope of the roof.

Shouts and rumbling voices punctuate the air, but I refuse to look at the vague shapes moving on the street above. Stones fall, strike the roof, and roll down on either side of me. The trolls are hurling missiles at us. One good hit will crush my skull, pulverize my brains.

Up ahead, Lir yanks open what looks like a trapdoor. "In!" she shouts, motioning for me to hurry. I don't hesitate for a second. I plop down on my backside, swing my legs of the edge, and drop into the darkness below. The rattle of falling stones sounds like hail overhead. Lir jumps down beside me and pulls the trapdoor shut.

It's completely dark. I'm blind. Helpless.

"This way!" Lir's voice hisses close to my ear, and her hand grasps mine. I hold tight for dear life as she leads me through the darkness down what seems to be a winding stair. I'm vaguely aware of movement, of other living souls close by. But the household trolls make no move to stop us, and only once do I hear a questioning cry of, *"Hrik hrik?"*

We burst out into the open street. Only we're further down in the city than we were before, further away from the palace and possible safety.

"Follow me!" Lir says and nearly yanks my arm from its socket, hauling me after her up the street. We duck between two buildings. Not fast enough.

Trollish voices ring out in triumph—we've been spotted. Those first voices are echoed by others, all around us, hemming us in.

I shouldn't have done this. I shouldn't have put Lir in such danger. I wish I could apologize, but I can't even catch my breath. I can do nothing but run and run and run, hoping the adrenaline rush will drive my tired body far beyond my limited endurance.

Lir takes us through a back alley, up a steep incline, then out into another street. We run five more paces before Lir stops. I peer around her. Six trolls stand in our way. One of them is the beautiful troll man, pale as alabaster, tall and broad and muscled. He wears almost nothing, like the other trolls, only a gray sarong tied loosely at his waist. Cooled and hardened lava clings to his hair, his shoulders, his torso.

His mouth curls in a grimace, flashing those jasper teeth of his.

"Ror ithortor!"

Lir snarls, wordless like an animal. She lets go of my arm and plants herself in front of me. "Mistress," she says, her voice trembling. "When I say run—"

The trolls rush straight at us. Lir just has time to scream, *"Run!"* before she flings herself forward, grappling with the beautiful troll man. She manages to throw him into one of the stone-hided trolls, knocking both of them off their feet and tripping two others.

I don't wait to see what happens next. I turn and run as fast as I can.

12

POUNDING FOOTSTEPS BEHIND ME REVERBERATE
through stone, causing me to stagger. My only advantage
is being smaller, nimbler, better able to turn abruptly and
change course.

I pivot on my toes and dive into a narrow alley on my right.
One of the trolls roars with frustration, but the other two crash in
behind me, breaking chunks off the walls in their efforts to follow.
I dare a single look back and desperately wish I hadn't. They're
much closer than I thought.

I emerge in a wide street but spy an open doorway in a building
across the way. I throw myself at it, manage to duck inside just
before the trolls behind me are able to squeeze out of the alley and
burst into the street in a cloud of dust and debris. Out of breath,
I stand with my back against the wall, hidden in the shadows,

struggling to draw gulps of air without making a sound.

The two trolls roar and pound each other angrily. I don't have to understand their language to know they're blaming each other for my escape. I see their shadows moving, see their heads draw together. Then they part ways, one heading up the street, the other down. Neither approaches my hiding place. Yet.

Where is Lir? I shake my head, gritting my teeth. I can't believe I left her behind to face those trolls alone! Granted, there's not much I could actually *do* in an outright brawl. I don't have any weapons, no means of defending myself. Gods above, I didn't even bring a quill and spellbook along!

Well, I can't stay here forever. Slowly, I crane my neck and peer out into the street. My ears prick, straining for some sound of Lir's voice or of battle near at hand. Somehow, I'm a little further up in the city than before, far enough that I can actually see the topmost dome of the palace citadel from here. I gaze longingly up at it, wishing to high heaven I was there right now.

Cautiously, I emerge from my hiding place and begin to creep up the street, clinging to the sides of buildings, hoping I can stay at least partially hidden. I make it approximately twenty paces, just far enough to start thinking I might slip away unseen, when a voice cries out: "*Stop, human!*"

I freeze. Then I turn very slowly to look back.

The pale troll man is there, flanked by half a dozen enormous stone-hided trolls. They all look a little battered and worse for wear. But there's no sign of Lir anywhere.

My heart drops to my stomach. I turn and run again. The rough paving stones shred the soles of my soft leather shoes, and pain spikes in my feet. I ignore it and just keep running.

"Grok kortarko!" The troll voice rings against the stones, echoing around me, nearly drowned out by the thunder of my own pulse in my ears. My breath is tight, and pain spasms in my side. I have moments, mere moments before those trolls will catch me, crush me with their massive brick hands.

My foot catches on an uneven paver. I trip, arms splayed, and land hard.

I don't even have time to catch my breath before something grips the back of my gown and lifts me clear off my feet. I find myself face-to-face with the pale troll man, his features half crusted in lava. *"Hrar hrar,* little human," he says. Diamond teeth catch the starlight as he smiles. Then he draws back his fist.

A *shing* of metal lances across my senses.

I blink.

A blade of pure *virmaer* steel glints before my eyes. It turns slightly, the razor edge pressed up against the troll man's throat. "Well met, Anj," a rich, golden voice says. "You seem to have found something of mine. I'd be grateful if you relinquished it."

My eyes swivel sideways.

The Prince stands before me, one arm extended, hand grasping the hilt of a delicate sword. He's dressed in blue silks with broad epaulettes and long, trailing sleeves that are so entirely incongruous with the setting, it makes him seem almost unreal. His eyes are bright and full of violent threat as they fix on the troll man's face. A dangerous smile curves his lips.

The troll man turns. The edge of the blade slides along his neck, leaving a thin line of blue. *"Rujabor korgra,"* he snarls.

"I couldn't agree more," the Prince answers with a tilt of one eyebrow. "But I'm sure Darling here is very sorry for her impudence. No need to go about skull crushing, not for a first infraction anyway."

The troll man's eyes flash. He snarls again, his words so jarring, they make my head throb.

Both the Prince's eyebrows rise slightly, forming puckering lines. "A *soromskunar?* How quaint! And perhaps a bit antiquated. But then"—he shrugs and whips his sword away from the troll's throat, backing up and twirling the point in delicate figure eights—"I'm always keen for a tussle."

Before I have a chance to understand what's happening, the troll man marches several yards up the street and sets me down between his massive stone-faced companions. My knees buckle. I fall heavily, but manage to lift my head, tossing hair out of my face. I see the troll man square off, shoulders set, fists clenched. He rises to the balls of his feet, knees bent.

With a mighty roar, he hurls himself straight at the Prince.

Time seems to slow and then strangely warp, and my vision expands with it. I see the Prince—how small he is before the breadth and power of that troll. He stands there, his sword held off to one side, his head tilted, his gaze downcast, not even looking at the doom bearing down upon him. The troll draws back his arm, his mighty fist clenched, ready to deliver a death blow.

The Prince drops his sword.

Then he lowers his head, sets his jaw, and rushes to meet the troll head-on. Unarmed.

My breath catches. He's going to be crushed, ground to dust, right there before my eyes! I open my mouth, ready to scream.

At the very last second, the Prince ducks and, using the troll's momentum against him, hitches an elbow into his stomach and sends him hurtling over his shoulder. The troll crashes flat on his back, staring up into the distant sky.

The Prince is already in motion. He dives at the troll, plants a knee against his throat, and delivers a single, brutal punch straight into one eye. The troll roars and twists, turning onto his stomach, knocking the Prince partially off-balance. Fast as lightning, the Prince grabs the troll man's arm, yanks it up to a horrible angle that draws a scream of pain from the troll's lips. That scream still echoing, the Prince grabs him by the hair on the back of his head and smashes his face into the street.

The troll's limbs go limp. His head lolls to one side.

The Prince stands, rolling his shoulders, then carefully smooths his long hair back from his face. He turns.

His mouth curves in a smile.

"That was the shortest *soromskunar* of my life. A bit disappointing if I'm honest. Anyone else game for a go?"

The trolls around me exchange looks.

Then, as a single body, they lunge.

The smile vanishes from the Prince's face. His lips form a single word—an expletive, I think, but I cannot hear it for the thunder of pounding feet exploding in my ears. The next moment, the trolls block him from my view. I can see nothing but massive, churning bodies, flying fists, stomping feet, mouths gaping in wrathful roars. Suddenly, two of the trolls topple, knocking several more over as they go. It looks like a game of dominos, only with more howling and flailing limbs.

The Prince emerges. His trailing sleeves torn, his hair in disarray, he speeds up the street, eluding several grasping stone fists, and swipes up his sword. Scrambling, I manage to get to my feet just as he reaches me. "Fancy a stroll, Darling?" the Prince says, catching my hand.

We run. I'm not sure where I find my second wind—perhaps it's some magic of the Prince's flowing from his palm through my body. However it may be, I pick up my heels and run faster than I ever have before in my life, in close step with the Prince. He darts and weaves through alleys, between buildings, choosing side streets, and always, always, heading up.

We come to the end of one alley, and he pauses momentarily, peering out. Somewhere not far off, I hear troll voices barking at each other. The Prince withdraws into the alley and makes me stand against the wall. I take a long, gasping breath, the first full breath I've managed in far too long. As I let it out, words tumble in a painful whisper: "Can't you order them to leave us alone?"

"You'd think that would work, wouldn't you?" he replies, turning to look down at me. With no further explanation, he tugs my hand, drawing me after him into the street. I groan, but somehow make my legs keep going, force my feet one painful step after another. We reach the end of this street and start to turn up the next before the Prince yanks me roughly back.

"This way!" he hisses and pulls me nearly off my feet into a nearby doorway. We step into the dark shelter, and the Prince murmurs something I don't understand, sweeping his arm in a wide, circular motion. Then he turns and, pushing me up against the wall, plants his hands on either side of me, leaning so close, his chest presses against mine. His mouth is close to my forehead; warm breath pants against my skin.

"What is—" I start.

"Hush!" he hisses sharply.

The wall behind me begins to shake, the ground beneath me to rumble. I close my eyes, grit my teeth, and feel the tide of trolls passing just outside our little hiding place. So many of them, far more than I had thought were even interested in us. The *boom, boom, boom* of their footsteps echoes against the stone buildings all around, deafening and devastating. I half expect the building above me to crack and crumble, burying us alive.

Finally the noise lessens, and the rumbling dies away. I'm still standing there, my back to the wall, drawing in ragged gasps. I open my eyes and peer up. All I can see is the Prince's sharp jaw as he looks back over his shoulder. His arms are very close around me, and I could swear I feel his heartbeat.

He looks down so abruptly, our noses bump. He pulls back a little, his startled eyes meeting mine. "Well, Darling!" he says, with a faint chuckle.

I stare up at him, unblinking, unspeaking. Then, with a sudden shake of my head, I gasp, "Lir!"

"Don't worry about your maid," the Prince says. "The *Hrorark* aren't interested in her this time. Just you."

I shake my head. "What are *Hrorark* exactly?"

"Followers of the Old Ways. What you might call *zealots*." The Prince shrugs and smiles. "They don't accept me as their ruler, don't accept anyone but other trolls really. They hate librarians most of all and would rather see this whole city torn apart by Noswraiths than allow humans to live in their midst."

He cranes his neck again to see beyond the hiding spell he's wrapped us in. I take the opportunity to work my hands up and push against his chest. "They've gone, haven't they?" I whisper.

The words are scarcely out of my mouth before the ground begins to quake again. Another wave of trolls goes pounding by, and once more the foundations of our little shelter rattle under my feet. The Prince presses close, his head bowed. His lips hover at my ear, which is the only reason I can hear his voice above the din when he says, "You'll have to endure this proximity a bit longer, Darling. But cheer up! Better a bit rumpled in a doorway than crushed to bitty pieces under a troll's heel, eh?"

I close my eyes, trying not to be too aware of the scent of him—a startlingly heady combination of ink and candlewax with an underlying spice I cannot place but which tingles in my nostrils. The Prince shifts his weight, leaning his elbow and forearm against the wall, creating a firmer barrier between me and the street outside. "While I have your attention," he says, his deep voice now tickling my other ear and making gooseflesh rise on my neck, "I really must ask what in the seven gods' names you were thinking, venturing into the City Below."

I hesitate, my jaw working. Then: "I was looking for my children."

"*Your* children?"

I turn my head, meet his gaze, and hold it. "Yes. *My* children."

For a moment, his façade cracks. The haughtiness and mockery melt away, revealing a strange conflict of emotions: anger, yes, but more as well. Things I'm not certain I can name. The muscles of his throat tighten, and his teeth flash in the starlight. I brace myself for whatever he's about to say. At the last moment, however, he turns away and takes a step or two back, removing the warm solidity of his body. I breathe in deeply, sagging against the wall. Strange that I should feel suddenly so cold.

The Prince looks out into the street, his brow stern. He nods and takes my hand once more. "Come, Darling," he says, pulling me from the doorway into the street. "If you've quite caught your breath."

I haven't. But he drags me along after him, and I've no choice but to run again. Gods on high, I'm a librarian! I'm not used to this much physical exertion. My legs feel as though they'll fall right off the moment I slow down.

"Don't lag," the Prince says, taking my elbow to offer extra support. "If we can just make it above the *jrorkra* district, we should be safe enough. *Hrorark* never venture that high if they can help it. We're not far now."

He stops suddenly, poised like a wildcat, sniffing the wind for some telltale scent. His eyes flare. "Gods blight," he whispers. Then, with a shake of his head, he turns and retreats down the street.

"What is it?" I demand, my voice tight, fighting against my own heaving breaths.

"I'm not sure. A feeling. But I've learned not to doubt such feelings."

We've progressed no more than eight more paces, when suddenly the pale troll steps out from the shadows of a looming building and squares off in front of us. His eyes are swollen, the alabaster skin an ugly purple, and one of his arms hangs dislocated from his shoulder. His lips roll back, revealing bloodied gums.

"*Hrothtoli ror ithortor!*"

"Really, Anj," The Prince presses a hand to his heart. "Must you be so hurtful?"

The troll throws back his head and roars. In response, more trolls pour out of the buildings and alleyways and streets. The Prince whips out his sword, and I just have time to wonder what good a sword will do against such stony hides, when the first of the trolls is upon us. It swings a heavy fist, aiming for the Prince's head. The Prince ducks low, narrowly avoiding the blow. His sword flashes. I hear a roar, a thump. A severed arm rolls down the steep incline of the street.

Three other trolls are upon us the next instant, clambering over their wounded comrade. The Prince's sword is a blur of motion, striking hits with each turn and sweep. He keeps one arm back, always aware of where I am, always holding me behind him. It's like I'm part of a strange and terrible dance.

I feel helpless, desperate. There are too many trolls. Even those the Prince has wounded pick themselves up and rejoin the fray, as though severed limbs are nothing to them. They crush in closer and closer, until there's scarcely any room for either the Prince or me to move.

He turns and wraps one arm around me, pulling me close. "Hold on, Darling," he gasps. "This might get—"

A flash of light—yellow, like the sun itself suddenly blazing to life. The trolls scream. It's the most horrific sound, the shriek of breaking stone. I scream as well, shutting my eyes fast, and press my face into the Prince's chest. The ground quakes beneath my feet. I would fall were it not for his arm around me.

At last, the troll voices fade. The vibrating earth settles down once more. I pull my head back, lift a hand to shade my eyes, and peer up into the sky. It's as though a star has found its way down into the lower city, hovering just ten yards or so above the street. Here in Vespre, under the twilit sky, it's too bright, too painful.

Even as I look on, however, the glow begins to dim. It shrinks back, drawing into itself, until I can see the outline of a person at its center. A woman. A glorious woman with long, golden hair and golden skin and great feathered wings sprouting from her shoulders. She holds a whorl of light between her hands, her fingers moving in an intricate pattern as though she's shaping and kneading that energy into existence.

She lowers herself, her flapping wings driving dust and debris into my face. I wince but manage to look up again just as she lands. Her delicate feet are clad in sandals, the straps winding up her bare calves all the way to her knees. She wears a white tunic embroidered in patterns of sunbursts that mimic the glow she holds in her hands.

She folds her wings and, in the same moment, brings her palms together, squishing the light out of existence. I'm left momentarily blind by its absence, but my eyes swiftly adjust, for her glittering skin gives off a light of its own, as though her very blood is on fire. Slowly, she turns her head, taking in the carnage on the street, all those severed troll limbs.

Then she lifts her gaze to us, passing right over me as though I'm not there and focusing on the Prince. "How now, Castien," she says in a voice as bright as daybreak. "Is this how you go about ruling your subjects? Cutting off bits and pieces and littering the streets? I suppose that's one way to keep them in check." She kicks at an enormous finger near her feet, sends it rolling down the paving stones. "Or is this your way of spreading joy to the masses?"

The Prince, whose arm is still wrapped tight around my waist, lets out a heavy sigh. "Ilusine."

The winged woman smiles and saunters toward him, her hips swaying. As she nears, her wings seem to melt away, and she herself shrinks until she is no longer towering a full head taller than the Prince but is now an inch or two shorter. He takes a step back and gently but firmly moves me to stand behind him. The winged woman stops in front of him, gazing up into his eyes for a long moment.

Then she catches the front of his shirt and pulls him into a kiss.

13

I DON'T KNOW HOW TO REACT.

My mouth drops open, and I stumble back two or three paces. Heat rushes to my cheeks, and I quickly look away. But looking away is no better, as I become suddenly aware of all the dark windows and doorways surrounding me, of unseen eyes peering out of shadowed depths. I'm also standing rather too close to a severed arm for comfort.

Shuddering, I wrap my arms around my middle and dare to glance up at the Prince and the golden fae woman. He pulls back from her kiss, clears his throat, and plucks her hand off his shirt. "Careful, Ilusine," he says. "Sarlana silk wrinkles at the least provocation."

She arches a brow. "That was quite a little display of swords-manship. I seem to remember the last time we spoke, you insisted that you were *not* a fighter and had little desire for such warlike exhibitions! I dare say, this performance puts the lie to your words."

"Not at all," the Prince responds with an elegant shrug. He lifts his sword arm and makes the tip of his blade flash in an intricate dance. "I may have little desire for swordplay, but I'm perfectly capable in a pinch. I simply have no interest in seeking out opportunities to demonstrate my skill."

"Opportunities like the Rite of the Thorn?" she asks.

"Quite."

Her expression hardens. For the first time, she flicks a glance my way. "What is *this?*" she asks, her lip curling slightly. It's the same tone she might use upon spotting an insect in her wine.

"This," the Prince replies smoothly, "is the reason for today's demonstration."

"Oh?" The golden woman looks perplexed. "Dare one ask *why?*"

"Certainly. Anj and his goons were set on grinding her bones to make their bread, as it were. I was against the notion."

The golden woman blinks. She looks as though she's trying to understand some bizarre concept. At last, she shrugs and simply dismisses it, pursuing a different tack. "If you don't want mayhem in the city streets, you'd best make your way back up top quickly. When I set out from the palace, your captain of the guard was mustering her troops. I have no doubt she'll be kicking down doors and routing the citizens if she doesn't soon see you safe and sound."

"Dear Khas," the Prince says with a smile. "I'm doubly blessed in warrior women willing to hurl themselves into battle for my sake. But then, who could blame them?"

Ilusine tosses her head, uttering the brightest, most crystalline laugh. She links her arm with the Prince's and pats his hand. "Don't flatter yourself," she says, leading him up the street.

I stand where they left me in the middle of all those troll appendages, watching them go. How small and dull and mousy I suddenly feel. It's almost a relief to see the golden woman putting distance between us, even if it means I'm alone in this street, surrounded by hostile trolls. But the Prince casts a glance back over his shoulder. "Keep up, Darling!" he barks.

Swallowing hard, I pick up my feet and hurry after them. My heart thunders with a strange storm of feelings: relief at having so narrowly escaped a grim fate; worry over Lir and my little troll children, somewhere behind me in the City Below; and, more pressingly, panic and survival instinct still roar in my veins, refusing to let my body calm, refusing to let me fully accept that I might actually be safe.

But there's something else as well. Something I cannot quite name. Something sharp and unexpected at the sight of the Prince walking ahead of me arm in arm with the gorgeous fae woman. I close my eyes . . . and just for a moment, feel the warmth of his body pressed close to me in the doorway, feel the beat of his heart pounding in synchrony with mine . . .

A little growl burbling in my throat, I pick up my pace, hurrying after the two of them. Why should I be surprised that the Prince has a paramour? He *is* a prince, after all. While he may be a half-human Hybrid, he's still the son of King Lodírhal, one of the most powerful rulers in all Eledria. I suppose part of me thought fae women would reject him simply for his half-human blood, especially once his father cut him from the line of succession. Then again, perhaps I'm thinking too little of fae women, assuming they're all like Princess Estrilde, only out for their own gain. Perhaps this Ilusine is different.

Also, it's none of my business.

I tuck my chin and hasten up the street. I'm so tired! Now that adrenaline fades, exhaustion floods through my veins, makes my limbs shake. I stumble, right myself, and stumble again. My feet are throbbing, bleeding through the ripped soles of my shoes, and I suspect I may have a few cracked ribs. My head pounds where I hit it during one of the wild jumps with Lir. I'm just so . . . so . . .

I slump. Sink to my knees in the middle of the street. With an effort of will, I try to hold myself upright. It's no use. I fall forward onto my hands, see the paving stones whirling in front of my eyes, very pale and white. My vision tunnels.

"Now, now, Darling." The Prince's voice is in my head, bright but not bright enough to drive out the closing darkness. "None of that!" A strong arm catches me around the shoulders, draws me back against a broad chest. I utter a little mewling protest but can't form any words. I have just enough awareness to feel my whole body lifted up.

Then I give in and let the darkness claim me.

THE PRINCE

S HE FEELS FRAGILE IN MY ARMS. LIKE A STRAW DOLL ready to disintegrate into tiny pieces.

I peer into her face, so pale and drawn. Her eyes are closed, but when I place my ear close to her lips, her shallow breath warms my skin. My heart, which had constricted into a tight knot in my breast, relaxes and begins to beat properly once more. She's alive. Alive. Worn out from fear and exertion, that's all. Her mortal body wasn't meant for the rigors of this treacherous troll realm.

It is strange, though—strange how a being so strong, a spirit so great, a will so ironclad, could be contained in so frail a frame. I could crush her against me, shatter her spine without a thought. Yet I fear it is she who holds all the power between us.

"Did it break?"

Ilusine stands behind me, casting a long shadow. She angles her head to get a better look at the girl. Her lip curls slightly. "Humans do that. Break, I mean. Such weak little creatures, they don't hold up well under strain."

A bitter reminder that I myself am half-human springs to my lips. I bite it back and instead simply rise, cradling the girl against my chest. "This one is stronger than she seems," I say. "And definitely more trouble than she's worth."

"If that's the case, why don't you leave it?" Ilusine glances around at the tall buildings and the echoing, apparently empty street. "Surely one of your trolls could fetch it later."

A bone in my jaw clicks. "Trouble or not, I paid a hefty price for this particular Obligate. I won't risk losing her."

With that I set out, marching up the street. Ilusine picks up the edge of her skirt and hastens after me, falling into step by my side. "This is why I don't keep Obligates," she says. "They're always causing problems with their little rebellions and flashes of will. It's far too much bother trying to break them into manageable behavior."

I shudder but offer no answer. My body still reverberates with the force of dread which had so recently filled me. Somehow, I'd known she was in trouble. Some instinct, some unconscious pull dragged me from my office and sent me scouring the city streets. Leading me with a sense of terrible inevitability straight to her.

The sight of her surrounded by those *Hrorark* was almost enough to undo me. To set me blasting them all to oblivion and damn the consequences! I could have murdered Anj and not slept the worse for it tonight. I very nearly did.

But no. I can't. I can't care so much. So intensely. It's wrong. Worse still, it's dangerous. For me and for all this doomed city of mine. Besides, the girl was warned, wasn't she? Whose fault is it if she ignored all reason and placed herself in such needless danger?

I look down at her again. Her head is pillowed against my shoulder, affording me a view of her soft cheek and brow. There's an ugly bruise on her forehead. The sight of it makes my blood boil, makes that murderous rage swell inside me once more. Why? Why did she have to go and do this? What is it about those children that makes her so reckless? She's determined to help them, to care for them. To love them. And I . . . I . . . I'm not jealous. I simply wish she would channel that energy in other ways.

I remember how her body felt, pressed up against mine in that doorway. How her breath hitched, how her heart raced.

She's not wholly immune to me. Is she?

"Prince!"

I turn sharply. Lir runs up from a side street toward us, her hair wild, her eyes frantic. She staggers, stumbles, and throws herself on her knees before me, reaching up to grasp Clara's hand in both of hers. "Oh, my poor mistress!" she cries. Tears stream down her pale cheeks. "My poor, poor mistress!"

"Enough," I growl. "The fool girl is fine. Just a little overwrought from all the frantic comings and goings, I should think."

The maid doesn't relent, but draws Clara's hand to her face, weeping over it and kissing it. "Please, my Prince," she begs, lifting red-rimmed eyes to mine, "forgive me! I should never have let my mistress put herself in such danger. I tried to warn her, tried to talk her out of it, but . . . but . . ."

"Really, Lir, if you don't stand up and cease this blubbering at once, I'll have you thrown in my deepest dungeon. I'm perfectly aware how convincing Darling here can be once she's set her mind on something. That being said," I add, leveling a stern look at the maid, who rises and wipes her nose with the back of her hand, "if you ever let your mistress wander these streets alone again, particularly while fleeing a hoard of ravenous zealots . . . well, I shall have to become quite stern with you. Do I make myself clear?"

"I will never—" Lir chokes and tries again, "*Never.*"

"Yes, well. See that you don't." I start to move, but the maid reaches to take my burden from me. A sudden rush of heat roars through me. Fury. Rage. It doesn't make sense. It doesn't fit within my realm of understanding or reason.

But it doesn't matter. The only thing that matters is that I do not wish to hand the girl over. The idea is about as palatable as cutting off my own arm.

I stop, shake my head. This isn't right. I've been so careful, so cautious. So aware of my danger. I've taken such pains to ensure I did not let myself become entangled in this deadly snare.

I look down at her face again. So mild and peaceful save for a faint line drawn between her brows. My chest burns, a mingling pain of loathing and . . . something else. Something I don't like to name. Coiling in my gut, burning in my veins.

"Here." I push her into Lir's outstretched arms. "Take her and begone."

Lir nods. "Thank you, Prince," she stammers and turns to go.

My heart gives an ugly wrench. "Wait!"

Lir stops. Turns back. Once again I can see the girl's face, now resting against her maid's shoulder instead of mine. I feel the coldness, the bare spot against my chest where she had been but a moment before. I ache to reclaim her, to restore her to her proper place.

"Be sure you have her patched up in time for dinner. I won't have Cook holding courses for her tardiness. Understood?"

The troll maid blinks several times. Then she dips her head. "Of course, Prince," she murmurs. The next moment, she slips away, hastening up the street ahead of me. And I must let her go. I must stand here and watch and let her go.

A brush of fingers against mine. Startled, I turn to find Ilusine's golden gaze fixed upon me. Though my heart gallops painfully, I force my face into a warm smile and offer her my arm. "That's taken care of," I say brightly. "Now then, Ilusine, my sweet. Tell me what brings you to my fair city."

She tucks her hand through the loop of my elbow, pressing her warm and willing body close. "Oh, a great many things, Castien, dear," she purrs.

CLARA

14

I WAKE TO SOMETHING COOL AND DAMP ON MY
forehead. Moaning, I put up a hand, trying to touch whatever
it is. My brow puckers. I can't seem to make my hand do
what I want. My body feels like lead. Except for my feet. They
feel like fire.

"Don't try to move too soon, Mistress. You've had a nasty bump."

My eyes flare wide. "Lir!" I gasp. Before she can stop me, I sit
bolt upright. A mistake. The room spins, and my stomach pitches,
and my vision starts tunneling again. I groan, drop my head into
my hands.

The next moment, Lir's arm is around me, pulling my head to
her shoulder. "There, there, Mistress," she croons. "Didn't I tell you
not to move too soon? You should listen better, you know. Here.
Try this."

Before I can question what *this* is, she holds something under my nose. I breathe in a startled gasp as a sharp burning sears up my nostrils. I jerk my head back and groan. But the vapors do the trick. When I open my eyes again, the room has stopped spinning, and I'm a bit more clearheaded than before.

I blink and look up at my maid. She doesn't seem the worse for wear, despite all her brawling. There's a bruise on one cheek, and her hair is a bit ratty. Otherwise, she's as smiling and beautiful as ever. "Are you all right?" I ask breathlessly.

"Who? Me?" Lir blinks. She looks surprised that I would even ask. "Why, of course I'm all right, Mistress! You didn't think a couple of *Hrorark* imbeciles could hurt *me*, did you?"

I did. When I remember that swarm of enormous rock monsters, every one of whom dwarfed Lir with their massive, rocky bodies . . . well, yes. I admit, I'd thought very much that they could hurt her. But then, I don't know that much about trolls. Perhaps throwbacks boast superior strength as well as superior beauty to their more rough-hewn counterparts.

Lir fetches a cup of water and holds it to my lips. I drink gratefully. There's more than water in the brew, for I'm suddenly flush with unexpected energy and lightness. Enough energy, in fact, to catch my maid's eye and ask, "What about the children? Will they be all right? Will they be punished?"

"Punished? Oh no." Lir shakes her head emphatically. "No troll, not even a *Hrorark*, would hurt a child of the Deeper Dark. They won't move to *help* them, but they certainly wouldn't *hurt* them."

Something sour knots in my belly. "How exactly is it not *hurting* them to send them down into that mine?"

Lir gives me a sympathetic look and pats my knee. "Remember, Mistress, trolls are meant for the deep places. At least, theologically speaking, they should be happier the deeper they go."

"Theologically speaking, maybe. But in practical terms?" I raise my eyebrows. "The truth, Lir. I see an awful lot of trolls living up in the higher parts of the city. And the children keep coming to me, keep trying to get me to adopt them. If they were happy in the Deep Dark, why would they seek a place up here in the palace?"

Lir looks uncomfortable. She swirls the last of the liquid in the cup. "What a troll *ought* to want isn't always what a troll *wants*," she admits slowly.

I wait just in case there will be more forthcoming. When there isn't, I offer a rueful smile and take her hand. "I suppose humans are much the same. But I'm not giving up, you know. I believe those children chose me to be their *mar* for a reason. I believe I'm meant to help them, meant to take them in, just as your family took you in. I understand this might put them outside of the . . . the *vo . . . va . . .*"

"*Vagungad*," Lir supplies.

"Yes. It may put them outside the . . . the holy cycle. But they will enter a new cycle. A cycle they cannot fall from. A cycle in which they will always belong, no matter what." I catch Lir's gaze and hold it. "And I believe Lumruil will smile upon them."

Lir drops her eyes, her pretty face lined with thought. She

doesn't look convinced. But I glimpse a tear trailing down her cheek. With a little sniff, she lifts her face and pats me on the head. "You humans discolor so easily!" Her fingertips trail across my forehead.

I wince at the unexpected pain. There must be an ugly bruise. "How bad is it?"

"Not as bad as it was. Don't worry, Mistress! I've applied *maalik* juice, and if you rest easy for another hour or two, the color should be back to normal in plenty of time."

I nod and, at Lir's urging, lean back into my pillows and allow her to apply her cooling cloth again. After a few minutes, however, I frown and open one eye. "Plenty of time for what?"

"Plenty of time to make ready for dinner tonight."

"What dinner?"

Lir tilts her head. I get the distinct impression she's feigning surprise. "Why, dinner with the Prince, of course."

I sit back up so fast, the room whirls around me again. My stomach pitches, and I close my eyes and hunch over, groaning. For a moment, I feel again the strength of the Prince's arms around me, lifting me from the ground. Was that a memory? Or a dream? No, definitely not a dream. Does that mean I really did faint in the middle of the street, and he really did carry me up to the palace like a sack of potatoes? All while that beautiful, glittery-skinned fae woman looked on?

I shake my head. Then, with a growl, I look up at Lir. "I'm sure there's some mistake. The Prince cannot want to have dinner with me again. He . . . I'm fairly certain he has a guest already."

Lir's lip curls. "Yes. Princess Ilusine."

Princess Ilusine? Of course. Of course she's a princess! How could such an incredible creature be anything less? I wrack my brains, trying to remember what little I know of Eledrian courts and their families. Ilusine must be from the Daylight Court, Solira. I've seen members of that court before, the great angelic beings who have visited King Lodírhal in Aurelis. They are ruled by Queen Immianthe, who is famous for having twelve daughters, each more lovely than the last.

It is odd, though: The Daylight Court folk tend to view themselves as vastly superior to everyone else, including the Court of Dawn. I wouldn't have expected a princess of Solira to take an interest in the disgraced and disinherited Prince of the Doomed City. I close my eyes—and see again that moment when she'd grabbed his shirt, pulled his head down to hers, claimed his lips. Princess Ilusine had certainly done more than *taken an interest.*

I swallow. My throat is dry and a little scratchy. "Yes. Princess Ilusine. Surely he will not want to be disturbed while entertaining his guest."

Lir sniffs. "It's not my decision whom the Prince chooses for his company." She gives me a look. "He's chosen *you* for tonight. So you must be presentable."

Presentable? If I'm to dine in company with Ilusine, it really won't matter if I'm presentable or not. While she might be swathed in several layers of fae glamours like any other Eledrian Princess, she gave the distinct impression that she didn't *need* glamours to be absolutely stunning.

The very last thing I need is to go to this dinner.

"Come now, Mistress," Lir says, dabbing my forehead with that cool cloth. "Best make the most of it. I'll have you fixed up in time, don't you worry. You can trust your Lir."

I sigh. "Do whatever you like with me. It appears I have little choice."

It hardly matters what gown Lir puts me in or how she styles my hair or what cosmetics she applies to my face. She does her best, of course. And, to give her credit, she does well with what she has to work with. I'm sure I've never worn a gown so fine, so perfectly tailored to my figure, the color so ideally matched to my complexion. I'm sure I've never had my hair styled with such intricate care, every curl and braid woven and rewoven with delicate combs and jeweled pins.

It simply doesn't matter.

The moment I step through the doors out onto that open balcony dining space, the moment I set eyes on Princess Ilusine leaning on the far balustrade above the city, I know how utterly and completely eclipsed I am. She's simply too radiant for words. Her gown is of gold, draped in such a way that the fabric seems to drip from her shoulders and pool about her feet. It's so close in color to her glittering skin, that at first glance, she almost seems naked. But no—the way the gown clings is more sensual than mere nakedness would be. And she knows how to wear it, both how to move and how to be still. I could never dream of such poise.

She and the Prince are standing quite close to one another when Lawrence opens the doors and ushers me through. I pause on the threshold, staring at the two of them. Ilusine is leaning close, her hand on his shoulder, her lips close to his ear. The moment is . . . intimate.

I don't belong here.

Face heating, I turn to make my escape.

"Darling!"

A bad word springs to my tongue. I close my eyes, think of Mama, and bite it back, then carefully paint my best, blandest smile in place. It can't disguise my flushed cheeks, but I hope it will at least distract from them as I turn and face the Prince.

Leaving Ilusine at the balustrade, he steps around the big banquet table to greet me, pausing long enough to pour something sparkly into a jeweled goblet. "You're late," he says, offering me the drink.

I stare at the swirling liquid, then lift my gaze to meet his, blinking mildly. "I didn't realize there was a set time."

"Dinner is always served promptly at eight bells," he replies.

I blink again. "No, it isn't."

He shrugs. "Well, it *ought* to be. Come, Darling! You've had a day of it. You must be famished." So saying, he sweeps a hand to indicate the table. It's ornately set, much like last night. The goblin waiters have already come and gone, leaving behind mounding platters of food. There are settings at the head and foot of the table, and one more placed exactly in the middle, facing the open view.

I accept the offered drink from the Prince and carry it to that middle seat. The Prince trails after me and, to my surprise and consternation, holds my chair. I shoot him a swift glance then turn my gaze Ilusine's way. She's ignoring me. In fact, I'm not even sure she's aware of my arrival.

I hesitate a moment. I'm not at all certain what the accepted mode of behavior is when a Prince offers to assist one of his servants. Trying to disguise my discomfort, I murmur, "Thank you," and sit, setting my drink down and folding my hands in my lap.

The Prince smiles and moves to the head of the table, calling as he goes, "Shall we wait for you, Ilusine, or do you prefer to maintain that decorative pose while the rest of us dine?"

Ilusine turns slowly, a languid smile on her lips. Hips swaying, she saunters to the far end of the table and perches gracefully on the edge of her seat. She surveys the meal, then lifts her gaze to the Prince. "And do your trolls not care to serve their betters?"

"I've always found myself perfectly capable of spooning food onto my own plate," the Prince replies and sets about doing just that. Wielding a silver knife, he cuts a roast and arranges it very prettily on a plate with a helping of vegetables and some spicy sauce. Then he rises, carries the plate to my place, and sets it in front of me. "There you are, Darling. Eat up."

I gape. I can't help it. This so wrong; the Prince should not be serving me! What sort of game is he playing? I cast another glance Ilusine's way. She raises an eyebrow. Then she stretches out one gilded hand and selects a piece of sugared fruit from a nearby bowl. She takes a slow, thoughtful bite, and daintily wipes a bead of juice from her chin. The Prince does not offer to serve his other guest. He returns to his seat, heaps food onto his own plate, and begins to eat with good appetite.

I look down at my plate—the red meat in its sauce, the colorful vegetables roasted to perfection, an entire color palate arranged so temptingly. My stomach growls, loud enough that I'm quite certain it's audible to both ends of the table. I clap my hands against my gut and feel Ilusine's disapproving gaze flit over me once more. I can't bear to meet her eye. Instead I pick up my fork and take a bite. A delicious explosion of flavors fills my mouth but turns to dust when I try to swallow. I choke it down with an effort.

"Clara Darling," the Prince says, drawing my gaze sharply back to him, "is the newest member of our little bookish coterie here in Vespre."

Realizing he's addressing Ilusine, I dare another glance the fae woman's way. She looks faintly perplexed, as though she can't understand why the Prince would bother to inform her of something so banal. "Oh?" she offers eventually.

"Indeed." The Prince carves his cut of meat with great precision. "She has single-handedly bound two minor nightmares and quite recently contributed to the binding spell for one of the Greater Noswraiths. She's showing far more promise than I'd dared hope."

He speaks of me like he might speak of a new hunting dog—appreciatively, but as a master would discuss his possession. My ears burn. The smell of the food on my plate is no longer appetizing but turns my stomach. Why has he insisted I be here tonight? Is this my punishment for venturing into the city? If so, it's a strange but undeniably effective punishment. I try to take a bite but simply can't. I set my fork down and let my hands drop back into my lap.

"Really, Castien," Ilusine says, tossing the pit of her fruit in an arc out over the balustrade to fall to the distant rooftops below, "I don't know why you insist on staying put in this place. Librarians and Noswraiths and trolls and I don't know what all distasteful things!"

I try not to bristle. I try not to feel anything.

The Prince takes another bite, chews, and swallows slowly. Then he leans back in his chair and swirls his wine. "It's rather more fun than you make it out to be, my dear. In truth, it's become something of a game: how long can I keep doom from falling on the Doomed City? Great sport."

I shoot him a swift glance before dropping my gaze again. I reach for my goblet, take a sip. Only as the shockingly sweet liquid burns down my throat do I realize my mistake: this is a fae drink. Even one sip is enough to make me tipsy. Two sips will make me rash, and at three, I might lose my head entirely. I need to be more careful.

Ilusine is talking again. I force myself to listen to her words. "Surely you've been playing this game long enough. With Lodírhal nearing the end of his life, it's time you took a serious look at your future."

"You shock me, Ilusine," the Prince says, sounding not in the least shocked. "How callously you reference the death of my father!"

She rolls her eyes and shrugs one perfectly formed bare shoulder. "Please! Don't try to convince me you have any tender feeling for him. That would be so grossly *human* of you, Castien, I'm sure I could not bear it. Besides, everyone knows he was only too eager to ship you off to Vespre where no one could be reminded of your existence. Hardly the doting parent!"

"I volunteered to take on the responsibility of Vespre."

"Yes, so you *say*. And believe me, I understand the urge to save face." Ilusine tilts her head, shining curls tumbling over her shoulder like a waterfall of molten gold. "But everyone knows there was more to your dismissal from the Court of Dawn."

The Prince holds her gaze for a long, silent moment. Then, sighing, he pops another bite into his mouth and takes a long time chewing and swallowing. "It's true," he says at last. "I was forced into the role . . . for the simple fact that *no one else could do it*. My Hybrid nature makes me the only candidate for the job of binding and containing human magic on such a vast scale."

"Perhaps that was so back then," Ilusine acknowledges. "Back when the library was first established. But since those days, the terms of the Pledge have grown lax. There's been a renewal of fae-human couplings, though I cannot *think* why," she adds with a shudder. "Still, the result is the spawning of more Hybrid children. Granted, most of them don't possess much magic as the humans themselves seem to have lost their former magical aptitude. But surely someone could be found and trained to take your place at the helm. Perhaps one of your own librarians."

"My librarians," the Prince says, "are a formidable bunch. The best magic-users the human world has to offer."

"There you are then!" Ilusine cries as though she's scored a point. She waves a hand vaguely in my direction. "Let this creature take over."

The Prince raises an eyebrow. "Clara Darling as the Princess of Doomed City?"

My heart rams in my throat. I stare down at my plate even as Ilusine's dismissive sniff tickles my ear. "Don't make me laugh, Castien dear. The city would require a fae overlord or lady, naturally. I'm simply saying you could appoint one of your humans to manage the library. No need for you to be here all the time."

The Prince shakes his head, chuckling softly. "I'm afraid it wouldn't do. They need me, you see. There are things even my brave librarians cannot accomplish on their own."

"So you'll *die* for them?" Ilusine leans forward suddenly, planting one fist on the table. Her eyes spark fire. "Don't pretend with me, Castien. I can *smell* the curse on you, I can *smell* how it has strengthened. You keep using your human magic to manage these Noswraiths. And it's killing you." She sits back again, draws a deep breath. "You *must* stop. Before it's too late."

"If I were to stop, Vespre would surely be lost."

"Let it be lost then! Lodírhal has a failsafe in place—he'll simply cut the island adrift in the Hinter Sea. Let it and the Noswraiths be banished forever to the Great Expanse."

"Along with all the city's inhabitants?"

"Trolls." Ilusine tosses her head. "They won't mind it much. They'll simply sink into their rock state and never know the difference."

"Nightmares can penetrate even stone." The Prince's voice is eerily soft.

"Why should you care? They're just trolls."

He makes no answer to this. Instead he rises from his chair, picks up his drink, and walks to the balustrade overlooking the city. But not before I glimpse the livid expression on his face. Or perhaps I'm mistaken. He turns his back so quickly, I'm not entirely certain what I've seen.

Ilusine watches him, swirling her drink and taking little sips. Finally, she sets her goblet down, rises, and, moving with silky grace, joins the Prince at the rail. I duck my head, trying not to eavesdrop. But her voice carries bright and clear, and I cannot help but hear. "Castien." She places a hand on the Prince's arm. "You know I say these things only because I care. I believe you are the future Aurelis needs. Not Estrilde. Not Ivor. *You.*"

"With you at my side?" The Prince turns a cold stare upon her. "Come now, Ilusine, let us not pretend. With eleven sisters between you and your mother's throne, you see me as your best bet for a crown of your own. Is that not the truth?"

"Not at all." Her smile curves like a cat's. "I could always have Ivor for my husband."

My stomach dips, and I catch my breath. I really, *really* don't want to be here right now. I cast about, looking for escape.

The Prince's dark chuckle rumbles in the still air. "I'm afraid you'd have to go through Estrilde if you want to take your throne that way."

"I'm not afraid of Estrilde." Ilusine takes the Prince's hand, draws it to her, presses it against her heart. She gazes up into his face, her long lashes wafting gently, soft as butterfly wings. "I could have Ivor if I wanted him. But I don't. It's *you* I want, Castien. Gods above know why! But I've long ago ceased to question my own heart. I simply know. It's *you* I seek to share a throne, a crown, a kingdom with. That's why you must demand the Rite of the Thorn. For you. For me. And for Aurelis."

"And Vespre?" the Prince asks.

"Vespre can burn for all I care." She takes a step closer, her lips drawing close to his.

Time for me to go.

I push my chair back and slip from the table, silent as a shadow. Pulse thrumming, I fairly sprint for safety, lifting my skirts clear of my feet. I reach the door, try the latch, find it resistant. Biting back a curse, expecting the Prince's commanding voice to stop me in my tracks at any moment, I push harder.

The latch gives; the door swings open. I burst out into the

passage beyond.

It's very gloomy after the light of the lanterns and the stars out on the balcony. I don't care. I pull the door behind me, not quite shut for fear of the sound it will make, and hasten down the passage, stumbling a little in the dark. How badly I need to find my room, to dive into bed and bury my head under the pillow! I don't want to think about Vespre being cut adrift, left to the horror of the Noswraiths. I don't want to think about Har, Dig, Calx, and Sis, forced to turn to stone and yet still preyed upon in their dreams. I don't want to think about Nelle and Mixael and Andreas struggling hopelessly to fight back the onslaught of horror.

Struggling, failing. Succumbing.

One by one.

And me? Would I stand with them? Facing that horror without hope, without help?

"Darling."

I stop.

I'm nearly to the end of the passage where it branches to the right and left. A single lantern hangs overhead, shedding stark light directly down on me. Knowing how visible I am, I take care to pin my smile back into place. "Prince," I say, turning and dropping a neat little curtsy.

He strides toward me. I can't see his face at first, only an impression of movement. Then he steps within the circle of lanternlight, so tall and unexpectedly stern. He wears robes of silver trimmed in red, and a stone crown rings his brow. I've rarely seen him look so princely. The faintest vibrations of fae glamour permeate the air around him, and though I know it's only the glamour that makes me feel this way, my heart aches at the sight of him. Only . . .

Only I realize suddenly that he's *not* wearing glamours. Not anymore. The instant he stepped into the light, they melted away. In this moment, he's merely human. Or mostly human. Tall, with narrow shoulders, a trim waist, thick black hair, and a beautiful, strong-featured face. Imperfect. And undeniably compelling.

He looks down at me, his eyes bright in the lantern glow. "Where are you off to?" he demands, folding his arms.

"Your pardon, Prince." I incline my head, focusing my gaze on the scarlet embroidery across his chest. "I am tired. It's been a long day."

"I suppose it has. What with your trying to impede Captain Khas in her work this morning, offending the *Hrorark* this afternoon, running around like a madwoman across the City Below, and then fainting in my arms." He chuckles and takes another step toward me. "You *did* faint in my arms, you know. Quite like a romantic heroine."

Heat flares in my cheeks. I don't know what to say. The best I can come up with is "You shouldn't leave your dinner guest waiting, Prince."

"*You* are my dinner guest."

My gaze flicks to meet his. "I was obliged to be here tonight. Not invited."

A sharp expression I cannot quite name flashes in his eyes. He hides it quickly with a blink, then takes yet another step, closing the little distance between us. "Is that fair, Clara Darling?"

"I don't know that fairness has anything to do with the matter. I am an Obligate; you are my Obliege Lord. There the matter stands."

"So it would seem." He's so close now. Too close. Close enough that I'm starting to remember how it felt to be encircled by his arms, his lips close to my ear as he sheltered me from enemy eyes. I can almost feel the beat of his heart once more, pulsing in time to my own.

His gaze moves from my eyes to my forehead. "Lir has done well tending your hurts. I can see only the faintest discoloration now. Tell me, does it still hurt?" He reaches out, brushes my forehead with the tips of his fingers.

A little gasp catches in my throat. "Yes," I manage, pitching my voice low.

Gently, slowly, he slides hair from my face and tucks it behind my ear. "Darling," he says, very softly, "come back to dinner."

I shake my head.

"It would please me if you returned. Does that mean nothing to you?"

"I think your guest would prefer to have you to herself."

"And how does that make you feel?"

My smile mask has slipped. Hastily I fit it back into place. "I feel nothing. Merely tired."

"Merely?" He echoes the word, his voice a low rumble. "I think perhaps you feel more than that."

"Think what you like, Prince." I lift my brows ever so slightly. "May I have your leave to depart?"

"I could make you return."

"You could."

"I don't want to."

I say nothing.

"I want you to return of your own free will. Or not at all."

"Then I will not return."

He's still standing there, his fingers resting against my cheek. His gaze moves from my eyes to my lips. I hold my breath. It's as though everything inside me has suddenly lost the ability to think or feel. Nothing makes sense anymore. I'm trapped in this single instant of forever, and the Prince is looking at me, and I'm wondering . . . wondering . . .

"Mistress!"

I start and take a step back, turning quickly to one side. Lir approaches from the end of the side passage. "Oh! Lir, what is it?" I gasp. Do I sound as stammering and foolish to her as I do in my own ears? The Prince withdraws a step. He's angled so that Lir cannot see him from where she stands. By the way he moves, I get the distinct impression he does not *want* her to see him.

Lir pauses, wringing her hands. "Oh, Mistress, I'm glad to find you here! Have you finished your meal? I do hope so, for you have a visitor."

"A visitor?" I blink, shocked. Then I shake my head. "That's not possible." Who would be visiting me? Who would . . .?

My heart stops.

Danny. He said he wanted to break my Obligation. He said he'd found a way into Eledria. But no. No, I've been very clear with him. I've begged him to let the idea go! He wouldn't ignore my wishes, would he?

"Who is it, Lir?" I ask, so afraid I can scarcely get the words out. "Who has come?"

"It's Lord Ivor Illithor of Aurelis, Mistress."

15

YOU COULD KNOCK ME DOWN WITH A FEATHER.

"Ivor? Lord Ivor?" I sound like an idiot. I know I do. But I can't seem to stop myself. "Lord Ivor has come to Vespre?"

"Yes, Mistress!" Lir's eyes are bright in the lantern light. "He is most insistent upon seeing you. Captain Khas has him waiting in the solarium, and she sent word for me to fetch you. Have you quite finished dining? I wanted to bring him to the dining hall, but he insisted on seeing you alone."

At this, I cast a sideways glance down the passage where the Prince stands just beyond Lir's range of sight. Only he's not there anymore. There's nothing but the faintest impression of glamour in the air. Did he use his fae magic to disappear?

I face Lir again. "You're *sure* it's Lord Ivor? That is, you're certain this person is who he says he is? Not an imposter?"

Lir gives me a look. "Of course, I'm sure. He couldn't give a name that wasn't his to give, now could he?"

This is true enough; the fae aren't capable of lying. They thrive on deceit and trickery, but outright lying is beyond their powers. And they certainly would not use someone else's name. That would go against everything it means to be fae.

I suck in both lips, biting down hard. What should I do? Lord Ivor is *here.* Here to see *me.* I remember the last time I saw him—how Estrilde's command that I not speak to him nearly caused me to choke to death in his presence. How he held me in his arms, realized what was happening to me, and vowed to make it right, storming off at once to speak to Estrilde.

As a direct result, she sold my Obligation to the Prince of the Doomed City.

But that wasn't Ivor's fault. He meant to help me, not to send me into this dangerous place. Why is he here now, though? Yes, he always *seemed* to show me extra interest, but I never let myself believe I was more than a favored pet in his eyes. A cute curiosity that served as a distraction when he was home in Aurelis and not off campaigning for his king. And if sometimes I thought I saw something more, something warmer in his gaze? Well, I've taken care to squelch those thoughts when necessary. I won't be deceived. I know what happens to girls who let themselves believe fae lords have fallen in love with them. It never ends well.

But Ivor is here. And whatever his reasons, I can't ignore him. I must deal with this situation. Now.

"Very well, Lir," I say, surprised at how calm my voice sounds. "Take me to him, please."

Lir leads the way, setting a brisk pace. I follow a little more slowly. My poor feet are still so sore after my mad run through the lower streets of Vespre. I wish that for once everyone would just leave me *alone*. Let me rest, let me recover. Let me get my thoughts in order. But that isn't how life works in Eledria. Particularly not in Doomed City.

"How was your dinner, Mistress?" Lir asks with rather too much interest. "Did you enjoy yourself?"

I huff and mutter, "The less said about it, the better."

"Oh. Well, pardon me." She sounds offended. But I haven't the energy to care just now.

I don't know the way to the solarium. I didn't even know Vespre had a solarium. It doesn't make sense in a place where the sun never shines. Thus I'm more than a little surprised when we arrive and Lir throws open the door to a scene of soft golden sunlight and rich green growth. Warm air hits my skin, and I hear the faint, pleasant buzz of insects.

"What is this?" I gasp, peering through the door into a huge space. There are enormous potted plants everywhere, some of the pots so big, they almost count as miniature gardens in and of themselves. Overhead is a crystal dome, not unlike the one at the top of the citadel. Sunlight pours through—pure, unmistakable sunlight.

"There's a spell on this room," Lir says with distaste in her voice.

She hangs back from the doorway, and when I glance her way, her arms are crossed, her expression tight. "The Prince made it for his mother so she could come and grow her human plants here. That light is carried all the way from Solira. Ugh!" She shudders. "It's too bright." Then she gives me a plaintive look. "Do you want me to stay with you, Mistress?"

She is a troll, after all; I shouldn't be surprised by her aversion to sunlight. "No, Lir. You may go."

Gratefully she bobs a curtsy and departs. There's nothing left for me to do but venture into the solarium.

It's a greater relief than I expect to step into that enchanted sunshine. I've become so used to the perpetual twilight of Vespre, I hadn't realized until now how much I missed the sun. And the flowers! I can scarcely believe the sheer abundance of blooming things, the colors, the smells. Climbing roses, creeping nasturtiums, gaudy and glorious peonies, towering gladioli, all in such profusion it dazzles the eye. Little buzzing creatures flit from blossom to blossom. At first I take them for bees, but on second glance, I realize they're hartlings—multi-colored, with trailing, lacy wings and faces reminiscent of tiny deer with huge, faceted eyes. Everywhere they flit, they leave trails of sparkles in their wake, which coat petals and leaves and make everything glitter.

I take no more than four steps into this thriving greenery before I can't see the door anymore. Several narrow paths of polished marble tiles lead winding routes through the foliage. I pick one and follow it, pushing through low branches. Leaves and petals cling to my skirts, and the sparkles left by the hartlings tickle my nose.

I'm just starting to think I'll have to call out for Ivor if I'm to have any hope of finding him in this jungle, when suddenly the path spills me out into a circular space in the center of the solarium. A fountain bubbles cheerfully in a blue stone basin. The water reflects the sun so blindingly, I'm obliged to put up a hand and shield my eyes until they adjust.

When they do, I see Ivor sitting on the lip of the basin.

I stop short. I'd nearly managed to forget the sheer beauty of this man. One would think in Eledria, where such beauty is so common, one would eventually become numb to it. But that's the danger of fae beauty—human senses *cannot* be numbed to its allure. We must always find them overwhelming, and if we don't, the fae simply increase the potency of their glamours until we do.

My pulse races, my head spins. All the riotous colors around me dull to sad grays. I try to gather my wits. I can't just stand here, staring at him, waiting for him to notice me. I must speak. But what can I say? Even a simple greeting seems foolish in this moment.

Before I can decide, Ivor looks up suddenly from his contemplation of the water. "Clara!"

He speaks my name with such tenderness, as though it *belongs* in his mouth.

Only it doesn't. Ivor shouldn't speak to me like that. And he really, really shouldn't look at me that way! As though I am the brightest object in this lovely garden, as though I am the source of all light and delight.

I take a step back. Beneath the thrilling pleasure flooding my veins is a thread of panic. That thread tenses as Ivor rises and strides toward me. I remember all over again what it felt like when Estrilde's command choked the air from my lungs, leaving me writhing and desperate on the floor.

There's no magical chokehold this time, however. There's nothing but my own heart, beating wildly as Ivor closes the distance between us.

"My lord," I say, dropping into a deep curtsy.

Ivor stops. "Clara," he says again, with that same devastating warmth. "I'm so glad to have found you. I cannot tell you what I felt when I learned Estrilde had sold your Obligation to . . . to *him.*" He speaks the word so bitterly, as though the idea of saying the Prince's name is poisonous. "I fear I am to blame. When I went to Estrilde, I intended only to help. It wasn't right that she should treat her own Obligate so harshly! But the princess has such a vengeful nature."

How am I supposed to respond? Estrilde may not be my mistress anymore, but that doesn't mean I'm safe to speak ill of her. I dip my head and say demurely, "My former mistress was well within her rights, Lord Ivor, as you must know. I do not complain of my treatment at her hands."

"*Do not,* perhaps," Ivor acknowledges. "But I know very well how you *could* if you chose. Ah! Clara! The torments I suffered to learn of your loss! I was not informed until many days later, and then I could not slip away from Aurelis until now. King Lodírhal keeps a tight hold on me, now more than ever."

This doesn't surprise me. Ivor is the newly named heir to the throne of Aurelis. Lodírhal must depend on him a great deal as his own life nears its end.

What doesn't make sense are these protestations of his, these claims of torment and woe. It isn't reasonable. How could someone like Ivor feel so strongly over *me?* Guilt bites at my conscience, as though I'm somehow responsible for enticing and entrapping this powerful man, all without trying.

"Gods on high, Clara," he continues, "I'm so glad to find you well and whole. I've been imagining all manner of horrors— Noswraiths plaguing the streets, trolls rampaging at will. And you, sweet, gentle creature that you are, trapped in the midst of them." He shakes his head. "It was too much to be borne."

I hastily clear my throat. "You need not have worried, my lord. As you see, I am quite well."

He looks me up and down. Am I imagining approval in his gaze as he takes in my figure, displayed to fine advantage in the lovely gown Lir chose for me? He reaches for my hand. His fingers close around mine, and when I try to withdraw and back away, he grips a little tighter. "I've come to rescue you, Clara." He inclines his head toward me, long locks of hair falling over his shoulder. "I've come to purchase your Obligation."

"What?" The word bursts from my lips in a little bleat.

"I've come to take you back to Aurelis with me. You'll be safe there. As your Obliege Lord, I won't let anyone harm you."

I open my mouth, close it again. I'm dazed, confused, unable to think straight. "But . . . but Estrilde—"

"Estrilde won't like it." Ivor chuckles. "But there's nothing she can do about it. You'll be under *my* protection. And soon I will be King of Aurelis." He smiles then, a smile that sets my blood pulsing all the way to my core. "Perhaps then I will be free to follow in the tradition of the previous king . . . if you understand my meaning."

Dasyra. He's speaking of Dasyra. Of King Lodírhal's wife, his *human* wife. The Fatebonded bride he made his queen to the shock and fury of his entire court. He defied all expectations and exalted Dasyra until she became more powerful than any fae lady of the Court of Dawn.

A vision flashes to life in my head—a vision of myself, seated on a throne upraised on a dais in Biroris Hall. The king's court kneels before me, everyone, including Estrilde. And beside me, Ivor, seated upon a throne only a little larger than mine, wearing a crown of golden leaves set with living-fire gems. Magnificent, powerful. Handsome beyond all reason. And he turns to me, looks at me, just as he is looking at me now—

No!

I take a step back, yanking my hand free from Ivor's grasp. What am I doing? Why am I letting myself think this way? It's stupid, stupid, *stupid.* Ivor cannot be serious. This must be some sort of game to him.

I turn my back, holding my shoulders very straight. When I'm not looking at him, my pulse calms, and my breathing levels out. "You needn't concern yourself with my well-being, my lord," I say, battling to keep my voice steady. "I am quite well here, you see."

"Perhaps you are." He takes a step closer. I feel the warmth of his presence just at my back. The next moment, his hands grip my elbows. "But *I* am not well so long as you are here. I am not whole, have not been since the very instant you stepped through the Between Gate and left Aurelis behind."

I close my eyes. My mind is a storm of emotions, and my body insists on responding to those emotions, filling with heat, with lightness. Every bit of my awareness seems to focus on the pressure of Ivor's hands. On the way he draws me slowly, slowly back against his chest.

"I won't ask anything of you," he says softly. His lips are near my ear, his breath tickling the delicate skin of my neck. I imagine how it would feel for his mouth to press against my skin. "You can return to your duties in Aurelis Library," he persists. "You can help old Thaddeus Creakle care for the volumes collected by the former queen. Hunt pixies."

This last bit is accompanied by a chuckle that brings vividly to mind my last pixie hunt, when Ivor arrived unexpectedly to lend his aid. He'd even risked the discomfort of iron for my sake. How many times had this great and powerful lord humbled himself? For me?

In light of that humility, how can I refuse what he offers?

"Clara." The pressure of his hands turns me slowly to face him.

There's so little space between us now. My breath hitches. I stare at the indentation between his collarbones. His skin is so pale, almost translucent, but shining with its own inner light. The muscles of his chest are hard, sculpted like the marble statue of a god.

He lifts one hand, runs a knuckle down the curve of my cheek. "Clara, say the word. I will take you away from all of this. You don't belong in darkness. You don't belong in Vespre." His finger comes to rest under my chin. He tilts my face up to his and smiles. Such a gentle smile on such a proud, strong face. He tilts his head to one side, lowers his lips toward mine.

"Say the word, Clara," he breathes. "Say *yes* to me."

My lips part. I let out a small, shuddering breath.

"And *this* was my mother's personal favorite: *respenia* blossoms. You see how they always grow in pairs? Quite an unusual little specimen and rarely found thriving in domestication like this. But then, Mother Dearest always had a knack with vegetation."

The bright crisp voice rings out across the solarium, followed by the sound of bootheels against stone tiles. I spring back from Lord Ivor, breaking his grip on my arm, and whirl just in time to see the Prince and Ilusine appear through the foliage.

The Prince looks straight at me and smiles. "Ah! Well met, Darling."

16

THE PRINCE SHIFTS HIS GAZE FROM ME TO IVOR. "As I live and breathe," he says with a wide smile that shows far too many teeth, "if it isn't my father's favorite hound. Has the king sent you sniffing about my home, Ivor, old boy, or have you broken your leash and gone a-wandering?"

Ivor's jaw hardens, but he offers the merest inclination of his head. "Prince," he says coolly, then turns to Ilusine. "Princess Ilusine," Ivor says, with only a little more warmth than he'd used to address the Prince. "It's been some time."

"Indeed it has, Ivor," she replies, her voice a silky purr.

"I could always have Ivor for my husband." Her words from dinner seem to echo in my head. Seeing the two of them together now, I can't help but think how right she was. They are both so beautiful, so golden. So well matched.

Shame floods my cheeks with heat. Had I *really* believed Ivor was about to kiss me just now? Had I *really* believed he was offering, not only to buy my Obligation, but also to make me his queen? I must be mad. Delusional! Standing here, looking at Ivor and Ilusine together, I see only too well that they belong to a different world altogether. A world that has no room for someone like me.

"And what brings you to Vespre?" Ilusine asks Ivor innocently. She holds a long-stemmed white rose in one hand. When she brushes her fingers over the edges of the petals, they take on a golden sheen, and the whole blossom sparkles.

"I come on business," Ivor responds with a smile. "And you, Princess?"

"Pleasure," she says, snaking a hand through the Prince's elbow. "And business too. I find the one more palatable when combined with the other." She glances then from Ivor to me, her brow puckering faintly as though she cannot begin to imagine why we would be found together.

Now is probably a good time for me to leave. Bobbing a quick curtsy, I start to slip away from the fountain, hoping to disappear into the greenery while the fae folk are distracted. No such luck.

"And where are you off to, Darling?"

I bite back a curse. Turning slowly, I meet the Prince's gaze and offer a curtsy and a smile. "I am weary. I beg leave to retire for the night."

The Prince's eyes narrow. "I don't believe I can give leave just yet. If I'm not much mistaken, Lord Ivor's business has something to do with you."

"Indeed, it does," Ivor responds at once.

Oh gods! Is he going to make the offer for purchase right *now?* He is. He is, and there's nothing I can do to stop him. If I even *want* to stop him. Which I don't. Or I shouldn't. I mean, of course I want to escape Vespre and its darkness and its Noswraiths and its man-eating zealot trolls. Of course I want to get back to Aurelis, a world of light and laughter, where the books in the library won't actively try to eat me. Of course that's what I want.

But I stare at Ivor in open-mouthed dismay as he addresses the Prince: "I have come to purchase Clara Darlington's Obligation."

There. It's spoken. Now my whole life will change. One way or the other.

I hold my breath.

The Prince nods. His lips purse as though he's considering the idea.

Then, quite simply, he says, "No." He turns and waves a hand, speaking to Ilusine. "And you see over there? Tucked away amid the hollyhocks? That's a rare specimen of *thejyre.* Quite tricky to grow anywhere in any world. One of my mother's great prides."

"No?" Ivor's voice echoes against the domed crystal overhead. "You would deny me without hearing what I am prepared to offer?"

The Prince glances back over his shoulder. "My dear Ivor, there's nothing you might offer that would tempt me to part with so useful an Obligate."

"Useful?" Ivor spits the word. "You speak of her *use?"*

"Why, yes." The Prince raises an eyebrow. "What else were we discussing?"

"This young woman is worth far more than the sum of her *usefulness."*

The Prince turns about, fixing the full force of his stare on Ivor. "Is that so? Tell me, old chap, if it's not her *usefulness* that interests you, why have you come so far to make this purchase?"

"That is none of your business."

"When it comes to the potential future and well-being of my Obligates, it very much *is* my business. I have no wish to sell the girl into service that may be beneath her."

Ivor draws himself up even straighter, his eyes flashing. "My intentions for Clara's Obligation are entirely honorable."

"Then state them outright."

"What I do with my own Obligates is *my* business. As to intentions, you must and will trust my honor as a warrior and a gentleman."

"I *must* and *will* do nothing of the kind."

Ivor's jaw works, the muscles in his throat tightening. "In that case, state your own intentions. Everyone knows you came to Aurelis for the sole purpose of taking this girl back with you. That you took advantage of your cousin, manipulated both her and your father to make certain you got your way. Do you deny it?"

"Why should I? It was a pretty bit of negotiation if I do say so myself. Though I would hardly call it manipulation considering *you* were the driving force behind my cousin's desire to sell."

"You don't deny that you came to Aurelis to take this girl?"

"Of course not. I needed a new librarian. One of mine was recently *eaten,* you understand. We tend to go through librarians rather quickly in these parts."

"And you hold her life so cheaply!" Ivor snarls. "You would steal her away, out from under my nose, and throw her like fodder to your cursed Noswraiths."

The two of them stalk closer to each other as they speak, one step after another, until they are now nearly nose to nose. The Prince's shoulders are back, a supercilious expression on his face, but Ivor clenches his fists. "You have the look of a man itching for a fight," the Prince says. "Do you intend to strike me, Lord Illithor?"

Ivor draws a long breath. They stand like so, as though caught in a spell of stone.

Suddenly, Ilusine laughs. It's such a sharp, unexpected sound, it seems to break the very air around us. She claps her hands, the glittering rose she carries flashing and dropping petals. "Go on, Ivor!" she urges. "Go on, throw the first punch! The Rite of the Thorn will commence at once, and I am most eager to witness the result."

I'm not sure what is happening. There's something here, some acknowledged truth the three of them understand, but which escapes me entirely. Judging from the expression on Ivor's face, he's just lost a fight. He draws several long breaths through flaring nostrils.

Just when I fear the moment will explode into violence, however, he takes a step back and smooths his hair with both hands, like a lion grooming his mane. "Now, perhaps, is not the best time for negations," he says in a cooler voice than a moment before. "I will beg a room for the night, Prince."

"Beg?" The Prince smirks. "That I should like to see."

"Don't be an ass, Castien," Ilusine trills and pats the Prince's arms in a proprietorial manner. Then, as graciously as though she were the ruling Princess of Vespre, she turns to Ivor and says, "A room will be made up for you, my lord. I trust your stay will be comfortable. Come! I'll walk with you."

Ivor looks momentarily confused but allows Ilusine to take his arm and lead him away. He shoots one last meaningful look at me before they disappear into the greenery. And just that abruptly, the brewing storm dissipates to nothing.

I draw a huge breath. I'd not realized how tight my lungs were until that moment. I let my breath out again, swaying suddenly as the world seems to tilt sideways.

The Prince is there in an instant, his hand on my arm. "There now, careful," he says, helping me to the fountain, easing me to sit on the edge of the basin. "Don't want to go fainting into my arms a second time today, do you? You've had a sip or two too many, I fear. Not to mention that Ivor—he'll go straight to any girl's head. Many a boy's too, for that matter."

I frown, rally, and push his hand away. "I'm fine!" The words come out in a snarl. "I don't need any help."

The Prince holds up his hands and takes two steps back. But he doesn't leave. I wish he would. Closing my eyes, I try to wish all this away, the whole encounter . . . basically the entire day from the moment Captain Khas informed us of an intruder in the palace. I rest my head heavily in my palms, elbows propped on my knees. This has been, I'm quite sure, the longest day of my life. I need for it to end.

Instead I feel the Prince's gaze fixed upon me.

Finally, I lift my head. I don't even bother trying to smile. I simply glare at him and snap, "What?"

The Prince folds his arms and tilts his head a little to one side. "Is this what you want, Darling?"

"What do you mean, *what I want?*"

"For me to sell your Obligation to Lord Ivor. To return to Aurelis with him."

I stare at him, taken aback.

"It'll mean leaving behind the library, of course," he continues in that same measured tone. "Not that I fancy you'd mind overmuch. Hard to be homesick for a load of ravenous Noswraiths. But I'd like to think you'd miss the librarians somewhat. Nelle and Mixael and Andreas." He shrugs. "And there's your children to consider."

"*My* children?" I shake my head, anger and frustration roiling together in my gut. "You mean the children you refuse to help? The children you refuse to let me help? Those children?"

"The same."

"What does it matter what I want? What I *want* is not to live under Obligation at all. What I *want* is freedom to return to my own home, my own life, my own people. What I *want* is not to be Obliged to anyone. Ever."

The Prince sniffs. "Come now, we both know that's ridiculous. We're all of us obliged to *someone* every day of our lives. Even the likes of Ivor and Ilusine cannot do and act wholly without consideration for others, or they wouldn't last long in the courts of Eledria."

I rise in a rustle of skirts and hold his gaze. "You know perfectly well there's a big difference between social responsibility and a gods-blighted Obligation curse. I don't *belong* to myself."

"And if you did?" The Prince takes a step closer, dropping his arms to his sides. "If your Obligation were to end today, what would you do?" He seems suddenly taller than before, though I can't tell if he's using a glamour to make himself seem taller or if it's merely my own perspective.

Either way, I refuse to back down. I plant my feet more firmly, digging in my heels. "I would return to Oscar. I would go home to my brother and care for him."

"Care for him?" The Prince utters a dark, bitter sort of laugh. His eyes flash like twin lances, piercing my skull. "Darling, you are a coward."

"What?"

"You heard me," he says. "A coward. Through and through. You're afraid. Afraid of your power, afraid of the obligation such power naturally invests. The obligation to use your power to protect."

"You don't know what you're talking about." I speak through gritted teeth. "I am responsible for Oscar. He's the one I'm meant to protect. I'm his sister."

"And what of Vespre? What of Aurelis? What of all Eledria, and all your world as well? Don't imagine that once the Noswraiths have finished with Eledria they won't infiltrate your world next. They can't manifest in physical form there, but make no mistake, they can be just as deadly. They'll poison the minds of humanity, living nightmares breathing through the bodies of those poor souls they inhabit. They'll wreak destruction until your whole world is bathed in blood, in chaos. And who will care for Oscar then?"

His words seem to close in around me, like darkness. I realize there are tears on my cheeks and dash them away ferociously. "How dare you?"

"How dare I? Rather easily. I don't like cowardice." The Prince draws a long breath and lets it out slowly. "You pretend you're all love and concern, all caring and devotion. But in truth, Darling, you just want to run away from everything you know you could be. You would rather use your brother as a shield than face the truth of who and what you are."

"And who are you to make such judgments?" I demand. "You, who don't even care for the people of this city, people you were given governance over, people you're meant to protect. You make a show of things, you battle the Noswraiths up here in your high tower, while down below, *children* are made to slave in the darkness. And you make no move to stop it!"

The Prince actually looks taken aback. Then his teeth flash in a snarl. "You know nothing of Vespre."

"Maybe I don't." Tears clog my throat, but I force the words out relentlessly. "What I do know is that four needy children have begged me to take them in, to care for them, to love them. And all you've done is set spells around my room so they cannot see me. You've sent your captain and her guards to hunt them down when they try to find me, you've turned a blind eye to what's being done to them in the City Below. I don't have to understand the ways of Vespre to understand *you*."

"I've never pretended to be better than I am," the Prince replies. "I, at least, am honest. But you? You pretend to care. When all the while your *caring* and your *sweetness* and your *gentleness* are little more than excuses. Excuses to hold back the power inside you, the very power Vespre needs."

"What do you want from me?" I throw open my arms, gesturing broadly, futilely, tossing my head back. "I've given everything I have! I've studied and faced and fought Noswraiths. I've taken my place among the librarians. I've risked my life again and again, and have you heard me complain? But it's not enough for you, is it. *What do you want from me?*"

The Prince moves so fast, I scarcely have time to register what's happening before he's grabbed my upper arm and drawn his face very near to mine. It seems as though a cloud has passed over the sun above, throwing the solarium into sudden darkness. His face shadowed, the Prince's eyes glint bright, and his teeth flash in a snarl. "I want . . ." His voice is thick, hoarse. "I want *you.*"

I stare at him, unable to blink, unable to breathe.

His grip on my arm tightens. "I want you," he continues. "I *need* you. To be *whole.* To be *strong.*" He drops his gaze to the ground, his jaw working as though he struggles to find the words. Finally, he growls, *"Vespre* needs you to be strong."

He lets me go. I stagger back, my heels hitting the base of the fountain. For a long moment, we hold each other's gaze, unspeaking.

Then, without another word, he turns on his heel and marches away. As he goes, the cloud overhead passes by, and sunlight returns, shining through the skylight and warming my head and shoulders. I watch him disappear into the foliage.

My knees give out. I sink heavily to sit on the lip of the fountain. At first I can do nothing. Nothing but sit there, shivering.

A little whimper trembling on my lips, I drop my face into my hands and let tears flow.

17

I'M SLOW AND SLUGGISH THE FOLLOWING MORNING.

"You look like something the *riroarat* left in the *hirrah toar*," Lir comments as she bullies me out of bed and into proper clothing.

I don't bother to ask what she means; I don't have the energy to care. She makes me sit at the little table and all but threatens to spoon feed me herself if I don't start eating the breakfast she's brought. I manage a few mouthfuls, but even though I ate next to nothing at that awful dinner last night, I can't seem to work up any appetite.

My gaze keeps drifting to the corner of the room where the shadows are deepest. Even now, with the overhead lanterns lit to their brightest setting, it seems darker than it should be.

Six bells are already ringing by the time I finally leave my room and make my way to the library. I know I should hurry, but I simply cannot summon the strength. When I finally step through the doors into the uppermost floor of the library, a loud bray rings out, echoing all the way to the dome overhead. I turn wearily and see Nelle's wyvern perched on the back of her chair, peering out from her cubical.

The next moment, Nelle slides her chair back into view. Her bountiful white hair is twisted into a knot on top of her head, held in place with a couple of old quill pens. I'm struck all over again by the strange combination of youthfulness and age in her face. It's almost as though the wrinkles and age spots are nothing but a flimsy mask disguising the true beauty lurking beneath.

She blinks several times, her eyes adjusting after presumably many hours of poring over her writing. "You're late, girl."

"Sorry."

"Out too late drinking with the Lords and Ladies, eh?"

At this, I snort. "Hardly!"

Nelle gives me a narrow look. Then she shrugs and turns back to her work. "Andreas left a stack of potentially compromised spellbooks on your desk," she tosses over her shoulder. "Sort through them, see if any are on the verge of a breakout. Bring anything to me that looks like it needs a proper seeing to."

Glad for a task, I nod and hasten to my desk. There I find quite a sizable stack of spellbooks, all supposedly containing Noswraiths. The minute I touch the topmost volume, I feel the living power inside. None of these are particularly dangerous wraiths, of course;

they wouldn't be on my desk if they were. But I know enough by now to treat any Noswraith with due caution.

I sort through the volumes slowly, daring to open a few, keeping others firmly shut. All of the spells are well on the way to breaking down, but only one or two feel as if they need immediate attention. I set these aside to take to Nelle. The rest can wait a few more weeks by my estimation, so I load them on a trolley to be shelved in the waiting room.

At first the work is engrossing enough to keep my mind fully occupied. As I go, however, little bits and thoughts start creeping in around the edges. Will Ivor breakfast with Ilusine this morning? Or perhaps he and the Soliran princess will take a stroll together through the labyrinthine passages of the palace or enjoy a heart-to-heart in the solarium, discussing the future of Aurelis's throne. After the events of last night, would Ilusine decide to give up on the Prince as a prospective husband and turn her attention Ivor's way?

My heart gives an inexplicable little thud. I pause, holding a spellbook tight in both hands. The nightmare inside wriggles. Setting the volume down with a *thunk*, I plant my elbows on it and rest my head in my hands. Oh gods! Why can't I make my imagination settle down? Why can't I simply do the task before me, keep my focus centered? I'm not looking for trouble. I just want to get through my time here in Vespre in one piece.

I need you.

To be whole. To be strong.

Well, I'm not strong. I never pretended to be. And great gods above me, what does it *matter* if the Prince wants me to be anything at all? I owe him my Obligation, not my loyalty. I squeeze my eyes tight, trying to drive out his voice in my head. Trying to drive out the memory of his eyes gazing deep into mine, of his hand gripping my arm.

I need you.

Vespre needs you.

"Stop it," I whisper. "Stop it! I don't care what you need. Oscar needs me. That's all that matters. That's all!"

I breathe. In and out. Let all those other thoughts and worries float away with each breath. I shouldn't let myself be distracted by anything. Not Ivor. Not troll children. Certainly not the Prince. I must remember what really matters. And that's my brother. Nothing else.

Something stirs.

I drop my hands, sit back in my chair. Stare down at the book in front of me. It's gone still; the Noswraith is dormant once more inside its containment spell. Whatever I just felt, it wasn't coming from the book. I glance at the stack of spellbooks, searching for a culprit. They're all quiet.

But that something—that inexplicable, subtle *something* deep inside my head—whispers.

You know . . .

You know . . .

I stand abruptly, pushing my chair back. For a moment I stay where I am, fists clenched.

Then, slowly, I turn and walk to the rail around the center of the citadel. Gripping it in both hands, I lean over and gaze down the many stories, down to the darkness far below.

You know . . .

You know . . .

Silence.

I draw three long breaths, let them out through my nostrils.

Then—

Clara!

I look to the right. Then to the left. No sign of anyone else—not Nelle or her wyvern, not Mixael, not Andreas. Certainly not the Prince. I might as well be totally alone here in the echoing vastness of Vespre Library.

Knees trembling, I walk to the nearest book lift and, after a moment's guilty hesitation, climb inside, shut the gate, and begin to lower myself. Though it's nerve-wracking to hang suspended over such a terrible drop in nothing more than a little metal cage, this is much faster than using the stairs. Not to mention I'm less likely to bump into one of the other librarians.

Working the ropes and levers, I lower myself down, down. The lower I go, the darker it gets. I feel the pressure of the Noswraiths growing. But I don't stop. Not even when the cage slides from the starlit gloom of the ninth floor into the deeper darkness below level ten. I keep going, working the ropes until my arms ache.

I don't stop until I arrive at the thirteenth floor.

For some moments I can't make myself move. It's so dark—absolute pitch. When I crane my head, looking up through the bars of the book lift cage, I can't even see starlight shining through the dome overhead. It's as if I've entered a different world. Maybe I have.

Feeling my way, I find the cage door, open it, and step out onto the floor. There's a lantern hung from a hook a few feet from where I stand. It burns bravely against the darkness but can't illuminate more than a few feet radius. I hasten toward it, panting softly. An alcove set into the stone beneath it holds a spare lantern, which I quickly light at the first one. The pale moonfire glows through silver filigree, painting strange shadows and highlights on the walls around me.

Clutching this light for dear life, I begin to walk.

On my right are a series of doors set with barred windows: the vaults of the Greater Noswraiths. I feel the swelling pressure of nightmares contained within. Most of them are dormant, suppressed under powerful spells. Some, however, are awake, gnawing away slowly at their bonds. Unless the librarians move to interfere, those bonds will break. Then the Noswraiths will escape, and Vespre will be overrun.

My stomach clenches with dread. Every instinct tells me to return to the book lift, to close myself inside, to haul on those ropes and pull myself back up to the higher floors and relative safety. But I don't. I continue.

Until I reach the thirteenth vault.

This door is no different from any of the others I've passed. It's just as thick, set with a barred window and a huge mechanized bolt. Nothing about this door sets it apart from any of the others. Yet something draws me back here. Just as it did once before.

I stand for several long heartbeats, holding my lantern high, staring at that door. When I close my eyes, I can't feel anything on the other side. But I know this is where I'm meant to be. This is where the voice in my head called me.

This is *my* Noswraith.

Part of me still doesn't want to believe it. How can I? Noswraiths are born of the deepest, darkest parts of humanity, called to life by magic far beyond my comprehension. None of that makes sense for someone like me. I'm not a monster capable of creating monsters. I'm just me. Just Clara Darlington.

So why does the voice in my head sound so familiar? And why does it keep calling me back to this door?

Maybe the Prince is right. Maybe I *am* a coward. I can't deny the dread I feel, standing here, staring at that door. The last thing I want is to know what lurks on the other side. What if I look at it, what if I see its face . . . and I remember? What if, faced by this horror that I called to life, I'm faced as well with the memory of what led me to create such a horror in the first place?

What if, in discovering the Noswraith, I also discover myself?

I draw a long, long breath. Then, slowly, I reach for the huge lock. It's a wheel of complex levers and tines, and at first I think it will be much too heavy for me to budge. To my surprise, however, it gives quite easily when I apply just a little pressure. This vault is meant to keep things in, after all, not out. I turn the wheel, and gears clunk and tines clink, and the big bolt draws back.

With an ominous creak, the door swings outward.

I should push it shut again. I should turn the wheel, reset the bolt. I should put my back to this place and go. Now. While I still can.

But I need to find out. I need to know.

Holding my lantern high, I approach the door, pull it a little wider, and step into the chamber. It's a large, square space, maybe twenty feet wide and thirty feet deep. Bigger than I expected. There are shelves on each wall, extending from the floor all the way up toward a ceiling that my lantern glow cannot illuminate. I get a sense that it's very high indeed, though the air in this room feels close, smothering.

There are books everywhere. On the shelves, piled three deep and more, shoved in every which way. On the floor, in unruly mounds, stacked and then fallen and then stacked again. I turn slowly, shining my lantern across them. It takes me a moment to notice that they're all paperbacks—all the same size, thin, no more than a hundred pages each, if that. Not at all like the big grimoires and leatherbound volumes I've grown accustomed to working with.

I kneel and pick up one of the little books, holding it up to the lanternlight. The paper quality is cheap; it feels on the verge of disintegration. There seems to be some sort of line art illustration on the cover and a thick, bold text, but for some reason, when I hold it close to the light, my vision blurs, obscuring the title. I shake my head, blink several times, and hold the book as close to my face as possible. It's no use. It's like some spell has jumbled the words, rendering them illegible.

The illustration, however . . . that I can see. It's a tall, narrow, spectral figure clad in a white shift. Shoulders bowed. Arms hanging loose on either side, palms forward. The head sags heavily, and long dark hair falls across the face, hiding the features.

I stare at that image. A creeping sense of familiarity comes over me. If I could just make myself read the text, I believe I would know exactly who that illustration is, would know exactly what story this book contains. But I can't. Or won't. I'm not sure which.

I drop the book back on the pile. A shivering susurrus ripples through the room. All the little books stir, pages flapping, whispering. Then, as suddenly as they began, they go still.

I tremble so hard, my lantern wavers, casting its strange shadows across the room. Once more I tell myself to retreat. To run, get off this floor, get back to the upper stories of the library where the starlight still shines. Go, now, while I still can.

But I don't.

I take another step into the room. Then, biting my lip, I reach behind me and draw the door shut. The pressure in the air increases tenfold. It's so sudden, it shocks me into another standstill. I feel as though my skull will burst and my brains will spatter across the books around me. I'm dizzy, ill. There's a tickle on my lip, and when I put up my hand to touch it, my finger comes away smeared with blood.

I wipe the blood on my skirt. Forcing my body to obey, I take another step. Then another. I can't move without stepping on books. They litter the ground and pile up the walls in uneasy stacks. Most of the books in Vespre Library, even the oldest, most broken and battered volumes, are treated with greater care, always carefully closed, and placed in orderly rows on their shelves, like treasures to be cared for and curated. Not here. Here the books lie every which way, as though tossed inside by the careless armload. Some of them lie open, pages half torn and sagging, spines broken, covers shredded. The librarian in me feels a surge of rage at such disrespect shown even the cheapest of paperbacks.

A pedestal stands in the center of the room, and a great grimoire lies there, waiting. It's so different from the other books in this chamber—a huge black thing with leather straps and silver buckles shaped like demon heads binding it shut. Its rough-textured pages bulge between the bindings, enough to contain at least a hundred of these smaller books.

The pressure in the room stems from that grimoire. I'm sure of it.

I draw near. There's energy inside that black cover. That book is as alive as all these paperbacks surrounding it are dead. I can't help the vivid, horrible feeling that they are sacrificial corpses littering the ground around the altar of a glutted god.

A stool of three steps waits before the pedestal, leading up to the grimoire. I stand below, craning my neck, trying to see the book. Hesitating.

No one knows I'm down here.

The realization hits me like a blow to the stomach, followed after by an overwhelming rush of vulnerability. No one knows I'm down here. It could take them hours to realize I'm missing, hours more to find me. If they ever did.

The books around me stir and whisper again. All those long-dead corpses, those broken things. I turn my head sharply, and the whispering stops. I know I imagined it. I *know* I did.

Squaring my shoulders, I turn to the pedestal again. My feet are heavy as I lift them, climbing the stool. There's a place beside the book for my lantern, so I set it down. It casts its white and black silhouettes across the room, its abstract, elegant patterns dancing across the dead books and the packed shelves. I grip the edge of the pedestal with both hands.

The darkness on the borders of my vision stirs.

He really loves you . . .

. . . you know . . .

I shudder. "Who are you?"

When no answer comes, I reach for the silver buckles. Three of them. One by one, I ease them loose. The life inside the book rouses, eager, but the book itself is sedentary. It looks sturdy as well. Surely I don't risk letting the Noswraith loose.

Before I can talk myself out of it, I flip the book open to the first page. The words scrawled there are written in a familiar, scratchy, awkward hand—Nelle's writing. The sight of it gives me a sudden surge of strength. If Nelle wrote this binding spell, it must be strong. Strong enough even for me to read.

I bend over the page, studying the words. At first, they're blurred and jumbled, just like the titles on the paperbacks. But as I force myself to look again, the light from my lantern seems to wash away the confusion.

I read:

They were brother and sister, but people observing them might almost mistake them for mother and son. Not for any great difference in their age—they were only two years apart—but by the way she cared for him. As though he were the only thing in the world that truly mattered to her. One could see in a glance that she would give everything for his sake, even her life.

But she always knew it wouldn't matter. Not in the end.

A chill trickles down my spine.

I know this story. I don't know how or why, but I know it. I've read it before. Somewhere, sometime.

I turn the page, reading on. Another page. Another. My eyes widen as words fill my head, images take shape in my mind, sensations prickle through my awareness. It's real. It's alive. The shadows around me deepen. The dead books rustle their pages, filling the air with an insidious whisper that grows and swells into a roar. I pay no attention. I'm caught up in the reading, caught up in the story unfolding. My face draws nearer and nearer to those pages, pulled by a force I cannot name—

Something moves.

The words on the page bulge.

I yank back, my concentration broken, and take an unwary step. My foot finds nothing but air. I topple off the stool, away from the pedestal, and land with a thud on paperback books that crunch like dead leaves beneath me. Heart pounding, I stare up at the edge of the pedestal outlined by my lantern's glow.

I keep expecting to see a hand emerge over the side, pale fingers grasping the edge.

But there's nothing.

The darkness on the edges of my vision shivers with life. But I'm not asleep, I'm not in the Nightmare Realm. I'm here, in this world. Staring up at that pedestal and the grimoire it holds.

"Close the book, Clara," I whisper. "Get up. Get up now. Get up and close the book."

I feel the pressure mounting. I feel the shadows closing in. In another few seconds, the darkness will be complete, and I will fall into it.

"Get *up!*" I snarl.

With a vicious wrench, I gather my limbs under me, crawl up the steps, and pull myself up by the pedestal. My limbs tremble so hard, I fear I'll fall again, but somehow I manage to stay upright. I look down at the book, see the darkness moving just beneath the pages, bubbling, swelling.

I grasp the cover and slam it shut.

The shadows still.

They retreat.

The light from my lantern fills the chamber once more.

Trembling, I fasten the silver buckles. It feels foolish, futile—I know perfectly well those straps aren't what hold the monster inside. I know as well that the spell is breaking down, that by daring to read it, I may have caused it to break faster. But I fasten the buckles anyway, catch up my lantern, and leap off the stool. My feet crunch on dry, dead pages as I back away to the door, never taking my eyes off of that grimoire.

It doesn't move. The shadows remain where they're supposed to.

I reach the door, find the latch, push it open, and practically fall out into the passage beyond. A little whimper on my lips, I push the door shut again and turn the great wheel until the bolt drops in place. Then I back up five places and stand there, staring at the door, staring at the window into the vault.

A figure flickers past.

Just the barest glimpse—a bowed head, its face hidden by thick black hair.

Choking on a scream, I turn and flee up the passage. My feet slap against the cold stone floor but make no sound at all.

18

I TELL NO ONE OF MY LITTLE EXPEDITION DOWN INTO the lower vaults. As neither Nelle nor Mixael ask me about it, I assume they don't realize what I did.

The rest of the day passes in a fog. I work at whatever menial tasks I can find, reciting lists of Noswraith names in my head while shelving completed binding spells and checking the fourth floor for leftover bookwyrms from a recent infestation.

It doesn't matter. I keep thinking about what I saw.

Those books. Those titles I could not read. Those first few pages in the big grimoire.

I couldn't have written that story. Could I? It doesn't sound like something I would write, and yet . . . and yet . . . it was undeniably familiar. Painfully familiar.

It isn't until I'm back in my own room that evening, changed out of my work dress and seated in front of my vanity, starting to comb my hair, that I realize. "It sounds like Dad's work." I whisper the words, watch my own lips move in the mirror glass. The moment I've spoken, I know it's true.

I set my brush down. My hand trembles hard, and that tremble seems to travel up my arm to my shoulder, my neck, right into my brain. I close my eyes, bow my head—

"Oh, Mistress! Thank the gods, you're here!"

I yelp and whirl on my stool, one hand reaching for my hairbrush like it's a knife. Lir steps into the room, her hands full of a large tea tray, oblivious to my distress. With a nimble sashay of her hip, she shuts the door behind her, and carries the tray to the table by the window.

"Such news, Mistress!" she says, pouring a little milk into a teacup, then adding the dark brewed tea. "The Prince is hosting another dinner tonight for Princess Ilusine *and* Lord Ivor. Did you know that Lord Ivor is the heir presumptive to the throne of Aurelis? It's such a surprise to all of us—we've always assumed the Prince would inherit when his father died. But we're all rather relieved too, truth be told. If the Prince were to leave us, he'd have to appoint a new governor of Vespre, and I'm just not sure how the city would get by, what with the Noswraiths and all. Not that it's any of *my* business, mind you." She presses the teacup into my hands. Pausing a moment, she peers into my face. "Are you quite all right, Mistress?"

"Yes. I'm fine." I quickly set the cup down before my trembling hands begin to rattle the saucer.

Lir *tuts* sympathetically. "Worn out from yesterday, I imagine. Oh, I should never have taken you into the City Below! I knew it would distress you." She pats me gently on the head before crossing to the wardrobe, which she flings wide. The next moment, she disappears inside. I pick up my teacup, take a sip, idly listening to the sounds of her rummaging.

"Lir?" I say after an interval.

"Yes, Mistress?"

"Have you had any news of the children?"

Lir pauses whatever she's doing and looks around the wardrobe door, her brow puckered. "What would I have heard?"

"Oh, nothing. It's just . . ." I trail off lamely. My whole day yesterday was so jarred by the arrival of Ivor, I've scarcely had a chance to think about the children. "I just wondered if you might have asked after them. Considering what we saw yesterday."

"There's nothing to ask after," Lir answers with a frown. "You have now seen for yourself where they are. You must trust it is where they belong, whether or not they like it."

I want to argue. For the moment, however, I can't summon the energy. I turn back to the mirror, rubbing at my temple with one hand as I drink the last few mouthfuls of tea. They have surprisingly good tea here in Vespre; better than one might expect from a city of trolls.

I pause suddenly and look at Lir in the mirror. She's pulling gowns from the wardrobe, looking them over, and shoving them back again, all with an air of purpose. "What are you up to?" I ask.

Lir looks at me over folds of dark red silk trimmed in black beadwork. She pulls it out of the wardrobe, gives it a once-over and then, satisfied, carries it to the bed where she lays it out, stroking the fabric reverently. "It's for tonight, Mistress. Won't it just suit your complexion?"

"Tonight?" I blink dully. Then I shake my head and set my teacup down with a clatter. *"Tonight?* You mean I'm expected to *attend* this dinner? *Again?"*

"Why of course, Mistress!" Lir laughs. "Didn't I say so? I'm sure I must have. But of course, you must have realized the Prince expects you to attend."

"Why?"

To this, Lir merely shrugs and goes about selecting fresh petticoats, stays, a crinoline, all the accoutrements necessary to wear a gown like that. "Perhaps it's for Lord Ivor's sake. He *did* come all the way from Aurelis just to see you." She gives me a close look, obviously hoping I'll elaborate on this mystery, but much too polite to ask directly.

I turn on my stool, face the mirror again, and pour another cup of tea, which I gulp down too quickly, scalding my tongue. Lir seems to accept this as all the answer she'll get to her unspoken questions and sets to work styling my hair. She maintains a steady stream of chatter all the while. Apparently, troll servants are as keen on gossip as any other species, and everyone is agog with news of Lord Ivor and Princess Ilusine.

"They were seen strolling about the palace together all day," Lir says, coiling locks of my hair around her fingers and pinning curls into place. "Shork is quite distressed about it; she considers the Prince practically *married* to Ilusine and says she will just *die* if Ilusine goes and breaks his heart! Which is ridiculous, of course. Anyone can see they are great friends! Lovers, though? Can't say I'm convinced, but Shork is such a romantic at heart."

Shork's romanticism notwithstanding, I remember the kiss I saw Ilusine plant on the Prince's lips yesterday. If that was *friendly*, I'm not sure I want to know what *amorous* looks like.

I close my eyes, trying to unsee that moment—and instead I see Ivor once more, standing in the brilliant solarium sunlight, gazing down at me with such apparent ardor. I could have sworn he was about to kiss me. Only that doesn't make sense! None of it makes sense. Even if he considers me valuable enough to travel all the way to Vespre to fetch, this doesn't explain his attempt to kiss me or any of those strange, suggestive comments he made.

"No one knows what they were discussing, of course."

Lir's voice breaks through my thoughts, dragging me back to the moment. I open my eyes, catch her gaze in the glass. "Who?" I ask.

"The Prince and Lord Ivor," she replies. "They spent several hours shut away in the Prince's private office, and no one knows what they were discussing. No one but Lawrence, that is, but nobody can get anything out of him." Lir sniffs disdainfully.

She goes on to speculate further, but I scarcely listen. My heart is thumping again, and all my exhaustion seems to melt away in place of a sudden surge of suspense. The Prince and Ivor . . . shut in his office . . . Doing what? Negotiating my Obligation, no doubt. Was the Prince taking Ivor seriously, or had he merely jumped at the opportunity to torment the lord, teasing him into believing he might actually sell?

Perhaps he would. Perhaps I want him to. Of course, I want him to!

Unless . . . unless maybe I don't . . .

I groan and bury my face in my hands. "Come, Mistress, don't spoil your hair now!" Lir says sharply. "Stand up, if you please, and step out of that shift. I'll have you laced up in no time at all. To think, you'll be dining tonight with princes and princesses and heirs to the throne!"

"Yes. To think," I echo dully.

Lawrence is waiting for me at the balcony door. He smiles at my approach and murmurs a polite, "Good evening, Miss Darlington," as posh and proper as though I were a lady and not a servant the same as he.

I nod uncomfortably but can't quite manage to return his smile. My stomach is in knots as he opens the door and motions me through. Summoning my strength, I step into the doorway and peer out on the scene.

The three diverse members of this little dinner party are positioned as far away from each other as they can possibly get. The Prince sits at the head of the table, one foot up, his chair tipped on its two back legs. He idly swirls a drink in one hand, watching it become a small maelstrom. Ivor stands at the balcony rail, his right hand clutching his left wrist at the small of his back. His stance is wide as he gazes out across the darkness of Vespre to that distant, magicked view of Aurelis, bright on the horizon.

Meanwhile, Ilusine perches on the rail on the opposite end of the balcony, overlooking a breathtaking fall. Her wings are not visible, but her confidence isn't dampened in the least. Tonight she wears a rose-colored gown that gives the impression of being no more than a flimsy bit of gauze, neither buttoned nor stitched, merely draped across her golden skin. Her hair tumbles in bounteous curls over one shoulder, held in place by glittering gemstone combs.

Ilusine pays no attention when Lawrence announces me, but the other two react. Ivor whirls to fix me with a gaze so intense, I fear I might melt on the spot. The Prince merely tilts his chair down, letting its other two legs strike the stone with a *crack* that makes me jump in my skin.

"Well, now," he says. "We're all assembled. Shall we eat?"

Feeling as though I'm the main course in a room full of tigers, I move to sit in my place between the Prince at the head of the table and Ilusine at the foot. To my dismay, Ivor takes a seat directly across from me. I cannot escape the force of his gaze. I try not to look at him. But in my head, I hear his voice again, urging: *"Say the word, Clara. Say* yes *to me."*

Oh gods! How am I going to survive this meal?

The trolls enter with their massive platters, which they arrange up and down the table. One of them approaches Ilusine and lifts the platter lid. She makes a face, pokes at whatever is on the plate with one finger, then waves it off with a sneer. The troll replaces the lid and shuffles away from her, his stone face expressionless.

"Really, Castien," Ilusine says, lifting her chin and calling down the length of the table, "I don't know how you manage it, surrounded by trolls every hour of every day! I should start to feel positively *crushed* under the weight of them before half a week was through."

Though I don't know what I expect from him, I glance the Prince's way. He lifts his glass in salute to Ilusine but says nothing. The trolls, having finished serving, line up, offer their synchronized bow, and file out once more, all without a word.

Ilusine watches them go, her face thoughtful. "I suppose one might get used to them eventually," she says as the door shuts in their wake. "But *should* one? That is the question, isn't it? My mother scarcely permits trolls to visit her court anymore. Why, I don't believe I've seen one at Solira since Trug the Terrible paid us a call. You remember Trug the Terrible, don't you, Lord Ivor? Styled himself as King of the Trolls and stirred up some rebellion or another. Whatever happened to old Trug, I wonder?"

"I killed him," Ivor says.

My stomach tightens.

"Ah!" Ilusine laughs lightly. "Well, that would certainly explain his absence from the social calendar, now wouldn't it?"

Ilusine continues her lively chatter in much this same vein while the rest of us eat in silence. Or rather, while Ivor and the Prince eat. I stare down at the food before me. Though it's bountiful and smells delicious, and I'm absolutely ravenous, I can't seem to make myself take a bite. Ilusine's words burn in my ears. Since when did I become so sensitive about trolls? I'm not sure. I only know I can't bear to hear Ilusine talk about them so callously. And is she to be the future Princess of Vespre?

Feeling a sharp gaze upon me, I look up and catch the Prince's eye. He quirks one eyebrow. Quickly I look down at my plate again. Picking up a fork, I shove a mouthful between my teeth and chew determinedly. I have no idea what I'm eating.

Ilusine keeps up a steady stream of talk, punctuated here and there by Ivor's short remarks or the Prince's acidic retorts. When at last there's a lull, however, the Prince suddenly says, "It may interest you to know, Darling, that I spent the better part of the day in discussions with Lord Ivor. Specifically pertaining to your future."

The food in my mouth turns to ash. I feel as though the whole table in front of me is slowly rocking back and forth. I set my fork down and surreptitiously grip the arms of my chair, but I make certain my face wears its habitual smile mask when I turn the Prince's way. He seems to be waiting for an answer. I blink and say only, "Oh?"

Ivor growls. The sound is so sudden, so vicious, it draws my gaze back to him. He glares murder at the Prince. "You're a fool, Castien," he says through gritted teeth. Hearing the Prince's given name gives me a shock. On Ilusine's tongue, it sounds intimate. Coming from Ivor, it's disrespectful.

The Prince turns his tiger smile Ivor's way. "Such is the popular opinion, I'm given to understand. I can live with it."

"You'll never get a better offer," Ivor persists. "Think of it! Think what you might do with it!"

The Prince rubs his upper lip with one finger, musing. "A favor from the future King of Aurelis. To be paid at any time and in any manner I see fit. Indeed, it is a handsome offer."

My mouth drops slowly open. I can't believe it. There must be some mistake. The fae never, *ever* place themselves under obligation to one another if they can possibly help it, not even for a single favor. The risk is too great. And a future king of Eledria? A favor from him could be world changing.

I glance at the Prince, my mouth dry, my heart stuttering in my breast. He really *is* a fool to turn down such an offer. For *me*.

"The offer stands," Ivor says, desperation tingeing his voice. "It stands until midnight, but no longer. Don't waste the opportunity."

The Prince shrugs and lifts his goblet. "Ah, but I'm in a wasteful mood!" He takes a delicate sip.

With a snarl, Ivor pushes back his chair and stands. His hand grips his goblet, knuckles whitening as though he is physically forcing himself *not* to dash its contents in the Prince's face. Finally, however, he simply turns and bows to Ilusine, murmuring some polite nothing. He shoots me a last loaded glance before striding from the balcony, his scarlet capelet billowing behind him. Lawrence rushes to open the doors, and Ivor vanishes into the passage beyond. Lawrence shuts the doors and resumes his polite, servile stance in front of them.

"That was close," Ilusine says, drawing my eye. The golden princess of Solira traces the lip of her goblet with one finger. Judging from the gaze she flicks across the table at the Prince, she's not entirely against throwing her wine in his face either. "Had you provoked him a little further, you may have gotten results."

"Results?" The Prince smirks. "Do you mean I might have drawn forth insult enough to demand satisfaction by blood? Are those the results you had in mind?"

"The Right of the Thorn," Ilusine responds coolly. "A battle to the death and your father's crown as the prize."

"I'm not certain a duel over splashed wine would *quite* count as the sacred rite you're picturing. Nor would it justify anyone's death."

"Why not?"

"Well, for one thing, this vintage isn't worth all that much. Now if it was that bottle of Fifth Age *qeise* I have down in the cellar, that might be a different—"

"Don't play the fool. If the insult is great enough, the demand for blood is entirely justified."

"I've been insulted before. No doubt I will be again. It's not healthy for a man to go dueling about at the least provocation."

"Everything *about* Ivor is an insult to you." Ilusine's face is suddenly pale beneath her natural golden sheen. "He's taken your place at your father's side, soon will take your place on his throne. Why does this not gall you? Why do you not demand your rights as son, as the king's own blood?"

"Half-blood. Don't forget that little detail."

Ilusine tosses up her hands. "It was Lodírhal's choice to take a human for his bride. He cannot fault you for that."

"I don't know if a Fatebond counts as a *choice,* per se. Seems to me he didn't have much choice in the matter."

Ilusine does not respond at first. She holds the Prince's gaze in a silence so tense, I'm afraid one wrong move on my part may set off a spark and cause the balcony to explode. I hold my breath, gripping the arms of my chair, waiting for I know not what.

Finally, in a measured voice, Ilusine says, "While *you* might not care about your future, Castien, *I* do."

The tension is broken. After all that, there's no explosion. The Prince merely wipes his mouth and stands. "I find all this caring exhausting. As I still have work to finish, I'll bid you good evening, fair Ilusine."

He bows. First to Ilusine. Then to me.

I don't know which way to look. He shouldn't have done that. He shouldn't have bowed to me. Especially not in front of the princess! He is my Obliege Lord. I am his Obligate. I shouldn't even be here, seated at the same table.

Acting as though there's nothing improper about his behavior or the situation at large, the Prince glides from the table. Lawrence opens and closes the door and this time remains on its far side.

I find myself alone under the starlight with the princess of Solira. And wishing myself anywhere else. I still have a bite of food in my mouth. It feels like a leaden lump, but I make myself swallow. Quickly patting my lips with my napkin, I begin to rise.

"I don't think much of human magic as a rule."

I freeze. Is Ilusine actually speaking? To me? I glance her way, but the princess isn't looking at me. She nibbles at a bite of bread and cheese. Her teeth, I notice, are strangely sharp and deadly looking. "Most humans," she continues, as though musing aloud to herself, "seem frail sorts of vessels for the magic they wield, if they wield any to begin with. But Castien seems to think *you* are possessed of both significant magic and the potential to wield it properly."

Only now do her brilliant eyes flash up to meet mine. This is the first time she's looked at me, truly *looked* at me. "I hope he's right," she says. "I hope you can learn to use the power he believes you possess and soon. Because if Castien is forced to use his human magic one more time, he will surely die."

I gape at her. I don't know what to say. I'm not sure I could make myself speak even if I knew.

Ilusine rises and comes around the table, pauses beside me, and places a hand on my shoulder. "Think about what I've said, mortal maid." Her voice is neither cold nor cruel. Instead it is deeply, shockingly earnest. "We must save him from himself."

With those words, she leaves. I don't turn to watch her go but listen to the sound of her silken gown trailing behind her, the gentle creak of the door opening and shutting. I feel the emptiness in the balcony at my back. I am alone.

I sink into my chair. For a long while, I can do nothing but sit there, gazing out across the city rooftops to the magicked view of Aurelis on the far horizon.

19

I MAKE MY WAY FROM THE BALCONY, VAGUELY INTENDING to return to my room. But once I'm in the stone passage, I can't quite bear the thought of a long night in my quiet, lonely chamber. Not now. Not yet. Not with my thoughts all in a clamor.

Instead I head for the library.

Some small part of me tries to whisper that I'm hoping to meet the Prince there. After all, he did say he had work to finish tonight. But no, that's ridiculous. I certainly don't *want* to see the Prince. I'm only going to the library because I have nowhere else to go. That's it. I could try to find the solarium again, but I rather suspect I'll bump into Lord Ivor there . . . and right now, I absolutely cannot stand to be around Lord Ivor.

He offered a favor for my Obligation.

A favor.

How have I managed to become the object of strife between two such powerful beings as Lord Ivor and the Prince of Vespre? It's madness! Absolute madness. I'm just Clara Darlington of Clamor Street, lower westside. Edgar Darlington's unimportant daughter. Oscar's elder sister. Kitty Gale's friend and Danny Gale's . . . I'm not even sure what. Nothing important. Not the means for saving Vespre City, certainly not a potential queen of Aurelis. I'm not meant for such things. I don't *want to be* meant for such things.

Oh! Gods on high, just let me survive and make it home again!

The library is quiet when I slip inside. Not just the usual quiet one expects from a library; this is true *stillness*. The books are dormant on their shelves. Even the pressure always so present rising from the lower floors seems less than usual. Somewhere, I know at least one librarian is still at work. There's always someone on hand in the library, for the Noswraiths should never be left to their own devices. But whoever is working tonight is nowhere in sight or hearing.

I make my way to my desk and take a seat. There's a stack of wyrm-eaten books in front of me, and I pick one up, page through it dully, then set it down again. I reach for my gray quill, pluck it from its stand, spin it once, put it back where it belongs.

With a sudden groan, I close my eyes and hunch over, gritting my teeth.

"Clara."

I bolt upright, turn in my chair. "Lord Ivor!" I gasp, completely taken aback. For Ivor is indeed there, just climbing to the top of the nearest stairwell, coming up from one of the lower levels. "What . . . how . . . What are you *doing* here?"

"Searching for you." He approaches my desk, and I jump up from my chair to face him. Almost unconsciously I pluck up my quill again, gripping it like a weapon, though why I should feel the need for a weapon, I can't explain.

Ivor stops a few paces away.

"You shouldn't be here," I say. "The library is dangerous."

"So I'm told." His stern warrior's face breaks into a small but lovely smile. "All these books! All this human magic gathered in one place! A library is indeed a wondrous thing. But I've learned not to fear it. Our time together in Aurelis Library has given me much more courage in the face of all this written power."

I shake my head. "These books aren't like those. They're . . . what they contain is much more dangerous."

"Ah, yes. The famous Noswraiths." Ivor shrugs easily. "I don't pretend to understand it all. I'll have to trust your word for it."

He takes a step toward me, and I start and slide away. But he approaches and sits on the desk itself, drawing one leg up and resting his elbow on his knee. "Monster spells or not, the atmosphere still brings to mind those days in Aurelis Library," he says and tilts his head my way. "Do you remember like I do, Clara? How patiently you would sit with me, teaching me to see and name those strange little figures. The *alphabet*."

I smile hesitantly. "You were . . . determined."

"Stubborn, I think you mean." He chuckles. "I'm sure I must

have seemed such a simpleton to one of your learning. But I seem to remember most of our lessons ending in laughter."

I blush and duck my head. "I certainly never intended to laugh at you, my lord."

"Perhaps not. But I like nothing more than making you laugh. Perhaps sometimes I played the dunce rather more than necessary just for the chance of seeing that solemn mouth of yours twitch."

"Really?" I shoot him a disbelieving look. There's such sincerity in his face. Sincerity and vulnerability, which feels so strange coming from a being of his might, his power. Folding my arms tight across my chest, I pitch my voice lower and say again, "You shouldn't be here. Especially not the lower levels." I frown. "What were you doing down there anyway?"

"I told you, I was looking for you." His eyes change from laughing to serious. "But I've found you now. Only . . . only I've lost you as well. The Prince has refused my offer, refused to sell your Obligation. I've tried everything. *Everything.* But I've failed you."

I don't know how to react. Am I supposed to be sorry? Perhaps I am. A little. He looks so sincerely distressed, and I wish I could fix it. I don't want him hurting because of me. "It's all right, my lord," I say, hoping he'll take my words as comfort and not notice the relief in my voice.

"It's not all right." He stands suddenly, drawing himself straight and tall. "It's not all right, I tell you. In fact, nothing has been right, not since the moment you left Aurelis."

My heart thuds in my throat. I try to swallow, try to draw a proper breath. But Ivor is gliding toward me now with the smooth tread of a stalking wildcat. I'm overwhelmed by his presence, lost in the hypnotic intensity of his eyes.

He reaches out, takes my hand. "I've not given up, Clara," he says, lifting my fingers. His lips brush ever so softly against my knuckles, causing the hair on my arm to prickle with sensation. "I'll never give up. Not until I can bring you safely home. To me."

The next moment, he's gone.

I blink. What just happened? Was it magic? He was here one moment, holding my hand; I can still feel the warm pressure of his grip. But now I'm alone, standing in the vast gloom of Vespre Library.

I grip my quill pen tightly behind my back.

With a huge sigh and a little, "Oh!" I grab my chair, turn it around, and sink into the seat. For some moments, I can't do anything but wait for my heartrate to calm. Did any of that really just happen? Or did I somehow dream it? I can't deny, I've had similar dreams before, dreams that made me wake up warm and blushing and determined to forget.

But this wasn't a dream. This was real.

"Oh gods!" I groan and hide my face in my hand. "Gods on high, what am I supposed to *do?*"

Something moves.

I don't see it—my eyes are closed.

I don't even hear it—the library is absolutely silent.

But something, some *impression* of something makes me lift my head and turn sharply to one side. Just in time to glimpse a figure slip out of sight by the far rail, across the open center of the citadel. It vanishes straight into the bookshelves, into the wall.

My eyes are playing tricks on me. That must be it. I blink, shake my head—and in the darkness behind my eyelids, I see the afterimage of a pale figure, head down, dark hair falling to cover her face.

My eyes flare open, staring again across the rail to the far side of the floor. All is still, silent. Empty. Starlight shines through the crystal dome above, and none of the shadows shiver with movement.

Shuddering, I spring to my feet and bolt from the library. I don't stop running until I reach my own room, slam the door behind me, jump into my bed, fully clothed, and pull the covers up over my head.

THE PRINCE

I STAND IN THE DOORWAY OF MY OFFICE. UNSEEN, UNOBTRUSIVE.

I stand there and I watch Ivor lift her fingers to his lips. Kiss them.

Something in me burns. Something wild and dangerous. A beast straining at its tethers, determined to be unleashed. I want to burst from this room, charge to her cubicle, and slam his head against the stone edge of her desk. This is what Ilusine has been urging for after all, is it not? A deathmatch? Only what I'm envisioning is not some sacred battle-rite.

No—this is murder churning my heart. Bloody, brutal murder.

I grip the doorframe. Steel my will. This impulse, this drive, it isn't me. It's a trick. A ploy of the gods, meant to warp me according to their pleasure. But I will not be manipulated. I will not answer the cry of my blood, the roaring in my soul.

Ivor leaves. At last. And still she remains for some while, sunk back into her chair, her face covered with her hands. What is she feeling? Despair that her handsome rescuer did not manage to free her from her enslaving master's clutches?

Have I truly become the villain in this little tale?

I want to go to her. To assure her she's better off without the likes of Ivor. To draw her up from that seat, wipe away those tears, pull her into my arms. I want to press my lips against her temple, murmur into her hair. Breathe in her sweetness, and—

Gods!

I step back into the office quickly, pushing the door shut. My heart pounds in my throat. What is wrong with me? I know better. I know better, damn it! I know how perilous this yawning pit at my feet may be. One wrong step, and I will fall. Lost forever, never to be recovered. I've seen it happen before. I cannot allow it to happen to me. I cannot make myself so vulnerable. Certainly not for *her* of all people. The one woman I hate above all others.

Only . . .

Only I don't hate her.

Gods damn me, I never did.

I storm across my office to the window, staring out across the twilit city to that distant, hazy view of Aurelis, shimmering on the far horizon. Slowly, slowly, my breath calms and the pounding in my head recedes. I am still my own master. I'm not some weak-willed swain ready to fall at the feet of a pretty maid. I am Castien Lodírith, Prince of Vespre, son of the King of Aurelis. My heart and mind belong to me, and I . . . and I . . .

I need some space.

"Shat," I breathe softly.

I must purge myself of this ravenous hunger. And why shouldn't I? I have the means. Ilusine is here, and she's offered . . . a great deal in fact. Her loyalty, her aid, her warriors. Her body.

An image of her in that gold dress swims before my mind. I see her, every detail of her. The way it hugs her curves, the way she moves and shimmers. Each line of her is carefully designed to make a man's blood turn to lava in his veins. I well know how she feels in my arms, the taste of her lips on mine. She would give me more, gladly. And it would be a relief to take everything she offers. To let this ache inside me know release, to give vent to this fire. Perhaps it would steady me. Bring me back to a foundation of reason.

I try to picture it. To see myself, standing at her back. Slipping that golden garment from her smooth shoulders. Sweeping back her hair, letting my lips, my tongue, my teeth explore the column of her neck, the curve of her shoulder. She laughs.

Only it isn't her laugh. And when she turns, gazes up at me, it isn't Ilusine I see.

It's her.

Clara.

Clara, who I drag into my arms.

Clara, whose mouth I claim.

Clara, whose body presses up against mine, whose arms encircle my neck. I pick her up, and her legs wrap around my waist, and I bend her back over my desk. Her skin is warm under my hands, her breast rising and falling fast as I strip away her gown. I kiss her, I taste her, feel the flutter of her pulse as my lips dance across her throat, her collarbone, drifting lower, lower . . .

With an angry snarl, I open my eyes, pound my fist against the stone frame of the window. The glass shakes, cracks. I would like to shatter it and send the shards scattering to the shadows far below. Possibly cast myself after them.

I need to get away. There's no other choice. Not now, not anymore. I need to put some distance between me and that girl before it's too late. I dare not stay in her proximity a moment more.

I'm far too close to the edge as it is.

CLARA

20

I SEE NOTHING OF IVOR THE NEXT DAY. NOR OF ILUSINE either.

I glimpse the Prince only in passing while going about my duties in the library. He neither speaks to me nor looks my way.

Instead I train in spellwriting with Mixael, drill Noswraith names with Andreas, and practice minor bindings under Nelle's supervision. I don't venture anywhere below the upper five stories. I don't glimpse any phantom apparitions. The day passes as normal . . . or whatever counts as normal in a place like Doomed City. And when the evening bells toll at last, signaling the end of my work period, and I return to my room, no dinner invitation has arrived.

"I don't understand!" Lir mutters as she goes about tidying my already spotless room. "I had a perfectly lovely dress all picked out for you and everything!"

"Please, don't fret," I tell her. "I prefer to eat alone anyway."

Lir sighs. "Maybe it's just as well. Lord Ivor has gone from Vespre, and the Prince and Princess are dining together tonight. While I don't particularly approve of Princess Ilusine as a choice for the Prince's bride, it's inevitable they will become betrothed sooner or later. And I suppose it'll be good for the Prince, what with one thing and another. What do you think, Mistress?"

She casts me a sly look. What is she hoping for? Some sign of disappointment on my end? Some indication that I care with whom the Prince spends his time or may choose to spend his life?

Because I don't. All I can think is *Ivor is gone.*

Am I relieved? Undoubtedly. Am I also disappointed? I'm not sure. I do know it's good that he is gone. Better. Safer.

I gratefully eat the meal Lir brings to my room, then sink into a bath, letting steam and scented soaps wash away my fears, however temporarily. Not until much later, when I'm curled up in bed with my head deep in my pillow and my eyes firmly closed, does the irony occur to me: I feel safer at the prospect of staying in Doomed City than of returning to Aurelis with Ivor.

Strange.

The next morning, I return to the library promptly at six bells to find no one at my desk yet again. It's been many days now since the Prince met me here. Hadn't he said I was to train with him every morning?

Irked, I march up to Nelle's desk and demand to know whether or not the Prince intends to continue my training. "Is he not satisfied with my progress?"

Nelle looks up from her work. There's a smear of ink across her cheek, and her eyes look tired. "Well, I don't know about any of that," she says, dipping her quill in the ink pot. "But I do know you won't be training with him today or anytime soon. He left this morning. With Princess Ilusine."

My stomach gives an uncomfortable twist. I ignore it and say with careful nonchalance. "Oh? And where have they gone?"

"To Solira Court, or so I imagine." Nelle sniffs. "Maybe after all this time, the two of them have come to an understanding. If so, he'll have a devil of a time getting Queen Immianthe's approval! But if Ilusine's got him worked up and thinking he ought to make a play for his father's throne, the queen might go for the idea." The old librarian shakes her head heavily, looking at the great spread of work before her. "I don't know what we'll do without him if that's the case."

"Do you think it's possible?" I ask quietly.

"Who's to say? All I know is that Ilusine has been making a play for him, and our Prince . . . well, he may be half fae, but he's also half human, if you know what I mean. There ain't a human man alive who wouldn't like to have a woman like that making eyes at him!"

I quickly bring an end to this conversation, asking Nelle if she'd like me to find Mixael and assist him. Nelle agrees, as she has several small bindings to get through. "And I need to begin the fresh binding for old Boney Long Fingers soon. His book's breaking down fast, and I don't want it to get out of hand. Off with you now, girl! Mixael will find work enough to fill your day."

I make my escape. But even as I start down the nearest stair, ostensibly in search of Mixael as ordered, I pause partway down, gripping the rail. My mind is in turmoil. But why? It's not as though I care where the Prince has gone or with whom. If the Prince wants to marry the Princess of Solira and leave Vespre in order to pursue a glorious destiny as King of Aurelis, what do I care?

With a determined growl, I push these thoughts to the back of my head. Today has enough trouble in it without borrowing from the future. I've got a library to care for.

I work with Mixael and Andreas by turns, and even manage to write a successful summoning spell to draw three bookwyrms out of a wyrm-eaten volume. Mixael is obliged to step in to draw the last dozen or so out himself, but I take pride in my victory, however small.

At last, seven bells toll in the belltowers, and Mixael dismisses me for the day. I always feel guilty leaving before the other librarians. I've never seen any of them end their workday at seven bells like I do. In fact, I'm not convinced they ever leave the library. It wouldn't surprise me if I were to someday discover a series of bookshelves-turned-bunkbeds in one of the tucked-away stacks, and Andreas curled up asleep under a pile of research.

Chuckling at this thought, I open the door to my room. Guilty or not, I'm grateful to return to my own quiet place after a long day, knowing there will be a fire, a meal, and possibly a hot bath waiting for—

"Mar! Mar mar mar!"

I just have time to suck in a breath before an avalanche of small, rock-hard bodies knocks me off my feet. With an *"Oof!"* and a *thunk,* I hit the floor, protecting my face with my hands as little troll children surround me, poking and plucking and shouting at the tops of their voices. I draw air into my lungs and bark, "All right now, settle down!"

The effect is immediate. The children flop to the ground and gaze up at me with huge, adoring eyes. I sit up, my hair tumbled out of its bun and flopping down one side of my face. Turning slowly, I take them in, one after the other—Dig, Har, Calx, and little Sis. The three boys, like living boulders carved by an inexpert hand, and their sister, a being of such delicate and ethereal beauty, poets would die just for a glimpse of her. They all beam up at me, flashing small gem teeth.

I cannot help grinning back.

I reach out and grab the boy in front of me in a big hug. The others cry out in protest and wrap themselves around me, determined to have their share of affection. I try to hold them all, dropping kisses on hard little heads and wiping tears from Sis's soft, pale cheeks. "What are you doing here?" I gasp. "How did you get in? Weren't there wards set around my room?"

"No wards!" Dig declares with rumbling delight. "Dig come check and no wards! He go find *ortolarok*. We come for *mar!*"

"Mar! Mar mar!" They start up again, chorusing so loud that it echoes down the stone passage. I'm half convinced Captain Khas or members of her guard will come storming down on us, ready to drag the children away. But no one comes, not even Lir with her disapproving face.

The wards are lifted? I shake my head, uncertain what to make of this. The Prince has been very clear that I am *not* to have the troll children in my room. Is there a chance he lifted the wards on purpose? Surely not. Perhaps the magic simply faded in his absence from the city. Which means he'll send the children away again as soon as he returns.

I wrap my arms around the little ones, making myself as big as possible to hold as many of them at once as I can. They nestle close, smearing my dress with dirt, filling my nostrils with stink carried up from the City Below. I don't care. I close my eyes and lean my cheek against the top of Calx's head resting on my shoulder. This time, I won't give them up. Before the Prince comes back, I'll figure out a way to keep these children with me. I swear it.

21

L IR DOESN'T DISCOVER US UNTIL MORNING.

I make certain I'm up before my maid arrives. Slipping out of my suddenly rather crowded bed, I wrap myself in a dressing gown and sit at my little table by the window to wait for the door to open and Lir to appear.

I've been thinking all night, scarcely slept at all. Going over everything I've learned about trolls and their practices where orphans are concerned. I don't want the children to suffer the way Lir has suffered. But I also cannot bear to send them back to the mines. There has to be some way to appease the *Hrorark* trolls and still keep the children with me. After hours of tossing and turning the problem around in my mind, I think I have an idea. But I need to talk to Lir.

She arrives not long after I get up, carrying a large breakfast tray in one hand. The moment she steps through the door, she stops. Her eyes widen, her nostrils quiver. Her gaze shoots first to the four snoring lumps in my bed before swiveling to fasten on me. She speaks not a word, but I feel the disapproval rolling off her in waves.

"Please, Lir," I say, keeping my voice down so as not to disturb the children, "hear me out."

She shuts the door and carries the tray to the table. There she sets it down with a clang that expresses more than words, then steps back, folds her arms, and glares at me.

"I know what you're going to say," I continue patiently. "I know you're worried about how these little ones will be treated if I keep them."

"They will fall out of *Vagungad.* They will be outcasts. Forever."

"If another *troll* took them in, of course," I acknowledge. "That would not be trusting the God of the Deeper Dark. But what if a *not troll* were to intervene?"

Lir's eyes narrow. She looks faintly confused but interested.

"Your family was *not troll,*" I point out. "And the *Hrorark* trolls did not rise up and storm the palace when they adopted you."

"No," Lir admits. "But I am still outside of *Vagungad.*"

"Are you though?" I persist. "Have you spoken to someone who might confirm this?"

"You mean like . . . like the *grankan-umog?* The Priestesses of the Deeper Dark?"

"Yes. The priestesses."

"No," Lir admits. "I've never been to see them. Because I'm outside of *Vagungad*. Those outside of *Vagungad* are not allowed to approach the *grankan-umog*."

"But how do you know you're outside the holy cycle if the priestesses have not confirmed it?"

Lir opens her mouth. Closes it again. Her brow puckers.

"I am not trollfolk," I continue slowly, treading carefully in this uncertain territory, "so I cannot be in or out of the holy cycle. Is that not true?"

Lir swivels her head in something not quite a nod but not quite a shake.

"And as I cannot be either in or out of the cycle, I cannot offend the God of the Deeper Dark?"

"Maybe?"

"In that case, what if I were to approach the Priestesses of the Deeper Dark? Having not offended their god, I may approach them, mayn't I?"

Lir nods, somewhat reluctantly. "It is possible."

"And if I were to approach them, I could request their permission to care for the children. If they give me permission, this must be a sign to the *Hrorark* that the God of the Deeper Dark has chosen to provide for his orphans via new means. Who are they to argue with a god's decision?"

I can't quite read Lir's face. She's usually so expressive, it's easy to see exactly what she's feeling. But her expressiveness plays against her now, so varied are the emotions passing over her lovely features—confusion, clarity, intrigue, frustration, hurt, hope, and a host of others, all jumbled together. Finally, she says, "I don't think the priestesses will give permission."

I acknowledge this with a nod. "But I might as well ask, right?"

Lir considers. I wonder if she's also considering the implications for herself: whether or not this workaround might apply retroactively to her own situation. "The *Vagungad* is in the deeps of the turn now," she says after a thoughtful silence.

"Yes?" I wait a moment. Then, "What does that mean?"

"It means the priestesses have gone into deep seclusion and will be in *jor*. That is, they will be close to the stone."

"Do you mean *inanimate,* perhaps?" I guess.

She nods, though I'm not sure she knows the word. "They will not receive anyone when they are in *jor*. But . . ." Her voice trails off for a few moments, and I can see that she's considering her next words very carefully. Finally, she says, "When the cycle turns, I will take you to the House of *Grakanak*. But I cannot promise they will see you, Mistress. And you will have to enter the house alone. I dare not risk it."

Her ominous words send a chill to my bones. I nod solemnly. "Very good. You must let me know. And meanwhile . . ." I look over at the little ones piled in my bed. "Meanwhile, they're to stay here with me. Do you understand?"

Lir chews her lower lip. "The Prince won't like it."

"The Prince isn't here."

For a moment, I fear she's going to argue. But in the end, Lir simply sighs and heads for the door. "Where are you going?" I call after her.

"To fetch four more breakfasts," she responds, and slips from the room.

I sit back in my chair and smile. That, at least, was a victory. A small victory, but a real one. I'll savor it while I can.

Life falls into something of a pattern.

I rise early each morning to enjoy a few quiet moments to myself before the children wake and before I need to prepare for work. I've spoken to Lir about the possibility of finding rooms for the children close to mine, but Lir says she cannot make household arrangements without the Prince's approval. So for the time being they stay in my room with occasional short excursions, during which we take extra care to avoid Captain Khas.

Every morning, I subject all four children to baths. So far, no one has drowned, though from the howling put up by Dig, Har, and Calx, one would think I was trying to commit bloody murder. Sis, by contrast to her brothers, seems to enjoy the experience and will afterwards preen in front of my vanity mirror for hours, running a comb through her silky white hair and singing to herself in a rumbling low troll voice. She will *not* submit to clothing. Yet. I figure there's plenty of time and decide to pick my battles.

From six bells in the morning until seven bells at night, I

work in the library as usual. The Prince has yet to return from his excursion to Solira, so my more intense training has ground to a halt. I continue to develop what skills I can under Nelle and Mixael's tutelage, and Andreas coaches me in the Noswraiths names until I can rattle off a list of some two hundred, complete with corresponding titles and proper spellings.

There is no further word from Aurelis. I wonder if Ivor has forgotten about me. I rather hope he has.

Several times I find myself wondering if the Prince will return from Solira married to Ilusine. Perhaps that's why he's been gone so long; weddings take a little planning, after all. But every time the thought pops into my brain, I push it out again. It's not my business. And I don't care, anyway.

The days pass, one after another. Then it's been a week. Then two weeks. Then more. I begin to wonder why I ever thought the Prince's presence in Vespre necessary at all. We seem to manage well enough on our own. The Noswraiths are uncharacteristically quiet. Even Nelle comments on the peace, though she follows it up with an ominous: "It can only mean they're brewing up for something bad. Best hope the Prince returns soon."

But I don't hope that. I want him to stay gone until after the *Vagungad* turns, so I can pay my visit to the House of the Deeper Dark. I'm sure I'll have an easier time convincing him to let me keep the children if I've already received permission from the priestesses.

My head is full of such thoughts one evening while returning to my room after a long day in the library. I need to summon Lir and ask her when the cycle will turn, when I can expect to make this visit. I'm not sure how I'll fit it in on top of my regular duties. I might even have to use my one free day . . . not an idea I relish. Can I truly justify neglecting Oscar, even for the children's sake? I shake my head, turn the latch, and open the door to my room.

I stop short.

For a moment I stare at what's in front of me, blinking dully.

Then I gasp, *"What?"* Frowning, I shake my head and look again. "What is *this?*"

My room is filled with thread. Thread festooning everything, strung in wild, tangled snarls, knotted to the bedposts, the wardrobe, the vanity and chair, the table, the curtain rod, even the stalactites overhead. It looks like some fat spider came along and exploded in my room. I can scarcely see anything through the mess of it.

"Dig?" I call, pushing a hand through the first few threads. They aren't sticky; that's a mercy at least. "Har? Calx? Sis?"

A little giggle sounds from somewhere near the floor. I turn sharply but can't see anything but more snarls of thread in myriad colors.

I push a little further into the room, pulling threads as I go. They snap with sharp *twangs*. Fibers wrap around my feet, cling to my skirt. Here and there I come across random objects suspended in the snarls, wrapped up like insect carcasses. Some of them are rocks of various shapes and sizes, taken from who knows where.

But I also find my brush, comb, mirror, several shoes. Even a corset rolled up tight.

Another giggle draws my eye. I whirl just in time to see two stony little feet disappearing under my bed. "Calx!" I cry. "Get out here and explain yourself. All of you! I mean it!"

Silence. Then, reluctantly, four small faces peer out from under the bed and blink up at me. I can barely see them through the mess of threads.

With a growl, I pull down several big swaths and push my way deeper into the room. Calx and Har duck back under the bed, but Dig and Sis remain in place, Dig wide-eyed, Sis smug. The truth is, it's difficult to stay mad at a sweet and pretty little face like hers.

Bundling threads under my arm, I march to the bed, crouch, and hold the bundle under their noses. *"What is this?"*

"Is *gubdagog*," Sis answers promptly.

I shake my head. "I don't know what that means. What is . . . is . . . goob dah gog?"

"Is for *grukk ungagh*." Sis tilts her head. "Yes?"

This is the problem with adopting children of an altogether different species. The language barrier alone is problematic; trying to fathom the intricacies of troll culture is a different matter altogether. I can't believe there was a time I thought trolls little better than crudely animated rocks.

Sighing, I sit cross-legged and look around at the chaos wreathing the room. My gaze fixes on a shoe suspended a few feet over my head. It all looks so chaotic and yet . . . am I mistaken in thinking there's a sort of *purpose* here? A purpose beyond bored children making messes?

Well, whatever it is, I can't very well leave it all up. Clambering to my feet, I set to work tearing the threads down. "Come on, you four," I tell the children. "Help me, or you're all going to bed without supper."

This threat works wonders. Soon three busy little bodies are leaping and climbing all over the room, pulling down snarls from even the highest reaches. Sis alone refuses to help. She crawls out from under the bed, sits on my vanity, arms folded, her face fixed in a sulky scowl. "Is my," she insists, smacking her brothers whenever they pass by carrying great armloads of broken thread. "Is my. My!"

"Mine," I correct. "And it's *messy.* Don't you know it's rude to make messes in other people's rooms? And to take other people's things to make your messes with?" I add, pulling down my wrapped-up corset.

I'm still trying to unwind the last thread from around the corset when Lir steps through the door, a big dinner platter in her hands. She takes one look around the room and her eyes bulge. "What is this?" she gasps, then turns on the children and cries, *"Horknuth viguka gubdagog?"*

"Korkor! Korkor!" Sis leaps from the vanity and spins in a circle, clapping her hands. "Is my *gubdagog!"*

"Do you understand what's going on here, Lir?" I ask, ripping at a particularly stubborn knot caught in the trimming of my corset.

"Oh, Mistress!" Lir sighs dramatically even as she deftly fends off troll boys, who are making wild leaps for the dinner platter and growling like so many hungry puppies. "It looks as though the children have tried, very badly, to make a *gubdagog*."

"Yes, so I'm told." I tug at the thread again and hear a discouraging rip. "But what exactly is a *goobda*-whatsit, pray?"

Lir frowns. "In your language you might say a . . . *tangle?*"

A short laugh bursts from my lips. "Well, that's certainly apt! But do you have any idea why they would tangle up my room like this?"

"Children do sometimes." Lir puts the dinner platter down, then growls a few words at the boys. Something in that growl works wonders, for they all three sit promptly on the floor. They watch her, eyes big, all but panting as their little noses snuffle the air. Sis joins them, looking strangely graceful and petite next to her brick-like brothers. Lir begins to serve up food, saying as she does so, "Most children attempt a *gubdagog* at some time or another. I know I did back before . . . well, back before. Never quite this big," she adds, glancing up at the threads still wafting between stalactites and caught in the lanterns overhead.

"But what *is* it?" I persist. "Is there a point to it exactly?"

"That I couldn't say." Lir thinks about it, then shrugs. "It's a *gubdagog*. That's all I know. It's something troll children do."

She goes on serving food, and the children fall to eating with noisy enjoyment. I continue taking down threads, unwinding my various articles of clothing and collecting bits of broken rock. The children must have ventured far beyond my room to gather these rocks, and I can only hope they weren't spotted going to and fro. I rather suspect Captain Khas already knows they're hiding out in my room and is simply choosing to turn a blind eye.

"How long until the holy cycle turns again, Lir?" I ask, suddenly uneasy. "I want to speak to the priestesses as soon as possible."

"Oh, not until after the *Hugag*," Lir replies.

I shake my head, once again perplexed. "I don't know what that means."

"Ah, the *Hugag*. The night of the Great Flight. It's glorious!" Lir smiles. "It's the one night a year when the moon rises fully to the apex of the sky above Vespre, and the *hugagug* moths hatch from their cocoons and fly free. Everyone in Vespre celebrates the *Hugag*. There will be dancing and singing . . . troll dancing and troll singing, you understand, which might not look the same to you. The palace folk always join in the celebration. It's quite wonderful."

I nod and try to accept Lir's enthusiasm, but my own questions are still pressing. "Yes, but when is this special night?"

"In three days' time, Mistress." Lir opens her mouth to continue, but in that moment, Sis grabs her skirt, demanding more food. Lir responds in trollish, and Sis raises her voice, and I give up trying to get answers just now.

Three days. I unwrap another shoe from strand after strand of snarled thread, considering. Three days until I can hope to visit the priestesses. Even then, it will mean another journey into the City Below . . . not a prospect to relish. I look around at the children eating happily out of their various bowls, spilling and slopping and making a terrible sight of themselves. A fond smile plucks at my lips. It'll be worth it if I can just find a way to make them safe.

But what will I do if the priestesses won't agree to my proposition?

"I'll just have to think of something else," I whisper.

Then I reach up and yank another swath of threads, which fall on my head in a thick white jumble. *"Tangle,"* I mutter like a curse.

22

YOU LOOK TIRED, MOTHER."

Mixael's voice draws my attention away from my work. I'm crouched in front of a casement, sliding books into place on the lowest shelf while Mixael perches high on a ladder above me, working the upper shelves. He holds on, one elbow looped around a rung, torso twisted as he turns to the nearest spiral staircase.

Nelle pauses on the stair, gripping the rail with one thin hand. Her knuckles stand out stark and white. The blue wyvern, her ever-present companion, wraps around her shoulders, one wing flapping in her face. She pushes it irritably out of her way and offers her son a weary half smile. "I am tired," she responds, "and I don't mind admitting it."

"Was the binding worse than usual?"

Nelle harrumphs. "Maybe. Maybe it just feels that way because I'm getting old."

Mixael snickers, and with good reason. While Nelle is old—a good three hundred years and more—here in Eledria, breathing Eledrian air, she need not show or feel her age unless she chooses to. In Eledria, she could live very much like an ageless fae if she so willed. Mixael told me that Nelle let her age creep up on her since the death of her husband a year ago . . . but even so, I've never seen her *act* old, despite appearances.

"Was it the Tall Man you were binding today?" Mixael asks with mild interest. "Or the Eight-Crowned Queen? I know she's been rather restless of late."

"No," his mother replies. "It was the Eyeless Woman."

They both go quiet. There's a sudden tension in the air that wasn't there before. I flick my gaze from Mixael to Nelle and back again. Neither of them looks at me or even at each other. Mixael's taken a sudden interest in the state of his fingernails. "I thought the Eyeless Woman was bound for another good week or more," he says, breaking the awkward silence.

Nelle shakes her head. "The binding was breaking down faster than I like. I don't know for sure, but it looked to me as though someone had been messing with it."

"Messing with it?" The words blurt from my lips with surprise. I sit up on my knees. "Someone was *messing* with one of the Greater Noswraith spells?"

"Apparently," Nelle answers, again not quite looking at me.

"But who would do that?" An unpleasant idea occurs to me. "It . . . it couldn't have been Vervain, could it?"

Nelle rolls her eyes. "Not likely, considering she's locked up in the west tower." Then, abruptly, she fixes me with the full intensity of her stare. "It looked to me like someone who didn't quite know what they was doing had been reading the book. You wouldn't know anything about that, would you?"

Another painful silence. My heart beats a little faster than before. It's been a few weeks since I ventured to the thirteenth floor on my own and tried to read the grimoire in the thirteenth vault. But surely that couldn't have caused any damage! And it was so long ago. If there were going to be a problem, it would have occurred by now.

But Nelle's expression is set, her eyes a little too knowing for comfort. Is it possible that this . . . this *Eyeless Woman* . . . could it be *my* Noswraith?

I meet Nelle's gaze. Though I can feel the blood draining from my cheeks, I offer her a bland little smile. "I . . . no. No, I wouldn't know anything about that."

The old librarian's pale blue eyes search my face. I hold her gaze hard and hold my lie a little harder. The last thing I want is for any of them to know I'd been stupid enough to enter the vaults on my own. "Did you successfully rebind the Noswraith?" I ask, keeping my voice carefully level.

Nelle purses her lips, then offers a short nod. "That I did. No harm done in the end. Still, it bothers me no end to think of someone paging through the Great Grimoires. I'll have a word with Khas about security, make sure she's doing her part to keep us all safe."

With that, she continues up the spiral stair, moving heavily. She pauses after a few steps, however, and peers back around the curving banister. "Oh, one more thing! I heard tell the Prince will be returning for the Great Flight."

A flush heats my face. I quickly turn away, back to my bookshelf, even as Mixael says, "Is that so? About time, I should think!"

Nelle grunts. "He's bringing Princess Ilusine and a whole party of folk from Solira with him, or so I'm told. They've got a taste for novelty, it would seem, so our Prince invited them to Vespre for a little ogling of trolls and trollish ways." She snorts, obviously displeased with such nonsense. "There's to be a proper ball held. And we're all invited."

"What?" I blurt.

Neither of them notices, for Mixael lets out a cheerful whoop. "You mean to say, we're going to be hobnobbing with the Lords and Ladies of Solira? Now *that* I call good sport!" The junior librarian laughs and grabs his lapels, balancing precariously on his ladder. "I'll put on my best dinner jacket, polish up my dancing shoes, and claim a dance with a pretty fae lass or two before they realize I'm not one of them!" He looks down at me and winks. "Don't look so glum, Miss Darlington. It'll be a grand time for all. Tell me, Mother, do you know if *all* the household members will be invited to attend?"

Nelle merely grunts a noncommittal reply and continues up the stair out of sight, leaving us to our work. Mixael slides down the ladder and pushes it along the rails to the next casement over. "You'll enjoy the Great Flight, Miss Darlington," he says, grabbing another armload of books from the trolley. "It's always a good time. We librarians usually venture to the Upper Round in the city to observe the troll dance. This time will be different with the Lords and Ladies in attendance, but I can't wait to see some of those dainty Solira fae trying to dance with the trolls! It'll be a sight, that's for sure."

He goes on for some while, rarely stopping for me to reply. That's one of the best things about Mixael—his ability to hold most of a conversation on his own, leaving me to my own tumultuous thoughts.

He's coming back.

He's coming back.

Why does it matter to me so much?

Well, of course, it's because of the children. I don't want the Prince's return to throw a wrench in my plans for them. I need to keep them out of his sight until after I've spoken to the priestesses. That's all.

I'm not wondering if he's returning to announce a betrothal.

Or if he's already married.

And he probably is—one or the other, betrothed or married. He's bringing Ilusine back with him, after all. He wouldn't do that if they hadn't fixed on some understanding, surely. Does this mean she's convinced him to fight for his throne? Or is she simply willing to give up her own ambition for love and become Princess of the Doomed City? I can't quite picture that.

The bells ring eight times. I rise and dust off my skirts. "I'm due up top for a lesson with Andreas," I call to Mixael.

He gives me a little wave and wishes me luck, and I make my way up the spiral stair.

At the top, I meet Nelle rolling a trolley from the book lift on the way to her desk. She gives me a stern look as she passes. "I'm surprised to see *you* here this morning," she says.

I frown. "I'm always here, aren't I?"

"Yes, but today is your off day. Didn't you remember?"

A stone drops in my stomach. *"Today?"* How could I have forgotten? How could an entire month have gone by since my arrival in Vespre, and I'd failed to notice? Oh gods, how much time have I lost? Has Oscar realized what day it is? Has he been watching for me, despairing of my coming?

Does he think I've given up on him, abandoned him?

"Well, go on girl, if you wants to go," Nelle says, waving a shooing hand. "You've still got a few hours, I should think. Go see your people!"

I gasp out a thank you and hasten from the library.

The shivering pain of traveling through worlds fades from my senses as the familiar contours of my own kitchen solidify around me. I blink several times, drawing steadying breaths.

On the third breath, I know something is wrong. The house is so still. A tense sort of stillness. A stillness full of pain.

"Oscar?" I call quietly and glance out the murky window. Judging by the light, it's already late afternoon. If Oscar did realize what day it was, if he knew it was my off day and I was supposed to visit him, he would have long since given up looking for me.

I hasten to the bottom of the stair and call up, "Oscar, are you there?" Not waiting for an answer, I start to climb. Oscar's face as I'd last seen it swims vividly before my mind's eye—pale, lined with shock, his eyes dazed with green *rothiliom* light. What became of him in the last few weeks? Did Danny and Kitty convince him to stay on at their house, to let them care for him? Or did he reject their offers as he has so many times before . . . only to run headlong into the next bout of self-inflicted pain and torment?

Is he even alive?

Dreading what I'll find, I creep to the door of his room. It's cracked open. I peer inside, my gaze first going to the bed. Empty. The window is open, letting in the cold and damp. I pull it shut before turning and looking around more carefully. There are signs of recent habitation: a spilled glass of whiskey, a half-empty bottle. A dusting of white powder spilled from a small packet. And there, on the desk . . . a vial of *rothiliom* standing atop a pile of loose pages.

I snatch up the vial, holding it tight in my palm. He might hate me later, when he discovers I've gone through his things. I don't care. I've been on the receiving end of Oscar's hatred before. I can take it. I'd rather be hated than wracked with guilt over his death.

I pocket the vial and turn toward the door. Then pause. Frowning, I look at the desk again. Ordinarily, I would expect to find sheafs of paper covered in Oscar's half-crazed scrawl. He's always fitfully working away at some story or another, determined to make his great breakthrough.

This time, however, I see clippings. Lots of clippings from various magazines—*The Wimborne Observer, Penny Illustrated, The Morning Chronicle, Bard Times* and more. The first one I recognize as the Filverel and Luris review which had so devastated my brother all those weeks ago. But the others?

I rifle through them, one after another. My heart sinks. It would seem that write-up from Filverel and Luris was the only positive review Oscar's story garnered. There are plenty more, however, and the words and phrases seem to jump off the cheap printing paper and stab my eyes:

A poor attempt to mimic a greater talent.

Derivative.

An interesting voice, but pales under mediocre ideas.

Poor execution.

But that isn't the worst of it. The worst is the name I see appearing again and again in every one of those reviews.

Edgar Darlington

Edgar Darlington

Edgar Darlington

Over and over, without fail. My brother's name, thrown into contrast with our father's. The apprentice's talent, always compared to the master's.

I sink onto Oscar's bed, my hands shaking as I hold those clippings. Tears blur my eyes. I tilt my head back, staring at the ceiling, trying to force down the lump in my throat. If Oscar comes back, I don't want him to find me like this.

Suddenly I blink, sniff. My brow tightens.

I know where my brother is.

Crumpling those reviews into a ball, I leap up, stride to the window, haul it open, and throw the lot of them out. Let them rot in the gutter where they belong!

I close the window and latch it fast, then hasten downstairs. Across the living room, through the kitchen. To the narrow door in the back of the house. The door with the broken latch and several kicked-in panels.

Slowly, I push it open.

A familiar stench of mold and rot and cold stings my nostrils, bringing with it a rush of memories. Memories of sitting on those steps, poised between the darkness below and the light on the other side of the door. Memories of my arms wrapped around my trembling brother. Memories of waiting, hoping, praying that Mama would come and let us out. Soon, soon, soon . . .

I stand there a full minute, eyes closed, waiting for the dizziness to pass. Then, very softly, I call, "Oscar?"

An abrupt shuffling sounds below. Too big to be a rat.

I bite my lip and push the door open wider to allow as much light into the cellar as possible. One step after another, I make my way down. The treads creak ominously under my feet. "Oscar, I know you're there. Won't you come out, darling? Please?"

"Go away, Clara."

I stop.

I've been straining my ears for a little boy's voice. For some reason, I'd not expected to hear a man's. Low, rough. Broken.

A shudder races down my spine. "It's just Oscar," I whisper. "It's just Oscar."

It isn't . . . it isn't Dad.

He's dead. Gone.

He can't be down there in the dark. Not anymore.

Drawing a steadying breath, I feel my way down the steps. When I reach the bottom, I have to stop and wait for my eyes to adjust to the gloom. Finally, I see the hunched form pressed against the far brick wall. He's got his legs drawn up to his chest, his face buried in his knees. But he's upright. He's alive.

"Oscar," I breathe. Moving cautiously, I cross the little space, my head low to keep from hitting the ceiling. "Oscar, what are you doing down here?"

"What do you think I'm doing?" My brother's voice is a low snarl. "I'm where I belong. I know that now. I should have known long ago. I'm where I belong. In the dark. In the dirt."

I swallow with difficulty. Crouching before him, I reach out to touch his hand. He feels so cold. "Please, dearest. Please, come out. Let me fix you something to eat, yes? You must be hungry."

Slowly he raises his heavy head. The light shining from the stairway gleams in his eyes, revealing the dull swirl of green in his irises. "I thought you weren't coming back."

I hold my breath, refuse to let out a rising sob. How could I have done this to him? How could I have let myself become so caught up in the doings of Vespre, in my own foolish concerns, that I lost track of the days? How could I spend so much time thinking about little troll children, who aren't even really mine, when my real responsibility was here? Suffering. Alone.

"I always come back, Oscar." I squeeze his hand. "You know I do."

He gazes at me long and hard, his eyes moving strangely in their sockets. "I'll never be free of him, Clara," he whispers. "He's always here. In my head. Everyone knows it. Everyone. I can't escape his shadow." He moans and buries his face in his knees again. "Can no one save me?"

Bitter bile rises in my throat. "I'll save you, Oscar. I will!"

But he shakes his head. "You can't. You're as trapped in the dark as I am."

"We'll save each other then."

"How?" He sounds pathetic. The deepness in his voice melts away, and I can picture my baby brother again. So sweet. So innocent. So wounded.

I move to sit next to him, lean my back against the cold wall. Wrapping my arm around him, I rest his head against my shoulder and press my cheek to his messy curls. I have no words. There are no words, not for him, not for the pain he's in. I can offer no real comfort, only understanding, which is never enough.

I begin to rock him slowly, speaking in a sing-song voice, "Once upon a time, there was a sister and her little brother, and he was very brave. As long as they could be together, they were both very brave, no matter what happened. One day, their mother said to them, '*You must venture into the Dark Forest, my children. For your father is sick, and it is up to you to find his cure. But you must be brave, strong, and always loyal to one another, or you cannot hope to survive the journey.*'"

Oscar lets out a gut-wrenching sob. He turns and wraps his arms around my neck, shaking and weeping. My voice breaks, and I simply hold him in the dark for a long, long time.

23

"CLARA?"

I start at the sound of the voice coming down the stair. Shifting in place, I groan. I'm still sitting in the coal cellar. Oscar's head is in my lap, and he snores softly. I must have dozed off as well.

"Clara? Oscar?"

It's Danny. I wince. I'm not sure why, but part of me had almost hoped I would get through this visit without seeing him. My life has been busy enough, but not so busy that I've forgotten that kiss we shared . . . oh! It feels like an age ago! Neither have I forgotten the passion in his voice when he spoke of trying to free me from my Obligation.

Still, I can't refuse help in this moment.

"We're down here!" I call out tremulously. I'm half afraid I'll wake Oscar, but he's sunk deep into drug-induced sleep following the high of the *rothiliom*.

A sound of footsteps on floorboards overhead. Then a silhouette appears on the wall near the base of the cellar stair. "Clara? Is that you?"

"Yes. I've got Oscar with me. He needs help."

The next moment, Danny descends, peering into the darkness. His gaze finds me against the far wall, and his brow puckers. Ducking his head, he approaches and crouches in front of me and Oscar. He places two fingers against Oscar's throat, just under his ear. Grunting, satisfied, he looks up at me. "What are you doing down here?" His voice is low and full of worry.

I bite my lips. I don't like to speak the words out loud. "Oscar . . . he got some bad reviews."

Danny waits. Apparently, this isn't explanation enough. I swallow and continue. "Dad used to lock him down here. As . . . as *punishment*. For anything. For nothing." I sniff and look down at my brother, gently stroking his curls. "Oscar got the worst of things, you know. As the son."

Danny is silent for a long, long while. Then, very gently, he says, "I don't know if I believe that."

I choke on the sudden thickness in my throat. "I used to sneak in here with him. When Dad wasn't looking. I hated that he would be down here in the dark by himself. So I'd sneak in and leave the door open a crack so a little light would shine through. We'd sit on the stair and wait. Mama always let us out eventually, when Dad

328

finally . . . when he . . ."

Something stirs in the darkness. In the deepest shadows of the cellar. I start, turn, stare into that darkness. My eyes are better adapted to the gloom by now, and I can see that there's nothing there. Just an empty coal skuttle.

But very faintly, in farthest recesses of my brain, I hear a breath of a whisper: *He really loves you . . . he really . . .*

Danny's voice cuts through, bringing me back to myself. "You've always tried to protect him. I know you have, Clara."

"Someone spittin' has to," I answer. Then I blink, shocked at my own language. I shake my head and glance up at Danny. "I'm sorry."

His face is very still. He probably didn't think me capable of speaking so viciously. But he simply shakes his head and touches my hand. "Don't be sorry. Your love for your brother does you credit. Come! It's cold down here. Let's get him up to bed."

Between the two of us, we manage to get Oscar off the ground, hauling him out of the cellar and up the narrow stair to his room. It's still bitterly cold, so I go through the house, hunting up whatever blankets I can find, along with Oscar's coat and a few spare shirts. I pile everything onto my brother. Danny, meanwhile, fetches his medical bag and mixes a tincture. He holds Oscar's head up and manages to get him to swallow a few mouthfuls. Afterwards, he checks his pupils and looks in his mouth.

"How long has he been like this?" he asks me.

I shake my head. "I'm not sure. He's on this again." I pull the vial of *rothiliom* from my pocket.

Danny's face is grim. "After you left us last time, Oscar stayed with us for three days, unconscious. During that time, I broke into this house and cleared out everything, his entire stash. When Oscar woke, he was angry. He swore at Kitty, threw a vase at the housemaid, took a swing at me, and stormed out."

I can't look at him. I stare down at my brother. "I . . . I wish I could apologize for him," I say softly.

"It's not his fault," Danny answers quickly. "It's the influence of the drug. I've seen it before. The substances may be different, but the aftereffects are the same." He sighs and takes a seat at the desk. "I've looked in on Oscar a few times since then. He either called me a thief and demanded to know where I'd taken his things or refused to see me at all. I haven't given up, of course. I keep coming. But I'd hoped Oscar wouldn't be able to get hold of more of *that*." He indicates the vial in my hand.

I nod, perching at the foot of Oscar's bed. Someone must have brought him the *rothiliom*. The new lover Oscar told me about? Or someone else? Someone determined to ruin my brother . . . though for what purpose, I can't begin to imagine.

Wiping two stray tears, I meet Danny's gaze and try to smile. "Thank you. For watching over him. For doing what you can."

He looks at me solemnly. "You know, Clara, you cannot protect him from himself. That's not a battle you can hope to win."

"I know," I answer softly. "Maybe if I was here . . ." I take Oscar's hand, study his face. He looks almost peaceful now, bundled up under all those blankets. Danny's tincture seems to have brought a bit of color back to his cheeks.

Suddenly, Danny's hand comes to rest on top of mine. "You could be here, Clara."

I close my eyes, shake my head. Then, with a sniff and a quick straightening of my shoulders, I turn to him. "How did you come to be here anyway? Were you checking on Oscar again?"

"I knew this was your day to visit," he answers softly. "When the morning went by and you still hadn't come to see us, Kitty and I began to worry. We always worry, Clara. We worry that one of these months, you simply won't return. And we'll never know what happened to you."

I hold his gaze. "I'll always come back," I say more firmly than I feel. "Always."

The expression on his face is enough to wring my heart. "That doesn't make me worry any less." He reaches for me then, cupping my cheek in his hand.

I spring from the bed, step around him, and go to the window. Standing there, I can still see one of the crumpled-up reviews I'd flung out onto the roof. Perhaps I should fetch it, take it down to the kitchen. Burn it. My hand moves for the window latch, but just then a cold wind blows, sending the little paper ball flying out across the city.

The floorboards creak under Danny's feet. I feel him behind me, warm and solid. I tense, but he doesn't touch me.

"I can't help feeling as though there's something you're not telling me," he says after a long silence.

I bow my head. "There are many things. So many things I'm not telling you."

"You know you can tell me anything, don't you?"

I know he *wants* me to tell him anything. Everything. And part of me longs to unburden myself, especially to so willing and sympathetic a listener. But I can't. If he knew even half of it . . .

No. He simply can't know. Ever.

It's in that moment that I realize the truth I've been avoiding for too long. It doesn't matter what happens to me. Even if I survive my Obligation, even if I return home in ten years' time, it won't make a difference. I'll never be able to marry Danny Gale. There are too many secrets between us.

The sun is getting low. I turn to look at Oscar in his bed. How I hate to leave him! This will be the second time in as many visits that I've gone away while he slept without saying goodbye. "Can you stay with him?" I ask Danny tearfully. "I just . . . I don't want him to wake up alone."

"Of course," he agrees. We both know the vitriolic rage that Oscar will hurl at him upon waking. But he doesn't hesitate. "I will stay."

I nod once. Then, impulsively, I take Danny's hand, squeezing his fingers. "Thank you. For everything."

"Clara—"

Before he can say anything more, I flee the room, back down the stairs. I step into the front room just as the gate to Eledria shimmers into existence, a scar of light cutting through layers of reality. Forcing back tears, I duck through, leaving my own world behind me once more.

24

THE NEXT DAY PASSES IN A BLUR.

Throughout my regular work hours, I'm aware of a background energy stirring in the city below the palace. Every now and then I peek out the citadel windows and glimpse signs of activity in the streets. I'm so high up, I can't see much, but enough to know the trolls are more energetic than usual.

"It's the *Hugag*," Mixael says, joining me at the window during one such interval. "It's the biggest celebration you'll find in these parts. All of Vespre participates. Even the trollfolk from the City Below will come to the Upper Round. None of them want to miss the flight of the *hugagug* moths."

The excitement is infectious. Though my heart is still sore from the events of yesterday, I cannot deny my eagerness for what the night will bring. The rise of the moon, the flight of the moths. The troll celebration and dance.

The return of the Prince.

No, that last part doesn't make me excited. It fills me with a nervous suspense. But he should be busy with his guests tonight at least. With Ilusine. I can't imagine he will have time even to notice me or the children I'm hiding in my room. He'll have other things on his mind.

I'm down on the third floor when a sudden burst of sunlight streams through the crystal dome overhead. It's so stark, I let out a little scream. Then I rush to the rail, join Nelle there, and we both crane our necks and peer up, shading our eyes against the glare. Nelle's wyvern lets out an irritable bleat and flees to hide in the closest bookshelf, shoving itself between volumes.

"Ah!" Nelle says, dropping her face and blinking as though to readjust her half-blinded eyes. "That would be the Soliran folk arriving, I'd wager."

I glimpse a flash of wings and remember Ilusine's arrival of a few weeks ago, how she'd shone like a small sun. This is a much greater glow than that, enough to illuminate the whole library as bright as day as the beautiful beings pass by overhead. "Won't they interfere with the moths' flight?" I ask.

"I should hope not," Nelle answers with a snort. "They'll dim their brightness a bit once they've settled in. The Prince won't stand for them going about *radiating* like that."

It's nearly impossible to focus on work the rest of that day. I pretend I'm not watching the library door, half expecting the

Prince himself to come striding in. He's been away from Vespre for some weeks now. Shouldn't he check on his librarians, make certain everything is running smoothly in his absence?

Of course, I'm not actually *hoping* he'll come.

"Will all the librarians be attending the dance?" I ask Mixael at some point. "Doesn't someone need to watch the library?"

"Oh, we'll take it in turns," Mixael answers with a grin. "Don't you fret, Miss Darlington, you'll have ample opportunity to enjoy yourself at the revels! We always split up the night duties amongst ourselves, and the Noswraiths are generally quiet during *Hugag*. They don't care for the full moon."

Mixael goes about his business, but I slip back to the window again, gazing down at the streets below. From this angle, I can see the main road leading up to the palace front door. I let my gaze follow that road down into the city to what I believe is the Upper Round everyone keeps talking about. It's too far away for me to get more than an impression of movement and activity, but I believe the trolls are decorating it in readiness for tonight's event.

Nearer movement catches my eye. I turn my head slightly and see one of the open walkways that make up the lower regions of Vespre Palace. Figures move along that walkway—ten or fifteen total, a mixture of ladies and gentlemen, all gorgeously golden and shining with inner light. They don't wear their wings at the moment as they sweep along together toward some part of the palace I do not know.

"Are you going to finish stacking those books, girl, or do you plan to spend the rest of the day ogling fancy folk?"

I start at Nelle's voice and turn quickly from the window, blushing. The senior librarian gives me a look, then waves me on about my tasks. While I finish loading the stack from the book lift, she inspects them, turning each one over with care. I work in silence for a few minutes before venturing, "I wouldn't expect the Prince to entertain much here in Vespre."

"He doesn't as a rule," Nelle answers, tossing one book carelessly back onto the book lift, then selecting another from my stack. "In fact, in the three hundred-odd years I've been here, I don't remember him ever having such a large party out."

I turn my next question over in my head several times before asking, "Do you think it has something to do with . . . with the succession in Aurelis? Do you think the Prince is mustering support to make a bid for his throne?"

"I do *not* think anything of the kind." Nelle picks up another book, turning it round and round as though studying it, though I doubt she's seeing it at all. "I don't think anything of the kind because I choose not to think on things beyond my range and scope. There's enough bother to keep me busy as it is."

Despite these protests, I can tell she's concerned. She masks it well, but she's even more aware than I am how vital the Prince is to the safety of Vespre.

I grab another few books to add to my stack. The top two slip free and drop to the floor with loud *thunks*. I stoop to retrieve them, but Nelle stops me. "No, no, girl, I can't take more of your fidgetiness just now. You go on. Go make yourself pretty for the party. I'll see you later."

"But it's hours yet until the party," I protest. "Don't you need me to help with—"

"I need peace and quiet is what I need." Nelle rolls her eyes but softens her words with a half smile. "The librarians will meet back here at nine bells, then we'll venture to the Upper Round together. All save Andreas, that is; he's volunteered to take the first watch tonight. Someone'll have to pry him from his books at some point and force him to enjoy himself a little."

Chuckling at this apt observation of my fellow librarian, I make my getaway. As I hasten through the stone passages of the palace back to my room, I tell myself that I'm *not* watching for the Prince. No, for he's off somewhere entertaining his guests, enjoying Ilusine's lovely smiles, planning his future, and none of it matters to me in the least.

A brilliant laugh breaks through my thoughts and freezes me in place. That laugh is followed by another and another, a whole chorus. But that first laugh still stands out from the rest: Ilusine.

I dive into an alcove just as a dozen glorious golden figures step into the passage. Hidden behind a rather musty old tapestry, I watch them go by—tall and beautiful as one would expect, powerful Lords and Ladies of Eledria. With their golden skin and shining hair and glittering eyes, they look like angels come down from heaven to light up the perpetual gloom of Vespre.

The Prince is with them. He walks at the front of the throng, arm in arm with Ilusine. This is the first I've seen him in many weeks. He stands out among his golden guests. Compared to them, he looks almost plain, and yet my eyes can't seem to look away from him. He wears silver in contrast to their gold, and his hair is so black, his skin so dark. There's something strangely human about him this evening, some quality I couldn't name if I tried.

My heart gives a little hiccupping start at the sight of him. Though I can't think why.

I force my gaze from him and look at Ilusine instead as they draw near. She's even more beautiful than I remembered, clad in a shining gown with golden roses draped across her collarbone and shoulders and little drops of liquid gold strung together like beads down her well-shaped arms. The gown clings in such a way to emphasize the perfection of her figure, and she's so tall, so statuesque, she towers above all others in the party, even the Prince. How proud he must be to have a woman like her on his arm.

Of course, he will marry her. How could he not?

The party passes on by, laughing voices ringing against stone. When they've reached the end of the passage and turned into another, out of my sight, I slip from behind the tapestry. I'm glad I've seen them, glad I've seen the Prince. That first sight was always going to be the most jarring. It's over now. I know how I feel, and I know how to compose myself for whatever the night will bring.

Ducking my head, I hasten on to my room, the laughter of the golden folk still echoing in my ears.

"Arob korgulg!"

It never ceases to shock me how guttural and vicious Lir's voice becomes the moment she starts speaking her native language. She's such a pretty creature and so sweetly spoken most of the time that I forget that she is a troll through and through.

She startles me now when, in the midst of styling my hair, she breaks into a stream of trollish. At least her ire is directed not at me but at the children, who are hard at work creating their usual mayhem. Dig, Har, and Calx have put on one of my dresses—one dress for all three of them, stacked on each other's shoulders. Calx's ugly little face emerges from the top, grinning like a rock devil, while Har's stubby arms stick out awkwardly through the sleeves, and Dig's heavy, flat feet stomp around, tripping over the hem. They careen about the room with Sis chasing after them, laughing and screeching uproariously.

Lir catches my eye in the vanity mirror, her expression despairing. She's got me in her clutches and has been determinedly creating an elaborate hairstyle for the last hour. I can't quite see what it is, but it involves numerous fat braids tied up in fantastical configurations involving more pins than I can count. With her hands thus occupied, she can only bark at the children with ineffectual fury.

"Leave them be, Lir," I say with a laugh. "I don't much care for

341

that dress anyway. And they need *something* to do."

"They *need* to be out of my way," Lir snarls, and jabs a pin into my scalp with more force than necessary.

I wince but don't try to argue. She's right, after all: the children should not be kept cooped up in this room all the time. It's not good for them. I've got to figure out what constitutes proper upbringing for young trolls, not to mention arrange for their daily care while I'm at work. Shutting them in my room with stern warnings not to leave won't do, and it's not fair to expect Lir to keep an eye on them while I'm at the library.

"There," Lir says, sticking a last pin in place and stepping back. She nods, satisfied, and holds up a small hand mirror. "Tell me what you think, Mistress."

I accept the mirror and turn around in my seat, trying to get a good angle on Lir's creation. It is truly magnificent—three fat braids wound and feathered so as to look like three enormous rosettes on the back of my head. Little tendril curls hang softly about my ears and neck, and bright combs glint like stars amid the coils. The overall look is softly romantic. And there are enough pins in place to hold it steady through hurricane gales!

"It's incredible," I say with honest admiration. "Truly, Lir, it's too much! No one will even notice, I'm afraid."

"*Someone* will notice," Lir says definitely. Before I can even think to question her, she pushes through the madness of laughing children and pulls something from the wardrobe. It's a gown I've not seen before. A full skirt made from yards and yards of soft, sheer fabric that looks as though it's woven from spiderweb silk. The light from the lanterns catches it just so to reveal glimpses of iridescent hues.

Though I try to discourage Lir's penchant for dressing me above my station, I cannot help a gasp of delight. "Where did this come from?" I cross the room and run a fold of the skirt between my fingers. "I've never seen this one before!"

Lir smiles slyly. "All the dresses in your wardrobe come from the Prince, of course."

My face heats, but I quickly disguise it with a smile. "Oh? Well, one must certainly give him credit for taste then, mustn't one? Even if half the time he seems incapable of keeping his own shirts buttoned."

Lir looks puzzled. "Is that a problem, Mistress?"

I try not to laugh. Lir, though raised by humans, is trollish in her own choice of dress . . . which is to say, she chooses to wear very little and probably would wear nothing at all if left to her own devices. I've already begun to wonder if I'll *ever* be able to get Sis into clothing. With Lir as an example, I rather doubt it.

Regardless, Lir is eager to dress me, like I'm her personal fashion doll. I acquiesce without complaint, allowing her to help me into proper undergarments and outer skirts. The bodice is fitted with boning, so there's no need for a corset. The neckline is wide and elegantly draped, and the long sleeves end with delicate points over each hand.

Once Lir has finished doing up the dozens of tiny buttons on the back of the bodice, she hands me a half-mask trimmed in rosettes and gemstones. "What's this for?" I ask.

"The ball tonight. It's a masquerade."

"Why?" I snort. "It's not as though we won't all recognize one another. It's hard to mistake Mixael's hair or Nelle's hunch. And Andrea's spectacles will look rather odd over the eyeholes of mask, don't you think?"

Lir shrugs her pretty shoulders. "Masquerades bring out the mystery in those we think we know."

I shoot her a doubtful look, but gamely hold the mask up to my face and turn to the children. They've finished their wanton destruction of the gown and are now seated in a row at the foot of my bed, watching me with eager, blinking eyes. "What do you think?" I ask, making a little spin. My skirts swish magnificently, like a silvery cloud.

"Oglub!" the three boys declare with great enthusiasm, while Sis's voice pipes loudly over theirs, crying, *"Tasty!"*

I laugh and drop a kiss on each of their little heads.

"We go to Big Dance tonight?" Dig asks, standing up and swinging from one of the bedposts. The other three echo his question eagerly, bouncing and rolling about until the mattress squeaks and strains.

I shake my head sadly. "I'm afraid you'll be taken away from me if you're seen outside this room. No, until I've spoken to the priestesses, you really must stay hidden."

They look so crestfallen, I promise copious treats when I return.

This elicits a chorus of promises to be *so* good, none of which I trust for a minute. Still, even if they do sneak out, I hope that in all the bustle tonight, four small children won't be noticed.

I turn to Lir. "Will you be at the dance?"

"Oh, certainly! I will see you at the Upper Round, Mistress."

"Why don't you join me and the other librarians?" I suggest. She looks startled, but I persist. "Truly, Lir, I would be delighted to attend the event *with* you. Please?"

The smile that breaks across her face will warm my heart for days. "In that case, I will! You go along to the library now, and I'll meet you there soon. I've a few things to finish up here first."

I nod. In the distance, the bells ring the three-quarter chime. It'll be eight bells soon and time to meet the others. "Don't be long," I urge my maid, hastening to the door. I open it, stepping out into the hall, and call back to the children, "And you four, behave yourselves tonight! If I come back and find any more gowns torn to ribbons, there will be no cakes, do you hear me?"

"No cakes at all? Not even a little one?"

I nearly jump out of my skin. Moving on instinct, I yank the door shut, whirl, and fix my gaze on the figure lounging a mere two steps away.

It's the Prince. Leaning at a jaunty angle, one shoulder against the wall, one hand resting on his hip, one leg bent and crossed behind the other. He's wearing golden robes in the Soliran style, but his crown is dark stone. He smiles, one sardonic eyebrow upraised. "Well met, Clara Darling."

My mouth drops open, unable to form coherent words. But I can't stand here gaping like a codfish. "Prince!" I gasp. Then, rather after the fact, I drop a curtsy. "I . . . I . . . didn't see you there."

"Didn't see me through a solid stone wall? A likely story." His smirk grows fractionally. "Now someone more curious than I might ask whom you were enjoining to behave just now."

Suddenly, I wish I'd thought to don the mask Lir gave me. Anything to disguise the sudden heat rushing to my cheeks. Putting it on now would be odd, however, so instead I hastily blink and paint my blandest smile across my lips. "Oh, that? That's just . . . Lir and I have a little joke, you see."

"Indeed?" The Prince pushes off from the wall and folds his arms, an imposing stance belied by the twinkle in his eye. "You are a woman of many talents, Darling. Lying, I'm afraid, is not one of them."

I lick my lips. The last thing I want is to give away the presence of my little ones. "Can a lady not keep her secrets?" I say, pairing the words with the faintest, teasing pout.

His eyes flash. "I suppose that would depend on the secrets in question. If, however, this particular secret involves a passel of small but extremely noisy troll children, then no—a lady is unlikely to keep her secrets." Though I try, I can't hide the surprise in my face. He snorts. "Come, Darling, I could hear their screeching from the next wing over. Did you really think you were pulling one over on me?"

My throat goes very dry. I swallow hard, staring up at the

Prince. Any moment now he'll speak to my Obligation, force me to turn the children over to Captain Khas and be done with them. But I won't go down without a fight. I plant myself squarely in front of the door. "They're not harming anyone. And I have a plan. A plan to make things right with the Priestesses of the Deeper Dark, a plan to keep them all in the *Vagungad*. That should appease the *Hrorark*."

The sardonic expression on the Prince's face melts into real surprise. "You know about the *Vagungad*?" His lips quirk into a smile which, if I didn't know better, I might almost mistake for sincere. "You've been busy, haven't you? It's a rare human who takes the time to learn anything of troll ways."

I drop my chin and look down at the toes of my shoes peeking from under the hem of the spiderweb gown. "I have trolls I care about now. Naturally, I must take an interest." I force my gaze back up again and hold his. "I sincerely want to do right by these little ones. Not just as children, but as trolls."

The Prince nods slowly. "I doubt very much the priestesses of the Deeper Dark will agree to see you. But if you have a plan in the works, I'm willing for you to try. After all, I've already lowered the wards and let the children through. We're rather committed to the cause now, like it or not."

I blink. "You *let* the wards down?"

"Of course." He frowns. "Didn't you realize I must have? How else did the little urchins get in your room?"

"I just . . . I thought . . ." I bite my tongue. Not once had I considered that the Prince would take the wards down on purpose. Even now, I can't quite comprehend it. Why would he do such a thing? For what purpose?

For me?

Blood rushes in my ears. I dip my head again, hoping the Prince can't see how this news has affected me. "Thank you," I say quietly.

"Well," he answers, "let's hope your plan works out, and we don't soon have bloodthirsty *Hrorark* pounding on our doors."

I look up and catch his smile. I also catch the way his eyes travel up and down, taking in my gown. His gaze comes back to rest on my face, locking with mine. "You look well tonight."

I flush. "So do you." Gods, did I really just say that? Am I really standing here exchanging compliments with the Prince of Vespre? This man who is my master, my Obliege Lord, who brought me to this dark city against my will? This man who thrust me into the middle of a war for which I am wholly unprepared? Everything about this moment feels so strange, so uncomfortable.

Yet I cannot make myself look away from him.

He takes a step nearer. "Darling," he says, his voice suddenly softer than before. There's something in his gaze I don't understand, something I'm not sure I want to understand. "Darling, I have not stopped—"

"Castien! There you are."

I start back, pressing my shoulder blades against the closed door as a flare of light fills the dark corridor. I shade my eyes against the glare, blinking as the figure at the end of the passage slowly comes into view: Ilusine, magnificent in the same gown I glimpsed her in earlier. Now she wears a half-mask, radiant beams of golden sunlight dripping with gemstones which frame her incredible eyes. It's not a disguise so much as an augmentation of her splendor.

"I've been hunting high and low for you," she says, gliding gracefully toward us, a semi-transparent impression of wings floating in the air behind her. "I was just beginning to think I'd have to venture into your beastly library!"

"No indeed, fair Ilusine." The Prince pulls a more modest mask from his inner jacket pocket and slips it over his own face. It emphasizes the cut of his cheekbones and casts his eyes into deep, mysterious shadows. "I'm off duty tonight, ready to play the doting swain."

Ilusine gives him an arch look. "You? *Doting?* I shudder to think."

With that, she tucks her arm into his and sets off, leading him after her. All without once looking my way. It's as though I don't exist, as though I simply *cannot* exist in conjunction with a being so great and glorious as she. I stand where I am, pressed against the door, watching the two of them go. Seeing anew how beautiful they are, how well matched in every particular.

I'm not waiting for the Prince to look back at me.

He doesn't.

They vanish around a bend. I let out a huge breath and sag where I stand. The next moment, I stumble slightly as the door behind me opens. I catch my balance and look around, meeting Lir's questioning gaze through the crack.

"Is he gone?"

I nod.

"Zugath torg!" Lir sighs dramatically.

"Yes," I answer, glancing again down the empty passage, which still seems to glow with the afterlight of Ilusine's coming and going. "I couldn't put it better myself."

25

LIR AND I GO TOGETHER TO MEET THE OTHERS AT THE
library. In honor of the evening, Lir has donned a traditional
troll belt made up of small animal skulls interspersed with
little crystal flowers. More of those same crystal flowers adorn her
head in a circlet, but her mask is bone and rather chilling. It's all
very rough and ready, very trollish, and somehow only makes Lir's
natural beauty that much more striking.

We enter the library arm in arm, not at all like lady and maid.
Truth be told, I prefer things this way. I haven't had a personal
maid since my family moved to Clamor Street when I was still a
child. Though I value Lir's assistance, I prefer to think of her as
my peer rather than my servant. She has proven resistant to the
idea, persisting in calling me "Mistress" and maintaining a certain
deferential manner. But tonight, she grins and squeezes my arm,

making me hope some of the barriers between us are crumbling.

Mixael and Nelle wait for us on the upper floor, also dressed for the occasion. I almost don't recognize Nelle at first. She looks *young*. Not youthful, but certainly not the wrinkled crone she's been since before I met her. I would guess her age at around fifty, with a head full of magnificent hair and an extremely pretty, delicate face. Freckles dust her nose, but beneath those freckles, her skin is creamy and smooth with only the most delicate tracings of lines around her eyes.

"What are you staring at?" she demands, catching me gaping.

Mixael makes dramatic gestures behind his mother's back. I hastily hide my surprise with a smile and say only, "Your dress. It's lovely. That color just suits you."

"This old thing?" Nelle looks down at her forest-green frock. Its puffed sleeves are slashed to reveal the white undergown beneath, and the belted waist sits low on her hips, emphasizing her lithe feminine figure. The fashion is several centuries out of date yet so perfectly tailored that it looks brand new. "Never thought it suited me much, but . . ." Her expression softens just a little. "Soran always liked it."

Before any of us can react to this moment of softness, she turns away and barks, "Worm! If you're coming, come now, else I'm leaving and eating all the *mog* cakes without you!"

With a squawk and a hiss, the wyvern emerges from under Nelle's desk. It waddles to her on its hind legs, its wing-arms upraised awkwardly, its fat belly wobbling in front. It flares its crest up and down in irritation, burbling to itself until it reaches Nelle's feet. She crouches, extends one arm, and it quickly climbs up and drapes itself around her shoulder. "All set?" Nelle asks, turning to us once more.

Mixael offers his arm. "That we are, Mother dearest, that we are." He's looking particularly handsome tonight in a deep blue jacket with gold trimming and a blue half-mask to match. Now that Nelle wears her young face, it's easier to see where Mixael gets his good looks. That being said, his jawline is much squarer than hers, his brow wider. Perhaps those features came from his father.

"Where is Andreas?" I ask suddenly, noticing the absence in our ranks.

"Oh, he's around here somewhere," Nelle replies. "Probably got his nose stuck in a stack of research books. Not to worry. We'll make certain Andreas joins the festivities for a little while at least. He won't like it, but it's good for him to remember he's more than a brain with legs now and then. Now, are we ready?"

The four of us make our way down from the citadel and through the halls of Vespre Palace. The night is nowhere near as dark and gloomy as usual. Moonlight, brilliant and clear, falls through the windows and sends shadows racing for cover. I delight in that glow, and my heart begins to lift with anticipation for whatever festivities lie ahead.

"What is that?" I ask Lir as we reach the lower floors of the palace.

"What is what?"

"That sound."

It's a low, hollow moaning underscored by deep, rhythmic booms. It rolls round and round on itself, just verging on chaotic but never quite crossing that line.

"Oh!" Lir nods. "That is *bugdurash*—troll music."

Music? I wouldn't have called what I'm hearing *music* exactly. There's no discernable melody, at least not to my ear. It's almost like listening to another language entirely. But it's undeniably beautiful, eerie, and haunting in a way that sinks deep into the bones.

As we near the great entrance hall at the front of the palace, the *bugdurash* song fades, drowned out by brilliant laughter and an ongoing murmur of bright voices engaged in bright conversation. Lir, the librarians, and I reach the end of the passage and gaze into the hall. It's alive in a way I've never seen before, full of yellow light that feels so foreign in this world. The enormous globe lantern hanging from the center of the high ceiling burns with moonfire, but it pales by comparison to the glow radiating from the skin of the Soliran fae. They mill about, talking with each other, sampling from refreshment tables and sipping from tall, clear glasses.

Though I try to pretend otherwise, my eyes search out the Prince amid the glorious throng. He's looking directly at me when I finally spy him, his eyes bright through the holes of his mask. I turn away quickly, but not before I see him raise a hand in greeting. Nelle and Mixael lift their hands in response. The wyvern lets out a bray that echoes to the ceiling above.

A silvery tinkling interrupts the murmuring conversation in the hall, clear as a chiming bell. I look up again to see the Prince tapping his glass. "Friends!" he cries, drawing all eyes his way. "Let us now make our way to the Upper Round that we may witness this great event. Then back here for dancing and feasting until moonset!"

His guests set up a cheer of delight. The next moment, they're pouring through the open doors in a golden stream. Once outside, their shining aura dims, however, and they become pale figures under the moonlight.

Nelle and Mixael set off after the others, and Lir tugs me into place behind them. The giant front steps make for an awkward descent for us humans, though Lir and the fae spring down lightly as gazelles, their robes and gowns billowing behind them. Once we reach the bottom, we're a little behind the others, but Mixael takes his mother's hand and runs merrily into the street. Lir and I exchange smiles, then set off after them, Lir tugging me along to keep pace with her long-legged stride, me hiking my bounteous skirts out of my way.

We follow the golden fae through the troll city until we come to a great clear outcropping set a little apart from the city proper. Here, enormous crystals stand in a circle, and I can't tell whether they have grown here naturally or been "planted" by the trolls. This is the *Gluronk,* or so Lir informs me—a place of sacred ceremony among troll kind, otherwise known as the Upper Round.

We stand a little above this circle of crystals, observing what takes place within. Trolls are gathering from all over the city— mostly huge, lurching, stone-hided trolls, but numerous delicate pale trolls like Lir as well. I gaze out across the city. From this particular vantage, I can see far enough to discern other rings of light scattered here and there. "I didn't know there were so many crystals in Vespre," I whisper to Lir. "They're so big!"

"You can't see them most of the time," Lir explains. "They only come alive under moonlight."

At first, I'm so taken by the crystals that I don't notice much else. Then, slowly, I become aware of something interesting: threads. Thousands and thousands of pale threads drape between the crystals, snarl in tremendous knots, and hang with broken bits of rock and debris. It looks startlingly like the mess the children made in my room a few days ago. What was it Lir had called it? A *gubdagog?* It must be some form of decoration, then. Were the children simply trying to make my room look prettier according to troll standards?

I tug on Lir's arm and, when she looks at me, point at the tangled threads. Before I can question her, however, the troll music starts up again. Trolls file into the center of the crystal ring and begin to dance—a heavy, stomping, rolling dance that rattles the ground so hard, I'm obliged to grip Lir's arm for support. I struggle to discern the rhythm and sequence of the dancers. It all looks so haphazard! It's like reading a poem and searching for the rhyme, only to realize the rhyme occurs every ten lines. Once you recognize it, you can see it more clearly and feel the proper sequencing in the rest of the lines. But before you see it, it all feels random, unsettling.

As I watch the dance, however, I'm slowly caught up in the strangeness and otherworldly beauty of it. Soon, I've lost all track of time. The vibration in my bones is exhausting, but I fall into it somehow, become part of that balance of movement and stillness. I even think I'm almost, *almost* starting to understand it. It's like an itch in my brain that I cannot quite scratch. I feel the wildness of it, though. I'm caught in its grip.

Suddenly, both the music and the trolls stop.

I look round at the others—Lir, Mixael, Nelle, and the golden fae standing not far from my current position. They're all staring up at the sky, waiting. I look at the trolls again, both those in the dance and those observing it. They've all assumed the same pose, perfectly still, hands cupped in front of them, eyes raised. Moonlight bathes their ugly faces and seems, almost miraculously, to melt away the crags and crevices. It's as though I'm given the chance to see through the veil of ages to the beauty these creatures once possessed.

Eerie silence holds the world captive. It continues for so long that I shift my feet, bite my lip, and glance around again.

My gaze locks with another.

The Prince. Standing beside Ilusine.

But looking at me.

He offers a slow smile. Moonlight gleams in his eyes.

Before I can react, the air erupts with a tremendous shout—a massive, simultaneous roar uttered from the throats of every troll in the city. It's so huge and so startling, I scream and grip Lir's arm. My own voice is utterly drowned.

The next instant, a rush of wings fills the night. The *hugagug* moths, called from their nests by moonlight, crawl out from the deepest places and take flight. They rise from every part of the city in great clouds, rushing past me, brushing my skin in a million feather-light kisses. I watch as they flow in massive formation to the various crystals, their brilliant-colored wings catching the light and transforming the air into funnels of living rainbows, rising up and up and up. Soon the air is so dense with their wings, they block out the moon above.

As suddenly as they come . . . they're gone. Streaking away across the sky.

I stand breathless. Every sense is alive, overwhelmed by the wonder of what I've just witnessed. Who would have guessed such things existed anywhere in all the worlds? The trolls resume their dancing, slow, sedate, ponderous. But I still stand there, staring up at the moon and the empty sky

THE PRINCE

HER FACE LIGHTS UP LIKE THE MOON AS THE MOTHS swirl around her, pulling at the skirts of her gown and the loose tendrils of her hair.

I watch her. I don't care to watch anything else. No other sight in all this realm or any other could draw my gaze with such allure. Only her. Her and that smile of hers, so bright and shining. Not the demure, masking smile I've come to know too well. This is a true, impulsive, brilliant burst of light and glory which illuminates every dark corner of my heart.

I am unmoored. A ship tossed upon tumultuous waves, at one moment buoyed to heights of triumph, the next plunged into deep trenches of dread. How hard I've fought! How valiantly I've resisted! I'd thought distance would help, an escape to Solira in Ilusine's fair company. I'd thought I'd return stronger than I'd left, ready to meet her and feel nothing. No weakness, no pain. No burning heat. Nothing more than I might feel for any Obligate in my service.

But the truth can no longer be denied. Every day, every hour, every agonized moment I spent in Solira was like daggers piercing my soul. The more I fought to ignore it, the more painful it grew, until I could only wake each day with dread of the long, long hours spinning out before me.

The truth is out. I must face it.

I cannot bear to be far from her. Cannot bear to breathe any atmosphere save hers.

So I watch her now and draw in great gulps of air. Each breath is an acceptance. Of who I am. Of what I've become. Of the gods and their games and their triumph over my petty will. At least in this I might know some relief. To cease striving and give in. Even if . . . Damn it, even if there is little hope of what I feel ever being returned. But even this agony is sweeter than the agony of sheer denial. So I'll accept it, learn to live with it.

The moths spin in a whirlwind of wings and rainbow hues, shooting up and away into the starry sky. She watches them go. And I watch her. Drink in the sight of her. Memorize each subtle fluctuation of her face and expression, the luminous glow of the stars shining in her eyes.

I can never be whole again. Not until I make her mine.

CLARA

26

THE LORDS AND LADIES OF SOLIRA RETURN TO THE palace not long after the moth flight. We librarians trail behind them, though Lir casts several longing looks back at the trolls as we go. I wonder how hard it must be for Lir to be separated from her people. Yes, she was raised by librarians, but she is not truly one of them. She's a poor shadow creature, not quite belonging to either world.

I take her hand and press it. When she turns to me, I give her a warm smile—a smile shared between friends, not between lady and maid. Lir blinks. Then she answers my smile in kind, her whole face lighting up like the moon above behind her eerie bone mask.

The palace is alive with music and life when we climb the big stairs to the front entrance. This time the music is familiar—not fae music, for they do not make melodies of their own. No, this sounds like music stolen from the human realm along with stolen musicians. I would venture to guess they are Obligates brought from Solira, for I doubt very much the Prince keeps musicians on hand in Vespre.

By the time Lir and I make it to the top of the stair, the dancing is well underway. I peer through the doors, my gaze first traveling to the gallery hidden among stalactites overhead from whence the music falls, then down to the dance floor filled with golden figures. There are so many of them, more than I initially thought—at least twelve ladies and sixteen lords in total, all dancing together in various combinations of partners, sometimes three together at once. Though they are all masked, it's impossible to mistake the Prince and Ilusine dancing at the center of the throng. They whirl in a complex pattern of steps, she like a brilliant sun, and he a dark moon, moving in perfect synchronized orbit around her, always drawn back to her brightness.

I look away.

Mixael and Nelle stand off to the right of the hall, not far from a refreshments table. Lir points them out, and we steer that way, arriving just in time to hear Nelle saying in a loud, rather irritable tone, "Well, you'll never know unless you *ask* her, fool boy!"

Mixael tugs at the collar of his shirt. Spotting Lir and me, he cries, "Ah! Miss Darlington, Miss Lir! Kindly distract my mother from her haranguing so that I may enjoy the ball in peace."

Nelle *harrumphs*, which sounds singularly out of place coming from such a beautiful woman. "All I'm saying," she persists, "is that

Captain Khas looks lovely tonight, and it's a shame nobody here has the courage to invite her for a dance."

"Captain Khas?" I follow the line of Mixael's gaze. Sure enough, the powerful captain of the palace guard stands at attention near the front doors. She wears armor, of course, but also, unexpectedly, a flowing pale blue skirt with a startlingly high slit. No doubt it's intended to give her better range of movement should she need to spring into battle mode . . . but it also serves to show off rather a lot of well-shaped, muscular leg.

Lir laughs and playfully flicks Mixael in the ear. "I know for a *fact* she's hoping you'll ask her tonight!"

I didn't know a man's face could turn such a shade of crimson. "Is that true?" Mixael rounds upon Lir, his cheerful face for once very stern indeed. "You're not teasing me, are you?"

Lir merely laughs and slips away. I'm not altogether surprised to spy her a few moments later in the arms of one of the Soliran lords. Lir is easily one of the most beautiful women present; even Ilusine can't quite compare to her pale and perfect loveliness.

I catch Nelle's eye. She sighs and mutters, "I live in hope of someday becoming a grandmother. But as the centuries go by, it's easy for a body to start doubting."

Mixael groans and throws his head back. "Don't start that line again. Fine! I'll make a go of it just to get away from you. But if the fair captain pins me to the wall with a lance, don't go blaming me!"

He soon disappears beyond the dancers. I can't see Khas anymore either. With all the Lords and Ladies thronging the floor,

I've lost track of the Prince as well.

"You could dance too, you know."

I look sharply at Nelle. She's watching me rather too speculatively from behind a green, leaf-patterned mask for comfort. "Oh, no," I say. "I wouldn't dare dance with the fae. Besides, no one will ask me, surely."

"Eh. I wouldn't be so sure of that," Nelle says with a knowing raise of her eyebrows. She opens her mouth to say more, but her wyvern sticks its muzzle into her ear and utters a noisy, *"Meeeep!"* She swears, pushes its head away, and growls, "I know, I know, fool beast! There ain't any *mog* cakes left at this table. Let's go see if we can hunt some down elsewhere."

With that she glides gracefully away into the crowd. I watch her and the wyvern go. A little shiver creeps down my spine as I realize I'm alone. Alone in a crowded ballroom, which is much more alone than mere solitude. I rub my hands together nervously, wondering if perhaps I should call it an evening. My idle gaze travels through the crowd.

My heart stops. Then plunges straight to my stomach.

Ivor.

I blink several times, shake my head, and peer into the moving throng. Was I mistaken? I'm sure I glimpsed him just there on the far side of the ballroom. Golden and glorious, his face half-covered in a great lion's head mask. But I would know that jaw, that fine full mouth anywhere. Am I imagining things?

The song ends. The dancers part ways, affording a clear view across the hall once more. He's not there. There's no sign even of a lion mask. I must have dreamed him up. After all, why would Ivor return to Vespre so soon after his disappointment? He wouldn't. Which means it couldn't have been him.

My throat suddenly tight, I wipe my sweaty palms surreptitiously on my hips. Realizing what I've done, I look down at the shimmery fabric of my gown, afraid I've spoiled it. I feel like a gray ghost in this room full of golden sunlight, completely unsuited to my setting. I don't belong here among the glorious fae.

I want out. Now.

Sidling along the wall, I make my way to the nearest passage and slip gratefully into the shadows. Once there, I slip the mask from my face, glad to be free of it, glad to feel cool air on against my flushed skin. Lifting the front hem of my skirts, I hurry. The twilit stone of Vespre Palace closes comfortingly around me. When first arriving in this city, I never would have believed I could learn to be more comfortable in the semi-darkness than in the brilliant light of Aurelis Court. Now I'm relieved to leave the sunglow behind and reenter the gloom.

"Where are you off to, Darling?"

I freeze, mere paces from the end of the gallery. My heart springs to my throat. Slowly I turn, look back the way I've just come.

The Prince stands at the far end of the gallery. Though he wears golden robes like the Solirans, the moonglow turns them to silver. Slowly, he slips the mask from his face. His eyes glitter strangely, like a wild animal's.

I don't speak. I'm not sure I could if I tried. I watch him approach, one firm footstep after another. He passes through the rectangles of moonlight cast through the windows, stepping from light to darkness to light again in quick succession.

Soon he stands a mere five paces from me.

"Why are you not dancing?" His voice is deep and dark beneath the brightness of the distant music.

I lift my chin a fraction. "I make it a rule not to attend fae dances. It isn't safe for humans."

"Yes." The Prince nods. "But this is *my* dance and *my* home." He takes another step toward me. The space between us suddenly seems very small. "Surely you feel safe enough here."

"Safe?" I echo. "In Doomed City?"

His garments are many-layered and intricate but cut away from his throat and chest after the current fae fashion. His dark hair falls across his shoulders like liquid night. I lift my gaze, meet his eyes. No smile of mine will do any good to disguise my emotions. Not here. Not in this moonlit moment with that music playing in the background. Suddenly I wish that I'd not removed my mask.

The song comes to an end. But the silence that follows is somehow still full of music.

I find my voice again. "I will never be safe here. Isn't that why you brought me in the first place?"

"I brought you here to face your fears," he responds. "All of them. Including, apparently, an unpardonable fear of dancing."

He closes the last of the distance between us so swiftly, I don't have time to react. One of his hands slips around my waist, the other grasps my fingers. He stands close, so close, gazing down at me. I can't move. Can't breathe. A new song begins, echoing along the gallery. This time, instead of a wild, lively, laughing melody, it's something softer, lilting. But no less wild in its way.

"Dance with me?" the Prince says. Though he's holding me, he does not move. We simply stand there, like statues frozen in time.

I open my dry lips and manage to whisper, "Am I *obligated* to dance?"

The line of his jaw hardens. "When have I obligated you to do anything?"

Never. I realize it with the force of a thunderclap. Not once since the moment he purchased my Obligation has he made use of it. Oh, he's given commands with all the imperious confidence one would expect from a prince . . . but never with the accompanying force that would oblige me to obey. Always he has left me the right to refuse.

In the end, however, does it make any difference?

My spine stiffens. "But you could. At any time." I narrow my eyes up at him. "Knowing that, am I supposed to be grateful that you don't press your advantage?"

He holds my gaze for a long moment, his violet eyes searching my face slowly. Then abruptly he takes a step back, letting go of me. I feel the warm place in the small of my back where his hand had rested suddenly go cold. He retreats several paces and bows.

"Go where you will," he says. "Do as you wish. All that I ask of you, now or ever, is that you be whole. Courageously whole."

I stare at him, completely taken aback. My heart pounds with a sudden and inexplicable longing. It hurts. Hurts in a way I can't begin to describe or understand.

But as I stare at my own reflection in the depths of the Prince's eyes, I feel as though I see myself for what I could be. Someone who isn't afraid of her inner darkness. Someone who knows, not only what she is, but also everything she could become.

The night deepens, like a cloud has passed over the moon. At first I scarcely notice it. But when the Prince frowns suddenly and looks around, his expression consternated, I realize just how dark it's become. Even the lantern overhead has dimmed.

Something's changed. Something's wrong.

"Prince?" I say tentatively.

The next moment the air splits with the roaring clamor of bells. Not the bells which toll out the hours, no; these are bells I've heard only one other time. But their meaning is seared across my mind.

Noswraith.

27

THERE'S NO TIME TO THINK. THE PRINCE TAKES MY hand, and we are running for the library before my brain has caught up with my body. By the time I'm able to form a coherent thought, all I can think is how eerily like this is to the night when the Hungry Mother escaped. Only this time I know what those alarm bells mean. This time I know the kind of battle ahead of me.

Which makes it so much worse.

"How could this have happened?" I cry, my voice barely audible above the din of the bells. "Mixael said the grimoires were properly bound!"

"They were bound," the Prince answers grimly. "I checked every last one of them myself before the party tonight. They were secure when I left the library, even the weakest bindings."

"Then how could this have happened?"

He looks down at me. "The only way a Noswraith could escape tonight is if someone tampered with a book."

A cold chill runs down my spine. "Vervain?"

But the Prince shakes his head. "She's safe in the west tower. Come, Darling! We'll get our answers soon enough. We've got to find Andreas."

With that he tugs me into a quicker stride. I bundle up the front of my skirts with one arm. This gown is completely impractical for whatever lies ahead of me, but there's no time to stop and change. I worry about Andreas, alone in the library. He must have set the alarm bells ringing. Which means he's still alive, right?

The doors are shut fast when we reach them. The Prince tries the latch, finds it locked, and quickly mutters a spell, making a sharp gesture with one hand. Fae magic flares and bursts the doors wide. We both step through into the uppermost floor. "Andreas?" the Prince calls.

There's no answer.

"Quick," he says, drawing the doors shut behind him. "Find a book and quill. We can't know where the wraith is. It could still be here in the library."

I hasten to my own cubicle and hastily snatch up my magicked quill and a blank book. The Prince arms himself as well. He is just testing the ink in his quill when the doors open again, and Nelle and Mixael arrive, Captain Khas with them.

"Khas," the Prince says, hastening to meet her, "I need you and your guards to post watch around the perimeter of the palace. Right now, we must assume the Noswraith is still inside somewhere. I want an alert the moment it shows signs of trying to escape. The last thing we need is a Nightmare on the loose during *Hugag*."

I think of the poor souls out and about for celebration in the city below. If a Noswraith got in among them, what kind of bloodbath would ensue?

Khas salutes . . . and it's only then that I notice her hand is clasped in Mixael's. She doesn't look at Mixael, however, as she pulls free and strides swiftly from the library, silent and stoic as ever. I hate to see her go; I would feel braver knowing Khas was with us, even though I know she can't possibly subdue a Noswraith. At best, she can serve as a distraction.

I'm not much more use myself.

The Prince turns to Nelle. "Our first task is to find Andreas. He can tell us more."

There's an unspoken *If he's still alive* in the air. I hear it loud and clear, and I can tell by Nelle and Mixael's expressions that they hear it too.

"We need to work in pairs," the Prince continues. "Nelle, you stay with Darling here. The two of you must work the upper five floors. I'll take Mixael, and we'll search lower down. No one is to go lower than floor ten alone. Once we find Andreas, use the tubes to let the others know, then we'll congregate back here and prepare for the next step."

The next step being containing the Noswraith. That's *if* we don't bump into it on our way.

"Any idea which wraith we're dealing with?" Nelle asks as she tucks an extra quill into the hair piled on top of her head. "Bigger or smaller?"

"I'm as ignorant as you are on that score," the Prince says. "If I were to guess, I'd say it's a Greater Noswraith. Andreas is unlikely to sound the alarm for a lesser."

We exchange glances. I can't help wondering if there's a chance Andreas loosed this Noswraith himself, just as Vervain had done. I have trouble believing it of the studious, withdrawn librarian I know. But who am I to say how the madness of a wraith may prey on anyone's mind?

The Prince claps his hands once, smartly, drawing our attention back to him. "First we find Andreas," he says. "Then we figure out our next steps. Agreed?"

"Agreed," we echo.

"And remember, if you see the wraith, *do not engage.* Withdraw to a safe distance, stay out of the Nightmare Realm, and call for backup. We must assume it's fully liberated of its binding, which means no one should tackle it alone. Stay together. Stay safe." His gaze flicks to mine as he speaks these last words. Just for an instant—but an instant of such intensity, it nearly stops my heart.

He turns away, beckons to Mixael. Mixael presses his mother's shoulder, offers her and me an encouraging smile, then disappears behind the Prince down the nearest spiral stair. I listen to the sound of their footsteps as they hasten to the lower levels to begin their search. Panic flutters in my stomach.

"Do not engage, my eye," Nelle mutters, tucking a book under her arm. "What does he expect us to do if we come face-to-face with a Noswraith? Scream and run away?" She crouches, encouraging the wyvern down from her shoulders onto the floor. "This ain't no place for you," she tells it with a tap on its blunt little nose. "You scurry along to my desk and stay there folded up small, you hear me? I don't want you becoming a Noswraith snack tonight."

"*Meep!*" says the wyvern and waddles off obediently. I watch its scaly tail disappear into Nelle's cubicle.

Nelle rises and turns to me. "Got your book and quill, girl?"

I nod.

"All right then. Here's a satchel—put the book in that. Keep it with you, but no writing save as a last resort, you hear me? At the first sign of the Nightmare creeping into your head, you run, find your waking self, and get out. I'll do what I can to make sure we both stay fully awake. But if it's a Greater Noswraith, that'll be challenging. They draw you into their realm faster than you can blink. Now come!"

With a sickening plunge in my gut, I follow Nelle. We light a couple of moonfire candles, then begin to carefully circle the uppermost floor, searching for Andreas in every one of the cubicles, under the workstation tables, and inside every storage room. No sign of him. No sign of a Noswraith either, but that doesn't make me any less jumpy. I keep listening for something from the other two below. If they encounter the wraith, will they be able to make it to the speaking tubes to call for help before it draws them into the Nightmare? I hate being separated from them and can't help feeling we should have all stuck together. But Andreas's best chance is if we spread out and find him fast.

With no sign of Andreas on the upper floor, Nelle and I proceed to the second and begin the next round of our search. This floor is devoted to Magic of Antiquity, and though it brims with power, at least it isn't Noswraith power. I breathe a little more easily as we go, peering into storage rooms and between bookshelves, following the curve all the way around the open citadel center and back to the same stair where we started from. No sign of Andreas.

Why do I get the sinking feeling the world around me is getting darker? Maybe it's just my imagination.

We descend to the third floor. Here the sense of creeping movement in the shadows increases. Each time I turn and look directly, however, I see nothing. Just ordinary shadows.

"Steady," Nelle says, reaching out and touching my hand. "Got to have nerves of steel for nights like this."

"Do we have them often? Only, this is the second outbreak since I got here . . . and I've only been here a month!"

Nelle grunts. "I won't lie, there's been unusual amounts of activity lately. There's something off in the world. Like forces just beyond my range of knowing are working against us librarians. Probably because our numbers are at a disastrously all-time low after . . . well, after Soran. And with the Prince weakened as he is . . ." She shrugs and heaves a sigh. "It sometimes feels as though the doom of Doomed City is coming sooner rather than later. But"—and here she shoots me an encouraging smile—"*sooner* doesn't mean *tonight*. We'll get this wraith bound up again, never you fear!"

She lets go of my hand and ventures down a side passage, holding her moonfire candle out in front of her. I trail at her heels, hoping against hope that she's right, that her confidence isn't totally misplaced.

What will happen if the Prince uses his human magic tonight?

He's down on the lower levels. Totally exposed to whatever horrors the Nightmare Realm can throw at him. His only defense is his human magic.

Ilusine's words come back to me, a chilling whisper in the darkness: *"If Castien is forced to use his human magic one more time, he will surely die."*

"Nelle," I start to say.

In the same moment, she turns suddenly, looking back at me from the passage. Her eyes are very wide and white in the moonfire glow. "Listen!" she hisses.

I hold my breath.

Somewhere, outside this passage—a groan.

I reach out, catch hold of Nelle's hand. We stare at each other by the flickering glow of our candles. Every sense in my body prickles with awareness, and my pulse jumps in my veins.

The groan sounds again.

"That ain't a Noswraith," Nelle hisses. "This way!"

She sidles around me and out of the passage back to the main section of the floor. Though every instinct urges me to crouch and hide where I am, I don't want to be left alone, so I hurry after her. The groan sounds again and again. We follow it to the next passage over where three lanterns hang from the ceiling, leading down two long rows of bookshelves. Their light, combined with the glow of Nelle's candle, illuminates a crumpled figure.

"Andreas!" I gasp.

He lies at the base of a bookshelf, one arm outstretched, the other wrapped over his head, his whole body curled and tucked into itself. Nelle doesn't hesitate. She leaps into the passage, kneels beside the fallen librarian, and checks his pulse. "Alive," she declares, but her voice is grim. "He ain't here, I'm afraid."

I know what she's saying: his mind isn't present. He's gone into the Nightmare. I look at his oddly contorted body. What terrors is he experiencing on the other side of reality?

"How do we get him back?" I whisper, slipping a hand into my satchel.

Nelle looks up sharply. "Nuh-uh, none of that!" she snaps. "The Prince told us not to engage it alone. We'll call for him and Mixael and see if we can't get in there and get Andreas out together."

I'm momentarily relieved. But then Nelle gets to her feet and says, "You stay here with him. There's a set of tubes just at the end of the passage, out on the main circle. I'll be right back."

"Shouldn't we stay together?" I protest.

"We can't haul him with us," Nelle responds. "I ain't that strong, and neither are you. Chin up, girl! I'll just be two steps and a jump away. We'll get through this."

So saying, she slips past me, making for the end of the passage. I crouch beside Andreas's fallen body, touch his back with one hand, and watch her retreat. As her figure shrinks into the distance, the passage suddenly seems much longer than it was a few moments ago.

Just as she reaches the arch at the far end and stands there, silhouetted, I see it—the shadows outside the circle of her candlelight begin to move, churn.

"Nelle, *wait!*" I cry.

Nelle turns, looks back.

Then shadows rush in fast, blocking her from view.

28

I'M ALONE AT THE FAR END OF THE PASSAGE, SURROUNDED
by moving, energy-filled darkness.

Andreas isn't here. His physical body may be close on the
other side of reality, but he is not *here*. Neither is Nelle standing at
the end of the passage anymore. I'm alone in this dark place. Alone
in the Nightmare Realm.

The Noswraith. It must be close.

Slowly, cautiously, I rise. For a moment I can't see anything
around me at all. I blink until my eyes adjust, discerning
bookshelves through the film of darkness. None of the lanterns
hanging overhead are lit on this side of reality. They swing gently
as though in a breeze, though the air is painfully still. My candle
is dead.

I need to wake up. Now. I need to wake up and get out my book and start writing. Never mind what the Prince said! My book and pen are my only weapons against whatever is waiting for me in this darkness. I need to start writing, put up some defenses.

I squeeze my eyes tight then open them as wide as I can. I don't wake up. I smack my own face hard enough to hurt.

Nothing. I'm still in the Nightmare.

My trembling lips part, try to form Nelle's name. No sound will come. I simply can't speak. Are Nelle and Andreas in here with me somewhere? They might be. They *must* be. Close by, even. If I can find them, maybe we can help each other.

I hate to leave this spot where, just on the other side of reality, I know my body is crouching. But I can't stay here and wait for the Noswraith to find me. The need for action drives me creeping down the passage, keeping my back to the bookshelves. One footstep after the other, I inch my way to the end. There I peer out into the main circle, looking first one way, then the other.

Then I look across the rail, over the central opening, to the far rail and the dark walkway on the other side.

My heart stops.

Someone is there. Walking slowly. Here, on the third floor with me. A woman—small, slender, with long bony arms, wrists and hands extending far out from the ends of her sleeves. Her feet are bare, and she holds the hem of her white nightgown out of their way as she steps softly, silently, slowly.

Her head is bowed. Long black hair hides her face.

Step. Step.

Slow, deliberate.

Step. Step.

She's coming around. Around to this side of the floor. She'll be here soon.

And then . . .

And then . . .

"Wake up, Clara," I whisper, shaking my head and blinking frantically. But I don't wake up. I'm trapped. In the Nightmare.

With every blink, that pale figure gets closer.

I look from side to side and . . . ah! There's the spiral stair leading to the upper floors. While I hate to leave the level where my body lies, I need to get out of here. Fast.

Step. Step.

She passes behind one of the support pillars. Out of sight.

I need to move. Now.

Swallowing a whimper, I lunge for the stair. As I step out of the passage onto the main circle, I see the apparition again. Just a glimpse—but it's closer than I thought. I run, stumbling, panting, desperate.

I look back. It's closer still.

I grab the stair rail.

Something latches hold of my wrist. Pulls. I begin to scream but don't get a chance before I'm yanked away from the stair into another side passage full of books. A hand closes over my mouth. I struggle, flailing, but a voice hisses in my ear, *"Not that way, fool girl!"*

Nelle.

"You keep going that way, you'll end up deeper in the Nightmare and not be able to wake up. Best to stay close to your body if you can. Now, you gonna be quiet if I take my hand away?"

I nod. Nelle lets go and steps back. Here in the Nightmare Realm, she seems younger than ever. But all the color is drained from her face and hair, leaving behind a pale, ghostly version of her true self. She holds my gaze hard for a moment, and I draw strength from her firm confidence.

Suddenly she hisses, *"Down!"*

We both crouch, half hidden behind a protruding bookshelf. She peers out, and I dare to look over her shoulder to the end of the passage.

The woman in white goes walking by. Her head bowed, her arms dangling. One foot after another. She steps toe to heel, like a dancer, but her tread is heavy.

Step. Step.

Step. Step.

I don't know why—I can't begin to explain it—but the sight of that specter fills me with more dread than any ravening monster ever could.

Step. Step.

Step. Step.

She passes by. Out of sight. Continuing around the curve of the main circle.

I let out a breath.

"Come on," Nelle says drawing me to my feet with her. When she takes a step, I tighten my grip on her hand. She looks back at me, and I shake my head, eyes wide. *"Don't be afraid, girl,"* she says firmly. *"We need to get you back to your body. I can wake you, never you fear! I've done this before, you know."*

Everything in me tells me to resist. But I know Nelle. I trust her. She's faced more Noswraiths than I can imagine.

Nodding, I allow myself to be led from the passage. We're behind the Noswraith now—I can see it walking away from us, round the curve. Soon it will disappear behind a pillar. Nelle tugs my hand. I follow her, craning my neck to keep an eye on the Noswraith as I go. I can't help thinking the moment I look away, it'll speed up behind me, take me by surprise.

I'm not looking where I'm going. Which means I don't see the stray piece of paper lying on the ground before I step on it.

Crunch.

The Noswraith stops.

I freeze in place. Nelle's grip on my hand tightens, and I hear her catch her breath.

The Noswraith turns her head, slowly. Black hair falls over her shoulder. And her head keeps coming round.

"Run!" Nelle breathes.

The next moment, I'm scrambling frantically back along the rounded floor, through the churning darkness of the Nightmare. Nelle is behind me, guarding my steps, but I feel alone, so dreadfully alone. I've got to get back, got to find my body, wake it up. I've got to get out of here.

I see the entrance of the passage where I think I left my body behind. Ducking inside, I'm momentarily blinded by the dense darkness. I don't stop running but hurtle all the way to the far wall. My hands, out in front of me, hit the shelves, knocking a book or two out onto the floor. They land with dull thuds at my feet. I'm trapped. Caught in a dead end.

Wake up. Wake up! I've got to wake up!

I can't.

A chill ripples down my spine. I whip around, staring back the way I've just come. At the end of the passage, just outside the arch, stands Nelle. She lifts one hand, and a flaming dagger bursts into existence. By the light of that flame, I see her face, younger than I've ever seen it. Beautiful and fierce, vibrant, and determined.

For an instant, she glances sideways. At me.

The next instant, a pale cloud engulfs her. A churning, roiling chaos, it blocks her from my sight. There's a long moment of silence.

Then a scream—short, sharp. Full of surprise.

Then another scream.

And another. And another.

Screams of terror. Screams of pain.

I press back against the bookshelf behind me, my own mouth open in silent terror. The cloud whorls, turning scarlet like a spreading stain of blood.

Then suddenly, it dissipates into vapors.

The specter appears, walking through the cloud. Slowly, toe to heel, toe to heel.

Step. Step.

Stop.

It turns. Lifts its head.

Dark hair falls back. For the first time, I see its face. A delicate gentle face, bashed out of shape, mottled with bruises. The eye sockets are sewn shut with ragged, haphazard black threads.

Her bloodless lips move. A whisper creeps down the passage, tickles my ear: *He really loves you, you know.*

29

SOMEHOW, I KNEW. I COULDN'T SAY WHY, BUT THE knowledge was there in my mind from the very first moment I heard the alarm bells ringing. I'd known as I raced with the Prince through the halls of Vespre, as we broke into the library, as I hunted up my quill and book. I knew as I descended with Nelle down the spiral stair, lower and lower.

Seeing that face now is merely a confirmation: This is *my* Noswraith.

I gaze into that twisted horror. Horror that was birthed from the depths of my own mind, my own heart.

Whatever courage I had left betrays me. My legs give out. I sink to the floor in a mound of silvery skirts. Desperately I blink and blink and blink again, trying to force myself awake, to force my unconscious back into my physical body. But I can't. I'm trapped.

The figure at the end of the passage turns her whole body. Her shoulders angle oddly, her arms dangle limp, lifeless. She tilts her head.

Takes a step.

Then another.

The long threads at the ends of the ugly eyehole seams dangle down her cheekbones all the way to her jaw.

Clara.

That voice. I know it as intimately as I know my own. It is the voice I gave to my creation.

Her lips curve in a smile but otherwise don't move, even as her words ripple along the shadows to caress my ear.

Clara.

Claraaaaa.

"*What do you want from me?*" I cry, desperate. Tears stream down my face.

I want you to know.

I want you to understand.

Toe to heel. Toe to heel.

Step.

Step.

You must understand.

She reaches out with one hand. Long fragile fingers beckon softly—

A burst of light. Not pale ghost light, but brilliant yellow flame. A man's silhouette appears at the end of the passage. The specter whirls to face the newcomer. She throws back her head and screams as the point of a flaming sword pierces straight through her chest, protrudes out her back.

That brittle, narrow body sags. And vanishes.

Suddenly the Prince is there, standing where the Noswraith was just a moment before. His eyes are very wide as they search in the darkness. He spies me and holds out his hand. *"Quick, Darling!"*

Whimpering, I scramble to my feet, run to him, take his hand. I drag in a deep breath, choking on a sob as strong arms surround me, pull me close, and—

"Darling? Can you hear me?"

I wake with a start. The Prince's face swims into view. I blink quickly, forcing my vision to clarify, and find I'm lying on the ground, my bounteous skirts *poofed* all around me, my upper body held in the Prince's arms. He gazes down at me, his expression stern by the light of the lanterns overhead. The shadows beyond the lanternlight aren't moving or writhing.

"I'm back!" I gasp, catching the front of the Prince's robes and clinging desperately. "I'm back, I'm here!"

"For the moment," he replies and helps me to sit fully upright, one hand pressed against my lower back. I want to catch my breath a moment, but he urges me to my feet. Dizzy, I sway. He quickly slips an arm around my waist. "Steady, Darling. Steady. You'll be drawn back into the Nightmare Realm soon. This Noswraith is wholly liberated from her bonds. She's nearly at full power already."

I turn to him, frowning. "She's not dead?"

"Hardly." The Prince snorts. "It'll take more than a poke with an ephemeral blade to put that one to rest. Haven't I told you, Darling? There's no known way to *kill* a Noswraith. They can only be bound."

I see movement from the tail of my eye and turn, heart jumping. It's Mixael. He's got the unconscious body of Andreas draped over his shoulder. Mixael's face is very pale and lined in the cold lantern light.

"He's still in there!" I gasp, turning to the Prince. I realize I'm holding his hand and quickly let it go. "Andreas is still in the Nightmare. I couldn't find him."

The Prince looks grim. "We need to get him out before we bind the wraith, or he'll end up trapped as well."

I look around then, my brow puckering. "Where's Nelle?" The Prince does not answer. I turn from him to Mixael. "Where is she?"

"I don't know," Mixael replies. "We thought she'd be with you, but . . ."

The Prince reaches out and claps Mixael's shoulder. "You find her. Now. We're going to need her before this is through. But first take Andreas to the upper floor. Use the book lift."

Mixael nods and hastens to obey. I wish we could both go with him and even take a half-step to follow. But the Prince catches my wrist. "Not you," he says, and reaches into the satchel at his hip, withdrawing a book and quill. *My* book and *my* quill I note when he pushes them into my hands. "Quick now," he says, catching and holding my gaze. "There's no time to lose. You *must* write her name. To write her name will draw her directly to you. Then I can bind her."

"Her name?" I gape at the Prince and shake my head stupidly. "I don't know it. I tell you, I don't know it!"

"You must."

"But I don't! I understand that she's mine. I . . . I . . . Seeing her just now, I felt as though I *recognized* her. But I don't remember creating her, and I don't know her name."

The Prince takes a step closer to me, drawing his face near to mine. Moonfire light shines in his eyes, making them hard as diamonds. The lines of his face are drawn with pain, with exhaustion. I realize suddenly that he must have used human magic when he faced the Noswraith just now. Not a large spell, not enough to bind her. Just enough to drive her away temporarily. But it's taken a heavy toll.

"You must remember," he urges. "You're the only one here who can help us. You must remember, or we cannot hope to bind her without . . ."

He doesn't finish. He doesn't have to; I know what he's saying. We cannot hope to bind her without him exerting tremendous magic.

I shake my head, close my eyes. Somewhere, deep in my mind, there must be a memory. Something to aid me, something to remind me of what I've done and why I've done it. At first, I see only darkness.

Then the darkness shifts. Subtly.

It's now a different darkness—the darkness found behind a closed cellar door. Full of the stink of coal, the scuttling of rats. Mold. Damp.

Oscar, sitting on a step. Weeping, weeping, weeping as though his heart will break. His small body pressed up against mine, his bony shoulder quaking. I hold him close, my back against the door, my feet on the lower step. I won't let him go. I won't let him fall into that deeper darkness below. I'll hold him, and we'll wait. We'll wait together. We'll wait and we'll pray.

We'll pray.

Pray for . . . for . . .

"No!" I lift my head, my eyes flaring open to meet the Prince's gaze. "I told you! I don't know. I don't remember. I *can't* remember."

"Can't, Darling?" the Prince says quietly. "Or won't?"

He doesn't wait for my answer. He turns away, pulls another book from his satchel, opens it across his arm. "What are you doing?" I ask, my heart ramming against my breastbone.

"I'm going back in," he replies. "I'm going to find Andreas."

I pull in my lips, biting down. Then, with a little growl in my throat, I open my book as well. "I'm going with you."

"No," the Prince says sharply. "You're not prepared for this fight. The Eyeless Woman . . . she's different. She's not like the Hungry Mother. She's not like any other wraith I've seen."

"Even more reason why you shouldn't face her alone," I answer with more courage than I feel. "Besides, maybe the name will come to me when I see her."

The Prince gives me a look but makes no further protest. He simply starts writing. I watch his eyes, see the moment when he suddenly splits, disconnects. His hand is still writing in this reality, but another, larger part of himself is gone. Stepped into the Nightmare.

Time to prove the merit of my words.

I lick the tip of my quill, put it to the page, and begin to write: *Once upon a time, in Vespre Library . . .*

30

WORDS SPILL FROM MY PEN ONTO THE PAGE, fast and cramped and jumbled, studded with odd punctuation and poor grammar. But the energy of the words is there: the truth, the intensity. I can feel the power they generate rising from the book, filling the air around me.

My eyes slowly shut.

When I open them again, I'm back in the Nightmare. The Prince is here as well, looking at me. He carries a drawn sword in one hand and what looks like a large sack in the other.

"Are you ready?" he asks.

"A moment," I reply, and in the other reality, scribble harder. Here in the Nightmare, I look down to find my enormous ballgown gone, replaced by a much more practical work dress. My searching hand finds a dagger in a sheath at my waist. I draw it, pretending

to test its balance, pretending I have any idea how to use a weapon like this.

Then I meet the Prince's gaze. *"I'm ready."*

For a moment he looks as though he's about to say something, something he has to fight back. He wants to talk me out of this, I know. He wants to convince me to wake up again, to stay in the waking world where it's safe.

Instead he nods once. *"This way."*

I follow the Prince to the nearest stair. The treads creak and the metal rail groans as we begin our descent. *"Andreas will be down on the thirteenth floor,"* the Prince says, tossing the words back over his shoulder as he rounds the curves. *"The librarians of Vespre are trained in a certain protocol for situations such as this. If you find yourself trapped in the Nightmare, unable to wake yourself, you are to make your way as swiftly as you can to the one place the Noswraith is unlikely to go."*

"Where is that?" I ask.

"The vault."

Of course. A Noswraith, especially one of the Greater Noswraiths, would hate to go anywhere near the vault and especially the broken grimoire it has just escaped. So naturally there is no better hiding place in the Nightmare. Andreas's body is still alive, which means his dream self must still be living as well. We can only hope he followed protocol and made his way to the thirteenth floor.

The Prince holds his flaming sword high, lighting up the darkness as we spiral lower and lower and lower. Below the fifth floor. The sixth. Down to the eighth. Shadows crawl and writhe on the edges of our light, but I feel relatively safe within its glow. I stick close to the Prince, scarcely more than a pace or two behind him, taking care not to tread on his trailing robes. We reach the ninth floor, the tenth. Down to the eleventh.

Suddenly, he stops.

"Back up," he says. Then, in a frantic whisper, *"Back up, back up, BACK UP."*

A pale light glows around the bend in the stair.

The Noswraith. She's coming.

I whirl and stumble over my own feet, scrambling to get back up the stairs. The Prince hastens behind me, sometimes pushing me along ahead of him. I feel as though my feet weigh a thousand pounds each, as though I'm wading through thick sludge.

Reaching the tenth floor, I leap out of the stairwell and nearly fall on my face. The Prince, just a step behind, catches me and sets me back on my feet before grabbing my hand and dragging me after him into one of the side passages. There we press our backs against the wall, the edges of bookshelves digging into our shoulders. I struggle to breathe without gasping aloud and giving away our position.

All around me, the books stir. Other Noswraiths. Still caught in their bindings but sensing the liberty of one of their sisters. Their eagerness, their hunger, is palpable.

From my angle, I can just see the stair. The spectral woman steps off onto the floor. Her lank hair covers her hideous, maimed face once more. She turns to the left. Then to the right, toward us where we hide. I can feel her reaching out with her senses, trying to discover where we are.

The Prince murmurs something beside me and makes a short, sharp gesture with one hand. I'm not sure what he's done, but the air around us darkens still more. I blink, wondering if something is wrong with my eyes.

The specter tilts her head slightly to one side. I can feel her considering, curious. My heart pounds in my throat, my pulse jumps with dread. She knows we're here. She must. She *must*. Otherwise, why would she linger so? Any moment now, she'll continue, straight toward us, and then . . . and then . . .

But she doesn't.

She turns to the left and wafts away. One slow step after another. Until she's out of sight.

I let my breath out in a long, shuddering sigh. My relief is short-lived, however, for the Prince grabs my shoulder and turns me to him. *"Her name,"* he says. *"What is her name? You've got to know!"*

"I don't." I shake my head, holding his gaze. *"I wish I did. But I don't, I just don't."*

The Prince growls and lets me go. For a moment, he stands in place, drawing slow breaths. Then, with a short shake of his head, he steps out of the passage and beckons me after him. The specter has rounded the bend out of sight by now. We creep to the stair and resume our descent. Down and down, round and round, until we come to the thirteenth floor.

The pressure is intense. So much greater here in the Nightmare than it is in the waking world. I could almost swear I see the vault doors bulging out from the walls as the Noswraiths within strive against their bonds. But as strong as they are, the spells holding them at bay are stronger still. Despite my fear, I feel a swell of pride. The librarians of Vespre are true magicians!

The Prince stumbles. It's so sudden, it takes me by surprise. I bite back a little scream as he staggers to one side and leans heavily against the wall. *"Prince!"* I gasp and reach out to touch his arm. *"Prince, what's wrong?"*

He shakes his head. His breathing is rough, ragged. He's already used too much magic. It's taking a heavy toll on him.

"You should go back." The words leave my lips before I realize I intend to speak. I grimace, wish for a moment that I could take them back. Then, with a determined shake of my head, I press on. *"You should go, get out of here. Don't use any more magic! I will find Andreas and bring him up."*

The Prince raises his heavy head. *"Don't be daft. I'm not leaving you."*

"Why not? It's my Noswraith. It's my fault we're in this danger." I swallow hard, then set my jaw. *"I can do this. I can get him."*

"Brave words, little warrior." Closing his eyes, the Prince seems to summon strength from deep inside himself as he pushes off from the wall. He sways, firms his stance, then looks at me again. *"No way in the nine hells am I leaving you. Now come! Let's find our man."*

The door to the thirteenth vault is blasted from its hinges. It lies in a twisted, broken mess in the middle of the passage. I wonder if it will look the same in the waking world. Either way, there can be no doubt this is the source of the outbreak.

The Prince and I approach cautiously and peer through the open doorway. *"Andreas!"* I gasp. He's there. Curled up in a little ball beneath the pedestal, his arms wrapped over his head. He does not move at the sound of his name.

"Quick, Darling," the Prince says. *"I'll stand watch."*

I nod and slip into the chamber. All of the paperback books have been blasted from the center, many of them blackened beyond recognition. They plaster the wall and mound in piles, broken, tattered, torn. My shoes slap against bare stone floor as I cross to Andreas. I crouch beside him, grip his shoulder, roll him over.

My stomach gives a sickening twist. He's beaten black and blue. His face is swollen almost beyond recognition, his cheekbones and nose broken, his lip cut and oozing blood. *"Oh, Andreas!"* I whisper. Bending down, I press my ear to his chest. A heartbeat. Faint, but present. Does that mean he's still alive in the waking world as well? If I can just get this version of him back into his physical form, will he be all right?

"Darling."

I turn.

The Prince stands just outside the doorway in the middle of the outer passage. He's braced for battle, his sword arm upraised. He flicks a glance my way. *"Now would be a good time for you to remember that name."*

A pale glow lights up his face. Not moonfire. No, this is a ghostly aura.

The specter approaches.

Suddenly white mist rolls along the floor, billows around the Prince's feet, climbs his legs, and obscures him completely. *"No!"* I cry, springing to my feet.

It's too late. I hear a single, bloodcurdling scream.

The cloud turns red.

For a terrible moment I stand as though frozen, staring at that cloud. Every sense strains for something, anything. Another sound, another glimpse. Something to tell me the Prince is still there, still somewhere inside that churning red.

The vapors thin, part. A figure comes slowly into view. The raw redness fades back to white, and the cloud peels away more and more, until I can see clearly who stands in the doorway.

Her.

Her hair streams back from her face. The black threads of her sewn-up eyes waft like grotesque eyelashes.

Listen to me!

Her voice is a whisper, but it rings like a shout in my head. I cry out, clapping my hands to my ears, and crouch over Andreas.

Listen to me! The voice says again, though the specter's lips never move. She steps over the threshold into the room. *Listen to me, listen to me!*

All the broken books surrounding me begin to murmur and

move and shiver. She takes another step. The pale mist crawls in around her, filling up the space, creeping around me. It covers Andreas. I cannot see him.

I reach out, take hold of the only thing my hand can find— one of the many dead books. Springing upright, I hurl it at the specter's head. It strikes true, knocking her face to one side. Her dark hair falls, covering her battered, purple features.

She takes a step back. The mist retreats. Just a little, just enough that I can see Andreas once more. Then she tosses her hair back over her shoulders.

You must believe me.

Her lips twist open, revealing red-stained teeth, black gums.

He really loves you. He loves us all.

He's in so much pain.

We have to help him.

You have to help him.

Her head turns. Those eyeless sockets fix upon me.

He's in pain.

Suddenly, the mist overwhelms me, blinds me, fills my nostrils. I open my mouth to scream, but it pours down my throat into my lungs. I stagger back, hit the podium, trip, fall.

Pain explodes in my head.

I scream, but my voice is cut off as something lifts me off the ground. I'm hurtled through the air, strike the wall, fall to the floor. Gasping with shock, I start to pick myself up, only to be caught up by some invisible force and hurled again, this time to the ceiling.

I'm pinned there, stalactites tearing into my flesh. I can't breathe. Whatever holds me lets go. I drop to the floor, ten feet at least. I put out my arms to break my fall. My wrist bones shatter on impact, and my chin cracks against stone.

Something strikes my side—ribs break. A blow to my head—my jaw shatters. My arm is caught, twisted behind my back, twisted hard, harder—snaps. I scream again, agony filling every sense. Something grabs the top of my head, draws it back, and smacks my face into the floor. My nose breaks, blood gushes. I see nothing but red, red, *red*—

Sudden, searing light.

I lift my head, peering through swollen eyes, through streams of blood. I see the Eyeless Woman, her head thrown back and twisting on her long neck, as though she searches, struggling to see.

The Prince is there as well. Just behind her, his sword in hand.

He's in pain! the Eyeless Woman cries.

"Aren't we all?" says the Prince.

With a brilliant flash his sword arcs, slicing the air. It cuts through her neck with a single stroke.

31

HER HEAD REMAINS POISED ON HER SHOULDERS
for the space of three throbbing heartbeats.

Then it falls.

It hits the floor with an echoing thud and rolls. Three times it rolls, round and round, before coming to a stop. Directly in front of me.

I stare at it. Stare at those sewn-up eyes, the threads so rough and haphazardly stitched. Through a haze of agony, through a storm of terror, I study that lifeless face, its mouth open in shock, in horror, in pain.

For an instant—an instant so painfully brief—I recognize it. I recognize *her*.

The Prince is already in motion. With two quick strides, he steps across the floor, plucks the head up by its hair, and stuffs it into his sack. He pulls the drawstrings tight, then turns, facing the body. It sways where it stands, as though confused and a little undecided. The fingers of its two pale hands twitch, playing with the folds of its skirt.

The Prince blows . . . and those headless remains disintegrate into a million dark particles, scattering away to nothing.

Turning sharply, the Prince drops his gaze to me, broken and mangled on the chamber floor. *"Darling,"* he says. *"Darling, I'm so sorry. I came as fast as I could."*

I try to speak. But I can't. Every part of my body has been battered, every bone broken. There's blood in my mouth, in my eyes, filling up my lungs, choking me.

He crouches, reaches out to me, takes my face between his hands. *"I don't have much left,"* he says. *"I . . . I only hope it's enough."*

My right eye is swollen shut. The other blinks fast, struggling to see through the sticky blood caught in my eyelashes. The effort is too great, so I close that eye too, just as he bends toward me.

I feel a gentle pressure against my forehead. Warm, soft. Like a kiss.

A flash of magic, pure and bright, goes through me like a bolt of lightning. Every atom of my body ignites at once, surging with life, with pain, with need. I open my mouth to scream and—

I come to slowly.

My physical body weighs me down. I'm aware of it in a way I never have been before. Aware of my ribs. Of my jaw. My arms, my legs, my nose, my spine. I let my awareness move from one to the next to the next, glorying with each discovery of wholeness. Nothing is shattered. Nothing is broken beyond repair. My head aches dully, but my skull is not cracked or caved in.

I let out a long breath, ending with a whimper.

"Miss Darlington?" A familiar voice plucks at my ear. "Miss Darlington, are you awake?"

Reluctantly I pry my eyelids open. At first there's nothing but a pale blur above me. Slowly Mixael's features come into focus. He breathes out a huge sigh. "Miss Darlington! Seven gods be praised!"

I'm lying on the floor. At first, I'm not sure where; definitely not the vault on the thirteenth floor. I look around and see the books on the shelves, recognize the volumes of Miphates magic and history. That's right. This is the third floor. This is where I started writing. In fact . . . I look down and see the book and quill still clutched in my hands.

With a groan, I push up onto my elbows then allow Mixael to help me sit fully upright. My numb hands fumble, drop my book. It falls open in my lap, and I see nothing but spatters of ink across the last several pages. Mixael quietly picks it up, closes the cover, and tucks it away under his arm.

Shuddering, I look around and spy Andreas lying close by. I shoot Mixael a quick glance. "Is he . . . ?"

"Alive." Mixael nods. "And in his own mind. Unconscious, but not lost. I think he will make a full recovery."

Good. That's good. We saved him. We . . .

I frown and look around again. "Where are the others?"

Mixael opens his mouth and tries to answer, but a spasm of pain flashes across his face. He turns away, his shoulders hunching. With an effort he masters himself, looks at me, and tries again. "The Prince. He came back," he says. "Jolted awake quite suddenly, and you were still asleep. He said you were in trouble down below and dived right over the rail. When I looked, he was sliding down the book lift cables. He's not come back."

I shake my head, and—flashing across my mind's eye, I see him again, standing in the vault, his sword arm in motion, his blade slicing through air, through cloud, through bone . . . It must have taken a devastating amount of magic to write that moment into being.

Was it enough? Did he manage to bind the Noswraith, even without her name?

"We've got to find him," I say. Using the nearby bookshelf, I pull myself to my feet and turn to Mixael. He looks paler than I've ever seen him, his face wreathed with some horror that, in the moment at least, I don't have time to fathom. When I try to take a step and stumble, he catches my elbow, helps me steady myself.

"I'm going with you," he says.

"What about Andreas?"

He casts his fellow librarian a quick glance. "We'll have to risk it. We need to know if it's done."

I nearly ask him about Nelle. But no. Judging from the look on his face, now is not the time. We need to focus. We need to find the Prince.

Carrying a moonfire lantern, Mixael goes first down the spiral stair, for which I am thankful. I fear I'll lose my balance and tumble headlong, but at least Mixael will break my fall if I do. I'm dizzy and sick, still in shock from a battering that never really happened. Every now and then I feel a stab of pain in some part of my body that still wants to believe it's broken. The sensation fades as we go, but I know it will linger on long after this night is through.

We reach the thirteenth floor. Mixael holds his lantern high, and I stick close to his side as we make our way along the curve. The doors to the Noswraiths' vaults no longer seem to bulge, but I still feel the pressure of the beings contained within. How much damage is being done to the grimoires tonight? The librarians will be hard-pressed to get these spells back under control again over the next few days.

We reach the thirteenth vault. The door is not broken and twisted on the ground, but it does stand wide open. Fearing what we'll find, we creep to the doorway and peer inside. Paperback books lie strewn every which way, fallen from their shelves and piled up on the floor. In the center, there's what looks like a blast radius, very like what I'd seen in the Nightmare Realm itself. The pedestal has fallen, and the grimoire which had contained the binding spell lies in tattered ruins beside it.

The Prince lies on his side in a corner of the room. Blood trickles from his nose and from the corners of his wide, staring eyes. He clutches a book in his hands. The cover ripples with the power of the being contained inside, trying to get out.

But for now, the spell holds.

I wait in the darkness of the vault while Mixael goes for help. Seated beside the Prince, I hold his hand, completely helpless. And absolutely terrified.

All around me the dead books seem to whisper: *He really loves you. He really loves you. He really loves you . . .*

What *was* that? What had I just experienced? What was that monster, that horror? I close my eyes and see again a mangled, hideous face, blind, sewn-up eyes. I feel again my own blindness when that cloud overwhelmed me, followed by those blows. Blows for which I had no defense.

Shivering, I open my eyes and focus on the Prince's face. It's difficult to see him in the gloom. I can only discern an impression of features. And blood. So much blood.

"I'm sorry," I whisper. How small and futile the words sound! But I whisper them anyway, forcing them through the lump lodged in my throat. "I'm sorry, I'm sorry, I'm so very sorry! I failed again. And now you . . . you're . . ."

Is he dying? Is it like Ilusine said?

Was that last spell—that magic he gave to me—his final undoing?

Gently, I push hair back from his forehead. Tears course down my cheeks and drop from my chin. "You're a liar." A hysterical little laugh burbles from my lips. "You're a liar! I can't believe I didn't see it before. I suppose I forget, because you're so beautiful, that you're not *really* fae. You *can* lie, and you *do*. You told me you would leave in a heartbeat if given the chance. You wanted me to believe you don't care. About this city, about these people. About any of us. But then you go and give everything. *Everything.* For me. For Vespre. For all of us to have a chance."

I lean in closer, place my lips close to his ear, and whisper, "You're a liar, Castien. But you can't fool me. Not anymore."

Sitting back upright, I lean my head against the wall and watch the door. Waiting. Praying for a glimmer of light. And in that moment, realization dawns—realization so strange and unexpected that it draws another hysterical laugh out of me. I *want* to be here. I *want* to be part of Vespre Library. I want to prove myself. I want to be worthy of this role.

For the first time in my entire life, I feel as though I have a chance of *belonging* somewhere. And that's a terrifying thought.

Footsteps echo down the passage. Then light. My heart jumps. For a moment, even though I know the Prince's binding is strong and will hold, I fear it might be the Noswraith returning. Then Mixael appears in the doorway, holding his lantern high. I let out a sobbing breath of relief.

With a nod to me, he steps into the room. Two more figures file in behind him—Khas and Ilusine. Ilusine is a shock to the eyes, still clad in her golden gown, her skin glowing with inner light. Her face is grim, fierce, and for the first time I get the impression that the youngest princess of Solira might be a warrior in her own right.

It's Khas, however, who takes action. At sight of the Prince, she utters a little cry, springs across the room, and scoops him up in her arms. The spellbook falls from his lifeless fingers, but I catch it before it hits the floor. The pressure inside the cover makes me gasp. I press it against my stomach, holding it shut.

Ilusine steps to Khas's side and checks the Prince's pulse. Shaking her head, she says, "He lives. Just." She addresses herself to Khas. As per usual, she does not acknowledge my presence in the least.

Khas turns to Mixael. "Is it safe to take him from this room?"

Mixael can only nod.

Without another word, Khas carries the Prince out the door, Ilusine trailing close behind. I start to follow, but Mixael catches my elbow. "Wait."

I look at him, then down at the book in my arms. I was about to carry it out of the vault.

Silently, Mixael rights the fallen pedestal and tests to make certain it won't topple again. He pushes bits of the old grimoire away, then motions for me to set the new spellbook in place. I obey, then step back quickly as Mixael touches a series of carved runes on the edges of the pedestal, murmuring words in a language I don't understand but which I recognize as Old Araneli. The runes light up with a pale red glow that leaves an afterimage even when they fade.

This done, Mixael turns to me again. "Let's go," he says.

I'm seated on the floor in a cold stone passage. Across from me is the door to the Prince's room. I think. I'm not entirely certain, for it blends into the wall almost exactly. But it was somewhere near here that Ilusine and Khas disappeared. So I've been waiting. Alone.

Lir finds me eventually and tries to convince me to come to bed. But I can't. I won't.

"What should I tell the children, Mistress?" Lir asks at last when she realizes I can't be either bullied or cajoled.

I bow my head, biting my lip until I'm sure I can speak clearly. "Tell them I'll be back as soon as I can," I say finally. "And . . . and please . . ." I look up at her, helpless.

Lir offers a small smile and pats my head like I'm one of the children. "I'll do it," she promises and leaves.

Again I face the door. It's very dark now that the moon has set. Twilight is a constant over Doomed City, but just now it feels much more like night. Every muscle in my body is tense with listening, with straining for some sign of something—anything—in the chamber on the other side of that wall.

Eventually I nod off, only to be awakened by someone settling onto the floor next to me. Mixael. He leans his back against the wall, draws up his legs, and rests his elbows on his knees.

"How's Andreas?" I ask quietly.

"Awake," he replies. After a few moments he adds, "In his right mind."

I nod. That's a relief at least. My throat thickens with the need to ask the next question. But I don't want to. I really don't want to. Finally, unable to look at Mixael, I whisper, "Nelle?"

He doesn't reply. His head drops into his knees. A moment later, I hear a choking gasp. There's nothing I can do but slip my arm around his shoulder, the way I used to with Oscar on the cellar stair. So that's what I do. And I sit there, tears streaming down my cheeks, as the man who is now an orphan weeps for the loss of his mother.

I'm alone once again by the time Lawrence finally opens the door and peers out. His gaze sweeps over the top of me at first, then he starts a little at the sight of me on the floor, surrounded by the billowing cloud of silvery ballgown skirts. "Miss Darlington!" he exclaims. "What are you doing down there?"

I scramble up, ignoring the loud rip when my foot catches in the delicate fabric, and quickly pull myself together. "Lawrence, the Prince? Is he . . . ?"

"He's alive." Lawrence glances back over his shoulder then

steps out of the room, pulling the door mostly shut behind him. He shakes his head, and I glimpse a sheen of tears in his eyes. "He's alive, but I don't know for how long. Princess Ilusine is doing what she can to restore him, but she can only influence his fae blood. It's his human blood that's killing him." He shrugs and looks so helpless. "I don't pretend to understand it, miss. I'm no doctor and no magic user. I don't know how to help him. I'm not sure anyone can."

His words echo inside me, in the hollow place in my chest where my heart once beat. But as the echo fades, something else springs into existence—the barest glimmer of an idea.

"Could a doctor help him, do you think?" I ask. "A *human* doctor?"

Lawrence looks at me strangely. "I'm not sure."

But now my mind is alive and racing so fast, I scarcely hear the exhausted defeat in Lawrence's voice. There's a chance. A rash, ridiculous, fool's chance. But any chance is better than none at all.

I leap forward and catch Lawrence by the hand, squeezing hard. "How quickly can you get the Prince ready to travel?"

He stares at me as though I've grown a second head. "Where are we going, miss?"

32

D OCTOR GALE! DANNY! KITTY! PLEASE, SOMEONE!"
I pound on the door of the Gale house, cringing
at each reverberating echo of my voice up and down
Elmythe Lane. It's late at night, which I hadn't been expecting
when Lawrence and I stepped through the Between Gate, carrying
the Prince between us. But this world and Vespre don't flow by the
exact same stream of time, so I oughtn't to be surprised.

Though the street is silent, I feel disapproval emanating from
each and every firmly shut door, as though the denizens in the
respectable houses on either side of me are shocked by my gross
impropriety. I silently curse them in my head and pound on the
door all the harder. *"Danny!"* I shout.

The door swings abruptly inward. Danny stands in front of me,
barefoot, his shirt hanging loose from trousers which sag on his

hips without suspenders to hold them in place. He looks tousled and tired and, in that moment, remarkably like the boy I used to know, not the man he has become. The familiarity sends a sharp pang through my heart.

"Clara!" He gapes at me, his eyes running up and down, taking me in. I've still not changed from the silver ballgown, which is much the worse for wear by now after my battle with the Noswraith, followed by my journey to the shores of Noxaur, not to mention my mad run from Clamor Street all the way to this doorstep. It's still magnificent, however, and far too sumptuous for a girl of my station. "What are you . . .? How have you . . . ?" He stops, looks me in the eye. His confusion sharpens to a single point. "Clara, what's wrong?"

"I need your help!" Impulsively, I catch hold of his hand. "Please, Danny. There's someone who needs you, desperately. He'll die if you don't come."

Danny stares at me a silent moment, his eyes full of confusion. Then without further question he nods and draws me into the foyer. "Give me five minutes," he says.

It's more like ten minutes later when he returns, properly dressed, his medical bag in one hand. Kitty appears at the top of the stair, clad in her nightgown, a shawl wrapped around her shoulders. "Danny, what is it?" she says through a yawn. "I thought you weren't on shift tonight." She peers over the banister, and her eyes widen. "Clara!" Fearful confusion washes over her face as she looks from me to her brother and back again. "What is going on? Is it Oscar?"

Danny pats her arm. "Don't worry, Kit. Go back to bed. I'm going with Clara. I'll be back as soon as I can."

Kitty looks as though she wants to protest, to delay us with questions. *"Please,* Kitty!" I beg. She catches my eye, seems to fight a brief inner battle. Then she nods shortly.

Danny descends the stair and steps out the front door. I cast one last grateful glance back at my friend before ducking out into the street. I wait impatiently as Danny fastens the door behind him. He turns to me. "Lead on."

I set a brisk pace. The tatters of my gown flutter wildly about me, like the wings of a wounded bird struggling to take flight. I know I must look a fright to Danny, but he doesn't turn a hair. He offers me his coat out of pure gentlemanly concern, but when I refuse it, quietly matches his stride to mine and keeps his mouth shut.

Only once we reach the end of Elmythe Lane and turn onto the next street does he ask, "Who is in trouble, Clara? It's not Oscar?"

I shake my head. How can I possibly explain? "Please, just hurry."

I can almost hear him biting his tongue. I should offer him some explanation, I know. But after everything I've just been through, I simply cannot find the words.

At last we arrive on Clamor Street. I rush ahead to the door, knock sharply, and call out, "It's me! I'm back, and I've got the doctor!"

The door cracks open. Lawrence peers out, his face illuminated by a single oil lamp. Danny stops short behind me and gives him a look of grave suspicion, which Lawrence answers in kind. I hastily make introductions: "Doctor Gale, this is Mister Lawrence. Mister Lawrence, this is the doctor I told you about. He can help us."

The two men exchange nods. Then Lawrence steps back, holding the door, and says with all the dignity of a consummate valet, "This way, sir."

Danny shoots me another sharp, confused look, but steps into the house without a word. I follow after, then quickly take the lead, guiding Danny from the little foyer into the main room.

Danny stops short. I hear him breathe, "Seven gods, what is this?"

The Prince lies on a makeshift bed in the middle of the living room floor, as close to the brick fireplace as he can safely be. I'd wanted to take him upstairs, but the only room with a proper bed is Oscar's. Though Oscar is out—I have no idea where and choose not to question it just now—I couldn't very well dump the Prince onto my little brother's tangled nest of blankets, old shirts, and who knows what else. So I'd gone around the house, gathering what cushions and blankets I could, piling them on the floor to make the Prince as comfortable as possible.

He looks very strange indeed, lying on those ratty old rugs and rags, still clad in his glorious golden robes. In this context, he is an utterly fantastical creature, larger than life despite the sickly pallor of his cheeks. Were he not so sick, his presence would be utterly overwhelming.

Danny looks from him to me. "Is that a . . . a *fae?*" He says the word in much the same tone he might say *spider.*

"Technically he's *half* fae," I answer rather lamely. I look into

Danny's eyes, trying not to wince at the expression I see there. "Please, I don't have time to explain. He's . . . he's *important*. Many lives depend upon him."

"Fae lives?"

I bite my lip. If I say *troll* lives, it would be even less likely to move Danny. How can I possibly express to him how much those lives have come to mean to me? Lir and the children, even the folk of the lower city, with their ancient beliefs, their devout practices, their *otherness* that is so much more complex and beautiful than I originally imagined. I think of the trolls dancing in time to their own eerie music, of the miracle of the *Hugagug* moths in flight, of the pale, stone-carved city under moonlight. All that would be lost. All that would be doomed if the Prince of the Doomed City perished.

"Danny, you know I wouldn't ask you if it weren't important," I persist. "Can you not trust me?"

Danny looks from me to the stranger on the floor. The Prince's head is propped on a limp gray pillow, his body covered in multiple blankets but shivering uncontrollably. Lawrence built up a small fire in the grate, but there isn't much fuel, and the blaze is pathetic. It seems almost to suck warmth from the room rather than to offer any back.

For a moment, I fear Danny will march from the room and turn a deaf ear to my pleas. He hates the fae so desperately, hates them for he doesn't even know what, exactly. Only that they took me away. I want to beg him, I want to clasp my hands and plead. But I can only stand there, watching him. Waiting.

Finally, he sets his jaw, strides across the room, crouches over the Prince. In brisk, efficient movements, he goes about inspecting his body, listening to his heart, lifting his eyelids, holding two fingers to his pulse. He places the back of his hand against the Prince's forehead and grunts. "He's running a dangerously high fever, but . . ."

"Yes?" I try not to let my voice betray the intensity of my feelings.

Danny sits back, frowning. "There's something else at work here. Something I don't understand. He's burning with fever, and yet there's this *coldness*. I don't know how to explain it. I've never encountered anything like it."

"It's a curse."

Danny blinks and looks up at me. He opens his mouth as though to protest; man of science that he is, he can't very well accept such a fantastical explanation. Then, frowning, he looks down at the beautiful being in front of him—a being so obviously *not* of this world. He swallows visibly. "Tell me this, Clara," he says, his voice edged with steel. He turns, looks up at me, and I see more of that steel in his eye. "Is this the creature to whom you are Obliged?"

I open my mouth. No words come. I told Danny long ago that I was Obliged to Princess Estrilde, but I'd not bothered to inform him when that arrangement changed. I didn't want him to know about Vespre, about my work among the Noswraiths. I didn't want him to worry unduly. And, truth be told, I didn't want him to know about the Prince. But when he asks me pointblank like this, how can I lie? I duck my head and answer softly, "Yes."

Danny is silent for a long moment. Then: *"Why? Why do you want me to help him?"*

"Good gods, man!" Lawrence mutters from a corner of the room. I send him a sharp warning glance. Thankfully, Lawrence has the grace to shut his mouth and hold his tongue.

I face Danny again, keeping my voice level. "You swore an oath, Danny—an oath to help all living creatures who fall under your care. This is one of those creatures. He needs your help."

Danny's lip twists. I don't remember ever seeing him look so ugly. The viciousness in his expression makes him seem like a stranger. "If I let him die, you'll be free."

My heart gives a sickening thud. I stand, brace my feet, and stare down into Danny's face. I think of all the arguments I could make, think of how I could beg. And I see at once that nothing I say will move him. Nothing except . . .

I draw a long breath through my nostrils. My stomach churns with sickness at what I'm about to do.

"If you let him die," I say very softly, "I will die as well. Part of my Obligation is to protect my Obliege Lord to the furthest extent of my ability. If I allow you to harm him, even through inaction, I am guilty of breaking my Obligation. And the penalty for such a break is to suffer the same fate as my master." I hold his gaze. "Do you understand me? If he dies, *I* die. So what are you going to do, Doctor Gale? What are you going to do?"

Danny blinks slowly. I can see the war waging in his eyes, can feel his will silently striving against mine. Will he detect the falseness in my voice? I've never lied to him before, and, as the Prince said earlier that very evening, I'm not very good at it. But I refuse to look away, refuse to so much as blink. I let that lie stand, brace myself behind it like a shield.

At long last, Danny sighs. "Very well, Miss Darlington." His voice is excruciatingly cold. "I will do what I can."

The room stinks of blood.

I force myself to watch as Danny performs the localized bloodletting, wielding a set of fleams with practiced care.

Lawrence tried to intervene. "I thought bleeding was considered a barbaric practice by men of modern medicine!" he'd said, clenching his fists as though he would take down the doctor in an outright brawl if necessary.

Danny gave him a look. "You are right, Mister Lawrence. But as the subject in question is not a man of this world, I rather doubt modern medicine will do much good. We need to try more creative solutions."

As he prepared for the bloodletting, he told us of a strange story, a short, nonsensical anecdote he'd discovered in an old medical book. In that story, a doctor treated a man known to have fae blood in his lineage. "His human blood had been cursed," Danny told us, "if I'm remembering the tale correctly. The doctor treated him by bleeding him until his blood ran blue—which meant the fae blood in his body was now dominant and was able, by virtue of its innate magic, to counterbalance the curse."

"But surely that's nothing but a fairy story," Lawrence protested.

Danny gave him a look. "Perhaps. Then again, perhaps fairy stories are more useful in times like these than all the medical journals in the world." He turned to me. "Tell me, this person is only half fae, is that true?"

I nodded in confirmation.

"Then this is the best I can offer. I cannot treat him using human methods if he is not human, and I cannot treat him using fae methods as he is not fae. But if I can make him more of one than the other, then perhaps his body will find a way to right itself, like in the story."

Lawrence didn't like it. "It's a trick, miss," he tried to tell me, drawing me a little to one side. "He wants you free of your Obligation; he has much as said it! We can't trust him."

"Yes, we can," I answered firmly. "I would trust him with my life, Mister Lawrence."

Now poor Lawrence sits at the Prince's side, watching every move Danny makes as he cups the Prince's blood, carefully measuring ounce after ounce. I cannot watch. The sight of all that blood makes me sick, woozy. Instead I go stand in the open doorway, gazing out into the night. All the way up to the stars above. Stars I've known all my life, but which now seem foreign. Like a host of strangers.

Where is Oscar? I searched for my brother upon our arrival, but his room was empty. As was the coal cellar. When questioned, Danny told me Oscar hadn't been home when he tried to visit the day before. He has no idea where my brother might have gone off to.

I have a few ideas. None of them good.

Still, at the moment we're lucky he isn't home. As hard as it is to see Danny crossing paths with my Eledrian life, I'm sure I couldn't bear to see Oscar in the same room as the Prince. It would be too painful.

A groan erupts in the room behind me. In an instant I'm peering back into the room, arms wrapped around my stomach. Danny's expression is grave as he presses a cloth to a wound in the Prince's arm and lifts the arm upright to stop the flow of blood. Feeling my gaze upon him, he looks up. "See here, Clara," he says, nodding to the bowl of blood.

Fighting lightheadedness, I draw near and peer into the bowl. Then I blink and look again. I'd been expecting red blood as I'd seen in the last several bowls. But this is purple.

"It's starting to bleed blue," Danny says, his voice hushed, awed. "Just like in the story."

"Will he be all right?" I ask, breathless.

"Time will tell." Danny shrugs. "Again, I'm working outside my range of experience here. The hope is he will be able to fight the infection—the curse, rather—now that we've removed that to which the curse was adhered."

He takes the bowl away to dispose of its contents. When he returns, he passes Lawrence, who has dozed off in a corner of the room, his arms still crossed, his usually pleasant face sunk into a stern scowl. He snores softly.

Danny turns from him to me. "You should try to rest as well," he says.

I shake my head. "I can't. Not until I know if he'll live."

"Clara."

I don't want to look at him. I don't want to see the expression that goes with that stern tone in his voice.

"Clara, what does this man mean to you?"

Nothing. Absolutely nothing.

Everything.

I swallow. "It's not about me, Danny. It's about Vespre."

"Who's Vespre?"

I close my eyes, shake my head heavily. I don't even try to speak, just hold onto my silence, my arms hugging my middle.

After what feels like a small forever, Danny rises and shuts his bag. "I'm due at Westbend Charity in two hours. I need to go home, speak to Kitty."

He'll have a long, difficult day ahead of him now, running on so little sleep. I look at him, hoping he can see the gratitude in my face. "Thank you," I whisper.

He nods. I walk him to the door. He steps out, his head bowed heavily. Then, abruptly, he turns and looks me in the eye. His mouth opens, and I brace myself for him to ask yet another question I cannot bear to answer.

Instead he reaches out, catches my chin in his hand, and kisses me—a firm, forceful kiss that shocks me to the core, stealing the breath from my lungs.

I take a step back, yanking my face away. "Danny!" I gasp, glaring fiercely. I don't say more. I don't need to.

He looks at me long and hard. I hold his gaze, refusing to back down, refusing to be cowed or embarrassed. Without a word, he turns and marches away. I watch until he reaches the end of the street and turns out of sight.

He doesn't look back, not even once.

Heart pounding, I shut the door and drop the bolt. Then I lean my back against it, releasing a long breath and rolling my eyes to the ceiling. Oh gods! Seven gracious gods on high, how has everything suddenly become so *complicated?*

A groan draws my gaze to the Prince. He stirs. It's the first time I've seen him move of his own volition since Mixael and I found him in the vault. It's just the slightest turn of the head. His brow puckers, relaxes, and puckers again.

"Oh!" I gasp and hasten across the room. Lawrence is still snoring away in his corner, and I don't bother to wake him. I kneel beside the Prince. Am I mistaken, or is his color looking a little better by the dawn light coming through the window? Are his cheeks less sunken, the lines around his mouth less severe?

I close my eyes, concentrating. Slowly I bend over the Prince, plant my ear against his chest. But it's not his heartbeat I listen for. I can just feel the simmering, innate fae magic that moves in the Prince's blood. His blue blood, his fae blood. Such magic is present in every fae, as much a part of them as their beautiful faces or powerful bodies. In the Prince, it isn't usually this strong. This morning, however, it is a pulsing aura, growing with each passing moment. Breathing a sigh of relief, I lift my head.

And find myself staring into a pair of violet-blue eyes so intensely vivid, they take my breath away.

I draw back swiftly. Heat floods my cheeks. I swallow with difficulty. Then, very softly, I say, "You're all right, Prince. You've had a rough time of it, but I brought you to a friend of mine. He's bled you, drained some of that cursed blood out of your body. Your fae blood is dominant now, fighting the curse. I'm not sure, but I think you'll make a full recovery."

His eyes move, traveling across my face. He opens his lips, closes them again. His eyelashes flutter heavily, then fall in dark fans across his pale cheeks.

I draw a long breath. Sitting back on my heels, I start to rise. His hand shoots out. Catches hold of mine. Startled, I look into his face, find his eyes open and staring up at me again.

He draws my hand to his mouth and kisses it.

I'm frozen. It feels like time itself has stopped as I kneel there beside the Prince, captured in his stare, feeling the warmth of his lips against my skin.

With a groan, his eyes roll back in his head, and his eyelids fall heavily. His hand relaxes, dropping hold of mine. Hastily leaning forward, I plant my ear on his chest again. There's a heartbeat, clear and strong. And his fever has finally broken.

I straighten up, hands in my lap. One thumb rubs against the place where his lips brushed. Finally, I close my eyes, bow my head, and whisper, "Oh gods!"

It's not the most articulate prayer ever uttered. But it's heartfelt. I can only hope any gods who might be listening will take it for what it's worth.

33

"MISS DARLINGTON?"

I choke on a snore and start awake, blinking and disoriented. The world seems to tilt, and my body jolts, bracing. It's another moment before I remember I'm seated in Mama's old rocking chair.

Lawrence's face clarifies before me. He offers a thin sort of smile. "There isn't much by way of food or drink here. I'll slip out and find us tea, shall I?"

I stare up at him uncomprehendingly for a moment. Then my gaze shoots to the Prince lying on the floor before the hearth. I try to speak but can't manage more than an inarticulate gabble of sounds.

"Never fear, Miss Darlington," Lawrence says, interpreting my meaning. "The Prince is resting easily just now. I dare say his color looks quite strong! Your Doctor Gale has worked wonders. He stopped by while you were sleeping and said the crisis seems to have passed. He promised to return this evening."

I nod, my face heating at the knowledge that Danny was here while I slept. Was I snoring then too? I groan and rest my head in my hand.

"Tea then?" Lawrence says.

"Yes." My voice emerges as a hoarse little croak. "Yes, thank you, Mister Lawrence."

With another tired smile, my fellow Obligate slips out the front door, shutting it quietly behind him. The house feels very still and very cold in his absence.

I sit up straighter, stretching my sore back and rolling my neck and shoulders. When I close my eyes, images flash through my mind: the spectral wraith approaching, one slow footstep after another—the red rage surrounding me—the blows—the fear.

I shudder and push up from the rocking chair, marching across the room to the kitchen. Now is not the time to dwell on dark things.

There's nothing in the cupboards when I search, just as Lawrence said. I sigh. How does Oscar manage to survive on his own? And where is he, anyway? I climb the narrow stair to check his room on the off chance he slipped in while I slept. It's still empty. I stand a moment in the center of his room, in the patch of sunlight falling through his window. There's such an air of *haunting* about this place. So many memories, most of them painful, which linger in every corner and crevice. What must it be like for my brother, living here alone? Surrounded by these memories, with no one to distract him. No one to protect him.

Shaking my head, I leave the room and make my way back down the narrow stair. I duck my head to keep from hitting the low frame at the bottom and emerge into the living room.

I stop short.

The Prince is sitting upright. He's got his back to me. Danny stripped him of his robes and shirt when he began the bleeding process, and now the moth-eaten blanket he's been wrapped in falls away, baring his shoulders and revealing a well-muscled back. He turns his head to one side, offering me a view of his profile. His brow is puckered, confused.

With a sudden twist of his torso, he looks over his shoulder, eyes flashing. When he sees me, however, his expression relaxes. "Darling," he says, "we seem to be in the human world. Or am I dreaming?"

"You're not dreaming." I step out of the stairwell and approach. Hoping my actions will be interpreted as brisk and efficient, I pick up the blanket and drape it back over the Prince's shoulders. "Try not to take a chill, if you please."

He frowns but obediently holds the blanket closed at his throat. He sniffs, nostrils flaring. His lip curls. "Is this *your* home?" he asks, looking up at me.

I nod. "It was."

"Dare I ask what we're doing here?"

Taking a seat on the rocking chair and folding my hands neatly, I launch into an explanation: how I convinced Lawrence of my plan, and how he, with much more difficulty, convinced Captain Khas. Then the three of us faced Ilusine together, explaining to her how a human doctor was the only chance we had of getting the Prince the treatment he needed. Ilusine was most resistant, refusing to so much as look at me. In the end, however, her concern for the Prince won out, and she agreed to let him go.

Khas traveled with us in the morleth carriage all the way to the shores of Noxaur. She carried the Prince in her arms to the brink of the Between Gate but refused to go any further. Her fear of the human world was palpable, overcoming even her devotion to her master. With extreme reluctance, she handed the Prince over to Lawrence and me, and we carried him through.

"In the end, it turns out I was right," I finish. "A human doctor was able to treat you successfully as the curse is on your human blood."

"What human doctor?" the Prince asks.

"Doctor Daniel Gale. He's quite excellent. I've known him all my life."

The Prince shoots me a narrow look. I wonder if he's picturing some white-haired family doctor, or if the sudden flush in my cheeks has revealed something more. I quickly paint a smile in place and blink blandly back at the Prince.

"This doctor," he persists, "did he *want* to treat me?"

I frown, somewhat taken aback. "Well . . ."

The Prince's gaze sharpens. "Answer me, Darling. You asked him to help me; did he comply willingly, or did you use force to make him treat me?" I open my mouth, blink, and shut it again. Before I can think of anything to say, the Prince groans, "Oh gods!" and covers his face with his hand.

"What?" I get up from my chair and hurry over to him, kneeling. My hand reaches for his shoulder but stops at the last second. "What's wrong?" I demand. "Are you ill? You lost a lot of blood. You should probably rest your head. Shall I fetch you some water?"

He drops his hand, looking straight at me. "Don't you understand? You saved my life. And I'm obliged to you."

"Oh. That." I shake my head, sitting back on my heels. "No need to thank me. I did what I felt I must. Anyone would have in my place—"

"No." The Prince's voice cuts me off sharply. His jaw works, the muscles of his throat tensing. "No, Darling, listen to me: I am *Obliged* to you."

I stare at him, uncomprehending.

Then my jaw slowly drops.

"Oh!" I breathe.

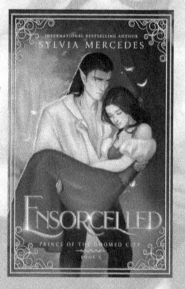

A CLEVER THIEF. A DISFIGURED MAGE. A KISS OF POISON.

THE SCARRED MAGE OF ROSEWARD

❖

For fifteen years, Soran Silveri has fought to suppress the nightmarish monster stalking Roseward. His weapons are few and running low, and the curse placed upon him cripples his once unmatched power. Isolation has driven him to the brink of madness, and he knows he won't be able to hold on much longer.

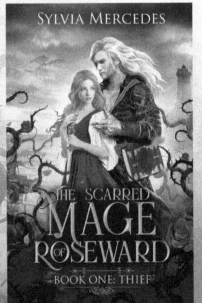

When a sharp-tongued, uncouth, and undeniably beautiful young woman shows up on his shore, Soran resolves to drive her away. He won't be responsible for another death.

But Nelle is equally determined not to be frightened off by the hideously scarred mage. Not until she gets what she came for . . . .

Can two outcasts thrown together in a tangle of lies discover they are each other's only hope? Or will the haunted darkness of Roseward tear them apart?

ABOUT THE AUTHOR

SYLVIA MERCEDES makes her home in the idyllic North Carolina countryside with her handsome husband, numerous small children, and the feline duo affectionately known as the Fluffy Brothers. When she's not writing she's . . . okay, let's be honest. When she's not writing, she's running around after her kids, cleaning up glitter, trying to plan healthy-ish meals, and wondering where she left her phone. In between, she reads a steady diet of fantasy novels.

But mostly she's writing.

After a short career in Traditional Publishing (under a different name), Sylvia decided to take the plunge into the Indie Publishing World and is enjoying every minute of it. She's the author of the acclaimed Venatrix Chronicles, as well as The Scarred Mage of Roseward trilogy, and the romantic fantasy series, Of Candlelight and Shadows.

Printed in the USA
CPSIA information can be obtained
at www.ICGtesting.com
LVHW091022040124
767924LV00109B/163/J